The

ROMANOV CODE

ALSO BY GAVIN COLLINSON

An Accident in Paris

The
ROMANOV
CODE

GAVIN COLLINSON

WELBECK

First published in 2023 by Welbeck Fiction Limited,
an imprint of Welbeck Publishing Group
Offices in: London – 20 Mortimer Street, London W1T 3JW &
Sydney – Level 17, 207 Kent St, Sydney NSW 2000 Australia
www.welbeckpublishing.com

A CIP catalogue record for this book is available from the British Library

Paperback ISBN: 978-1-80279-366-6
Ebook ISBN: 978-1-80279-367-3

Printed and bound by CPI Group (UK) Ltd., Croydon, CR0 4YY

10 9 8 7 6 5 4 3 2 1

'All around me there is treachery, cowardice and deceit.'
– Nikolai II Alexandrovich Romanov

'All warfare is based on deception.'
– Sun Tzu, The Art of War

PROLOGUE

The Schirn Kunsthalle Museum of Modern Art, Frankfurt, Germany. 2022

'Not so long ago, a private detective called Marc Novak was hired to investigate the final days of Diana, Princess of Wales. He discovered her death wasn't simply an accident in Paris. It was murder, gentlemen.' The woman paused. 'Uncovering that information seems to have annoyed a few people. Can't think why.' She leant across to the man sitting closest to her and rested her palm on his forearm. 'That's English sarcasm, my darling. Never certain how well it travels.'

One of the other two men at the table shook his head in apparent disbelief. 'What makes you think you will survive this night?' He pulled a flick knife from a side pocket of his suit and added, 'What makes you think we won't stretch you across this table and fillet you?' He pressed a button on his knife's rivet and a small blade sprang from its casing.

'Well, if you're going to attempt it with that paperknife, I hope you'll be using a general anaesthetic.'

The individual sat opposite the woman laughed. 'Madame,' he addressed her. 'My name is Jean-Pierre de Bray. I admire your courage in calling us here tonight.'

The four of them sat in the rotunda of the Schirn Kunsthalle Museum in the heart of Frankfurt. The woman had hired the venue for the evening and they were alone. Moonlight leaked

1

through the famous glass domed ceiling directly above them, but the large chamber was otherwise unlit, aside from a set of spotlights trained on the stone columns flanking the room's entrance. The table itself was an art installation. A circular piece of furniture constructed from oak. Solid. A slab of interconnected wooden beams that felt at once modern and medieval.

'And, Mr Doyle,' de Bray continued, 'put your knife away. We are not savages here. We are businessmen. Men of reason. But, madame, you have us at a disadvantage. From your accent, I assume you are English, but aside from that . . . For example, you know our names and yet—'

'You can call me Nemesis. My code name du jour. A tad theatrical, I grant you, but I never can resist a touch of the dramatic.'

Doyle used his knife to point at de Bray. 'You two can hugger mugger all you like, but when the other three get here, they'll be with me. They'll vote to kill the bitch. You know that!'

De Bray winced. 'The people responsible for the death of Diana are no longer with us. We benefited from their crimes. I suspect this lady is proposing a truce.'

She nodded. 'You three and all your associates must promise that Novak isn't harmed by any of you *or* your colleagues. Agree to that and I won't go public with the extent to which your businesses profited from the assassination.'

The third man, an American called Jefferson who had remained silent until this point, cleared his throat. He was, like the other two, in his mid-forties and dressed in a dark, couture suit. 'Nemesis – is that the correct pronunciation? Good. I have two points to make, if I may? Yes, we would like to accept your offer. At least, I guess, Monsieur de Bray and I would. But when the other three stakeholders arrive . . .' He glanced at his watch. 'Where are they, by the way?'

'They'll be dropping in shortly,' the woman assured him.

'Good, good ... Except, they are a little hot-headed. I'm afraid Mr Doyle's assessment is quite correct.' Jefferson paused, uncomfortable with what he had to say. 'They will kill you.'

'They wouldn't be the first to try.' She lowered her voice. 'Thank you for your concern. It means a lot.' Her polite but authentic smile suggested she was being genuine. 'You said you had two points, Mr Jefferson?'

He nodded. 'We can forgive the sins of the past. We can prevent the consequences that Marc Novak would ordinarily face. But we can't control the future.'

'Meaning?'

'Meaning, if my intel is correct, your Mr Novak will shortly be offered a proposition. To put it bluntly, he'll be asked to go on a treasure hunt.'

'Sounds fun.'

'The kind of treasure that's already drenched in the blood of countless men and women who have attempted to lay hands on it over many generations.'

'Still sounds fun.'

Jefferson shifted uneasily in his chair. 'If he becomes involved in the search for the Romanov treasure, he's on his own.'

'We must let the future take care of itself.' The woman nodded. 'But I want to confirm our understanding. Excepting the future developments you mentioned, Mr Jefferson, would you, and you, Monsieur de Bray ... Well, would you be willing to accept my offer of a truce?'

They both nodded.

'And Mr Doyle. You would not?'

'Listen,' he replied, 'Nemesis, or whatever you like to call yourself. The three guys we're waiting for will shoot you in the throat. For the threat you present. For your bloody impertinence. And for the hell of it. Out of my respect for them, I'll let them finish you.'

'By *respect*, you mean *fear*, of course.'

'I'd have cut you open myself,' Doyle hissed. 'But very, very soon—' He paused as everyone in the room heard the distant din of a Bell 427's twin engines and its four whirling blades. He smirked, folded his own blade and slipped it into his side pocket. 'That's them, missus!'

De Bray said, 'I'll give them five minutes to land the helicopter and another five to make their way here. Please . . . leave now, madame!'

She gripped Doyle's arm. 'Are you sure I can't change your mind? You were a good man, once.'

'People change!' He shrugged off her hold. 'I'm paying you no more attention! You're a mad thing! I'll spit on your warm corpse.'

'I'll make you apologise for that.'

'What did you just say?' Doyle glared at her. 'Fuck it!' He pulled a Glock 43 from his shoulder holster and aimed it at her head. 'Why wait? I'm gonna do them a favour and do you myself!'

'Mr Doyle.'

'Yeah?'

'You're an idiot. Which is fine. But you're cruel and crass. I deplore both characteristics.'

'You fucking bitch . . .' His finger tightened on his pistol's trigger.

De Bray and Jefferson simultaneously shouted, 'No!' but another noise drowned out their voices.

The sound of shattering glass and the deep rumble of a hovering helicopter.

A millisecond later, the body blurred past their eyes and smashed into the centre of the table.

All three men yelped in shock, swore and hurriedly pushed their chairs back, scrambling to get away from the cadaver

4

that had been tipped into the middle of their meeting. They leapt up, fell back from the table in stumbling steps, transfixed by the broken body that now dominated it.

'Jesus H. Christ,' Doyle murmured. 'That's Scalfaro! She killed him!' He looked wildly at the woman, shouting, 'The other two will hunt you down! You know that?'

She rolled her eyes. 'Well, guess what, petal?'

Thwack!

A beat.

Thwack!

Two more bodies crashed into the middle of the table. There was something obscene about the lack of time between their descents.

The three living men were frozen by the pile of dead men. Slivers and shards of glass from the ruined dome coated the bodies, moonlight reflected in every fragment. The noise of the helicopter changed in tone as it banked starboard, then faded as it soared into the Frankfurt night. Silence now, except for the sound of ragged, terrified breathing.

The woman remained seated. Unmoving. Calm. Completely unfazed by the corpses. 'Mr Jefferson. Monsieur de Bray. You may leave. With my thanks. Cheery-bye, my cherubim.'

They turned and ran from the room.

The third man remained planted to the spot, transfixed by the bloody mound on the slab of oakwood.

'And Mr Doyle . . .' Nemesis at last turned to face him. 'Do I have your attention?'

-1-

Three months later

'In the early hours of 17 July, 1918, seven members of the Romanov family, including Mother Russia's last Tzar and Tzarina, were murdered in the basement of a building known as the House of Special Purpose.

'All their jewels and treasures were taken to Moscow and these extraordinary riches, many of which predate Russia itself and were worn at the court of the Byzantine Empire, were catalogued and later sold at auction. Here's the thing. Not all the items listed in the first inventory of 1922 made it to the auction. We know of at least four major pieces that disappeared.

'Here is the other thing. Those four items are just the tip of a very large, jewel-encrusted iceberg. We know of six priceless Fabergé eggs which went missing after 1917. And we also know for certain that several individuals smuggled Romanov jewels out of Russia in bed linen, hollowed-out shoe heels and even chocolates. Imagine, Mr Novak, popping a truffle in your mouth, feeling something hard against your teeth and plucking – pop! – a diamond from your lips, large enough and perfect enough to fetch a king's ransom at any private sale in the world! And more, there were—'

I interrupt my guest. 'I'm sorry, Miss Karpin, but I'm not sure where this is heading. If you want to trace the Romanov jewels, you need a historian, not a private detective. And if you want to find the lost treasure, you need . . .'

'Yes, Mr Novak?'

'A healthy shot of realism. The lost gold of Russia's last emperor and empress sounds romantic, sure. It's a great story. But you might as well go looking for the Holy Grail, or Atlantis, or the Ark of the Covenant.'

My guest bristles and I guess she normally lives in a world of 'Yes, ma'am.' Ekaterina Karpin is tall and slim. A touch of aristocracy in her face, but without any haughtiness. Quite the reverse. There's kindness in her clear blue eyes. She's about forty. Wears it well. Her accent is Russian, but soft enough to suggest she's been in England for a fair few years.

'No, no, no! You speak of fictions! But the Romanov treasure is real, factual history!'

By the way, we're in my front room, which doubles as the central office of Novak & Stewart. I live alone, so I can't blame the sparse decor on anyone other than myself. We're seated, but now Ekaterina leans forward and lowers her voice as though she suspects we're being monitored.

'We *know* that it exists! And here' – she pulls an old, discoloured envelope from her Givenchy handbag– 'is the . . . treasure map, if you will, that will help us locate a small fraction of it. I say small, but acquiring it will make us . . . How do you phrase it in your country? Rich beyond your wildest dreams.'

'Well, I have some pretty wild dreams, Miss Karpin.'

'*Ya tozhe!*' She holds the envelope aloft. 'I have some pretty wild plans, Mr Novak.'

'Oh, I specialise in those, and so . . .' The cavalier nature of her reply means that for the first time since she mentioned the Romanovs, I entertain the idea that she may not be mad. Or at least, not entirely. 'You're serious, aren't you?'

'Yes. Absolutely.' Her pale, kindly face breaks into a smile. 'This quest for the treasure is more important than you can ever know. And I'm asking you to join me on it.'

Ekaterina Karpin stands and I automatically follow suit. She solemnly extends her open palm towards me, an invitation to shake hands, of course, but also a plea for me to accept her request.

'Will you help me, Mr Novak?'

-2-

'I'll shake your hand, but it doesn't mean I'm shaking on a deal.'

'Why not?' She suddenly sounds angry, as if my refusal to commit is a carefully crafted insult. 'What are you afraid of?'

'Very little. But the last time I took on a case connected with royalty . . .' I recall the blood and horror and duplicity that the investigation brought into my life. 'It didn't end well.'

'You failed?'

'No.' I reflect on how much I'm willing to share and simply add, 'I was failed.'

Ekaterina nods. 'I know that feeling.' She doesn't say these words with any wryness. There's sorrow in her voice, and understanding. 'It's why I want the Romanov Code.'

'What's the Romanov Code?'

'It's . . . Excalibur.'

'You say that like it's a private joke.'

'I didn't mean to. I'm sorry.' There's contrition on her face. But it's the contrition of a six-year-old straining with every fibre to appear remorseful for an act they secretly classify as entirely justifiable. 'You forgive me?'

I can't be bothered to reply, and in the next moment, as if she's completely lost interest in our conversation, she whirls around and walks away. She's aware I'm watching her, of course. Ekaterina is the sort of person you can't help but watch. She wanders over to a glass-fronted display cabinet that houses my collection of first editions and other antiquarian books. She stoops to read their spines.

'Do you have any Russian literature?'

I open the cabinet and hand her a first-edition Fleming. 'I'm afraid that's the closest I get.'

She looks at the rather beautiful cover artwork by Richard Chopping and, exaggerating her accent, reads the title. '*From Russia With Love.*' She beams. 'You people! You hear *Russia* and think of either the Kremlin or this!' She brandishes the book. 'James Bond! The Cold War! Exotic female agents in glamorous furs!'

'Don't forget beef Stroganov and ushanka hats.'

She steps closer to me. It's an invasion of my personal space and a mischievous challenge to see how I'll react. To be honest, I don't know whether to feel violated or invigorated. 'Is that why you're afraid of me, Mr Novak? You think I'm a Russian spy?'

'Are you?'

'No.' She shrugs. Steps back. 'I was. Once. Many years ago. But the money . . .' She pulls a face to imply it was derisory.

'Aren't you supposed to keep these things to yourself?'

'You won't take my case because you don't trust me.'

'If it's any consolation' – I carefully replace the first edition and close the cabinet door – 'I trust you as much as I trust any Russian spy.'

'That was a long time ago.'

'So was the Bay of Pigs,' I reply, 'but you still can't buy Cuban cigars in New York City.'

'You will help me find the Romanov treasure. You and your colleague, Mr Frank Harvey. You will help me.'

'Frank isn't my colleague. I've just pulled him into a couple of jobs.'

'And my job?'

'I'll think about it.'

'When the English say, *I'll think about it*, they really mean they'll think of a way of getting out of it.'

'You may have a point.' I'm becoming irked with the dance she's trying to lead. 'That envelope . . .' I extend my hand. 'Give it to me.'

She taps it against her lips as if considering my request. 'No. When you take my case, I'll show you, but—'

'It's time you were leaving, Miss Karpin.'

She gives me her best smile. 'You don't really mean that.'

I give her my best glare. 'You don't trust me? Fine. I don't trust myself half the time. But I don't trust you. Not one little bit. And we can file that away under "problem". You come in here knowing I'll be intrigued and thinking I'll fall for you. I imagine most men do. But it could be argued the Romanov jewels remain the property of the Russian state. So for me to go after that kind of loot, well, I'm going to need more than wide eyes and tall tales.'

She's fuming. If this was a cartoon, she'd have steam coming out of both ears. 'Mr Novak, the elders in the small village where I grew up—'

'And you can stop trying to sell me all this "elders in the small village" and "how do you phrase it in your country?" shtick, because I'm not buying it. You've been here a long time and you know what plays well. Good for you. But I've heard it all before and I was only mildly impressed the first time. And, by the way, a real agent of the Russian Federation wouldn't tell a total stranger she was once FSB. So who are you really, Miss Karpin? Is that even your real name?'

To her credit, she's not backed down. She stands a couple of paces away from me, her eyes boring into mine with something bordering on fury. 'I should slap your face.'

'Well, then I'd slap yours. And I'd do it harder. Which would be a pity.'

She walks across to the table. 'Yes, it would.'

Ekaterina drops the envelope back into her handbag and reaches inside for something else. I'm half expecting her to yank out a Makarov, but, disappointingly, when her hand emerges, she only has a business card between her fingers. She places it on the table. Gives me an icy stare.

'My coat.' She glances at her large, overly ornate wristwatch as if instructing me to get a move on.

I take a seat at the table. 'It's hanging up in the hall. You can see yourself out.'

She pushes her card halfway across the table. 'Call me . . .'

Ekaterina sashays into the hallway and dons her black, Balmain double-breasted trench coat. Thick wool, tapered waist and gold-toned buttons. I'd be lying if I said she didn't look catwalk-ready.

My guest opens the front door, looks back at me and adds, 'If you grow a pair of balls.'

'I'll be sure to check.'

She leaves. I laugh. Pick up the business card. It only gives her name and contact number. But, let's face it, I might as well put it on speed dial right now.

-3-

I wander through to my kitchen and make myself a coffee using a new Pacamara blend I haven't tried before. The label tells me it's 'ethical', which means the manufacturers have stuck a photograph of beaming pickers on the side of the jar so you can feel good about yourself, and stuck an extra fiver on the price per pound so their shareholders can feel equally good.

I sip it. Not bad. Drift into my living room and phone Frank Harvey. He picks up and gives me a groggy, 'Hello?'

Frank's a friend of mine. A former journo, I guess he's in his early seventies, not that he lets the decades slow him down. He smokes like he's got a personal vendetta against his lungs, but he's a tough, wiry, old battler. He's also one of the best informed people I've ever met. I'm certain that if anyone in England has an inkling of what happened to the Romanovs' possessions, it's Frank. He's bound to at least know something. His knowledge of anything in that line is extraordinary.

'What do you know about the lost treasure of the Romanovs, Frank?'

'Bugger all.'

'I'm being serious.'

'So am I, lad. It was a load of gold baubles and bangles that went missing over a century ago. Priceless. I doubt it's about to turn up in lost property, so who cares?' He stifles a yawn. 'Christ, what ungodly time in the early hours is it?'

13

'Frank, it's literally half past eleven in the morning. Do you know a woman called Ekaterina Karpin?'

'No. Why?'

'She seemed to know you.'

'I'd remember a name like that.'

'*Ekaterina Karpin*. Not ringing any bells?'

'Silence in the belfry. Maybe she was using a legend. Do you have a photo of her?'

'I can get one.'

'What did she want?'

'She claimed to have information about the treasure's whereabouts. She wanted me to help her find it and retrieve it.'

He hesitates. 'Don't touch this one, lad.'

'Why not?'

'Because . . .' Another pause. 'Sounds like a wild goose chase.'

'I'll get you the photo.'

'Novak!'

'Yeah?'

'I know you, son. You're going to poke your nose in whatever I say. But . . . be very careful with this one.'

'Absolutely.'

I know that right now my friend is shaking his head. 'I suppose there is one good thing about it.'

'That being?'

'This is the first conversation we've had in yonks where you haven't mentioned the Diana case.'

'Why's that a good thing?'

'We ran out of options, lad!'

'People don't run out of options, Frank! They run out of will.'

I've raised my voice, but he replies quietly, 'We did everything we could. The men directly responsible are all gone.'

'There's one left. Somewhere. You know that as well as I do.'

'You're a tenacious bugger. I'll give you that.'

'A tenacious bugger? Know anyone else that phrase applies to?'

He chuckles, but adds, 'Just watch yourself!'

'Sure.'

'Promise!'

It's my turn to hesitate. 'Promise.' After all, I suppose it's an easy promise to keep on a literal level. 'Speak soon, Frank.'

I hang up. Consider the conversation. It felt off. Something was wrong. There was the obvious irregularity. He warned me away from the case because it was 'a wild goose chase'. Believe me – that would normally be a reason for him to be all over it. He loves that kind of caper. Show Frank Harvey a wild goose and he'll be chasing it faster than you can say due diligence. But there was something else. Something more troubling. I can't put my finger on it exactly, but—

I push the problem to the back of my mind and focus on getting an image of Ekaterina. Across the room, close to the cabinet that houses my book collection, there's an old wooden clock that houses something more modern: a camouflaged 2.5mm lens that feeds into a surveillance system. I tend to covertly record new clients in case I need some kind of visual identification check. Sketchy, I know. But useful.

I pull a USB stick from the back of the clock. It should contain some decent images of my guest, especially as she wandered close to the lens when checking out my book collection. I stick the USB into my laptop, save the most recent recording to my hard drive and hit 'play'. I see what looks like a static image of my front room. Fast-forward a few seconds . . . I walk across the shot and I recall I entered the room ahead of Ekaterina. A few more moments of my current surroundings and then—

A storm of static interference, followed by total darkness.

I sit back. Smile.

'Bravo, Miss Karpin.'

I recall the Russian's huge watch, which I'm now assuming was simply the casing for a jammer. I've used them myself. Small ones are often built into jewellery or items of clothing and can knock out recording operations if positioned close to the camera. Larger ones are illegal but powerful enough to take out security across an entire street. The mini versions have been around for years. They're cheap and easy to get hold of, but still, I'm begrudgingly impressed that Ekaterina was cautious enough to use one when visiting me.

As I'm replacing the USB stick and considering what my next step should be, my phone rings.

'You're through to Novak & Stewart.'

I hear a female voice, so low it's barely audible. 'Is that Mr Marc Novak?'

'Yeah. Speaking.'

'I need your help.'

The urgency and fear in her voice suggest this isn't an idle inquiry.

'Are you in any immediate physical peril?'

'No . . . But without your help hundreds of children will be in danger. Immediate danger.'

Suddenly, chasing lost treasure with a woman who may or may not be a former Russian agent seems unimportant.

I ask, 'What kind of danger?'

No reply.

'Do you know where the children are located?'

Further silence.

I instinctively know she's considering hanging up, so I cajole her with, 'I'll treat anything you say to me in the strictest confidence. And I give you my word I won't take any steps without running them past you.'

'I shouldn't have called.'

'You contacted me for a reason. You want to help those kids. We can do that together.'

'He's too powerful.'

'Who is?'

'It's about a child trafficking ring.'

'Do the police know about it?'

She gives a slight laugh. 'He's got the police in his back pocket.'

'Can we meet?'

'It'll be difficult for me to get away. I'm afraid he might—'

'It's important,' I interject. 'If kids are in danger, we need to act fast.'

'Tonight,' she tells me. 'We can meet tonight.'

And with that confirmation, I feel a surge of relief.

-4-

Nikolai's Story
Yekaterinburg, Russia, July. 1918

Four minutes before the massacre of his family and closest friends, Nikolai felt a surge of relief. As he walked towards the staircase, a guard pushed his shoulder.

'Hurry, citizen!'

Months earlier, such disrespect would have been unthinkable. Now, it was unremarkable. He was carrying his son, Alexei Nikolaevich, in his weary arms and stumbled slightly, but regained his balance and began trudging down the twenty-three steps of the mansion his captors called 'the House of Special Purpose'.

He was that special purpose. Or, rather, his imprisonment, and that of his wife and children, was held to be. Special enough to warrant three hundred armed soldiers standing guard over a man in his fifties, his ailing wife, sickly son and four young daughters. Never let it be said that the Bolsheviks did anything by halves. Security, as with murder and hypocrisy, was something they committed to on a grand scale.

The shoes worn by Nikolai II Alexandrovich Romanov, the last Tzar and Emperor of Russia, King of Congress Poland and Grand Duke of Finland, had gradually become, like the rest of his clothes, badly worn. Holes in their soles meant his feet could feel the cold, dusty stone steps as he padded down them and into the semi-basement.

The chamber was half above ground level, half below. Rectangular and completely devoid of furniture, its small, single window was predictably barred.

And here, in this dimly lit room no bigger than the boot cupboard of his previous home, the Winter Palace, he saw four of his friends and fellow prisoners, huddled by the far wall with his wife, Alexandra, and their daughters: Olga, Tatiana, Maria and Anastasia, who held her tiny King Charles spaniel close to her chest. The relief Nikolai felt was overwhelming. When he'd been woken up and ordered downstairs, he'd feared that Lenin, or Trotsky, or the prison-house's commandant, Yakov Yurovsky, or any one of his countless enemies, had decided his death would be convenient.

But no. His wife was here. His girls were here. This gathering could not be for a massacre. He'd once joked that the Bolsheviks chose a red flag so the bloodstains wouldn't show, but Nikolai reasoned that even the most fervent revolutionary must realise that 'ordinary' Russian folk would baulk at the idea of slaughtering unarmed women and children. The word Bolsheviks meant 'the majority' and surely the vast majority of his people still retained an iota of humanity?

He asked for a seat for Alexei and although his request was granted, the commandant's assistant sneered, 'So, the heir wants to die in a chair?'

Nikolai assumed the rhetorical question was just another barb intended to unsettle him.

Yakov Yurovsky leant against the back wall and called for his prisoners to straighten themselves up and line up. He told them they were going to be photographed to provide proof that they were alive and well.

Nikolai nodded. It struck him as a reasonable request. A reassuring one, as well, suggesting their welfare remained a consideration. He helped organise two smart rows. His wife sat in a seat near the corner, their daughters were arranged behind her, and their friends, including their cook and long-standing doctor, positioned themselves a pace behind Nikolai, who stood by his son's armchair in the middle of the front row.

He leant forward slightly to inspect the line-up. *Yes, that should—*

A clatter of footsteps down the stairs interrupted his thoughts. Everyone in the two rows looked towards the steps as about a dozen men poured into the room. Some were drunk. Some were absurdly young and looked expectant, like fresh-faced kids about to set off on a school trip. All were heavily armed.

As they lined up to face the Romanovs, Yurovsky shouldered his way to the front of the divide between the soldiers and civilians. He read out the order for the Romanovs' execution.

The deposed emperor spluttered, 'What? What?' and the fatal words were recited once more. A little faster this time. Yurovsky wanted to crack on.

The gunfire was deafening. Alexandra tried to make the sign of the cross, but Yurovsky's right-hand man, Peter Ermakov, although hopelessly drunk, delivered a killshot to her head so quickly that the blessing was unfinished as she fell. Her husband didn't witness her murder. Yurovsky, in his zeal, had shot him thrice in the chest with his Colt pistol, and a little over three centuries after Michael I became the first Romanov Tzar of Russia, that nation's final official emperor lay dead at his son's feet.

But Nikolai's children were not so easy to kill.

-5-

The Scottish Highlands

One of the women says to me, 'You should never have come here.'

She's pointing the latest version of the Beretta M9 at my chest, so I tend to agree.

'I was in the neighbourhood.'

'You live five hundred miles away.'

'I didn't say which neighbourhood.' I offer a hopeful smile, which isn't returned.

Her boss has been running a child trafficking network for the past two decades. I'm standing in his study, in the manor house of his sprawling estate in the Scottish Highlands. Two of his bodyguards, a couple of tall, impassive women wanted for murder in half a dozen European countries, are keeping me company and they've both got pistols trained on my torso. Their employer's name is Alexander Paige, known to most as Sandy Paige.

Yes. *That* Sandy Paige.

Philanthropist, charity campaigner, ethical businessman and, in recent years, media personality and all-round national treasure. And, oh yes, a vicious, highly intelligent and staggeringly cruel bastard.

I've been investigating him for the past three months, beginning soon after the phone call that warned of children being in immediate danger. He's not terribly keen on me because my dossier on his business has grown fat enough to put him away for eighteen years with good behaviour.

He enters the room and shakes my hand. 'Good to see you, Mr Novak!' He beams at me, and in an aside to his bodyguards adds, 'If he tries anything, kill him.'

Not that Sandy Paige is big on good behaviour.

He nods to himself, sits behind his desk and gives me an open-palmed shrug like he's posing for a Sunday supplement. 'I instructed my colleagues to bring you here so we could chat.' He leans forward. 'Forgive the theatrics.'

I shrug. 'This is nothing. The last person who threatened my life was a Balinese dancing girl.'

'I have a proposition for you.'

'How exciting.'

'If you tell me which member of my organisation tipped you off about my activities, you'll die from a bullet to the head.'

'Not going to lie, Mr Paige. I'm not *loving* your proposition so far.'

'If you maintain your rather selfish silence, I'm afraid your death will be drawn-out and extremely painful. Beginning with the obliteration of your right kneecap.'

He gestures to my lower legs and for a moment I assume he actually believes I need help with the basic anatomical thrust of the threat. But no. It's an instruction to one of his staff. She points her Beretta at my patella.

'You have three seconds to give me the name I require.' He settles back into his chair. 'One.'

The study is spacious, full of bookcases and a huge log fire blazes away to my left. Paige's desk is a large, gorgeous piece of furniture. Cherrywood. Antique. To its right, an enormous free-standing world globe is open to display a dozen or so bottles of very good Scotch, vodka and vermouth. No gin.

Behind the desk, I can see a shield emblazoned with Paige's family crest over a pair of dirks – small, steel daggers – that are crossed as if locked in battle.

'Two.'

When I was shown into the room, the two women lingered outside, checking their sidearms for a moment. That gave me enough time to do one thing.

'Three!'

He nods.

I hold up my hand. 'I have a counter-offer, Mr Paige.'

'Oh? Now *that* is exciting.'

But this time I'm not smiling. I look this monster of a man in the eye and tell him my terms. 'Disband your organisation. Convert your assets to hard cash and spend all of it rescuing every girl and boy you have ever trafficked. I'll give you a year to do that. Then sell this place. All money from the sale goes directly to your victims. Then you move to some sunny little hellhole where there's no extradition treaty. Those are my conditions.'

I pause. Paige and his bodyguards exchange glances. The crackling of the fire seems louder.

'This is me being merciful, Mr Paige. It's a one-time offer and is off the table any time I feel like it, because I'm not a very merciful soul when it comes to creatures like you.'

I'm never entirely sure what a stunned silence is, but I'm pretty certain the quietude that follows my offer is a prime example. Eventually, Paige looks at the woman pointing a gun at my trouser leg. He nods to my right kneecap and she aims her pistol in its direction.

Paige turns to face me. He doesn't break eye contact as he orders, 'Cripple him.'

-6-

Aside from ghouls like Sandy Paige, I don't mind the people I'm forced to mix with. Killers, crooks, cheats and deadbeats. Half the time, they're a perk of the job and some of my best friends are sociopaths. Good company, and usually more honest than the forces that I nominally represent.

The death threats, frequent attempts on my life and having to give up bank holidays don't bother me, either.

It's my clients that kill me.

You see, just for once I'd like a nice, easy case from a returning customer. That never happens. *Never.* Because if I do my job well, my client shakes my hand, transfers payment into my meagre bank account and vows eternal friendship. They've forgotten my name before they've reached the end of my driveway, of course, because they just want to move on. Fair enough. And if I screw up the case, my client either winds up dead, which is bad for business, or they hold me responsible for the mess they got themselves into, which is worse.

But sometimes, like today, it's on me.

I visited Paige's mansion by choice. Gave him the ultimatum by choice. And I'm not going to back down, by choice.

The two women murmur, 'Yes, sir.'

But before they can pull the triggers, there's a light knock at the door and Paige's wife, Louisa, walks in. She's about the same age as her husband but looks a lot older than her sixty years. She's a kindly looking Scot whom I've chatted to more than once.

'Mr Novak!' she exclaims. 'I thought I heard your voice. Will you be staying for afternoon tea?'

Paige answers for me. 'Sadly not, my dear. I'm afraid our guest has only a little time left on this mortal coil.'

She wags a finger at him and says playfully, 'Oh, Sandy!'

It's remarkable. She knows he isn't joking but treats his criminal empire like it's a vaguely embarrassing hobby, as if he's building a model railway of the Bluebell Line in his attic.

He stands, rounds his desk and slips his arm across her shoulders. 'Why don't you wait for me in the drawing room, dear?'

I say, 'Why don't you wait here and see exactly how your husband runs his business?'

He responds with a calm, 'I'll give you one more chance. Who put you on to me?'

'I came here of my own free will. Your two clowns dragged me up here, but that's because I wanted to see you. Let that sink in . . . So, *your* final chance. My offer. Take it or leave it.'

He's impatient and incredulous, but impatient wins out. 'I'm getting bored of this. It's your lucky day, Mr Novak. I'll make this swift.' And to his bodyguards: 'Shoot him in the head.'

Louise asks timidly, 'Do you think that's wise, Sandy?'

A slight hesitation. 'You're right.' He takes a deep breath. 'Shoot him in the chest. Less blood on the Egyptian rug.'

I ask, 'Doesn't the condemned man get a final drink?'

My eyes flicker to my left. Almost time . . .

'No.'

'Pity. I'd have killed for a G&T. Navy-strength gin if you had it.'

'Oh, I have a couple of bottles,' Paige replies, waving airily to the open globe and its collection of spirits. 'I'll tell you what. In less than a minute, I'll pour myself a drink and toast the late Marc Novak. Fair enough? And now, I'm afraid, it's time for you to shuffle off this . . .' He glances over to the bottles. Pauses. Narrows his eyes.

In my peripheral vision, I see it's very nearly time . . .

'What's going on, Novak?'

'Mrs Paige. You might want to stand back.'

I look into the blazing log fire. Paige follows my gaze and spots the two bottles of gin I tossed onto the flames when I entered the room. He's about to say something, but I'll never know what, because at that precise moment the spirit in one of the bottles reaches peak temperature and three things – collectively known as flame jetting – happen almost at once.

The metal, screw-top lid blows off. The vapour from the bubbling hot gin ignites, drawing the flames into the bottle. And so, of course, as fire meets liquid that's 57 per cent alcohol, combustion takes place, skyrocketing the pressure in the bottle and forcing the spirit to expand and emerge as a jagged bolt of fire.

In other words, there's a bloody big bang, followed by a whooshing flame-jet that lashes out a good four feet into the room, with thick shards of glass spattering into the blazing air, just to add to the fun.

This dragon's breath of a reaction scorches into Paige's face. He screeches and falls back. His wife, who stepped away when I suggested, screams at her husband's anguish. But before the bodyguards can react, this first explosion triggers a second. The glass of the other bottle of gin shatters and the spirit, searing onto open flames, is spat into the study as a dispersed, fiery spray. A million droplets of alcohol forming a burning cloud that—

I launch myself forward towards the bodyguard that had been standing nearest to me. She hadn't been expecting the blast, and still reeling from its suddenness and force, she's off guard. I tear the Beretta from her grasp, take a couple of paces back and say, 'Phone an ambulance for your boss.'

The other armed woman has been knocked to the floor by the first explosion. I see half of her face is studded with slivers of glass and I'm guessing she dropped her gun, but I can't immediately spot it.

I ask, 'Are you all right?' as she staggers to her feet.

The other bodyguard supports her. They exchange a few words in a language I don't understand and one of them snarls, 'We're leaving!'

I'm covering them both with a loaded sidearm, but there's not a lot I can do to stop them as they limp from the scene. A corner of the Egyptian rug that Paige was so worried about is alight, and several of the books in the shelves to my right are starting to smoulder. Half of me wishes I was leaving with the bodyguards.

But Louisa is sitting on the floor and has hauled her husband across to her, so his head rests on her lap. He's unconscious, but the rise and fall of his chest tells me he's alive.

'You'll be all right, Sandy . . .' she tells him. 'You'll be all right . . .'

I pull my phone from my pocket and ring my contact with the local police. He understands the urgency of the situation, and yes, he'll send an ambulance. But the geography means it'll take his people at least twenty minutes to reach the estate.

I say, 'That's fine,' hang up and drop to my haunches beside Louisa.

The call took less than thirty seconds, but the bookshelf is now ablaze and it's clear we need to leave.

'Mrs Paige. We must get out of here as soon as possible if we're to—'

She looks at me with absolute fury. 'What have you done?'

'You asked me to look into your husband's business! You thought he was just running harmless drugs, but he was trafficking children! For two decades he's been—'

I'm not sure why I feel the need to explain myself, but whatever I've said isn't enough and she shouts over me, 'You're a liar!'

'I'll let you go before the police get here, so you can tell your children your own way and—'

'We don't have children!' Her voice drops to a murmur. 'We gave up trying . . .'

And that gap in my knowledge is on me. I've compiled a file that's forensic about his business- life but totally unconcerned with his private life.

But before I can digest that, she adds, 'We gave up trying twenty years ago.'

Twenty years ago. Around about the same time he began his child trafficking operations. This hits us both. Her face crumples and she gestures to me, inviting me in. Very soon now, this whole room will go up like a tinder box, but the wife of an ice-hearted killer is tearfully asking for a hug. So I lean across, embrace her and gently whisper, 'We'll get Sandy to safety and—'

'Mr Novak.'

'Yes?'

I feel her press something hard into my waist and suddenly realise what happened to the second bodyguard's Beretta.

'I'm sorry.'

I hear two muffled thuds and the pain through my stomach is excruciating. I topple onto the rug. Feel myself passing out.

Before the encroaching darkness claims me entirely, my vision blurs. But I can see flames. Lots of flames. And I can make out the woman who brought me into the case dragging one of the vilest predators I've ever known from the room, whilst I lie on his study floor, bleeding out onto a rug I could never afford.

Like I said, it's my clients that kill me.

-7-

My friends are all doing better than me. I don't mean at this very moment, although I'm guessing they're ahead on points as I lie in this impromptu recreation of Dante's *Inferno*. I mean in life generally.

They went the ways you're supposed to go. The safe jobs and safer relationships that I didn't exactly avoid but . . . Well, they avoided me. And so here I am. Alone in every conceivable sense of the word, whilst they have annual appraisals, friends round for dinner and shiny children they use to clog up my Facebook feed.

The other day, an old university pal told me about his latest venture, quietly informing me that he could let me in on the ground floor. I said it sounded like a long shot for someone approaching forty, and I'd rather be parachuted onto the balcony of the penthouse suite. I'm not sure he understood my response.

The flames are crackling closer, now.

I meant I didn't have the time to build the kind of life he's already constructed. But it's more than that, of course.

The fire's heat scorches the side of my face.

You see, for some of us, it's too late. It's a kind of trap, I suppose. And always was, from the moment we realise we don't care about being like the rest.

And now I don't know whether I can escape.

*

Just when I thought my day couldn't get any worse, the world blows up.

I'm lying supine on the floor of Sandy Paige's study. The heat against my skin and the pain in my stomach are both intense. I'm groggily coming to, and as my eyes flicker open, I see the open globe, full of bottles, explode as the raging fire engulfs the alcohol. Instinctively, I cover my face with the crook of my arm, but I feel something slice into my right temple.

The blaze has caught hold and there's no sign of Paige, his wife or any of their staff. I kneel, then manage to get to my feet. I'm consciously trying to ignore the pain in my stomach, but it's like walking on burning coals whilst telling yourself you're sauntering across a bed of feathers. The theory's great, but it still hurts like hell.

There's a bank of flames between me and the door that leads to the landing. The windows are barred and there's no other exit. I give the room a final scan and for some reason – I've no idea why – I grab a framed photograph that stands on top of the cherrywood desk. It shows Louisa, her husband and three kids all smiling. I suppose this was the picture that convinced me the Paiges had children. I glance at it. Shake my head. Place it back on the desk. *Let it burn.*

I turn and charge through the fire and don't stop running until I reach the foot of the grand staircase that leads to the large entrance hall.

I must have been out for some time, because the blaze has spread. I stand in the lobby of this huge, opulent house and shout, 'Is everybody out? Does anybody need help?'

'Looks like you do!' I spin around in time to see a firefighter march through the front door. She adds, 'We need to get you out of here right away!'

'I'm fine.' Her eyes dart to the blood seeping through my fingers over my stomach wound. 'Ish.'

'Out! Come on – you can lean on me.'

'We need to make sure there's no one left in the house.'

'That's kind of our job.'

More firefighters are rushing through the front door.

I tell her, 'I'll give you a hand.'

'Are you serious?'

'Not often.'

'You can barely stand.'

'*I'm fine.*'

'Oh, yeah?'

'Fighting fit.'

She yanks my right arm and begins pulling me from the house. I yelp in pain. She murmurs, 'Fighting fit,' under her breath and when we're outside asks, 'Do you need oxygen?'

'We all need oxygen.'

'Don't be a smart-arse.'

'I think this might need seeing to, if that's OK?'

I peel my left palm from my waist but don't look down, because seeing the injury always makes it worse. Every doctor will tell you that. Probably.

But the firefighter swears and pulls a massive grimace, which is never how you want a first responder to, well, respond.

I ask, 'Is it that bad?'

'You won't be doing sit-ups for a couple of days.'

I offer her my right, unbloodied palm. 'I'm Marc Novak.'

'Stacey Smith.' Her huge right glove envelops my hand. 'First time in the Highlands, Novak?'

'Yep!'

'Hell of an entrance.'

'It's the best part of my act. Thanks for getting here so quickly.'

'You got lucky. We were doing a drill just across the way.' She glances at the burning manor house. 'What were you *supposed* to be doing here?'

'What makes you think I'm responsible?' I'm trying to sound indignant, but it's hard because she's laughing at me.

'Call it a crazy hunch,' she replies.

And at this moment, out of nowhere – just when I thought things were calming down – it happens. And happens big.

-8-

The fire must have reached the generator in the mansion's west wing because my conversation with Stacey is interrupted by a gigantic explosion. Part of the building's façade, away to my right, is blasted apart and although we're not hit by any debris, the force of it knocks us both off our feet.

We land on the ground, on our backs. I glance to my left. Stacey eyes me like the whole thing is somehow my fault. Which you could argue it is. But she doesn't *absolutely* know that.

I give a defiant shrug. 'I only popped over to borrow the lawnmower.'

She laughs for a second, but stops when I wince. The blood is pumping out of me fast. Maybe the adrenaline is starting to wear off, but I suddenly feel nauseous and feeble.

Stacey says, 'We need to get you help . . .' and a lot of other words I don't hear. It's as though someone has turned the world's volume right down to zero.

I see the house engulfed by flames. Firefighters running towards us and suddenly—

Stacey's face, worried and intense. She's mouthing something. My name? A command? A question?

I start to tell her, 'Don't worry, I'm fine,' but feel myself passing out before I can reach the end of the sentence. I sense myself sinking into the ground and realise that, given the remote location of Paige's estate, there's every chance I'll have bled to death before medical assistance can reach me.

The world is still silent, but Stacey is directly above me. I think she's tending to my wound, but even that's stopped hurting. Small mercies, you could call it. I see her look up at my face, and she's shouting something in my direction. She's also weeping.

My head falls back and the sunlight dazzles me. Before I slide into unconsciousness, two things occur to me.

I didn't think firefighters wept, and it's far too nice a day to die.

Smoke drifts across the sun.

Leonid's Story
Yekaterinburg, Russia. July, 1918

Smoke drifted across the naked light bulb. Leonid Pavlovich Kiselyov, one of the Russian soldiers tasked with the execution of the Romanovs and their retinue, realised the 'procedure', as Yurovsky had phrased it, was becoming a bloody shambles. They'd been shooting at the civilians, who stood and sat just feet away, for several minutes and yet only Nikolai and Alexandra were dead. Maria Romanova had been wounded, but not fatally. Leonid had seen the intoxicated Peter Ermakov shoot her in the thigh as she'd scurried towards the room's rear doors.

But, that aside, the condemned prisoners appeared astonishingly, almost supernaturally, uninjured. Alexei remained bolt upright in his armchair, a pale picture of horror and bewilderment. His sisters were screaming. Jemmy, Anastasia's pet dog, barked incessantly. Eugene Botkin, the Romanovs' doctor and Nikolai's close friend, was yelling something – Leonid could not hear what exactly – before a bullet to his forehead finally silenced the physician.

And, of course, the noise of sustained gunfire in the confines of this small semi-basement was immense. Shattering.

Grey-white smoke from the hot barrels of the sidearms filled the room and when he inhaled, Leonid could taste the sharp chemical tang of cordite and feel its caustic burn at the back of his throat. Visibility was further worsened by a heavy snowfall of dust from the plaster ceiling, loosened by the reverberation of the shooting. And yet Leonid could see that Olga, Tatiana, Maria, Anastasia and Alexei were all clearly alive.

Before they'd entered the room, every member of the firing squad had been given rough instructions as to whom they should kill. Each soldier had nodded his compliance, as if agreeing to a minor matter such as manual labour, which was perhaps all that murder had become in Russia after so many years of warfare. But here, in this smoke-filled messy hell, the majority of them had opted to spend their ammunition on the adults. Even now, even here, the prospect of gunning down terrified young women was too unholy for most of the men.

Yet that didn't explain everything. Ermakov and a couple of the other drunken assassins had taken plenty of shots at the Romanovas who remained relatively unscathed. Leonid felt sure it was simply an illusion born of the smoke and chaos, or his own mind playing tricks on him, but it looked, once or twice, as if bullets were ricocheting off the girls and zinging into the surrounding brickwork.

He felt certain of one thing, though. Something remarkable was happening. The twelve gunmen were becoming panicked. Leonid looked across to Yurovsky, who by now had switched from his Colt to a Mauser. All across Russia, there was a scarcity of bread, Leonid briefly reflected, but there was never any shortage of guns. The commandant seemed on the verge of issuing an order, but before he could bellow any instructions, a burly soldier dashed into the room, shouting for the firing to stop.

Leonid recognised Alexey Kabanov, as had Nikolai many weeks earlier. He'd seen the former Tzar spot Kabanov whilst walking in the gardens. 'You served in my cavalry regiment, did you not?' Nikolai had asked. Kabanov confirmed he had, and this reply, overheard by Yurovsky, had singled him out as one to watch. A man who might harbour a secret allegiance to the prisoner. But now, the anguish on Kabanov's face was not caused by the sight of his former commander's corpse.

'The gunfire can be heard from outside!' he called across to Yurovsky. This came as no surprise to Leonid, who imagined it could probably be heard on the other side of Russia.

Yurovsky raised his hand and the firing died out. The noise of gunfire was replaced by worse: the sound of sobbing and wailing of the prisoners. Leonid could also hear the muffle of guards racing around in the rooms above, doubtless rattled by the unexpected shooting below them.

The young soldier to Leonid's right was staring at the miraculous survivors of the onslaught. Without taking his eyes from them, he murmured, 'They *are* divine! God Himself protects them!'

Before Leonid could reply, the flustered Kabanov continued, 'The whole neighbourhood is waking!'

Yurovsky didn't speak a word, but his expression said, *Well, what would you have me do, comrade?*

Kabanov said, 'Kill them using your bayonets! Much quieter.' He glanced at Alexei and his sisters. 'And quicker.'

Again, Yurovsky didn't open his mouth. He simply shrugged and swished his hand in front of his face; an irritated and impatient command to bludgeon to death a line of petrified young people and their friends. Appalled, Leonid hung back. The maniacal Peter Ermakov and a handful of his comrades felt no such disinclination.

Leonid suspected the next few minutes would define his life, and he was quite correct. Just not at all in the way he anticipated.

-10-

Even before I open my eyes, I know I'm in a hospital. The starched bed linen cocoons my body too tightly for one thing. The scent of the place is another giveaway. Disinfectant and, from further away, the aroma of food, which, although not inedible, remains unique to hospitals and D-cat prisons. But the sound is the main thing. That regular beep-beep-beep of close-by equipment and the more distant chatter, with its cheerful robustness that I always associate with NHS nurses, peg this place as an infirmary. The quality of the sounds suggests I'm in a private room, which is fine by me, as long as I'm not paying for it.

I could open my eyes but choose not to. I want to rest. But before I can drift off, I hear a male voice I half recognise.

'How is he?'

A female voice replies, 'He'll live.'

'Pity.'

OK. Now I recognise the voice 100 per cent. The less than dulcet tones of Jeremy Simmonds are unmistakeable. I met the guy on a case I worked a while back. Technically speaking, he hired me, which goes a long way to explaining the way I currently feel about my clientele.

He adds, 'He's very pale. I mean, *unnaturally* pale.'

'He lost a lot of blood.'

'Looks like he lost all of it.' I sense movement and his voice is nearer when he asks, 'Are you *sure* he's not dead?'

I open my eyes and Simmonds' face looms inches above mine. 'Don't get your hopes up.'

He looks genuinely disappointed, straightens his back and shakes his head, as if my survival is a childish prank designed to annoy him. 'I knew it was too much to hope for.'

'Good to see you, too, Simmonds.'

He coughs theatrically as I pronounce his surname and his eyes swivel to his right, drawing my attention to the presence of a medic stood a pace behind him.

'I'm Doctor Sharma.' She takes a step forward. 'How are you feeling, Mr Novak?'

'Oh, he's fine,' Simmonds assures her. 'Takes more than a bullet to stop this one.'

'And, believe me, he's tried. How am I doing, doctor?'

'Well, you were shot from close range. Never a good idea. But the bullets sliced through your body obliquely.'

'What does that mean?'

'It means . . .' She hesitates. I always get nervous when doctors hesitate. And now, to make matters worse, she repeats the last two words, as if she needs a proper run-up to her diagnosis. 'It means I have bad news for you.'

-11-

'Look, to be precise . . .' The doctor moves her hips and puts one hand on the side of her waist and the other on the front of her stomach. 'The bullets penetrated your lower abdomen at this point, travelled through your body and exited here.' She moves the hand at the side of her waist. 'So they missed your internal organs.'

I feel a degree of relief, but she doesn't sound too thrilled. 'That's a good thing, right?'

'You lost a massive amount of blood and suffered a degree of internal bleeding. Luckily, we were able to operate immediately and we saved your life.'

The news comes as more than a little disconcerting. 'You had to operate to save my life?'

Doctor Sharma doesn't hide her exasperation. 'You were shot in the stomach, Mr Novak. What did you think would happen? We'd put a plaster over it and send you home with our good wishes and a bottle of aspirin?'

'I'm very grateful for what you did, doctor.'

'You were airlifted to the nearest hospital, where I operated. Then your friend here ordered you to be moved to this place. You're in a village cottage hospital.'

I suppose Simmonds thought it'd be easier to keep an eye on me in this place. I ask Doctor Sharma, 'Will I be OK?'

Simmonds steps forward again, so now he's closest to me. 'Oh, don't be such a baby. Of course you'll be as fit as a fiddle in the morning – won't he, doctor?'

She shakes her head. 'Actually, the nature of the injuries means—'

'There you go!' Simmonds exclaims, interrupting her. 'Nothing to worry about!' He turns to face Sharma. 'Could I have five minutes alone with the patient?'

She looks hesitant. 'Mr Peters . . .'

Oh, that old gag. When I first met Simmonds, he was using the alias *Thom Peters* and I'm guessing he's at it again because he likes how manly the name sounds.

'Doctor . . .' His voice has hardened. 'You've seen my identification. My status *has* been explained to you.'

A pause. 'Five minutes, Mr Peters. That's all I'm giving you. Do not vex or in any way aggravate my patient.'

He nods. 'Perish the thought.'

As Doctor Sharma walks towards the room's solitary door, I lay my hand across the linen above my stomach and call out, 'Isn't there anything you can do about the pain, doctor?'

She replies, 'I'll give you more fentanyl when I get back.'

'I was talking about Peters.'

She laughs, leaves the room and Simmonds scowls at me. 'You haven't changed.'

'And I doubt you have, either.'

Jeremy Simmonds is part of British Intelligence. He doesn't work for MI5 or MI6 or any branch that's entirely official. I doubt his section has a short, neat acronym to define its purpose or standing. You see, his world lacks little things like 'neat'. And 'accountability' and 'ethics', for that matter.

When he hears the door shut, he pulls up a chair, sits down and says, 'Right. Let's get down to business.'

41

In the past few hours, I've been threatened with death, burnt, shot in the stomach and caught in the blast of a gigantic explosion. But this is the first time today I've felt nervous.

'You and I have no business.'

'Oh, but we do, old man. Now . . .' He slides his chair closer to my bed. 'Here's what we need from you.'

-12-

Jeremy Simmonds looks exactly how you'd expect a man called Jeremy Simmonds to look. He's late forties, medium height and no matter how expensive the suit he's wearing happens to be, somehow he always makes it look like he bought it from a supermarket on a whim after his wife sent him out to do the big shop. I doubt he *entirely* recognises this fact and suspect that every time he leaves for work he studies himself in the mirror and nods before turning away.

I say *entirely*, because somewhere deep down inside what I charitably call his soul, I'm guessing he's aware of his flaws. I mention this because in my mind it contributes to the unholy trinity that can make even the limpest man a threat. He holds a degree of official power. He retains ambition. But he remains an underachiever. More than this, I get the feeling he feels thwarted. These things combine to make him dangerous. And so no matter how pompous and poor he can be with people, if you are to fully understand Jeremy Simmonds, you must appreciate how hazardous dealing with him can be.

'All right, Novak. Just how involved are you in this child trafficking ring?'

I don't like where this is heading.

'I'm not involved in it. I was investigating it.'

'Same thing.'

'No. Woodward and Bernstein were not *involved* in the Watergate scandal.'

43

'I doubt Nixon would have agreed.'

Fair point.

'I've been *investigating* Sandy Paige for three months.'

There's a pause. 'You've been investigating Sandy Paige.' Simmonds silently acknowledges the news with the nod of a man who's crashed his car whilst taking his driving test and has just been informed he's failed it. He rubs the bridge of his nose. 'One of the UK's most respected businessmen. One of the Tories' biggest contributors and a champion of British investment for more years than I care to remember. Philanthropist. Friend of royalty. Media darling. Do you have any idea how careful and respectful we have to be with this man?'

'Yes. Yes, I do. The files of Operation Yewtree were groaning with the weight of men's names whom we had to be careful and respectful of.'

Simmonds shouts, 'Hardly the same thing! For Christ's sake!' He leans back. Lowers his voice. 'Right. Let's try to sort out this mess.' He speaks like he's doing me a favour. 'How did you get caught up in this in the first place?'

'Paige's wife approached me.'

'Louisa?'

'You know her?'

He's suddenly guarded. 'Know of her.'

I frown. 'How long have you been *involved* with the Paiges?'

'Don't try to be funny, Novak.'

'It's what keeps me going, Mr Simmonds.'

'So, Louisa Paige approached you and said what? *If you haven't anything on at the moment, would you be good enough to bring down my husband's criminal empire, Mr Novak?*'

44

The sarcasm is new, but his reluctance to believe anything I tell him is familiar.

'Those weren't her exact words.'

'Oh, get on with it, man!'

So I get on with it.

-13-

Just over three months ago, over a hot cup of Tanzanian peaberry coffee, Louisa Paige told me the esteemed Alexander 'Sandy' Paige was a criminal. She sat in my front room and explained that she believed her husband was involved in the distribution of narcotics. She further understood he may have hired men to commit acts of violence in order to make his business run smoothly. She harboured absolutely no moral qualms about any of this.

'If people want to do drugs – let 'em!' she'd exclaimed.

But Louisa had heard disturbing rumours that Sandy was also involved in child trafficking. She said she didn't believe the rumours but wanted her mind to be free from any suspicions.

'So she hired you,' Simmonds interrupts, 'to investigate her own husband?'

I nod. Looking back, when Louisa initially reached out to me, I believe she was secretly certain that Sandy Paige was involved in trafficking. But in the period that followed, she convinced herself it couldn't possibly be true of the person she loved, to the point that she ultimately saw me as the enemy for confronting him about his crimes.

'But why on earth did you believe her in the first place? How could you accept Paige is a criminal? He's so damned respectable.'

'Respectability is very much an artificial façade. You know that. It didn't seem such a stretch to believe Paige's façade was concealing something terrible.'

'And I thought I was cynical.' He sniffs. 'What have you got against respectability?'

'Nothing. I may even try it some day.'

'I wouldn't bother. It's overrated.'

After the sarcastic humour, his wryness is the second time he's surprised me today.

'Carry on!' he urges.

'No.'

'What?'

'Before I do, I want information from you. What the hell are you doing here? How did you know I was involved in this whole thing? I get shot and when I wake up, you're at my bedside. I thought I'd died and gone straight to hell. But how does that happen? Why were you keeping tabs on me?'

'You're a person of interest to several departments who all like to keep an eye on you, Novak. Especially after the Diana business. When you were seen to be poking around in Paige's affairs and child trafficking began coming up in the reports, well, bells started ringing. A whole bally peal of them.'

'I can imagine. That still doesn't explain your presence, though. The powers that be see I'm taking an interest in Sandy Paige. Why wasn't I just forcibly warned off? Tell me what happened.'

'No.'

'What?'

'We're sharing information, remember. Go on with your story.'

That seems fair enough, but I still pull a face like a child who's been told to eat his greens. 'Well, I accepted the case. Louisa thought she'd given me limited access to her husband's accounts, but she actually opened the door wide enough for me to see his kingdom. It wasn't a pretty sight.'

Simmonds slowly nods. 'I can imagine.'

'Long story short – I compiled a dossier on him.'

'Extensive?'

'It's got enough facts and figures to make even the most expensive defence barrister throw down their wig in despair.'

'You amassed *conclusive* evidence that Paige was implicated in child trafficking?'

'More than implicated. He was up to his Gordonstoun old school tie in it.'

'Give me details.'

'Kidnapping or acquiring the kids or babies is the easy bit.'

Simmonds murmurs, 'Usually from a country like Vietnam or Romania or Albania?'

'That's right,' I tell him. 'Getting them to the UK or US or wherever the order has been placed . . . That's also pretty simple if you know the right routes. The tricky bit is the documentation. If the client wants to adopt the child legally, or pretend he or she was their biological offspring . . . that all takes documentation and fixing. That's where our Mr Paige came in. Sure, he was involved in the set-up, acquisition and transportation, but his real genius was in making those arrangements.'

To his credit, Simmonds looks aghast. 'I imagine he exploited all his contacts and know-how and nobody suspected a thing when good old Sandy requested a favour. Christ! So, you compiled the dossier. I'll need that, by the way. What happened next?'

I shake my head. 'Your turn. Why wasn't I forcibly warned off the Paige case? Who called off the dogs?'

It's obvious Simmonds is considering obfuscation, but after a moment, he takes a deep breath and replies, 'Me. Stupidly.'

'What?'

'My new boss, the replacement for Miss Winters, told me you were investigating Paige and suggested that you were to be encouraged to abandon your inquiries.'

'But?'

'But I heard the case involved child trafficking. I said if something as appalling as that was going on . . .' Another hesitation. 'I couldn't think of a better chap to investigate and bring down the bastards at the head of the ring.'

'Technically speaking, you can't be at the head of a ring.'

'I also told my boss you were an eternal reprobate. An understatement, although—'

I interrupt him. 'Seriously? You stuck up for me?'

'No! God, no! I stuck up for the kids you were trying to help.'

It amounts to the same thing and I'm both touched and taken aback.

'Well, I have to say . . .'

Fortunately, a nurse breezes into the room, so we're both spared the embarrassment of me having to express gratitude.

She says, 'Mr Novak?' Her accent is Eastern European.

'Yes.'

'Good.' She looks into my eyes like she's caught me stealing the cutlery. 'You must drink this.'

I'd guess she's in her thirties. She's tall and slim with long dark hair that's been lashed into a ponytail.

I tell her, 'There must be some mistake. I ordered cocktails for two.'

Her dark eyes show no sign of amusement. 'There's been no mistake.'

I take the glass of clear liquid that she hands me. 'Glad to hear it . . .' I look for her name badge, but she isn't wearing one.

The nurse turns and walks away. I raise the glass to my lips. She reaches the door, turns to me and says, 'Goodbye, Mr Novak.'

-14-

I'm about to take a gulp from the glass that's just been handed to me. As I begin to tilt it back, Simmonds pipes up impatiently, 'Your turn, Novak!'

I pause. Lower the glass. 'I should take my medicine.'

'Oh, you can swig your Calpol later!'

As I place the still-full glass on my bedside table, he chivvies me along with, 'You compile the dossier. Well? What then?'

'A lot of people who assisted Paige did so because they thought they were helping with a legal adoption process. I didn't want those people hurt. There's more to it, I suppose, but the bottom line is I went to Paige and offered him a deal. All his cash to go to his victims and he could disappear to some backwater with no extradition treaty.'

'How did that go down?'

'My client shot me in the stomach.'

'So very nearly a happy ending!'

I recount the events that took place in Paige's study, then, using my phone, forward the dossier to Simmonds. I've just pressed *send* when Doctor Sharma bobs her head into the room.

'Right!' she declares. 'Time's up! We need to examine Mr Novak to make sure there's no collection of blood and—'

'I require just one more minute, thank you!'

Simmonds' peremptory tone clearly grates on the medic, but I give her a *'please, miss!'* nod and she snaps, 'One minute!' and disappears.

I ask Simmonds, 'So what happens now?'

He gets to his feet. 'I return to civilisation.'

'I meant to me.'

'The doctors do their bit. You convalesce. My people go after Paige.' He grabs his long cashmere coat from a hook on the wall. 'Christ knows what the PM will say about all this.'

'Yes, it must be *jolly* difficult for the poor old thing.'

'Oh, one more thing, Novak. Our sources tell us that Paige has already taken out a contract on you.' He slips into his coat. 'He's paid someone to have you bumped off.'

'That's a *one more thing*?'

'One was reluctant to mention it earlier. Didn't want to bring the mood down.'

'Very thoughtful. Will I get protection?'

'Shouldn't think so. Budget cuts. Public purse. Paperwork. You know how it is.'

'Thanks ever so.'

'Stop fretting!' He buttons up his coat. 'I was pulling your leg. I've ordered men to watch you whilst you're here. They should arrive within the hour.'

That's something at least, I suppose. 'Thank you.'

Simmonds stands over me, and as if he's being forced at gunpoint to say the words, he asks, 'Is there anything else I can do for you? Anything you'd like?'

'I could murder a drink.'

'I'm not a trolley dolly, Novak!'

'Was worth a shot.'

He gives another sigh and pulls a silver hip flask from his coat pocket. 'Here. I suppose you could do with this more than me right now.' He hands me the flask and walks towards the door, pausing before he opens it. 'Why do we do it, Novak? Do you ever stop to ask yourself that?'

'All the time.'

'And?'

'I haven't a clue.'

He gives me the ghost of a smile. 'For once, we are aligned.'

He opens the door.

'Simmonds!'

'Yes?'

'Thank you.'

He looks vaguely embarrassed and points a finger in my direction. 'I shall want that hip flask back, Novak!'

He leaves the room and I smile. God, I could do with a drink. I open the hip flask. Sniff its contents.

Oh, no . . .

I take a swig.

It's full of coffee. Bloody coffee!

If I wasn't so aggrieved, I'd laugh. It's zero alcohol and the real kicker is, it's terrible coffee.

I screw the lid back on as the doctor re-enters the room. 'How are you doing?' she asks.

I slide the flask under the sheets. 'I'm good, thanks.' As she approaches, I remember the medicine the nurse told me to drink, turn and reach for the glass. 'Just about to drink up, like the nurse told me to.'

'Nurse?'

'The lady who brought me this.' I raise the glass.

'This is a cottage hospital, Mr Novak. We only have one nurse. And he called in sick this morning. Right now, it's just me and Billy the porter.'

I attempt a smile. 'Just my little joke. Mr Peters poured me a drink from a bottle he sneaked in.'

She scowls at me. 'Well, you shouldn't drink it.'

I recall Simmonds' warning.

Our sources tell us that Paige has already taken out a contract on you.

I place the glass back on my bedside table. 'For once,' I tell the doctor, 'we are aligned.'

-15-

When the scans and checks are complete, Doctor Sharma informs me in mournful tones that I have '. . . a collection of blood'.

'Pardon?'

She repeats her assessment.

'All right. I don't know what that is. It makes it sound like I'm stockpiling haemoglobin as a side hustle.'

'It means you might die.'

'I think I prefer my interpretation.'

'I'm sorry to be so blunt, but you need to start taking this seriously.'

'Of course. Sorry . . . I'm just . . .' I'm just floundering. 'Is there anything you can do to help?'

'The collection of blood means our attempts to repair your veins weren't successful. At least not entirely. So we'll open you up and where the trauma wasn't repaired, we'll use grafting to seal the wounds shut. How does that sound?'

'Let's hope the operation isn't in vein this time.'

'That's your worst yet.'

'I was going to say it sounds like a bloody mess, but it felt too on the nose.'

She removes her glasses and gives the point some thought. 'No. That would have been more accurate. Believe me, Mr Novak, this whole thing *is* a bloody mess.'

'I take it I'm going to be moved back to the big hospital for the operation?'

'Sadly not. Your Mr Peters has insisted we undertake surgery here. Security concerns, apparently.'

'That doesn't sound ideal. Is this place suitable for operations?'

'Oh, there's a theatre. Hasn't been used since the Relief of Mafeking, but we can spruce it up. The main issue is getting the staff that we'll need over here. Medically speaking, that will cause a level of discomfort in the piriformis.' She sees me looking blank and clarifies, 'It'll be a pain in the arse.' She turns to leave. 'You've got some paperwork to fill in and then . . .'

'Yes?'

'There are a couple of gunmen who'd like to see you.'

I peer at her. She's not joking.

'Just a couple? I must be slipping.'

*

I hate paperwork. I especially hate medical paperwork. The form Doctor Sharma gives me to sign essentially states that if anything goes wrong with the operation, such as me dying in theatre, well, it's just bad luck. The document is an 'Oh, well!' waiver. A legal shrug of the shoulders. The medics responsible cannot be held to be responsible in any way.

Yes, I know it's all about insurance and indemnification, but it does nothing to boost my mood or my confidence in the people who'll soon be slicing me open and sifting through my veins and arteries like a chef examining the quality of a pan of linguine.

But still, I scrawl my signature at the bottom of the third page and hand it over to Doctor Sharma.

'Thank you, Mr Novak.'

'No problem. But I want you to know I've auto-set my account ahead of time. So if I do die on the operating table, I'll be leaving this place a very scathing review on Tripadvisor.'

'Good.' She checks my signature and nods. 'That might be enough to get me suspended on full pay. You'd be doing me a favour.'

'I've not just put ideas into your head, have I?'

She closes the document and begins to walk away. 'You may never know, Mr Novak. You may never know!'

'Always a pleasure to see you, doctor.'

'I'll send in the gunmen!'

'Thank you.' And momentarily alone, I murmur to myself, 'I remember when it was nurses.'

*

The 'gunmen' Sharma was referring to are the two bodyguards Simmonds drummed up for me. They're both built like bison and wear dark suits tight enough to ensure the outlines of their shoulder holsters and sidearms are clearly visible through their jackets. One introduces himself as Dave. No imagination. The other calls himself Emile. They both have English accents that suggest they hail from Lancashire or Yorkshire.

'Well, I appreciate you coming. But I'm hoping you're just here as a precaution.'

Dave is already looking around my small room and doesn't break off from his assessment. 'I'm afraid not, Marc. Mr Simmonds has already received some significant intel.'

'Significant intel?'

'That's right,' Emile confirms. 'All the intercepted comms point to one thing. There'll be a full-blown attempt on your life within the next twenty-four hours.'

56

-16-

P_re- and post-surgery, Dave and Emile always keep me in sight. It's hard to simultaneously represent an unpleasant reminder whilst remaining a reassuring presence, but this couple of guys manage it without even trying. After the operation, Doctor Sharma informs me the grafts have been applied successfully and a five-star review on Tripadvisor would be appreciated.

I get back to my former room, fall into a deep slumber and have insanely vivid dreams. Don't worry, I won't bore you with them. But the thing is, when I wake up, I'm not sure if I'm still dreaming.

A face is watching me. A very nice face. I half recognise its owner. She's someone I know, but not well. I try to say, 'Hello!' and the face smiles at me.

'How are you feeling?'

A Scottish accent.

'I'm good, thanks.' This time, I can talk, but my head still feels foggy.

'You don't remember me, do you?'

Of course, I don't.

'Of course I do!' I guess she's slightly older than me. She has big dark hair that's so distinctive, I can't fathom how I don't recognise her. 'How are you?' She's wearing a light pink tracksuit and long acrylic nails that make it look like she's grown a set of sparkly gold talons. 'And thank you for being here . . .'

'You're a detective.'

'And so, it seems, are you.'

'I mean, everyone in the village is talking about you. They're saying you brought down Sandy Paige.'

I don't reply, but push myself up and lean back into my pillows.

'Don't worry,' she tells me, 'they all hated him. Patronising wee fecker. They're over the moon you exposed him. Shame about Mrs Paige, though. She always seemed OK.'

'She shot me in the stomach at point-blank range.'

'Yeah, well, can't say I blame her. You have that effect on people, Novak!'

She laughs and I recognise her. Stacey Smith. The firefighter who took care of me at Paige's mansion.

'I should take umbrage at that, but I'm still indebted to you. I don't think I had time to say thank you.'

'You didn't.'

'Well, thank you.'

'Who's Precious?'

I choose to misconstrue her question. 'We all are, Stacey.'

She narrows her eyes. 'You kept saying her name when you were out.'

'She's just a friend.'

'An ex?'

'We were engaged. Then we weren't. She shacked up with another bloke, but that didn't take, either.'

'What happened to him?'

'Oh, he lost his head. Precious moved back to London. Haven't spoken to her in ages.'

Stacey nods, seemingly satisfied. 'Your colleague, Thom Peters . . . He interrogated me.'

'That must have been fun. But he's not my colleague.'

'Good. Smarmy wee bastard. He let something slip, though.' I don't ask what it was, but after a moment, she adds, 'He said your life was in danger.'

'I'm sure he was exaggerating.'

'No.' She shakes her head. 'I don't think so.' This hangs for a moment. 'You don't seem bothered by it, though.'

I should brush away her concern with a light one-liner, but there's something about the way she's looking at me, with such puzzlement and concern, that would make any kind of glibness feel discourteous.

She asks quietly, 'Why is that?'

It's not a question I want to think about, let alone find an answer for. But the porter arrives with impeccable timing, both knocking on and pushing open the door in one movement. 'How are you feeling?'

'I'm fine, thanks, Billy.'

He seems like one of the good guys. He talks in a staccato Glaswegian accent and always carries a clipboard, which, intentionally or not, gives him an air of propriety.

He tells me, 'There's a woman downstairs wanting to see you.'

'Did she give you her name?'

'I asked her, but she wouldn't.'

'Can you just show her up, please?'

He shakes his head. 'Insisted she speaks to you in the courtyard.'

Stacey's rage is instant. 'Absolutely not happening! He's nowhere near fit enough to go traipsing round outside!'

'I'm fine!'

It's as though she's not heard me and says to Billy, 'Tell her she can come up here or do one.'

'Please do *not* say that to her! Clearly, whoever she is, she wants to meet on neutral ground and my room is hardly that.'

I pause. 'Miss Smith has a point, though, Billy. I'm still feeling bleary and I'm not sure it's a good idea for me to go out.' I don't mention that I'd be a sitting duck for any snipers in the courtyard. 'Is that OK?'

'She said you'd say that.' Billy steps closer to me. 'Told me to give you this.' He hands me a piece of paper. I unfold it and scan its brief, handwritten contents.

Stacey asks, 'What does it say?'

But I'm lost in thought.

'Novak!'

I refold the piece of paper.

'*Is it her name?*'

'What? No. It's the names of four other people. Billy! Tell my visitor I'll be down in ten minutes, would you, please?'

'Will do!'

He turns, but I call out to him, 'Could you do me another favour?'

'Depends what it is.'

'Could you get me some magnetic powder?'

He looks at me like I've just requested a pound of crack cocaine. 'Magnetic powder?'

'Yeah. Thought you might have some around. Magnetic particles are used in quite a few medical applications, like MRI scans, cancer therapy – most obviously treatment of carcinomas – and even drug delivery in terms of—'

'I know what it's used for!' Billy exclaims. He pauses. 'We don't use it here, but we do store it.'

'I only need a light smattering. It's important.'

'I'll see what I can do.'

'And some gel tape.'

'Don't push it, laddie.'

'Thanks, Billy. Appreciate it.'

'Oh aye?' As he walks away, he adds, 'That makes everything tickety-boo then, doesn't it?'

'So,' Stacey asks, 'who's the mystery woman?'

I reply honestly, 'I have no idea.'

'But you've got to see her? Because of the names?'

I nod. 'Because of the names.'

-17-

Turns out I'm weaker than I thought. Getting out of bed, shedding my surgical gown and struggling into jeans, Derby boots and a thick woollen fisherman's jumper proves exhausting and afterwards I sit on the bed to recover. I feel alone, fragile and vulnerable. If Sandy Paige has hired people to kill me immediately, it's difficult to see how I'll be able to put up a fight, let alone stop them.

My phone rings. I pick up.

'Novak. Jeremy Simmonds, here. It's about your report on Paige.'

'I'm very well, thank you for asking.'

'Well, we can chat about your health niggles or cut to the chase with the good news. Thanks to your dossier, an arrest warrant has been issued for Alexander Paige and half a dozen of his top men. And the CPS are currently studying the file.'

'So you're ringing to say well done?'

'Of course not. I'm ringing to say the trail on Paige has gone cold. You investigated him for months. Where do you think he is? Best guess.'

'He could be anywhere in the world. He knows every trick in the book when it comes to invisible travel. The man nurtured an entire network devoted to moving people across borders without . . .' I tail off. Exhale. 'He's in the wind. We've lost him.'

'He must have a bolthole.'

'He must have several. But he'll have made certain they're untraceable and he'll have Swiss bank accounts and—'

'All right, all right! I get the picture. But your instinct is, he's fled the UK?'

'Yeah. No! Wait. Paige is good friends with a lot of very wealthy, very shady characters. Most of them still have huge mansions in this country that – realistically speaking – the police could never get permission to enter. Now, Paige knows about the file I compiled. He might be reluctant to use his networks in case they've been compromised.'

'So, instead,' Simmonds speculates, 'he opts to lay low in luxury right here in Blighty whilst he plots his next move.' He clicks his tongue. 'It's certainly a possibility. So, who are these rich friends of his?'

'Businessmen from Moscow that paid enough money and made enough of the right noises to keep their pads in Mayfair and mansions in Surrey. In other words, Russian oligarchs.'

I hear Simmonds wince. 'The ones we allowed to stay, Novak – we don't call them oligarchs anymore. We call them *refugees*.'

'Jesus.' There's a knock at the door. 'Look, I've got to go. Start checking out his *refugee* billionaire buddies. Let me know how you get on.'

'Sure. And, Novak . . .'

'Yes?'

'Well done with the dossier. And just for once in your life, stay safe!' Whilst I'm wondering how to respond to something bordering on warmth, he adds, 'God knows I don't need the paperwork that would be triggered by someone killing you.'

'And the real Jeremy Simmonds is back in the room.'

I hang up. There's another, more insistent knock at the door.

I glance at my bedside table and grab a biro from it, slipping it up my sleeve to be deployed as a makeshift weapon if necessary. It doesn't sound that dangerous, but I once stabbed a Montblanc fountain pen into an assassin's throat, and although it wasn't as effective as a combat knife, his windpipe was still a write-off.

'Come in!'

It's Billy with the tape and magnetic powder that I requested. I thank him and once he leaves, I carefully take a glass from the drawer of my bedside table. It's the one given to me by the woman who'd claimed to be a nurse. I'd stashed it away and now I hold it under the overhead light and tilt it until I can discern her fingerprints. I sprinkle a very light coating of powder across the marks and squint to see if my rather Heath Robinson approach is working. It's a delicate job and I'd normally use a magnetic fibre wand to layer the application more evenly, but out in the field a deftness of touch is all I can rely on.

Fingerprints are made up of protein, sweat and oil and the magnetic powder should cling to the latter. I blow very gently on the marks, and the arches, loops and whorls of the woman's prints become clearer. I place a stretch of gel tape across them and again, using adroit caution, lift it and position it across a piece of white paper I placed on the table. I grab my phone and take several photos of the fingerprints. The process and resulting shots aren't perfect, but they should be good enough to run with.

I call Frank Harvey and he answers almost immediately with a riled, 'Where the hell have you been?'

'Sorry. Not got time to go into that.'

'Are you all right, lad?'

'Yeah, I'm fine. Look, if I can get some fingerprints across to you, can you pull in some favours and get someone to run them for you?'

'What's going on?'

I give him a very brief précis of recent events and he responds with incredulity.

'So you went to have a quiet word with Paige and ended up blowing up half his house?'

'To be fair, he won't be needing it for the next eighteen to twenty-five years.'

'You drive me crackers! You're not safe to be on your own. You know that?'

'It's been said. The fingerprints. Can you help me?'

'Bung them across. Terry Potter still works for Durham Con. He owes me.'

'Thanks, Frank. You're a legend.'

We hang up and as I slip my phone into my pocket, a recollection hits me. It's odd how a scent or a taste or a word can trigger a memory from years earlier. In this case, the Proustian remembrance is from a few months ago. The conversation I had with Frank where I asked him about Ekaterina Karpin. At the time, I felt there was something off about the exchange.

'*Thanks, Frank. You're a legend.*'

Those words brought back a phrase he'd used at the time.

'*Ekaterina Karpin,*' I'd said to him, and asked, 'Not ringing any bells?'

He'd replied, 'Silence in the belfry. Maybe she was using a legend.'

That's what had bothered me. Frank had been using jargon. In this instance, 'legend' means a fake name tethered to an assumed background and biography, usually supported by forged documents and a plethora of memorised details and spurious anecdotes. Crucially, the expression only applies to members of the intelligence community. But I'd not told Frank that Ekaterina had claimed to be a former Russian agent. It's possible that without me telling him, he'd assumed my potential client had been a spy. But he had no grounds for the supposition, which means another scenario is much more likely.

Frank lied to me. He knows more about Ekaterina than he was willing to say, which suggests the two of them have crossed paths. That begs the question, what's the nature of their relationship? And, by extension, given the fact he's trying to conceal it from me, what's so dark and dangerous about their shared history?

-18-

I hear someone banging on the door and Stacey calls through, 'Are you decent?'

'Yes!'

'I won't bother coming in, then!'

I laugh and the stitching across my abdomen stings.

Stacey nudges the door open and pushes a wheelchair into the room.

I'm slightly aghast. 'Where did you get that?'

'Some old fella was using it downstairs, so I just tipped him out and hoicked it up here.' She shakes her head. 'We're in a hospital! Where do you think I got it? Billy said you could borrow it.' She parks it in front of me. 'Your chariot awaits, you wee scunner.'

'Scunner?'

'Nuisance. Go on.'

I manoeuvre myself into the wheelchair and Stacey spots that even this leaves me catching my breath. She moves forward, but I hold up my hand. 'I can manage!'

'You can manage nothin'! Come here! I'll push you.'

'I said I can—'

'And if you give me any lip, I'll shove you down the stairs in it.'

'Point taken! All right . . .' It's pretty clear I'm not going to win this one. 'The courtyard. And don't go over twenty miles an hour.'

She smiles. 'Aye aye, sir!'

*

As Stacey Smith pushes me down a hospital corridor, she says, 'So. The names. Are they friends of yours or something?'

We're being followed by Dave and Emile, who remain about three paces behind us.

'No. I never met them. But they all have one thing in common.'

'Well?'

'They're all dead.'

I didn't have her down as a diplomat, but she doesn't pursue the matter and I'm grateful for her silence.

We take a lift to the ground floor and quickly reach the set of double doors leading to the courtyard. I signal for her to stop and rise from the chair. 'Stay there, Miss Smith.' There's a key in the door to my left. I try to turn it, but it's already unlocked, so I just pull the door slightly ajar and cautiously peer outside.

It's a cold, windy, drizzly afternoon. The sky is thick with storm clouds and the light is so grey, so dark, it feels much later than it is. I shudder involuntarily.

The quad looks empty, but it's lined with columns and a dozen people could be concealing themselves behind the four rows. I call out, 'Hello?'

Only the rasping wind replies, and after a moment, Stacey says, 'Sit down.'

I comply, and before I can decide whether it's safe to go any further, she pushes me through the doors.

'Oh, let's just get on wi' it, Novak!'

She takes me to the centre of the courtyard. My two bodyguards begin to follow, but I ask them to stand guard on the other side of the doors. They're not happy, but I guess Simmonds told them to follow my orders, so they nod and make me promise to shout for them if I even suspect trouble.

The wind makes dead leaves surround us in broad, swirling circles.

Stacey leans down and whispers into my ear, 'Looks like you've been stood up, pal.'

'Wouldn't be the first time.'

'Probably won't be the last.'

'You're a beacon of comfort, Miss Smith. I don't know where I'd be without—'

I break off as I spot movement in the corner of the quad. A sleeve becomes apparent, edging half an inch from the fluting of the column.

I nod towards it and murmur to Stacey, 'Go inside.'

She murmurs back, 'Feck off.' Then shouts, 'Are you gonna stand there all day, hen? Coz I'm freezing my tits off here!'

Looks like her diplomatic skill set comes and goes.

I call across to the figure, 'I think you asked to see me!'

A moment passes and a woman emerges from behind the column.

-19-

Stacey whispers, 'Do you know her?'

'I do.'

'Friend or foe?'

She's dressed in a pale trouser suit and a long dark coat and despite the wind, her mid-length black hair remains perfectly in place.

'Friend. Very much so.'

Her name is Claudette Vale and she runs ACTION, a quasi-governmental agency that fights on front lines of the war against child trafficking. I met her twice whilst researching Paige's activities and found her shrewd, friendly and completely committed, whatever the risks. The first three letters of her organisation's name stand for Anti-Child Trafficking and the final three are – as is often the way with these things – a slight contrivance to make sure the acronym sounds short and snappy.

Now, there are several charities battling to end the sale and exploitation of kids, including ECPAT, Operation Underground Railroad and, of course, Save the Children. They do an amazing job in tough circumstances. But, in recent years, ACTION have been successful in reuniting families and proving that the traffickers are usually involved in other illegal activities. So when they've rescued girls and boys, they've gone after the monsters that abducted them and achieved notable victories, getting entire syndicates jailed for significant periods of time.

It goes without saying that these sentences have terminated, or at least curtailed, the crimes of those individuals, but their success has been such that they've become a deterrent, persuading even the most hardened profiteers that child exploitation is too dangerous a business to be involved in.

'Claudette,' I shout to her. 'What's with all the cloak-and-dagger stuff?'

She doesn't reply but walks swiftly towards me.

I like to think I'm not a vain man, or if I am, my vanity is not a blinding or controlling thing. But I'm glad to see Claudette, because at last I'm about to get a bit of praise. I've brought down Sandy Paige and so far all I've got for my trouble is a bullet in my belly and a hip flask full of instant coffee.

I stand as she nears me. Extend my hand. 'Good to see you, Claudette.'

I suppose my guard is down. I just want to hear the head of ACTION say nice things about me and my work, and yes, I confess, part of me is glad Stacey is hovering by my side to catch the praise that will be flowing my way.

I start to say, 'How have you been?'

But I don't quite reach the end of the question as Claudette Vale strikes me across the face. It isn't a light slap to my cheek. More a powerful punch to my lower jaw. I stagger back, see fury blazing in her eyes and know she isn't done. I raise my hands for protection, but she shoves me hard and I feel myself falling. Luckily, I land in the wheelchair, but Claudette strides towards me.

Stacey steps forward and pushes the other woman in the chest with such force that she stumbles backwards, almost toppling to the ground and only just managing to regain her footing. 'Back off, lady! Try that again and I will *flatten* you!'

I say, 'It's all right, Stacey. It's all right. Claudette, what the hell is this about?'

She glares at Stacey. 'Your boyfriend—' she begins, but we both interrupt simultaneously.

'He's not . . .'

'We're not . . .'

Claudette continues, '—has totally screwed over our organisation!' She directs her anger at me. 'You've done what all those child traffickers and bent barristers haven't managed to achieve! You've ended us!'

'I've not got a clue what you're on about!'

'Jeremy Simmonds, or Thom Peters, or whatever he's calling himself, told me the whole thing.'

'Well, would you mind filling me in?'

'ACTION is underfunded. You know that! We need at least 90K to even survive the year. Then, to expand as I'd wanted, to really make a difference, we need millions.'

'How have I done anything to prevent that?'

'The PM promised us that, using special powers afforded by a COBRA session, the government would seize the assets of any organisation found guilty of child trafficking. Those funds would have come directly to us!'

I'm starting to see where this is heading and already feeling sick about it.

Stacey asks, 'What's that got to do with him?'

'Everything!' Claudette screeches. 'He knew Sandy Paige was the head of a child trafficking syndicate! If he'd just gone to the police and told them everything, Paige would have been arrested and had his assets frozen. When found guilty, his cash would have come to us, allowing us to keep on going. Keep on rescuing and protecting kids.'

'I was trying to do the right thing. I was trying to help the people caught up in the process that were genuinely innocent. I was trying to achieve . . . justice.'

This infuriates Claudette even further. 'Justice? You talk about justice? We need money, Novak! We need the proper legal framework! Not your penchant for riding in like only you can single-handedly save the day whatever the odds!'

'Hey!' Stacey points a finger at Claudette. 'I was there! This guy was almost killed. He was dead on his feet at Paige's place, and you know what he was doing? He was seeing who else he could help!'

'Well, what a hero!' She gives us a moment of slow, sarcastic applause. 'Except the real world is no place for heroes anymore.' She shifts her livid gaze to me. 'And the twenty-first century doesn't need men like you. Your time is over, if you ever even had one.'

'I promise you, Claudette, I'm going to save this situation.'

'You've done enough damage!'

Stacey raises her voice, 'All right, you've said your piece! Paige has taken out a contract on him if that makes you feel any better.'

'I know. I heard.'

'And?'

'And if Novak had played this by the book, we could have saved more children. As it is, Sandy Paige has already switched most of his assets. ACTION will be lucky to survive the year. Don't expect me to shed any tears if Marc Novak doesn't survive the week.'

'I know you're hurting, pet,' Stacey says calmly, 'but it's best you're on your way.'

Claudette ignores her and focuses on me. 'And if everything I've just told you isn't enough . . .' She pauses. 'There's one more thing I need you to know.'

-20-

I dread what I'm about to hear and Claudette continues, 'Earlier today, I wrote down the names of four kids we were too late to save. I want you to hang on to that list and look at it every night. Then imagine all the names we don't know that are being added to it because of you trying to . . .' And using air quotes. She concludes, 'Do the right thing.'

'That's enough,' Stacey murmurs.

'Yeah.' Claudette nods. 'That's enough.' She gives me one last look of pure hatred, turns and storms away. She pushes open the doors to the hospital and a moment later I hear them slam shut.

For several seconds, despite the wind and light drizzle, there's a stillness in the courtyard.

Eventually, Stacey says, 'I don't think she's your biggest fan.'

She's trying to console me with humour. I know that. I'd do it myself. But right now it feels like an ill-judged kindness.

I counter with, 'What makes you say that?'

'Come on! Let's get you back inside.'

'Can you give me five minutes alone? I just need a moment to . . .'

'I get it,' she replies and pats my shoulder. 'I'll give you a bit of time to process.'

'Thanks.'

Stacey Smith follows Claudette into the hospital and I wheel myself over to the courtyard entrance, take the key from inside and lock the doors. Wearily, I push myself back to the middle of the quad. It's grown darker. Colder. I sit alone, staring at the clouds, feeling wisps of icy rain hit my face.

I half hear what I take to be the sound of thunder announcing a nearby storm.

Take a deep breath.

Claudette Vale had been right. Not about everything. But about enough to make me feel wretched. More than that, her words force me to question not just my actions, but the reason behind them: why I took that course without giving a fleeting thought for any easier alternative. I could have tipped off the police about Louisa Paige's suspicions or simply handed over the file when it was detailed enough to interest the Crown Prosecution Service.

I hear the crack of nearby lightning.

Yet I chose to take a harder path, which ultimately proved much tougher for everyone involved in the fiasco. So, Claudette is justified in her detestation of me. This hits me like a kind of grief.

This brilliant woman who has fought so fearlessly has rejected me as an ally and compelled me to question everything.

Because, you see, my instincts, my compulsion to act as I do, not only define my career, they define me.

I don't know about you, but sitting down to question something so significant seldom pays dividends for me. And so it proves now. The question itself is so big that my mind doesn't have space for the answer. It'll come to me as I'm driving home or doing the washing up or—

Lightning. Nearby lightning. I look up.

The darkness of this chilly late afternoon hasn't been punctuated by any lightning.

So what *had* I heard?

The adrenaline hits immediately. I rise from my chair and hurry to the double doors. Unlock them. Hear the bolt sliding back. I try to open the doors, but something inside the hospital is blocking them.

I push harder and the obstruction gives. I feel whatever it is being pushed aside as I lean against the door, which is now ajar by about a foot. I look down and instantly see what the obstruction is.

It's a body.

I can make out her legs, or rather the pink fabric of the lower half of her clothes.

'No, no, no . . .'

For all of a second, I use the narrow gap between the door and door frame to scope out what I can of the corridor. It seems to be empty. I thrust the door open, step into the hospital and look down on the corpse.

I didn't know her well and I didn't know her long, but her violent death appals me. Her dead face stares up at me. Unmissable and horrific, the cause of death is instantly apparent – two bullet holes in her forehead, so close together they form a filled-in figure of eight. Blood weeps from the wound, rolling down her face like red tears.

-21-

Leonid's Story (cont.)
Yekaterinburg, Russia. July, 1918

Their pale, dead faces were streaked with red. Leonid had seen war. Been close enough to the battlefield to taste the mud and the blood and feel the heat of his comrades' rifles blazing away at his shoulders. But he had never witnessed horror like this.

It had been less an execution, more a mismanaged, craven frenzy. Just over twenty minutes after Yurovsky had fired the first three bullets, the rampage came to a panting halt. The young people and the Romanovs' retinue who survived the initial shooting spree had been bayonetted, booted and shot in the head at point-blank range.

When it was all over, Leonid moved forward. He stepped cautiously but almost fell. The floor was so awash with blood, it was like trying to walk across an ice rink. He paused over the body of one of the Romanova girls and dropped to his haunches. Her killers were moving back, catching their breaths. One addressed Yurovsky directly, asking what was to be done with the corpses.

Silently, and without looking directly at any of the victims, Leonid began to pray for them. He realised, of course, that it was at best a worthless exercise and at worst a plea bargain with the Almighty for his own soul.

Another soldier, a young Muscovite called Pasha, joined Leonid and similarly crouched over the young Romanova. Moments earlier, he had been the one who'd murmured, 'They *are* divine! God Himself protects them!' And now, in equally low tones, he asked Leonid, 'Are you praying for her?'

The two men had become firm friends during their weeks serving under Yurovsky, but Leonid replied with a quick and cautious, 'Of course not.'

His gaze fell to the girl's slightly upturned skirt. Something on its inside hem caught his eye. He glanced over his shoulder. No one was watching. Leonid leant forward and tugged what looked to be glass from the bottom of the skirt. The sharp, transparent fragment had been sewn into its fabric. But more than this, now he'd spotted this one piece of mineral, he could see many others, both in the skirt and the insides of her torn upper clothing.

He peered at the bloodstained gem he held in his hand and whispered, 'Hardest thing known to man.'

The other soldier asked quietly, 'What is it?'

'God didn't protect them, comrade . . .' For a brief, reckless second, Leonid angled his body so his actions were hidden to all in the room except Pasha. He held his find aloft, momentarily transfixed by its shine. The shine of a pear-shaped diamond as big as a baby's fist. 'This did.'

-22-

The hospital corridor is horribly silent. Lifeless. I glance to my right. The corpse of one of my bodyguards, Emile, is splayed across the bottom few steps of the staircase. He's been shot several times in the chest. To my left, another couple of figures lie dead. I recognise them as male nurses who assisted with my operation.

I kneel beside the dead woman's body and using my thumb and index finger gently close her eyelids. 'I'm sorry, Claudette.'

I jog over to Emile and, more out of habit than hope, check his carotid for a pulse. Of course, there is none. I begin to frisk him and as I'm about to take his—

Footsteps!

I freeze. The footsteps are coming from an intersecting corridor. Slow but heavy. Deliberate. I stand and press my back against the wall so if the individual keeps walking, he'll stride past me and I'll be able to approach him, unseen, from behind.

But he pauses before reaching the corner of my corridor. He says in a low, growling voice, 'I know you're there . . . I heard you.'

Desperate to remain silent, I hold my breath. Weigh up my options. If he's armed and steps forward whilst opening fire, I've nowhere to hide.

I say, 'OK, after three I'll show myself.'

I slide the biro from my sleeve. Clasp it firmly in my fist.

'One!'

I swing around the corner, bringing the pen around in a blurred curve that—

I stop, confronted by the porter. Dazed, he takes a couple of steps back.

Billy is unarmed, of course, but, as usual, he's holding his clipboard, pressing it to his upper ribcage. He's also unnaturally pale – shock, I suppose – but I can't see any injuries.

'Are you OK, Billy?'

'Not really . . .' He lowers the clipboard to reveal a bloody cavity where his chest used to be. 'I feel . . .'

He topples backwards.

I drop to my haunches, and although it's obvious he's gone, I try to staunch the blood, offering quiet verbal encouragement and urging him to hang on. After about a minute, I check for a pulse but find none. I stand. The hospital is silent again. My woollen jumper is drenched in Billy's blood. I briefly revisit Emile's corpse, but as I'm taking something from him—

'Novak!'

Stacey's voice. Fearful.

'Novak, are you there?'

She's calling me from upstairs. I move quietly but quickly up the steps. Pause at the top of them, reluctant to turn the corner. Ahead of me, my other bodyguard, Dave, lies supine on the floor. As with Claudette Vale, he has a neat, red figure eight shot into his forehead.

I assume there are two shooters. One who goes for the larger target area of the chest, and another, more precise and skilled assassin who delivers a nucleated pair of shots to his victims' heads.

I cautiously peek around the corner.

The corridor is littered with corpses. Two hospital staff members lie face down halfway along the passage. Both ooze blood. And just beyond them, a few paces from my room, I spot the fallen figure of Doctor Sharma, obviously taken out by the killer who prefers to obliterate his targets' upper torsos.

And in the doorway to my room, pale and trembling, I see Stacey Smith.

She notices me but immediately averts her gaze so she's starring straight down the corridor. Now she calls out, 'Are you there, Novak? The gunmen have gone, but I need your help!'

It's obvious they're covering Stacey from within the room, using her as a Judas goat. It's not a bad strategy, but I know the gunmen won't want to remain in the hospital longer than necessary. They'll give this tactic a go for a couple of minutes, and then, if it's not worked, they'll kill Stacey and try to hunt me down.

Treading softly, I turn the corner and begin moving down the corridor as swiftly as I dare.

Stacey glances to her left and says, 'Do you want me to call him again?'

She's got guts. I know full well she's letting me know where the gunmen are located, but any sort of interaction with them presents an enormous risk.

She nods, then calls out, 'Novak! Let me know you're all right! Please!'

Her eyes flicker down to her right hand. I follow the glance and she unfurls two fingers, indicating we're dealing with a couple of assassins.

I nod. I'm only three metres from the doorway. Moments away from reaching Stacey and—

A man's angry voice: 'What the fuck are you doing?'

One of them has spotted her signal to me. I hear another voice shout, 'Bitch!'

Stacey dives to her left as her captors open fire. I raise the Beretta 96A1 I took from Emile's back holster. I know it was his spare because it's fully loaded – twelve bullets in the mag and one in the pipe. I empty all thirteen into the wall of my room, raking a line of fire across the area where I estimate the killers will be concealed.

The noise is immense but brief.

Mag spent, I'm already running into my room. A quick glance to my right reveals thirteen was an unlucky number for the two male figures peppered with bleeding bullet wounds. Neither man moves.

To my left – Stacey's dive clearly meant she avoided the gunfire and it's apparent I took out the hitmen before they could take further shots at her. She's on her feet, hurrying towards me.

We hug. No, it's more than that. We collide and hang on to each other. I say, 'Are you all right?'

I feel her nod as she replies, 'I'm all right, I'm all right . . .' in a tone that suggests she's anything but. I can hear her weeping and embrace her tighter.

'You're safe,' I tell her. 'It's over. It's over.'

But, of course, I don't believe that for a second.

Leonid's Story (cont.)
Yekaterinburg, Russia. July, 1918

One of the older soldiers shouted, 'It's over! It's over.'

Leonid slipped the diamond into his right boot, scraping it down between soft, worn leather and his ankle until it lodged by his sole. He stood up. 'Yes, they're dead!'

Pasha, his young friend from Moscow who stood by his side, said, 'Not quite the same thing, comrade.'

*

'Get a move on! This has to be done by first light!'

Leonid and Pasha helped load the Fiat truck. It was not a large vehicle, certainly too small for the many corpses it would have to carry. Leonid paused as he heard barking and turned around. He smiled as he saw Ortipo, Tatiana Romanova's French Bulldog. She'd always made a fuss of the pet; in truth, all the Romanovs had been fond of the dog, its happy overexcitedness often bringing joy into the grim world of Ipatiev House. Now Ortipo was running towards the truck, as though she somehow knew her mistress was—

'Bitch!'

The soldier beside Leonid ran his bayonet through the dog's body. She whimpered. He withdrew the blade, stabbed Ortipo again, bent down and picked her up.

'One more,' he said and tossed the bulldog onto the back of the truck.

*

The Fiat made slow progress across the boggy ground. Yakov Yurovsky, the man in charge of the Romanovs' incarceration and slaughter, had also been tasked with taking care of the dead bodies to ensure no one discovered the fate of the royal family. He travelled to and through the Koptyaki forest with the corpses, the drunken psychopath Peter Ermakov, Pasha and several soldiers. Leonid was part of a group that followed behind. Their job, Yurovsky had explained, was to strip the corpses, smash their faces, douse their bodies with sulphuric acid and finally to dispose of them.

Some of the soldiers had vomited when the instructions had been issued.

When Leonid arrived at the clearing where the truck had stopped, it was clear things were not running to plan.

Pasha sidled up to Leonid and whispered, 'Yurovsky is furious! Ermakov only brought one shovel!'

'Jesus . . .'

'And Ermakov's gang – the men who were waiting here for us – they're livid! They'd been promised that they could rape and kill the Romanovas. They're furious at—' Pasha broke off. 'Christ!'

Leonid looked at the scene unfolding in the clearing. Several of Ermakov's men were throwing the corpses from the truck onto carts intended to take them further into the forest.

But they'd reached the body of Alexandra, the last empress of Russia. Two of the men cheered. One lifted her skirt and slipped his hand into her undergarments.

'Stop! Stop!' the furious Yurovsky yelled. He marched to the men. 'We are here to do a job and then move on! Anyone caught looting or . . .' He nodded to the man who had abused Alexandra, 'Will be dismissed!'

Leonid murmured, 'What does he mean? Looting?'

Pasha replied, 'All the royals except Maria had huge amounts of gems and jewellery hidden about them. In their clothes and—'

Yurovsky's raised voice cut him off. 'Do I make myself clear?'

The men holding Alexandra made no indication that they would release her or obey him.

Yurovsky removed his sidearm. '*Do I make myself clear?*'

Ermakov nodded at his workers and they shrugged.

The man who had hoisted Alexandra's skirt now tossed her body onto one of the carts and turned to face the other soldiers. He grinned. 'I can die in peace!' he declared. 'I've touched the royal cunt!'

Leonid closed his eyes. 'This is madness.'

'This is what we have become,' Pasha replied.

'No.' He opened his eyes. 'This is not what I have become. I'm getting out. I'm leaving.'

'You're crazy!'

'I'm going to make a run for it.'

'Ermakov's men will shoot you down!'

'I can't stay.'

'You can't leave!' Pasha paused. 'You need to sell the diamond you stole and split the money with me! Attempt to run now and I'll call out! I'll tell Yurovsky the diamond is in your boot.'

Leonid had already been slowly retreating from the group and now both he and Pasha were several paces behind the other soldiers. 'You wouldn't . . .'

'Leonid! Why should you benefit and not me?'

'I took the risk!'

'You took the diamond!'

Leonid turned and began to jog further into the forest.

Pasha called to him, 'Comrade!'

Leonid looked over his shoulder and saw the other man raise his pistol, point it at his back and pull its trigger.

-24-

I phone Simmonds and tell him about the bloodbath. He's commendably horrified, assures me that he's despatching a team to take care of the situation and orders me to stay put. I agree and hang up.

Stacey asks, 'What's happening?'

'I'm leaving.'

'I'm coming with you.'

'Too dangerous.'

'You need someone to look after you. You need *me* to look after you.'

She's perfectly serious.

'Stacey, that's kind of you. But I've managed without you for almost forty years and I'm doing all right.'

Her eyes widen in sheer disbelief. 'If this is you doing all right, I'd hate to see you on a bad day.'

It's hard to argue with her when I'm standing in the aftermath of a massacre meant for me, wearing a jumper that's soaked in the blood of a man who was gunned down for simply being in the same building as me.

'I'll figure something out,' I tell Stacey. 'After I get changed, I'm leaving. And I'm leaving alone.'

*

We're heading south in Stacey's ancient Austin Morris J4, a former Royal Mail van that zips through the country lanes with a sprightliness that belies its age.

As dusk peters out into night-time, she switches on the headlights and says, 'My old da did it up for me. I use it for my job.'

'I thought you were a firefighter.'

'Just a volunteer. I'm a kind of white van man, except I don't have a white van and I'm not a man. Lots of folk, especially young lasses, they prefer having a woman help them to shift stuff. It's a good job. Decent coin and I'm my own boss.'

The engine of these old J4s is in the front compartment, between the driver's and passenger's seat. On the plus side, it means we're toasty warm, but the noise is loud and constant, forcing us to raise our voices as we converse.

'Sounds good!'

'You ever thought about jacking in the detective business and getting a normal job?'

'Only once or twice. A day.'

'Then why don't you?'

I pretend not to have caught the question and ask, 'How much further?'

'About an hour,' she replies and we continue to tear through the night.

*

We pass Inverness, pick up the A82 and eventually find a village just west of Loch Ness. Stacey has known where we've been heading since we left the hospital, and her choice definitely meets with my approval. It's a small, old-fashioned pub that looks like it was originally a pair of cottages converted into a single building. We booked ahead and reserved one of its two available guest rooms.

There's a log fire blazing in the main saloon and as we walk into the bar, the group of drinkers closest to it stand and start putting on their coats. Stacey swoops and grabs their chairs whilst I get a round in, buying a bottle of wine and a couple of double shots. The patrons that are leaving nod a cheery farewell and I sign us in. The landlord hands me the key to our room.

'How long have you known Stacey?' he inquires.

'Feels like forever.'

'Ach, well, she's a good friend to a lot of folk around here. You mind you treat her well, young man.'

It feels more like a threat than friendly advice.

I carry our libations across to our table, down my whisky in one and warm my palms on the fire.

As Stacey pours us both a glass of wine, she asks, 'Do you have kids?'

'God, no. Do you?'

'I've got a son.' She fiddles with her mobile, then hands it to me. 'That's him.' She's brought up a photo of a boy I guess is about four years old. Dark eyes. Wide cheeky grin. He's wearing an enormous sombrero and has both thumbs raised to indicate life is A-OK. He's sitting on the knees of a young man bursting with so much pride, it's obvious he's the kid's dad.

'Great pic. What's his name?'

'Liam.'

'Well, Liam has excellent taste in hats.'

Stacey laughs. 'No! Liam's my son! The bairn's Connor – his boy. My grandkid.'

I glance at the photo again. 'The bloke . . . You're his mum?'

'Aye!' She takes her phone back. 'What's so surprising about that?'

'Nothing.' I raise my glass. 'Cheers.'

'Cheers.'

'It's very different to my life. That's all.'

'Did you and Precious ever talk about having kids?'

'Precious thought I *was* a kid.' I take a sip of wine.

'And why was that?'

'Who knows? She was always very driven. Very ambitious. I think it got on her nerves that I didn't have this great masterplan for my career.'

'It's good to have a masterplan for something.'

'And what's yours?'

'Now that Liam's all grown up? I'm not sure. But I know I'd best get my skates on. It goes faster than you think, Novak.'

Stacey smiles at the photo on her phone.

'Having young kids?'

She doesn't look up. 'I meant life in general.'

'Ahh . . .'

She puts her phone away, asking, 'Do you have a business partner? Or an assistant or anything?'

'Not really. I used to have a young woman called Mishka Ramakrishnan on the books.'

'Mishka? Good name. What happened to her?'

'Wafted by a favouring gale – as one often sometimes is in trances – to the USA. It wasn't her decision to go, but she met someone whilst over there and stayed Stateside.'

'Good for her!' Stacey nods. 'Anyone else?'

'Just my original partner.'

'The Stewart in Novak and Stewart?'

I nod.

She begins, 'And what happened to—'

'I don't know.' I down the double shot I'd bought for Stacey. 'Stewart is still missing.'

'I'm sorry.'

'Don't be.' I give a tight smile. 'And I seem to have necked your whisky. Sorry. I'll get another couple in.'

'No! Don't be daft!' Stacey gets to her feet. 'My round.'

Whilst she's at the bar, I call Frank Harvey. 'Did Terry have any joy tracing those prints?'

'Bad news, lad. He did run them, but whoever the dabs belong to isn't on file.'

'So he didn't come up with her name?'

'If her prints aren't in the system, he can't magic them up! Bloody hell, Novak, he's Terry Potter, not Harry Potter.'

'Sure. Hey, thanks for calling in the favour. And thank Terry for me.'

'No problem. And will do.'

Stacey returns with a couple more large whiskies I noticed she didn't have to pay for, and going from my expression, she infers there's a problem. 'What's wrong?'

'Nothing. I'm tired. That's all.'

Stacey retakes her seat. 'You sure?'

'Sure.' I down one of the shots. 'It's nothing I can't handle.'

'So what's your immediate plan?'

'Lay low for a while. Heal.' I shrug. 'Take a month off. Travel around Europe for a few weeks, maybe.'

'Sounds good.'

We drink the wine and Stacey tells me about Liam and how his dad was 'a twat who did a runner the minute he heard I was up the duff'. But there's no rancour in her voice. Some people say 'what's done is done', but she seems to genuinely believe it. We finish the first bottle and I buy a second. More chat. She gets the third and we've almost sunk it when she abruptly changes the topic of conversation.

'You know we were saying about life. And masterplans? Well, I've just got one.'

'A life?'

'A masterplan. I'm going to join you! I'm going to be the detective's apprentice.'

'Do you have any idea how dangerous that would be, working with me?'

'And do you have any idea how persistent I can be? Come on! What do you say?'

She picks up her wine glass.

'The detective's apprentice?' I wearily shake my head but smile and we clink glasses. 'God help us both.'

'I'll get another bottle in to celebrate.'

'It's my round,' I reply, but she shoots me a grin.

'Aye, but it's on the house for me!'

Whilst she's getting us restocked, I think back to the phone conversation with Frank. It still niggles me. You see, immediately after asking Frank to help me with the prints, I'd messaged another friend with the same request. Within an hour, she'd replied with the name of the person whose dabs were on the glass, so I'm actually wondering why Frank lied to me. Again.

Stacey returns to the table and I begin to pour a glass of wine.

-25-

Leonid's Story (cont.)
Russia. July, 1918

Leonid finished pouring vodka into the cup and quickly glugged down half of it. His wife, Maria, emerged from their bedroom.

'What are you doing here? It's almost midnight and—'

'Darling! I didn't mean to wake you. But maybe it's no bad thing. How is Georgy?'

'He's well.'

'And how are you?'

'Leonid, what are you doing here? Oh my God, have you deserted?'

He took another mouthful of vodka. 'I saw Russia's future this morning. And it's murder and madness and savagery.'

His wife snatched the cup from his grasp. 'Tell me what's going on!'

'We have to leave!'

'The house?'

'The country.'

She stared at her husband. 'Leonid. We have a three-month-old baby! We can't leave Russia!'

'Yes, we have a three-month-old baby! That is why we *must* leave Russia!' He gently took the cup back. 'We can reach your uncle. He has a car! He can drive us to—'

'He despises us! He despises everybody. He would never agree to help us.'

'We'll make it worth his while.'

'How?'

'We'll give him this place and everything in it in return for money to get us started overseas and a ride to—'

'Stop!' Maria took the cup and finished its remaining contents. 'You're not making any sense!'

'Neither is the world, anymore. But I have this!' He tried to show her the gem, still stained with Romanov blood, but her eyes remained fixed on his. 'Look! This will bring us—'

'They shoot deserters!'

'They shoot anyone. Believe me, the Bolsheviks are not discriminatory when it comes to the redistribution of bullets. And—'

'What were you thinking?' Maria fumed. She'd seen the diamond and appeared enraged by its presence. 'You took this? Do you know how dangerous that was?'

Leonid nodded. They stared at the stone for several quiet seconds.

Maria asked, 'Is it real?'

'As real as death. It must be worth a fortune.'

'It's not worth your life! You're a fool!'

'I married you, didn't I?'

'You got lucky!' She paused. Nodded. 'We must hurry!'

'Thank you, Maria.' Leonid gently put his hand on his wife's face. Softly rubbed her cheek with his thumb. 'I love you. You and Georgy are all I care about in this world. As long as I have you . . .'

Maria embraced him. 'Always,' she said.

*

They packed quickly and lightly. Before leaving, Maria sat down to write a letter to her parents, and as she penned her farewell, Leonid took Georgy in his arms.

'We're going far away,' he told his son. 'But we will be safe. We will be happy. Daddy has this . . .' He showed the baby the gem. Pressed it into his palm. 'I call it the Red Diamond and, Georgy, I believe it will bring us good luck and great fortune. More importantly, I believe that one day it will do great good.'

-26-

The woman who masqueraded as a nurse at the hospital is called Yulia Protopopov. She did a little mule work about a decade ago, which is why her fingerprints are still on file, and since then she's changed her name to Julia Grant, moved a couple of times and is trying to live off the grid. But that's tricky these days, especially when you've got a kid.

Julia's daughter is called Willow and finding her through state education records is simple. I don't even need to hack any systems to confirm it's the correct Willow Grant. Her school has a helpful Twitter account and several months ago posted a few photos of a day trip to Bannockburn. And there, in one of them, I can see Julia in profile.

The following day, I wait at the school gates. A man meets Willow and walks her to a complex of apartments that's upmarket without being the province of millionaires. There's a small water feature in the atrium. A pool with a modest fountain and through its clear water I can see coins that people have tossed into it. I wonder if Julia has thrown loose change into the water, and what she wished for as her money sank beneath the surface.

Willow and the man enter a flat on the first floor. I make a note of the address. Google it. Looks like Julia works from home as she's listed as a masseuse using the premises for her job. I find an online advertisement for the business and call the number provided.

'Hello?' It's Julia's voice.

I feel faintly absurd putting on a fake London accent so she won't recognise me. 'Hi, do you have any appointments available, please?'

'What are you after?'

'Straightforward back massage.'

'What for?'

I suddenly realise I have no idea why people have massages. Are they supposed to relieve stress? Having a stranger pummel my flesh would only increase any anxiety I might be feeling, but I vaguely recall that's not the widely accepted view.

'Works been crazy recently,' I reply. 'Been under a lot of pressure.'

'I'm a professional masseuse. I don't offer anything extra. You understand that?'

'Look, a girl at work said back massages can help relieve tension. If you're busy, no problem. I can call somewhere else.'

This seems to reassure her and I book an appointment for the following morning.

*

When I ring the entry buzzer to her flat, I'm wearing a face mask, glasses and a beanie hat, so I doubt she'll recognise me, but just to be on the safe side, I dab the tip of my index finger onto my tongue and smear it across the lens of the video doorbell.

She buzzes me in after a brief conversation and meets me in her hallway.

'Thanks for getting here on time,' she begins. 'You've no idea how many . . .'

I've removed my glasses and mask and as I take off my hat, she clocks who I am and falls silent.

'It's all right, Julia. I'm not here to harm you in any way. I just need to ask you a few questions.'

I've been in this situation a million times and the people I've cornered react in wildly different ways. Some deny who they are. Others rage at me. I've had people physically attack me and some try to scarper.

Julia's reaction is by far the worst I've ever encountered.

Her lower lip trembles for a moment and she begins to weep.

'You're Marc Novak, right?'

'Yes. I'm a private detective. Julia, you're not in any trouble.'

'Not in any trouble?' She wipes a tear from her face. 'Novak, you've just murdered me.'

-27-

Julia Grant hands me a mug of coffee. We're in a space she termed her studio. A dimly lit room with bland decor and even blander music playing through a couple of speakers. Mahler's Fifth, I think. One of his dirges, anyway. I'm perched on a massage table. It's like a hard, padded bench with a mysterious hole at one end that seems to serve no purpose. Julia takes a seat at her bureau desk and revolves to face me.

'Who sent you to the hospital?'

'If I tell you, will you help me?'

'Why would you need help?'

'Because they'll be watching me. Or watching you. Probably both. Christ, I was supposed to be out of this. More and more of us are being sucked back in. It's not fair.'

'Do you think they'd harm Willow?'

'I doubt it. They'll probably just kill me.'

'Who?'

'Powerful men. Does it matter who they work for? The organisations change. Acronyms alter. But a bullet is still a bullet.'

'Give me a name.'

'Give me an assurance.'

I take a sip of my coffee. It's appalling, of course, but I make an effort not to grimace. 'What assurances can I give you?'

'You have contacts in British Secret Service? Yes?'

'One or two.'

'Get them to take me away. Then make them tell Colonel Maksim Bulatov that my daughter and my boyfriend are both nothing to do with my past life. They're to be left alone!'

'Who ordered you to go to the hospital? Bulatov?'

She nods. 'I worked for him back in the day. Now the international situation has become how it is, the ones who tried to walk away are being – how did he put it? – "called upon to do our patriotic duty".'

'Whenever anyone asks you to do your "patriotic duty", they mean there's no good reason to do what they ask.'

'His revolver seemed a pretty good reason.'

'What were you there at the hospital to do?'

'Just report on how you were looking. Bulatov received news you'd been shot. He wanted to know if you'd make it. I told him you would. That was it.'

'Why the hell was Colonel Maksim Bulatov so bothered about my well-being?'

'He told me you were swimming in dangerous waters. The Romanov treasure. The Court.'

'The Court?'

Julia's eyes widen. 'Oh my God. You don't know what you're mixed up in, do you? You don't know anything about this!'

'I'm a fast learner.'

'You're a dead man.'

She stands. Scurries from the room. I follow her. 'What are you doing?'

'Packing! I have to leave! Straight away!'

'I can help you, Julia!'

She pauses. Looks me in the eye. 'You're playing a game you cannot win, against forces more powerful than you can imagine. And you stand there, telling me you can help me? You're a fool.'

'Come with me now and I'll protect you.'

She hurries into her bedroom, talking over her shoulder. 'I built a good life here! I was happy!' I can tell she's fighting hard not to weep. 'Let me pack some remembrances. Collect me in half an hour.'

'We should leave now.'

'I can't leave it all behind.'

'Julia!'

'No!'

'All right.' I pause. 'I'll collect my car. Bring it to the front. I'll wait in the atrium by the pool. When I'm there, I'll phone you. You come down and we'll hit the road. I'll take you somewhere safe.'

She nods.

'And, Julia, don't phone anyone whilst I'm gone. And I'm only giving you quarter of an hour. I don't even like doing that, so get a move on, yeah?'

She nods again.

I take a spare key from her, leave, walk quickly to Stacey's van and phone Jeremy Simmonds when I'm behind the wheel.

'I'm bringing in Julia Grant, aka Yulia Protopopov.'

'Bringing her in? Where?'

'To you.'

'I don't want her! She was just a low-level mule. I was involved in her relocation when she retired from the scene years ago.'

'Well, Colonel Maksim Bulatov has unretired her.'

'Let me guess. You said you'd help her.'

'Something like that.'

He gives a sigh so deep it feels like it lasts half an hour. 'All right. Bring her down south. I'll see what I can do. Call me in an hour.'

'Thanks, Simmonds. You won't regret it.'

'I already do!'

He hangs up and I drive around to Julia's apartment block. I park by the main entrance and walk through the atrium, pausing by the pool. A couple of men are lingering near the complex's rear exit. Something about their demeanour – calm but vigilant – bothers me. I immediately phone Julia.

No answer.

I race up the staircase leading to the first level and sprint to her flat, unlock the door and call her name as I enter. 'Julia! Where are you?'

The only reply is a stifled cry coming from the kitchen. I dash towards it.

Another sound – this time a cry for help. 'Novak!'

I run into the room and see Julia is being held by her throat, pinned to the far wall. Her face is bloody, but she remains conscious. Her assailant is tall, broad-shouldered and, believe you me, in very serious trouble.

-28-

A kitchen contains all kinds of things that can be useful in close combat, from serving forks to carving knives, but I guess I see red and just attack the bastard with my bare hands.

Before he has a chance to even turn around, I send my right fist slamming into his torso. My strike starts low, builds power and crashes into his body just below his elbow. It's a sharp, stabbing kidney punch. My fist hits him directly below his ribcage and keeps going, driving into his renal cortex. He drops Julia immediately, of course, yelps in pain and tries to fall to the floor. But I'm not letting him off that easy and follow up with a left-handed blow to his other kidney. It's not as effective as my first punch, but he'll be pissing blood for a week.

He shrieks as he collapses. In the movies, he'd spring to his feet, but in real life, he won't be springing anywhere for a fortnight. There's a reason kidney punches are illegal in boxing and the gibbering gym bunny at my feet is a pretty big clue.

But Julia points over my shoulder. 'Look out!'

I spin around. The man reaching for his shoulder holster is lightly built, but if he's armed with the SR-1 Vektor he's going for, well, his diminutive size won't come into play. It's a Russian-made pistol, similar to a Beretta 92. Very efficient. Very destructive. His fingers reach its grip.

As he pulls the piece from its holster, I reach him. I'm looking him in the eyes and moving my right hand towards his chin, so he's expecting a blow to the face. But if he's armed with a Vektor, I need to take him down immediately.

So my left fist delivers a powerful shovel punch up and into his body, landing just beneath his lower ribs. It's a liver shot, one of the very few strikes that's even more painful than a blow to the kidneys. He's not expecting the move so doesn't defend for it and I see at once it's landed strongly and right on target. The guy looks at me like I've zapped him with a cattle prod.

You see, the kidneys are surrounded by nerves connected to the autonomic control system. This regulates the functions that keep us alive. Little things like breathing and heart rate. The body's response to an attack on it is to register extreme pain and, more often than not, enter shut-down mode. All of which means the man reaching for his pistol screams in searing agony as he crumples to the floor, where he whimpers, writhes and, given time, will probably re-evaluate his career path.

'Are you all right?'

Julia nods.

'Good,' I tell her. 'We need to get out of here.'

Julia assures me there's nothing remotely incriminating on her phone. So I take it and we swing by the local National Express station. I get aboard one of the coaches and have a quick word with the driver. As I ask about journey times, I drop the phone into the ticket bin and then make my way back to Stacey's Austin Morris J4. Julia is hidden in the back. She asks, 'What were you doing?'

'Making sure that if they're trying to locate you by tracking your phone . . .' I pause as I start the engine. 'Right now, they'll be on their way to Thurso. That's the northernmost town in Scotland and—'

'I know Thurso,' she snaps. 'There's a nice beach there. We took Willow last half-term.'

We head south in silence. Julia doesn't thank me for saving her life, but, to be fair, she doesn't chastise me for endangering it in the first place.

As we cross into England, she climbs over the passenger seat and sits next to me. 'What will happen to my daughter? And my partner?'

'They're together and they're being looked after. They're both OK.'

'When can I see them again?'

'Honestly? I don't know. I'm going to hand you over to British Intelligence. They'll question you and take it from there.'

Julia tuts. 'I have nothing that would interest them. This whole thing is crazy.'

'I agree. Why the hell would Colonel Maksim Bulatov send men round to kill you, simply because I'd visited you?'

'He might think we're working together.'

'No, I don't buy that. I've never met Bulatov, but we crossed paths when he was running guns out of Copenhagen.'

'Copenhagen?'

'Long story. Anyway, the point is, he's a tactician. I mean, he's ruthless and driven, but he's a cool, clinical thinker. This makes him look paranoid at best. Psychotic at worst. Can you think of anyone else who would benefit from your death?'

'You don't get it! No! Alive or dead, I don't matter! I worked very hard to be a nobody. God . . .' Her voice trails off. 'They never let you go.'

'Do you know a woman called Ekaterina Karpin?'

'Kat?' Julia shrugs. 'Yeah, sure.' She's astonishingly casual about it. 'She was in the game when I was on the scene. It's a small world.'

'Did you work together?'

'Yes. No. I don't remember.'

'This is important, Julia.'

She shouts, 'Do you think I don't know that?' and although I keep my eyes on the road, I feel her glaring at me.

We continue in silence for a couple of miles, and after several minutes, I sense Julia's anger ebb away.

'I was just a mule. She was always more important, you know? We never worked side by side, but we were involved in the same operations once or twice. Low-level stuff.'

'What did you make of her?'

'Scary lady.'

'What makes you say that?'

'You ask a lot of questions.'

'Let me know when you fancy answering one.'

Julia gives the tiniest of laughs. 'Ekaterina was so focused. There's something scary about that, because it suggests other things don't matter. And now you're going to ask, what was she focused on?' She pauses. 'Looking back, she was bothered about the operations, sure. But she was obsessed with the Romanov treasure. I mean, like a child. Stupidly.'

'Why stupidly?'

She's quiet again, but this time I infer she's thinking up the right response. Eventually, she replies, 'When I was a mule, I mostly shifted guns, drugs, money . . . The obvious stuff. But occasionally it was artefacts, you know? I was supposed not to look, but I always did. Sometimes I was taking artwork from one side of the world to the other. When I got bored, I researched it. I suppose I became fascinated with it. The secret world.'

'Go on.'

'There is something very strange. For well over a hundred years, mankind's greatest artistic achievements and its treasures have been vanishing. The crown jewels of Ireland were stolen from Dublin Castle in 1907. Michelangelo's priceless *Mask of a Faun* was lifted from a Tuscan castle in the 1940s.

The Florentine Diamond – poof! Gone! All of them are still missing. Have you heard of the Eagle Diamond?'

'Can't say that I have.'

'It was the second-largest diamond ever found in America. The thieves who took it in 1964 were found, but the gem itself was never recovered. Same story with the Comtesse de Vendôme necklace – valued at over thirty million dollars. And the men who seized the Marlborough Diamond were also caught, but the jewel disappeared.'

'Point taken,' I tell her. 'I'm starting to see a pattern here . . .'

'This isn't a pattern! Don't you understand? It is a *process*.' Julia is on a roll and continues without pausing for breath. 'The Ivory Coast Crown Jewels were stolen in 2011. Never recovered. Most of the treasure stolen from the palace of Prince Faisal in the so-called Blue Diamond Affair were never found. The Great Mogul Diamond, Tucker's Cross – the most valuable single object ever found in a shipwreck – all lost. And—'

I interrupt her. 'Wildly expensive treasures are stolen. Is it really so strange?'

Julia shakes her head. 'No, the strange thing is . . . nobody is interested! Missing items worth billions of dollars and do you hear about anyone trying to actually find them? I'm late on a council tax payment of a hundred pounds and the authorities are on it by return of post. The world's greatest jewels? No one even looks for them! Or, if they do, the search is so inept that nothing is ever found. *Ever.*' With an edge of triumph, she adds, 'Don't you think that's strange?'

'I suppose when you look at it *not* as a series of one-off thefts, but as a long-standing ongoing process . . . yeah, it's strange.'

'And guess what? It gets stranger . . .'

-29-

'What do you think is going on, Julia? Who's stealing all this treasure?'

'Don't be so dense! That's not the important question!'

I try to keep my temper in check and calmly ask, 'Then enlighten me.'

After driving through greenery for over an hour, we're entering a village and pass a few stone cottages and what looks to be a converted church. A sign indicates we're seventeen miles from Hexham.

'I think' – she points to the fuel gauge – 'we need petrol.'

'*What do you think is going on, Julia?*'

She shrugs. 'It's not just jewels.'

'Go on.'

'Many of mankind's greatest artworks are missing.'

'Is this another process?'

'It's part of the *same* process and it's both historical and ongoing. Da Vinci's *Battle of Anghiari*, Raphael's *Portrait of a Young Man*, Michelangelo's *Leda and the Swan*, Caravaggio's *Nativity* – these are all long-term lost masterpieces. But in the last fifty years, thousands – literally thousands! – of significant paintings have been stolen and never found. The vanished art ranges from the works of modern artists like Geddes, to Old Masters like Rembrandt and the greats including Degas, Cezanne and Renoir. All gone and never found!'

I get the impression she's happy to continue, but there are roadworks ahead and I'm forced to stop in front of a lanky young man wearing a needless hard hat, holding one of those STOP/GO signs. For a second, I'm on max alert. *Is this some kind of trap?*

But I scan the scene and see several burly blokes in high-vis tabards doing absolutely nothing except chatting, so I assume they're legitimate British workmen. There's a uniformed police constable walking towards them and he begins chatting to the only one who's holding a mug of tea – a fact that suggests he's in charge.

I say to Julia, 'It's all right. We'll be moving in a—'

For a moment, I think it's the sound of an open-bolt, blowback-operated submachine gun unleashing a brief hail of bullets, and so does my passenger. She flinches, half ducking, before realising it's one of the workmen testing his pneumatic drill. The guy in question spots Julia's fright and grins, holding up his hand by way of apology.

But the copper noticed her reaction too and seems surprised. He begins sauntering over to us. Julia swears under her breath and I put on my best 'nothing to see here' smile. He lightly raps on the passenger window. Julia lowers it. I lean across. 'Everything all right, constable?'

'I was going to ask you the same question, sir. The young lady seemed . . .'

He's not sure what the 'young lady' seemed, or, at least, he can't articulate it, but she herself snaps, 'I'm fine.'

I offer a more placatory, 'Thanks for checking. We're just a bit on edge.'

'What about?'

I think, *None of your bloody business*, but reply, 'We're running low on petrol.'

He nods in that slow, deep way that people always affect when they don't believe you. I get it a lot, and gesture to the fuel gauge as if to say, *I'm honestly not lying!*

The tall, thin youth with the sign spins it around to present us with GO. Julia glares at me and asks, 'What are you waiting for? Just put your foot down!'

If she's trying to antagonise the policeman, she's doing a first-rate job. He furrows his brow and opens his mouth to speak, but I get there first. 'Would it be all right for us to move along?'

'No. I think I'd better take you to the station.'

Julia yells, 'We haven't done anything wrong!'

I gently tell her, 'He means the petrol station.'

The PC nods.

'That won't be necessary, but thanks. We located one on Google Maps a few minutes ago. But thanks again.'

'No problem, sir.' He steps back and touches the front of his helmet's brim, like he's Dixon of Dock Green. 'Travel safe.'

I release the handbrake and we move away. It's obvious the constable has put Julia even more on edge, and to take her mind off the encounter, I return to our earlier conversation. 'Going back to what you were telling me . . . How much money are we talking about with these things? The missing works, I mean.'

'Hard to say.' I think she's going to leave it at that, but she soon warms to the subject, as if the PC's intervention has already been forgotten. She continues, 'Vincent van Gogh's *Poppy Flowers* was stolen from a Cairo museum in 2010. Never recovered, of course. At the time of the theft, that one painting alone was valued at fifty-five million dollars.'

'And you think Bulatov was involved in this process? Or at the very least interested?'

'Hard to tell. He gives the impression of being connected to everything and linked to nothing.'

I agree. 'Yeah, the Colonel plays his cards so close to his chest they're practically in his ribcage. What about Ekaterina?'

'She was only ever interested in the Romanov treasure. Oh, and the Amber Room. She seemed to believe its disappearance was somehow connected with the Tzar's missing jewels.'

'The Amber Room?' I'm on more familiar territory here. The Amber Room was an extraordinary chamber decorated with amber panels backed with gold leaf and mirrors, located in the Catherine Palace, near Saint Petersburg. It was dismantled during World War II and whisked away from Russia by the Nazis. It famously disappeared, however, and has never been located.

'People called it the Eighth Wonder of the World and its absence is a loss to the art world.' Julia pauses. 'But it was also a priceless piece of art. It was constructed from six tonnes of amber, gold and silver, with serious amounts of gemstones throughout it all. If it was found today, experts estimate it would be worth over five hundred million dollars.'

'And I thought rooms in London were getting pricey.'

'But it disappeared. Of course it did. All part of the process.' She sounds genuinely saddened by the loss of so much heritage but becomes animated again as she glances at the dashboard. 'Novak!' She jabs her finger at the fuel gauge. 'We really need petrol!'

I pull into a small station and something odd occurs. When I kill the engine, it's as though I've killed our conversation. For a moment, there's a loud silence. Julia looks reflective. I ask her if she's all right and she replies with an offhand nod. I get out of the Austin, top up its tank and tell Julia not to leave town.

She widens her eyes. 'Where do you think I'm going to go?'

'I mean, just stay in the van. I'll only be a moment.'

'Fine!'

I walk into the shop to pay. The guy in front of me has a succession of cards declined and starts arguing with the woman on the till. Eventually, he settles using cash and I pay for the petrol and a couple of bottles of water. It's starting to rain as I stroll back to the Austin Morris. I glance at the passenger seat. Empty. Dash to the rear of the vehicle. Unlock the doors and fling them open.

'Damn it!'

Julia has disappeared.

-30-

I jog back to the woman on the till. 'Do you have CCTV?'

'What?'

'Cameras! Do you have security cameras out there?'

'Aye! That we do.'

'I need to see footage from the past couple of minutes. It's important.'

'No can do, I'm afraid.'

'I said it was important.'

She lowers her voice. 'The cameras out there have been on the blink for the past six months, pet.'

'By *on the blink* do you mean they're—'

'Totally knackered? Yes, indeed I do. What's the problem?'

'It doesn't matter. Thanks anyway.'

A moment later, I'm standing in the rain wondering where Julia can have gone in the few minutes I was away from the forecourt. The garage is largely surrounded by open space and private residences.

There's a road leading to the heart of the village and I drive down it slowly, scanning the pavements and parked cars. Still no sign of her.

My phone rings and I pick up.

'Novak – it's me. Julia.'

'Where the hell are you?'

'The bank. The manager let me use his phone.'

'Are you safe?'

'I don't know.'

'I see it now. I'll be there in thirty seconds.'

As we drive from the village, I ask why she left the vehicle. 'There were two men acting suspiciously. It looked like they were watching me. So I ran.'

'Why didn't you just get me?'

She doesn't answer and I doubt she saw anyone. It's entirely plausible she was simply trying to escape from me, then realised I was her best bet if she ever wanted to see her partner and Willow again. Whatever the truth is, Julia's mood has changed. She seems forlorn and angry at the situation. And, truth be told, I'm momentarily forlorn and angry, but with myself for placing too much trust in her. No, it's more than that. I'm disappointed I couldn't imbue her with more faith in me.

We follow the North Tyne for a couple of miles, then join the A68. The rain is falling heavily now, beating a loud tattoo on the van's thin steel roof. What with that and the noise of the engine, I'm forced to raise my voice to be heard clearly.

'Before we stopped for fuel, we were discussing missing artworks and treasures. You seemed to have a theory about them.'

She gives a non-committal grunt.

'Is it anything to do with the Court?'

'I've been thinking,' Julia tells me. 'My only value to British Intelligence is what I know. So I think I'll start rationing what I tell you. My knowledge is the only thing I have that's worth anything, so why should I give it away free of charge?'

'Because I'm trying to help you.'

'You know what, Novak? I think you are. I think you're a good man.'

'Thank you.'

'And so I'll tell you one thing. For free. Don't ask about the Court. No good can come of it. And now . . .' She unfastens her seatbelt. 'I'm going to try to get some sleep in the back of this thing. The sound of rain always makes me sleepy.'

Julia kisses me on the cheek (I try to disguise my astonishment at this) and she nimbly climbs into the rear section of the vehicle. I'm guessing that it's a smaller version of what she tried to do back in the village. An escape from me. And after everything she's been through in the past few hours, I can't say I blame her.

We reach Oxford late in the afternoon. I park illegally on Catte Street and we walk to the offices where I'm due to hand over Julia. I meet Simmonds' operatives in rooms overlooking the Bodleian Library. They're excellent agents whom I've worked with before, but I'm still relieved to see the man I requested is part of the detail.

Sebby Hughes is a youthful looking forty-something. Sharp and thin, he's been many things, including a bodyguard and an assassin, so, in terms of experience, he's got both ends of the spectrum covered. Although he doesn't currently work for Intelligence, I persuaded Simmonds to temporarily hook him on-board.

As is his way, Sebby salutes me. 'Good to see you, Mr Novak, sir.'

'Good to see you, too.' I shepherd him to one side and whisper, 'Like I said earlier, Miss Grant's life is in danger. I need you to look after her. Like we discussed.'

'Affirmative. And don't worry about the lady. To kill her, they'll need to kill me first. And that ain't going to happen.'

I squeeze my friend's shoulder. 'Good man. You take care.'

He nods. 'Understood, Mr Novak, sir.'

I complete the paperwork and there's an awkward moment where Sebby and the operatives hang back a couple of paces so Julia and I can swap goodbyes.

She gives a half-smile. 'I thought exchanges were done in sunny parks or motorway service stations in the rain.'

'Or on curiously deserted runways.' I return her smile. 'We're dealing with the British government. It's all very white collar and red tape. Look, I know the people assigned to look after you. They're good. Especially Sebby. Do as he says and you'll be all right.'

She nods. 'If anything does happen to me, will you find Willow? Tell her the truth about me. And tell her . . .' Her eyes fill up and she purses her lips.

'You'll be safe, Julia. I promise you.'

She nods and we shake hands.

I arrive home late in the evening. Stacey, who'd taken a train down from Scotland, is waiting for me. She's buzzing about our trip around the Continent, but her tactful qualities kick in when she spots I've had a tough day. She says, 'Can I get you a small drink?'

I shake my head. 'No, thanks. But you can get me a large one.'

She mixes us both G&Ts that are heavy on the G and light on the T. We clink glasses. 'So, what happened, Novak?'

'A question I often find myself asking.' I take a sip of my drink. 'That's not bad. I might let you stay on.'

'Look, if you don't want to go into details, that's fine. But sometimes it helps to—'

Our conversation is interrupted by my phone. 'Do you mind if I take this?' She nods and I answer the call. 'Novak.'

'It's me.' I can hear the tension in the voice of Jeremy Simmonds and immediately fear the worse.

'What's happened to Julia?'

'The two men you injured at her flat were both shot before our people arrived. The shooters escaped. But both men were killed.'

'My heart bleeds for them.' I grip the phone tighter. 'Simmonds. *What's happened to Julia?*'

A beat. 'She's missing. Went to the restroom in a service station on the M4. Your man Sebby Hughes went in after her when she didn't show after three minutes. She'd vanished. There was a storage room by the cubicles which had a door leading to the outside. We think that's how it happened.'

I rake my fingers through my hair. 'Why would she do a runner? She knew she had to co-operate so she could see Willow again.'

'Well, there was something else.' Simmonds leaves an awful pause before continuing. 'Hughes found blood in the storage area. And signs of a struggle. He thinks Julia was taken.'

I remember my promise to her. 'Simmonds, you have to put every operative on this. You have to find her.'

'I'm going to do everything I can to get her back, believe me. But I need you to be realistic, Novak. If Colonel Bulatov's men took her – and that looks like the only explanation – it's more than likely . . .' Another pause. 'Julia's already dead.'

Three weeks later

I dip my hand into my inside suit pocket and prepare to leave Diana a remembrance. But in the hubbub of this public space, my choice of what to place here feels suddenly foolish. I should have brought a small bouquet, I suppose. Most people have left roses or photos of the Princess herself. Yet I feel she was given enough flowers over the years and I can't imagine she'd have wanted even more pictures of herself in the world. And so I brought her something that, perhaps uniquely, would mean something to us both.

I'm standing in a busy square in the 16th arrondissement of Paris, here to visit the memorial to the Princess of Wales. It's not officially any such thing, of course. *La Flamme de la Liberté* is a full-sized replica of the torch brandished by Libertas as depicted by the Statue of Liberty. Erected in the late eighties, it's just under twelve feet tall with a grey and black marble pedestal that serves as a base. The sculpture of the flame itself is a copper construction coated in gold leaf.

To tell you the truth, I'm not wild about it. I mean, its design is fine when stuck at the end of an arm that's raised about three hundred feet in the air, but here at eye level it appears curiously inelegant.

After Diana, along with Dodi Fayed and Henri Paul, was killed in the crash that happened in the nearby Pont de l'Alma tunnel in 1997, *La Flamme de la Liberté* became an unsanctioned memorial for the Princess, and over the years, thousands of men and women from around the world have left flowers, letters, photos and other gifts of remembrance here. The Council of Paris recognised this, and the square in which it stands, previously named after Maria Callas, was rechristened Place Diana in 2018.

To my left, there's a narrow road and, beyond that, the banks of the Seine. Across the river, ahead of me to the left, the Eiffel Tower. Sometimes Paris can seem too grey for me. A little too monotone. But today, as I gaze across the Seine and its background of azure skies and bright, almost silver clouds, the City of Light is looking luminous.

I start to pull my remembrance to Diana from my pocket, but pause to say a few words. I should stress, I never met the woman, but after my investigation into her death, I feel an odd, shared kinship with her. Yes. Ridiculous, I know.

I mumble something about how I'm sorry. How I'd tried my best for her and—

'Mr Novak!'

I don't bother to turn around. 'Hello, Ekaterina.'

She takes a step forward to stand at my side. 'I'm sorry to interrupt. That was thoughtless of me. Sorry.'

'How long have you been waiting?'

'Oh, all day. Don't you think it was terribly clever of me? To know you'd visit this place?'

'I'm travelling under my own name, so finding out I'd be in Paris can't have been too difficult.'

She pouts. 'Don't be so mean!'

'But guessing I'd be here—'

'*Reasoning* you'd be here!' she interjects.

'Was *terribly* clever of you.'

She beams, then frowns. 'Are you teasing me?'

'Just a little. Shall we walk?'

'We absolutely must.'

I drop to my haunches and place a photograph amongst the flowers left for Diana. I whisper a few words and stand.

Ekaterina says, 'I didn't have you down as a praying man.'

'I need all the help I can get, sweetheart.'

As we link arms, she asks, 'Who is that a photograph of?'

'A gentleman. And, more importantly, a good man. He was a mutual friend of ours.'

She responds with an only vaguely interested, 'Oh,' and with her arm looped through mine, we walk towards the Seine, away from Liberty's Flame and the photograph of Colonel Gerry Whittaker.

*

We stroll along in silence for a few minutes. It's a cold, bright day and, to our left, sunlight shimmers across the Seine's gentle waves. We're heading eastwards, away from the Pont de l'Alma tunnel, which suits me fine.

Eventually, Ekaterina says, 'Have you reconsidered my job offer?'

'I tend not to work for people I don't trust.'

'That must leave you with a pretty small pool to choose from.'

'Why didn't you tell me your real name?'

She's shocked but hides it well. 'How did you find out?'

'I found out because of one word that you used.'

'Just a single word?'

I nod.

She continues. 'Can we start again?'

'No.'

She stops. Holds the sleeve of my suit jacket. 'This time, I'll be honest with you. I swear.'

She's using her big blue eyes to good effect, deploying them to silently plead with me.

I look over her shoulder and see we're opposite the Palais de Tokyo. I recall that one of its restaurants, Monsieur Bleu, has good views and even better cocktails.

'I'll hear what you have to say on two conditions.'

She hurriedly replies, 'Name them.'

'One. I want full disclosure.'

'Agreed. And two?'

We link arms again and begin walking towards the Palais. 'You buy me a drink, Miss Romanova.'

-32-

Damian's Story

For Damian Gross, it wasn't about wealth or material acquisitions, or even stocks in blue-chip companies. It wasn't about holidays that had been designed with Instagram in mind, or cars that belonged in a Bond movie. Damian Gross had all these things, of course. His life was a wall of extreme prosperity. Shine a spotlight at any part of it and affluence was illuminated. But it wasn't all about that for him.

For Damian Gross, it was much, much worse.

Damian not only surrounded himself with luxury. He sought to elevate it and fuse it with everything that represented him, so it became a core principle of his identity. In short, he wanted to be synonymous with opulence. He wanted the sound of his name to be so potent that it made other men feel insignificant. Unworthy. Failures. He wanted people to find his success incalculable. Staggering. Insane. He craved to be part of an allure that others pretended to reject but fell for so completely that they would dream of him and wake feeling hollow, having to endure their world and not his.

He would go to any length to achieve this, because aside from that compulsion, he didn't care how he felt. He just wanted other people to feel shit about themselves.

He drove his neon cerise Lamborghini Gallardo through murky countryside, speeding through the Surrey Hills towards his huge property at the foot of the North Downs.

As he parked up, his phone rang. He took a look at its screen. It was past 9 p.m., but his lawyer was calling him. He pressed *answer*. 'Speak.'

'Damian – good news.'

Silence.

'Damian, I said I have good news for you.'

'I know. You wouldn't be calling me at this time of night if it was bad news. Just get the fuck on with it.'

'It's about the people who made statements about you.'

'Go on.'

'We got our best people on it.'

'I should hope so.'

'They're all old. Now, we knew that. But our guys have assembled enough evidence to imply they're all gaga.'

'And are they?'

'Christ, no! But they've made mistakes! Who hasn't? We'll be able to manipulate it, though. Make a convincing case that all three of them are losing their marbles so their testimony against you won't stand. Damian, this won't even get to court. You're in the clear.'

'About time, too. Like I said, that's what I pay you for.'

He hung up and stepped from his Lamborghini.

Lon Dugdale, the head of his private team of security guards, approached him.

'Evening, Mr Gross.'

'Everything all right, Dugdale?'

'Yes . . .'

'But?'

Lon Dugdale was a grizzled, well-built army veteran who Gross suspected preferred fighting in the Middle East to

123

looking after a mansion in the Home Counties. He seldom looked troubled, but at this moment his face held a trace of concern.

'It's nothing, sir. We had a slight blip with the pano earlier on. A couple of the lads called in ill. Dunno . . .' He looked past Gross, scanning the darkness. 'Just got a feeling something ain't right, tonight.'

'Call Red Fort and tell them to be extra vigilant. Do what you think necessary here. Double the perimeter guard if appropriate. Money no object, Dugdale.'

Red Fort was the company that maintained the electronic security for the estate, in addition to liaising with local police if any threat was detected.

'It's not just about money, sir.'

Gross studied the former infantryman. 'You've got one job, Dugdale.'

Convinced his head of security was allowing himself to be spooked by coincidences, Gross walked towards his front door and, ten minutes later, sank into his vast granite bath. He lit a cigar. Puffed on it, trying to enjoy his victory over the three people who had sought to hold him accountable. But it hadn't been a victory. It had been a phone call. A resolution. There was nothing about the outcome which enforced his brand. His dominance.

Gross reached across to his mobile and phoned his lawyer. She picked up after three rings.

'Christ, what the fuck were you doing?'

'Sorry, Damian. Is everything all right?'

'You're saying you can stop this thing – this fucking travesty of justice – from reaching court?'

'Yes, sir. Wheels already in motion.'

'I don't want wheels in motion. I want wheels in reverse.'

'I don't understand . . .'

'Try to keep up. I *want* it to go to court. I want the three old people who accused me of stealing their money to stand in the dock. And I want you to humiliate them in front of the world. Expose them as loony old men and women. Pile on so much stress they won't be able to speak. Make them weep. Apologise. Make them weep again. I want them to stand against me and I want the ordeal to be harrowing for them. I want it to end them. Do you understand me?'

'Are you sure that's the right way to—'

'Yes. I'm sure. Can you do it?'

His lawyer hesitated, but only for a moment. 'Yes, sir. Yes, I can.'

'Good. Phone me at nine in the morning with a full, detailed plan about how you're going to achieve it.'

'Yes, Damian, I'll certainly—'

He hung up. And for the first time that evening, he grinned.

His expression of satisfaction lasted less than a second, because as he reached for his burning cigar, one of his home alarms sounded and a light in the corner of the room began to flash red.

'What the . . . *Jesus*!'

He snatched up his phone and tried to call Dugdale. No reception. He cursed – less than a minute earlier, speaking to his lawyer, he'd had three bars. Why couldn't he call out now?

'Fucking red!'

The colour concerned him because it signified why the alarm had been activated. This wasn't some fault with a security cam or even protestors scaling an outer wall. The blinking red light indicated his home had been breached.

-33-

As we cross the Palais's spacious, striking foyer, Ekaterina inquires, 'Are you enjoying your holiday with Miss Stacey Smith?'

She says it like she's asking another question, but I'm not about to rise to it. Or sink to it, depending on your perception of tittle-tattle. 'It's not a holiday. It's a Grand Tour. Englishmen in the seventeenth, eighteenth and nineteenth centuries would—'

'Lounge around Europe and write poetry about it. I *have* heard of the Grand Tour, Mr Novak.'

'It wasn't just about verse. The journey was meant to arm people with a knowledge of classicism, art, antiquity. All that stuff. Getting to know the history and richness of other nations isn't a bad thing, surely?'

'Sounds like a rich boy's gap year.' We reach the long looping staircase that looks like it's come straight out of an Escher print. 'Is that what you were doing as you criss-crossed the Continent? Studying art and antiquity . . .' She mimics my accent to add, 'All that stuff.'

Her impression makes me smile. 'Yeah. I suppose your talk of the Romanov jewels and treasure made me realise I'm unaccustomed to it. To its physicality, if you like.' We start to wander up the curving steps. 'So I visited some of the great palaces of Europe. The Belvedere in Vienna. Schwetzingen Palace in Baden-Württemberg. The Royal Palace of Aranjuez.'

'And the Palace of Versailles?'

'God, no. Far too touristy. Even for me. They have some fabulous markets in Versailles, though. I'd rather wander through the Saint Louis Market than the Saint Louis Chapel.'

'Aren't you clever?'

She's teasing me this time, but I simply reply, 'Yes.' She laughs and I continue. 'What can you tell me about Colonel Bulatov?'

'He's dangerous.'

'Gee, thanks. Here's me thinking he's a vegan with a mania for pacifism.'

'He works for Russian Intelligence. He's pervasive. Power-ful. Currently working in the UK.'

'Is he? It's quite the invasion.'

'You think we're invaders?'

'Oh, we're all invaders.'

'I resent that. They call us refugees, now.'

'Yeah, so I've heard.'

'So, all these royal riches that you saw on your rich boy's gap year, what did you think of them?'

'Not much.' I shrug. 'The art's all right, but all the finery and crown jewels ... It's just bling with a bit of reverence thrown in.'

We reach the top of the staircase. 'And is that what you think the Romanov treasure is? Bling with a little reverence?'

'No. It's bling with a lot of bloodshed. And don't look so cross, Ekaterina. We're about to have cocktails overlooking the Seine. You could at least pretend to be happy.'

'I'm Russian, Mr Novak. Angry and happy tend to run in tandem.'

*

As it's out of season, the terrace section of the restaurant is officially closed, but Ekaterina – of course – knows the manager, who quickly ensures an outside table is prepared for us. The views are famously fantastic, with a postcard vista of the Seine and just beyond the Pont d'Iéna, the Eiffel Tower.

I plump for a Vesper Martini and Ekaterina, appropriately enough, goes for a Saint Petersburg. I also ask the waitress if she can whistle up a couple of blankets. Ekaterina looks amused by this request, but when two quilts are brought out, she swiftly cocoons herself in the thicker of the pair as I wrap mine around my shoulders.

Our drinks arrive and we clink glasses. Ekaterina says, '*Za vstrechu!*'

'To your very good health.'

'So, are you going to tell me how you found out who I really am? How you discovered I'm a Romanov? I covered my tracks well. You're so old-school, I thought you would draw a blank. You had no background information about me. No photograph or details about any friendships.'

What she just said strikes me as peculiar, but I put it to the back of my mind to worry about later. 'I had a phone number for you, but assumed you'd taken steps to make sure it was untraceable. However, I did have a photograph of you. Taken when you visited me.'

'How? I thought the jammer—'

'Oh, your jammer did the job on my internal security. Brought the Wi-Fi down so the data collected from the camera couldn't be stored internally and I just got a whole load of nothing. My outside camera, however . . .'

'Concealed?'

'Of course. It's 4K, but it's wired directly to a DVR, so it can't be jammed or hacked.'

'My God! That's virtually analogue.'

'As you say, old-school, Miss Romanova.'

She raises her glass to me. 'So, you have a photograph. What next?'

'I contacted a friend.' The friend I contacted is Molly Stone, the de facto head of a ragtag bunch of investigators known as the Next Time Crime Club. This group of former journos once helped out Frank Harvey when he in turn was assisting me on a case. 'I gave my friend your photo.'

Ekaterina furrows her brow. 'But what good is a picture? I mean – so what?'

'You were carrying a Givenchy handbag and wearing a Balmain coat and Stuart Weitzman shoes that I'm guessing you didn't get from your local Oxfam. You live in London. So I asked my friend to visit all the shops in the Smoke that sell clothes in that price bracket, and specifically those brands.'

'There must be hundreds!'

'There's fewer than you think. But she found nothing.'

Ekaterina smiles. 'I never shop in London. Too crowded.'

'Next, my friend tried the best gyms and spas. Nothing. A few of the fancier restaurants and cocktail bars. Still zilch. I gave it up, but then I remembered a word you used.'

'Go on.'

I take a sip of my Vesper and see it's almost done. Cocktails are something I enjoy, but I've never understood why they come in measures that wouldn't satisfy a Borrower.

'You called your country "Mother Russia". That was the telltale word. *Mother*.'

'Which tells you nothing! I don't understand.'

'It struck me at the time. And thinking about it later, it felt like a term of affection and pride. It wasn't forced. That's really how you think of your nation.'

'I don't agree with everything the Russian government does. Just as you probably don't agree with how your collection of crooks and liars run your country.'

'That's not what I'm driving at. Mother Russia. You're proud of it. You probably idealise it a little. And I guessed you miss it.'

'Of course.'

'So you do what every holidaymaker, tourist or émigré does when they're a long way from a home they think of fondly. You visit a restaurant that is a little haven of your country. In your case, you frequent a Russian eatery. I asked my friend to check out three such restaurants in London. First, Mari Vanna's. I thought that'd be right up your cobbled street. The chandelier. The lace. All the tchotchke. It feels so homely! But no. Then I suggested Zima, in Soho. Fantastic vodkas, except for the horseradish vodka. Tried it once and—'

'Get on with it!'

'My third guess was the charm. Your favourite restaurant. My friend could see the waiter she spoke to recognised your photograph immediately. He tried to lie, but she met him after work and a bottle of Grey Goose later . . .'

Ekaterina shakes her head. 'The guy drinks French vodka? That tells the whole story!'

'He said you often dined there with a male friend. There was no suggestion of him being anything other than platonic, by the way. And the waiter remembered you both celebrated a shared milestone birthday over a long, boozy lunch. So that helped with the question of how could you know him. University friend, maybe? Seems a fair bet as you're the same age. A little financial encouragement persuaded our friendly waiter to pull some records.'

'I'll have him fired!'

'No, just be more careful, next time. Anyway, this friend of yours paid by card, so we had his name. It wasn't too difficult to find where he studied. I think we got that from his Facebook page. We accessed the uni's records for his year group. Everything still on file, including photo ID. And there you were. Ekaterina Romanova.' I finish my Vesper and place the glass on the table. 'Busted.'

She drinks a little more of her Saint Petersburg. 'You did well.'

'I had help from the best. And like I always say, teamwork makes the dodgy-as-hell scheme work. Why did you lie to me?'

'I lie to the world. I've been Ekaterina Karpin for years. I couldn't risk telling you the truth.'

'And is that still the case?'

She bites her lip.

I lean forward. 'Look, Miss Romanova. One of two things is about to happen. Either I'm going to leave and have dinner with Miss Smith at Scarlioni's. I'm led to believe they do a very good Espresso Martini. *Or* you're going to order us a bottle of wine and, as we drink it, you're going to tell me exactly what the hell is going on.'

The waitress, spotting my empty glass, has wandered over to our table and asks if we want anything more.

I say to Ekaterina, 'Your choice.'

She tugs her quilt more tightly around her body. Glances up at the waitress. 'A bottle of my favourite. The Ruinart Blanc de Blancs, please.' Looks at me. 'Two glasses.'

I ask for a large vodka chaser. If Ekaterina is going to tell me the truth about her past and the Romanov treasure, and why she wants me involved so badly, I've a feeling I'm going to need it. As the waitress walks away, I ask her to make it Grey Goose and Ekaterina scowls at me.

-34-

Damian's Story (cont.)

Gross climbed from his bath, slipped on his silk kimono, hurried through to his bedroom and removed his Wilson Combat Supergrade Classic from his desk. Although an expensive handgun, many enthusiasts believed it was one of the most beautiful sidearms on the market. Gross's was a stainless-steel slide and frame model with a wood-grain grip. At just under nine inches long, it wasn't the most compact pistol available, but it consistently scored five stars in terms of accuracy, so for a non-shooter like Gross, who wanted aesthetic excellence as well as efficiency and reliability, it had been the obvious choice.

He gripped it in his right hand, slipped the safety to *off* and curled his index finger around its skeletonised trigger. He should have felt better. Safer. Instead, his stomach lurched. He was holding forty-five ounces of hardware and every last one weighed heavy. A reminder that he was facing a real, physical situation that no amount of lawyering up or buying off could resolve. This was him versus whoever had entered his home and the usually confident millionaire suddenly had a dry mouth and wet palms.

He edged onto his landing. Looked down across the reception area. Still. Quiet.

'Dugdale!' he shouted. 'Dugdale, for fuck's sake!'

He inched along the landing towards the stairs, muttering to himself, 'That prick is so fired in the morning . . .'

He reached the top of the stairs.

'What the fuck do I pay him for?'

Gross looked down and saw something that made his heart beat even harder.

The handle of the front door dipped. Someone was trying to enter.

He raised his sidearm, expecting the door to open, but it was apparently locked. The handle reverted to its usual position.

'Jesus . . .'

Gross heard a rattle in the lock. His finger tightened on his pistol's trigger. The handle dipped again, but this time the door was gently pushed open.

Shifting his weight uneasily from one foot to the other, he mentally prepared to shoot whoever stepped across the threshold.

Any moment now—

'Hey!'

The voice was close. To his left.

Gross almost dropped his weapon. He yelped something incomprehensible, stepped to his right and swung his sidearm round to point towards whoever had spoken. But the individual was too swift, grabbing the pistol and easily twisting it from Gross's hand.

-35-

'OK, Ekaterina . . . let's start with some of the big points,' I suggest. 'First question. Were you really a spy? And if you were, who were you spying for?'

'Do you remember when we first met, Mr Novak? I poked fun at the Western perception of Russian agents.'

'You mentioned we thought they were all exotic female agents in glamorous furs.'

'But it's not like that. I came to England when I was a child. I remember thinking it was so vivid and free! My mother knew I was afraid. I was in a completely new environment, away from all my friends and everything I'd ever known, so it was natural. And so she would point at your bright red postboxes, with the regal insignia – ER, which I now know stands for Elizabeth Regina. But my mother told me the letters stood for Ekaterina Romanova and that the people of Britain had had the postboxes specially made to celebrate my arrival.' She smiles at the memory.

I ask, 'So you stayed here for a few years?'

'Yes, I studied at the University of Reading and . . . Cutting to the chase, yes, I worked for the Security Services, but I never even thought of myself as an agent, let alone a spy.'

'How were you recruited?'

'I wasn't recruited! Not in that sense! The FSB didn't turn up on campus and offer a free Makarov for everyone who attended an induction class. What you've got to remember is this was the nineties! We weren't the enemy back then! Gorbachev's *perestroika* movement had led to *glasnost*, German reunification and the end of what America called the "Evil Empire". We were the good guys! Russia was cool! *I* was cool!'

'How lovely. *How were you recruited?*'

'They asked me to sell badges of the Soviet Red Star.'

'The Red Star?'

'Like I said, back then, Russia was cool. Students wore fake-fur ushanka hats with the Red Star pinned to the front. They carried their dirty washing back to Mummy and Daddy's in sports bags with the hammer and sickle on the side, just below the letters CCCP. They wore T-shirts depicting Lenin urging the proletariat onwards.'

'They probably didn't have a clue how many thousands of workers Vladimir Lenin butchered.'

'Quite so. So another student tells me that dozens of dodgy spivs are making good money selling knock-off Soviet iconography. Did I think that was right? He explains he sells goods authorised by the Russian government. Quality stuff! And the profits go back to Moscow to be distributed amongst the wives and children of soldiers who didn't make it back from the Chechen War. Could I help? I said sure! I'll help! So I sold a few badges and bags.' She shrugs. 'That hardly made me Agent Triple-X. But I imagine you can guess what happened next.'

'You were given more and more responsibility, but it all remained above board. I take it you even received messages from the families your efforts helped. And the Party invited you to swish parties and made you feel like a million dollars.'

'You've heard the tale before?'

'The beginning is always the same. It's how the story ends that interests me.'

The waitress arrives with our champagne in an unnecessary ice bucket. The temperature is dropping as the evening creeps in. She uncorks the wine, pours us both a glass and slips back inside.

I say, 'I'm guessing that when you left uni, although you didn't twig at the time, they made sure you didn't even get an interview for any of the jobs you applied for. Then a member of the team you'd worked with showed up and said they could fix you up with a position . . .'

She's been nodding along. 'Pretty much. They got me a job at a courier company. Sounds boring, I know. But we were transporting items all across the world. It was fun! Exciting! I got to travel, and at first the business I was involved with was legitimate. Then gradually . . .'

'You were asked to move items that were off the books. Then they asked you to conceal one or two pieces. And finally to smuggle them.'

'Exactly. I was told it was for tax purposes. It was all so gradual. So normal . . . You'll think I'm a fool, but I went along with it. I should mention the social life! Wow! To a young woman suddenly to be at these amazing balls and weekend get-togethers in Palm Beach, Melbourne, Monte Carlo . . . I'd often meet businessmen and my boss would say, did he talk about such-and-such? And I'd be asked to steer the conversation around so I could pick up inside pieces of information.'

I take a mouthful of the Ruinart Blanc de Blancs. 'So you were gathering intelligence?'

'Yes, but in my head it wasn't framed that way.'

'It never is. Miss Romanova, you mentioned your boss.'

'*Da?*'

'I imagine he was your case officer, yeah?'

'What's a case officer?'

'It's the person you report to.' I take my phone from my suit pocket. Open the photo gallery and select a pic. 'The contact to whom you passed the intel you gathered, for example. He or she will have looked after you. Acted as a friend. Taken care of anything you needed taking care of.'

'Ahh . . . Yes, I had a case officer.'

'Ekaterina . . .' I show her a photograph of Frank Harvey. 'Was it this man?'

-36-

Damian's Story (cont.)

'Dugdale!'

'Sorry, Mr Gross. You looked like you were going to shoot.' The head of security handed the Wilson Combat Supergrade Classic back to his boss. 'I noticed the safety's off.'

'It's not a lot of good when it's on!'

'Depends which side of the barrel you're standing, sir.'

'What the fuck is going on?'

'I noticed a recurring error in the security pano, sir. I think it's what caused the alarm to go off, but I told the lads to sweep the house and grounds, just to be on the safe side. Is that OK with you, sir?'

Gross normally forbade his guards from entering his home, but on this occasion he was prepared to let the preclusion slide.

'Of course! I want everywhere double-checked.' He looked down at the reception area and spotted one of his guards had entered via the front door. He murmured, 'That little shit scared the fuck out of me.' And louder, 'What kind of error, Dugdale?'

'Just a gremlin in the works. The network got an upgrade the other day. It's possibly something that needs a patch. That's all.'

Gross nodded. Both men heard a vehicle tearing across the gravelled driveway and seconds later it skidded to halt with a long sliding crunch. 'Christ!' Gross exclaimed. 'What now?'

*

The Red Fort van drew to a halt a few yards from the front door and a woman emerged. She wore her company's uniform – a navy blue jumpsuit with military-style epaulettes and her photo ID card affixed to the outer chest pocket.

Gross groaned when he spotted her. As she approached the house, he shouted, 'It was just a bug in the system! You can toddle off! Everything's taken care of!'

'Damian Gross?'

'Yes. I'm your client, so—'

'Our analysts came up with the same finding. Just a glitch.'

Gross shrugged. 'Brilliant. What are you doing here, then?'

'I spoke to your man Dugdale on my way over. He said phone reception dipped. Men off ill. Then this so-called glitch. I'd like to take a look around.'

'Not necessary. I've got an army vet in charge of security here. He's spent most of his life serving on the front line. You've spent most of your life serving in Côte. Do fuck off, luv.'

She unclipped her ID card and, raising it slightly, said, 'I'm Maggie Roberts. The alarm was tripped. I've got to talk to you and assess your property. Contractual obligation and I really think you ought to be taking this more seriously.'

'I'll give you ninety seconds. Come in, then!'

She followed Gross inside his home, asking, 'Do you have anything of value in this property, sir?'

'Anything of value? Seriously?' He stopped in the doorway leading to his sitting room and glared at her. 'Look around!

Everything in this place cost more than you'll make before you retire to fucking Bridlington.'

'I'm not talking about furnishings and artwork, sir. You should be safe there. Professional thieves tend to go after more exclusive targets. Nouveau riche stuff like this isn't highly sought after.'

Gross wasn't entirely sure what she meant by *nouveau riche*, but he lashed out anyway. 'Are you taking the piss?'

'Do you have anything unique? Maybe in a vault or a hidden safe? That could be what the thieves are after.'

'There are no thieves! You've spoken to me and seen inside my house. Contractual obligations observed.' Dugdale reached the woman's side. 'Take this girl back to her van.'

Maggie looked to be in her late fifties. Black hair. Grey roots. Big, serious spectacles. 'One, I don't appreciate the word *girl* in that context, sir.' She took a step forward. 'And two, I think your home is under attack.'

'And I think, if you don't leave now, Red Fort will have one fewer client in the morning.'

She paused. 'Your call, sir.'

'As you say, my call, sir.'

Gross turned away, but the woman's belief that something was awry had rattled him. And, as always, he knew exactly what he had to do.

-37-

Ekaterina looks at the picture of Frank Harvey. 'Give it to me.' I hand her my phone, and using her index finger and thumb, she expands the image until Frank's face fills the screen. 'No . . . no, I don't remember ever meeting this man. Who is he?'

'It doesn't matter.'

I slip my phone back into my pocket. Ekaterina is a pretty good liar, but I think she's telling the truth when she claims she doesn't recognise my friend. Her reaction when she studied the photograph suggested his face was unknown to her, so there goes another one of my theories. I take another sip of the champagne to console myself.

'Go on with your story,' I say. 'What turned socialite and fledgling spy Ekaterina Romanova into former agent Ekaterina Karpin?'

'There was a death.'

'A murder?'

She nods. 'It scared the hell out of me. Brought me to my senses. It was as though a mirror had been held to my face and I suddenly realised I was smuggling and gathering intelligence. My God, I was terrified!'

'You asked to leave but they said no.'

'Exactly! So I pretended it was fine. But I kept my eyes open after that.'

'Tell me about the murder.'

'I was pretty high up the network's food chain, but whenever I met new people who were in the know, I pretended to have more information than I did. It made colleagues more willing to share information with me.'

'Makes sense.'

'So, one night I'm in Rome, drinking wine and vodka with a boy who moves high-end items around central Europe. And he says, "Hey! You're a Romanov! They should have given you my job!"' Ekaterina shuffles her chair slightly closer to mine. 'He told me he was transporting items that belonged to the Tzar and Tzarina! I thought he was drunk. Just trying to impress me for a lay, you know? And I was right, I think. About him wanting to screw me. But the idiot had taken photos of his consignment! Showed me! A Fabergé egg! And a tiara! I couldn't believe it. I knew it was big, so I didn't want to know.'

'Hold on! You can't just leave it at that! A Fabergé egg? A tiara?'

'I think the Fabergé was the Alexander III Commemorative egg.'

I try to take this in. 'One of the most sought-after relics in history . . . And the tiara?'

'An item known as the Russian Beauty.'

'Never heard of it.'

'A pearl and diamond tiara that was created for the Empress Alexandra Feodorovna. Over two-dozen huge, natural pearls, hung from pointed diamond arches, floating over a gemstone base. Legend has it that the Empress Maria loved it so much that she used to wear it about the palace for no reason other than her fondness for it.'

'How the other half live. OK. So what did you do after he showed you the pics of these dinky little trinkets?'

'I plied him with more and more spirits so he would forget he'd let me see the evidence. Poured him into a cab and sent him on his way. I didn't sleep that night, I can tell you. I was sick with worry!'

'The boy who showed you the photos of the treasure. What was he called?'

'They called him Mr Pitkin. I think it was a sort of joke, but I never understood.'

Despite everything, I give a short laugh. 'This kid. Was he clumsy? Gauche?'

'Yes.' Ekaterina looks confused. 'How did you know?'

'Mr Pitkin is how Eastern Bloc countries knew Norman Wisdom. It was the name of a character he played in one of his early movies.'

'Who's Norman Wisdom?'

'A comic actor. Massive in Russia. He holidayed in Moscow in the early sixties and was mobbed. The Albanian government declared a day of mourning when he died.'

'Never heard of him.'

'Before your time. I just happen to like old movies. Anyway, go on. Did you get to know Mr Pitkin's real name?'

'When he was drunk, he told me it was Taras, but I think he was lying.'

'Surname?'

She sighs. 'I did not find out that evening and never got the opportunity to ask him. Mr Novak, less than one week after showing me the photos of the Romanov treasure, he was found hanging from the Ponte Milvio.'

-38-

I hazard a guess: 'His death was put down to suicide.'

'Absolutely. But here's the thing. He worked with a man called David Fenton. I also drank with David. He was smarter. We became good friends. Lovers, I think.'

Ekaterina is foggy about that last fact, as though it's a minor detail. She pauses and reaches across to the ice bucket, but I'm eager for her to continue. 'I'll get that. Please, go on with your story.'

'They made the runs together. Mr Pitkin and David.' As I refill our glasses, she adds, 'David, he was a real firebrand for the Party. David wanted Russian citizenship. Insisted Gorbachev had been a traitor. That Yeltsin should have been shot for allowing the dissolution of the Soviet Union. You know the type.'

'Only too well.'

'Well, he obviously gets scared after Mr Pitkin turns up under the Ponte Milvio because he disappears, too. I think he'll be found under another bridge, but no!'

The waitress reappears and asks if everything is in order. We say yes. I thank her and she leaves us. As she walks away, I notice the light is fading fast.

Ekaterina's hand emerges from her quilt cocoon. She takes another mouthful of the wine and resumes. 'A couple of days after David vanishes, I'm doing a job in Sant'Angelo.'

'Rome?'

'Of course!' She looks at me as though it's patently obvious which Sant'Angelo she's discussing. 'Anyway, I'm on my way to a pick-up. Two colleagues I don't know very well are taking me to some apartment. We're walking through those narrow roads around the Portico d'Ottavia.' She gives me an unexpected smile. 'I can still smell the fresh vegetables frying and the scent of fish being prepared in those little cafes that line the way!' Her smile melts away. 'But the two guys. They ask in Italian if I speak Italian. I can, of course. But I smile blankly. You know. Stupid woman! So they have this conversation. I don't hear it all, but it's clear enough that David has defected. Defected! And he's gone to England.'

'Whereabouts?'

'They didn't give me his address!' She shrugs. 'We did the job. I moved on. A few months later, I got my new ID and fled.'

'You never looked for him?'

'No.'

'And how did you get your new ID?'

Another smile. 'Another boy. During my work for the network, I came into contact with a freelancer who arranged new identities. He was a nice person. Really. But weak. I slept with him. Told him he must create a new identity for me, or I would tell his wife everything! And that's how I became Ekaterina Karpin. Travelled the world for a decade. Even stayed in Russia for a couple of years. Good times. Then, ten years after leaving England, I heard rumours that the network I'd worked for had been disbanded literally weeks after I left.'

'And do you believe those rumours?'

'Yes! It had been a time of massive change. I investigated, and yes, it was true. I felt it was safe to return to London, but kept my assumed identity. Settled down as Ekaterina Karpin.'

'And then?'

'I marry rich. I divorce richer. Life is crazy! But fun. Then, four years ago, I was approached by the Romanov Foundation. I don't think they even knew I was a Romanov, but it felt like destiny, you know?'

'I know.'

'They do good work, not only helping Russian émigrés, but anyone dispossessed who needs assistance. It's the first worthwhile thing I've been involved with, Mr Novak. After years of me-me-me, it felt good to give something back! Oh, you can smirk! But it's the truth.'

'Who funds the organisation?'

'Many of our members are wealthy and we sink our own money into it. But we still rely on donations from the public.'

I start laughing. 'It's all becoming clear! As Russia falls out of favour after recent and ongoing events, an organisation with a Russian name stops being a desirable charity to donate to. Your funds dry up.'

'And then I recall the Romanov treasure! It is mine by birthright! I'm a Romanov, after all! So I think – I will track down David Fenton and get him to tell me what he knows. Then we will seize the treasure. Sell it. And our foundation can continue to help people around the world.'

'But Fenton had vanished from the face of the earth?' She nods. 'But even if you could find him, his intel might be years out of date.'

She gives a one-shouldered shrug and, as if I'm an idiot, counters with, 'It might not be. Anyway, we have a difficulty.'

'I'd say we have several.'

'My former husband is now a member of parliament.'

'Congratulations. He can rely on my vote.'

'He does some digging around for me. British Intelligence wiped Fenton's file, so even they don't know who he is or where he went to . . . You see the problem?'

'Clearly. Even if we have contacts in MI5 or MI6, they can't help because the information was expunged years ago. Miss Romanova, I'm assuming you want me to find Fenton and you can take it from there.'

'You do understand!'

'But how on earth do you expect me to locate him after all this time?'

'How should I know? That's your job!'

'I suppose it is,' I concede. I divide the last of the Ruinart Blanc de Blancs between our glasses. 'Tell me about Yulia.'

'Who?'

'Yulia Protopopov. Also known as Julia Grant. She said she worked with you.'

'I can't remember every Yulia I ever met.' Her air of complete apathy suggests she genuinely doesn't recall her countrywoman. 'Why are you asking?'

'She's probably dead.'

Ekaterina tilts her head and for a moment I anticipate she's going to reply, *So what?* But she asks, 'Did you kill her, Mr Novak?'

She looks disappointed when I tell her I didn't. I explain that I believe Colonel Bulatov's men had been watching Julia Grant and later tried to murder her at her home, intending to make her death look like a robbery gone wrong. 'When that failed, he simply had her abducted.'

'I told you he was dangerous.'

Ekaterina has somehow managed to turn Julia's plight into nothing more than a vindication of her own words.

'So,' she adds, 'I have been honest with you. Told you the entire truth – as you demanded. Now will you take the case? Yes or no?'

-39-

Damian's Story (cont.)

Damian Gross watched the Red Fort van turn left at the end of his long driveway and disappear into the night. He closed his bedroom curtains and scurried downstairs to his study.

Dugdale had assured him that there were no intruders and the last of the security guards had vacated the house. Good. He was convinced that Margie Robertson, or whatever she'd been called, had been trying to unnerve him in order to subtly drive home the importance of her company's services. But still, there was something he needed to check.

He closed his study doors and, with his Wilson Combat Supergrade Classic in his hand, gave the room a perfunctory search, feeling faintly absurd as he glanced under sofas, behind the desk and in cupboards. But this was his home's one space that remained devoid of cameras and so he needed to be certain because . . .

He paused. Removed a book from a lower shelf and opened it. The tome had been hollowed out and a small control unit secreted between its covers. He removed it and entered an eight-digit sequence, paused and added five more characters. He heard a tiny click and pulled his shoulders back.

'I am Damian Gross.' He spoke loudly and clearly. 'Authorisation for opening: granted.'

He heard an artificial voice intone, 'Opening authorised.'

The sofa, tugged by underfloor electromagnets, moved back by about four feet. The adjacent chair also slid to one side. It was a weird sight, as if the items of furniture were being repositioned by the neatest and quietest of poltergeists. This shifting exposed an area of parquet floor that had been mostly covered and now an oblong section of this space dropped by about three inches and slid to one side. This revealed what looked to be a container, roughly the size and shape of an adult's coffin. A thick slab of Perspex covered it, but after a moment, this also slid to one side and the container began to rise, exposing metallic struts beneath its structure.

It reached chest-height and stopped. Gross stepped forward.

The container was full of files. It held a cache of corruption. Every dossier detailing every shady deal Gross had ever been part of; every paper chain linking ostensibly respectable firms and business people with his own, less legitimate ventures; every signed memo implicating members of the rich and powerful in criminal enterprises was stored here.

It was also a cache of complicity. It held sex tapes showing a failed prime minister and former exchequer; the dalliances of two presidents, although Gross doubted the footage of one of them would be of any use other than offering a kind of masochistic titillation. Sound recordings of the great and the good being less than great as they got up to no good. Photographs of public figures indulging in private vices.

The container was brimful of material that gave Damian Gross leverage, and, as always, looking at the hoard and running his fingertips across it was one of the few experiences that excited him sexually. He knew the contents by sight and ticked off every item from his memorised inventory, finally nodding to himself.

'Good . . .'

He stood back, preparing to return his study to its customary state.

'That's very impressive.'

Gross swore involuntarily. 'Fuck!' He whirled around and saw Maggie Roberts had entered the room. 'Christ! What the hell are you doing in here? I'll have you fired! I thought you'd gone!'

She appeared to be taken aback. 'My colleague left in the van. I told Dugdale I wanted one final sweep of the house.'

'And he was cool with that?'

'I told him you'd texted me and that the request came from you.'

Gross pointed a finger in her direction. 'You are in a world of trouble!'

The woman held his stare. 'All right. Let's drop the pretence, if only so you'll end this tirade of petty insults. I'm fairly thick-skinned, but it's exhausting, in a depressing OMG-there-are-still-men-like-you-out-there kind of way.'

'You'd better—'

'Hush! Now, Mr Gross. I warned you. I told you I thought something was wrong. I told you that you weren't taking the situation seriously enough. And I told you I thought you had a dangerous intruder in your home. Well, now I'm convinced of all three.'

'How can you be so bloody sure?'

She closed the door behind her and locked it from the inside. 'Because, Mr Gross, I'm the intruder I warned you about.'

'Mr Novak!' Ekaterina repeats her question. 'Will you take my case? Yes or no?'

'Let me think about it. I've thought about it. No.'

'What?' She looks staggered. 'Why not?'

'I still don't believe you're telling me the whole story, and even if you are, there are three problems.'

'And what are they?'

'The entire proposition is crazy, crazier and craziest.'

'You never intended to agree, did you?'

I remain silent.

'Then why did you have me tell my story?'

'Well, I fancied a laugh and I was enjoying the champagne.'

For a moment, I see the livid Ekaterina who regarded me with such fury when we met at my house and I told her I thought something was off. But watching her now, I see that anger seep away, slowly replaced by something smoother.

Guile.

'So you're just going to leave, Mr Novak?'

I nod. She shrugs.

'Okey-dokey, Joe.'

I stand and unwrap the quilt from my shoulders. Place it on my chair.

'By the way,' she says. 'At the Diana memorial, what did you say to the Princess?'

'None of your business.'

'Because it sounded to me like you were telling her you did your best. Which is another curious English expression. Roughly translated, it means *I failed*.'

'Like I said before, I was failed.'

She watches me with smiling eyes as she takes another sip of champagne. 'Sure, sure.'

I'm hovering when I should be walking, but something about her tells me she's about to play a card, and despite my better judgement, I want to see if it's an ace or a joker.

'You see,' she continues, 'from what I heard and read and researched, well, looks like you found the organisations responsible for the murder of Diana. But not the individuals.'

'It was a long time ago. Most of them are dead.'

'Only most of them?'

'Two disappeared. One of them turned up dead in Jakarta three years ago.'

She takes another deliberately slow sip of wine. 'And then there was one.'

I sit back down. 'You're bluffing.'

'Oh, if you believed that you'd be on your way out of the door.'

'Tell me what you know.'

She arches an eyebrow.

I take a breath. 'Please.'

'No!' she snaps. 'We tried that game. Me telling you everything I know. Wasn't much fun. You seemed very pleased with yourself at the end of it. Well, off you fuck.'

I hold her stare and after a few seconds say, 'How could you possibly know?'

'It's a mystery,' she replies. 'But it's almost as though I've moved in circles of people who make it their business to know about such individuals.'

I study her face to see if she's overplaying her hand. It's obvious she's enjoying the situation, but I can't discern anything more.

I get to my feet again. 'Goodbye, Miss Romanova. I'm sorry things didn't work out for us.'

She says nothing. Gives me a wave by waggling the fingers of her right hand.

I fasten the middle button of my suit jacket, turn and walk away. As I reach the doors leading inside the building, she speaks two words.

I stop dead.

The words are a name. And the name is that of the one man implicated in the murder of Diana who remains unaccounted for. He could be anywhere in the world and maybe he died years ago. But the fact that Ekaterina knows him, and implicitly knows something about him, suggests her card was an ace.

I stride back to the table. She says, 'Here's the new deal. You find Fenton and I tell you everything I know about the man you seek.'

'You might know nothing.'

'I might.' She nods enthusiastically. Childishly. 'But those are my terms. Oh . . .' She pouts sarcastically. 'Don't look so cross, Mr Novak. We're about to have more champagne overlooking the Seine. You could at least pretend to be happy.'

'I'm delirious,' I tell her and sit back down. 'I'm helping a former Russian spy track down loot belonging to the Kremlin so she can get very, very rich. What's not to love?'

Ekaterina doesn't smile, but she regards me, thoughtfully, for several seconds. 'If it would make you feel any better, once the gold and diamonds and the rest of the haul are found, you can keep them.'

'Are you serious?'

'If it means that much to you, yes. I'll finance the foundation some other way.'

'I thought your whole plan from the outset was for you to get your hands on the Romanov treasure.'

'I only want one thing that was lost all those years ago. Something of almost no intrinsic value.'

I'm suddenly glad I stayed. 'What is it? What would you go to so much trouble for? What would you give up an absolute fortune for? What is it you really want?'

'All I want, Mr Novak . . .' She pauses, then nods, as if to herself, 'Is the Romanov Code.'

-41-

I catch a cab and phone Stacey en route to our hotel. She doesn't pick up, so I leave her a message explaining we've got to get back to Britain as soon as possible.

As my taxi weaves through the backstreets of Paris, I replay my conversation with Ekaterina. She refused to tell me what the Romanov Code is or why it's so important to her and so I feel like yet again I've walked away with more question marks than full stops. And—

Maybe I'm getting paranoid, but I try Stacey's number a couple more times. *Why the hell isn't she picking up?*

One last time. Still no answer.

I reach the hotel and head straight to our room. It's large and airy with a Juliet balcony overlooking a street market and, in case you were wondering, twin beds. No sign of Stacey. I phone her again, but the call clicks through to her answer service.

'Hi, it's me . . .' I begin, rather obviously. 'Do me a favour and get in touch the minute you get this. Nothing's wrong. Speak soon. Thanks.'

I pour myself a G&T and phone Simmonds. 'I need a favour.'

'Oh God,' he replies. 'You're not getting married, are you? You're not going to ask me to be your best man?'

'Honestly, Simmonds, if Mount Rushmore was a tribute to delusional men, your face would be carved slap bang in the middle of the rock face.'

'I was joking, Novak. How can I help? What do you need this time? False passport? AK-47? Help with The *Times* crossword?'

'I need everything you've got on Ekaterina Romanova. You might know her as Ekaterina Karpin.'

'I'll need more than a flighty request, Novak.'

I tell Simmonds what she told me and he agrees to cross-check her story. I add, 'There's one more thing I need.'

'Well, praise the Lord for that. For a moment, I thought I was going to be able to get on with my job.'

'I'm heading back to England.'

'Europe's loss and all that.'

'So I might need a bit of extra protection.'

'More bodyguards? I doubt there'll be many chomping at the bit after last time.'

'God, no. I don't want anything like that. But you helped me out once before. Unwillingly. With that derringer. You told me it had been provided by the Toymaker.'

Simmonds sounds cautious. 'Yes . . .'

'Well, I'm wondering if there are any other toys I can play with.'

Our exchange lasts another minute or so and immediately afterwards I start packing. I'm almost done when I hear the door opening behind me.

I spin round. 'Stacey! Where the hell have you been?'

She's weighing up whether to tear a strip off me for being so rude or take a more amicable approach. Thankfully, she opts for the latter. 'I've just got off the Metro, so I've not had time to check your messages. Are you going to tell me what's rattled your cage?'

'I'm sorry. Tough couple of hours.' I tell her about my meeting with Ekaterina.

Stacey asks, 'But she wouldn't tell you what the Romanov Code actually is?'

'It's a riddle within a riddle within a riddle. And yes, the Russian dolls image was deliberate.'

'But unnecessary.' She grins at me.

'The bottom line is that I have to go after the Romanov treasure because she can give me something that's important to me.'

'She's dangerous. She's sketchy. She's trouble. Why not just walk away?'

'Because I need to do the right thing. You know, I once introduced myself with the words, *My name is Marc Novak and I've got the best job in the world.* It wasn't a brag. It meant I was doing something that was just and worthwhile. I'm not sure I could say those words and mean them today. But if I could ever speak them again with truth and conviction . . . Well, it would be redemptive, I guess.'

'Ach well, I don't even know what that means . . .' She suddenly embraces me. 'But I'm with you all the way.'

It's difficult to explain, but there's something about her total loyalty and faith in me that I find utterly heartbreaking.

*

We reach the Gare du Nord in good time and catch the 20:25 to Calais-Fréthun. It's a direct train that completes the journey in under two hours, which means we should be able to make the ferry setting sail for Dover at 22:30. But the weather's become stormier throughout the night, gathering in intensity the further north we've travelled. It's atrocious now – blowing a gale and lashing it down – and whilst collecting our tickets, we hear mumblings that crossings might have to be suspended until daybreak.

Despite this, Stacey remains adamant that she's not setting foot on the Eurostar service, insisting, 'I get anxious enough when it's a couple of stops on the London Underground . . . A train that goes under the ocean just isn't natural!'

Fortunately, the ferries remain operational, and a little after our intended departure time, our vessel begins cutting through the choppy waters to England.

We grab a couple of drinks in one of the ship's bars and take seats beside a window overlooking the dark water.

Stacey says, 'Do you want to talk about it?'

I filled her in on what happened with Ekaterina, but I'm not sure what she's driving at. 'Talk about what?'

'Well, you told this Russian lass that you're up for it. You'll find this David Fenton guy in return for the full SP on one of the fuckers that offed Diana.'

I'd have phrased it differently but say, 'More or less.'

'So how are we going to do it? Normally, we'd find a friend in the Intelligence Service, yeah? But that's out because his record was wiped. Ekaterina has given us nothing. He had a London accent, was roughly her age and . . . that's it. I'm guessing we could come up with a photo of him from his university days . . . but what then?'

I try some of my wine. I've been served a lukewarm Pinot Grigio, but I guess worse things happen at sea. 'You're the detective's apprentice. What would you do?'

She beams. 'Challenge accepted. Right, strikes me, like, that we know more about this Pitkin character than we do about Fenton. We know where he was killed and why. There are bound to be police reports about "his suicide".' She puts these last two words in air quotes. 'So we access those files. Get his real name. Maybe even find out where the body was transferred to after the Italian police had finished with it. That'd be a start.'

I'm impressed and tell her as much. 'The only problem is, I'm guessing the Italian police would have registered his death under the name of his legend.'

'What?'

'A fake identity set up by the Russians. So we could try to follow the body, so to speak, but after it left Italy, the Roman authorities will have taken no further interest. The Russians probably tipped him overboard and the trail goes cold at the bottom of the sea.'

Stacey gazes through the window and across the English Channel. 'Not the pleasantest of thoughts.'

'Good idea, though. Definitely outside the box.'

'So how do we trace Fenton? We don't know his real name or his assumed identity . . . We know nothing about him. And it's been donkey's years since Ekaterina saw him . . . I don't get how we're going to locate him.'

'It took me a bit of thought, to be honest. But I came up with a plan about an hour after we left Paris. Trouble is, if it's going to work, it'll be risky. Which would be fine, except I wouldn't be the one taking the risks.'

'I don't mind taking them.'

'I wouldn't let you, even if it could be you.'

'Right, I want to know what you've got in mind. But do you mind if we step outside? I'm dying for a gasper.'

'Why not?' I glance through the window and see the storm has grown even stronger. 'It's a glorious evening.'

-42-

Damian's Story (cont.)

Damian Gross watched Maggie Roberts nod to the raised container as she asked, 'What is it?'

'None of your fucking business! If you're not off these premises in sixty second, I'm pressing criminal charges.'

'Press away. We're both criminals. It might be fun. When did it start for you? School? Were you the bully or the bullied?'

'What? Who the hell are you?'

'The bully, I think. You see, I've known all manner of monsters. Psychopaths, sociopaths, MPs. But I've studied you, and you have absolutely zero empathy. It's remarkable. No soul. No kindness. No inkling of what it is to be human. Actually, aside from your biological make-up, I don't think you even qualify *as* human.'

He had been fixed on the woman's face. Appalled by her words, not due to their inherent meaning, but because they meant this individual held no fear of him. The realisation horrified Damian Gross, and as she finished dismantling his identity, he noticed she was holding a Colt Mustang XSP. The small but powerful sidearm was levelled at his chest.

'You've got me wrong. I've . . . I've faced hardships. That's what made me the way I am.' He suddenly realised why the woman might be here. 'Oh God, if I've caused you hardships in any way – I'm sorry! If you think I've wronged you in any way . . .' He spread his palms. 'I can put it right. How much do you want? I've a million in cash in the safe in my bedroom. I can get you that now. Right now. And you can walk away.' He heard himself adding, entirely out of habit, 'I won't even need a receipt.'

'You cannot get out of this with your blood money. Your sins are too great, Damian. Too heavy. They will crush you. Entomb you.'

'We can sort this out.'

'Confess your sins. It'll make you feel better.'

'My sins?' Gross's strained laughter made him sound like a terrified child. 'Look, I don't know what you mean.'

'Confession isn't for God, you know. It's for the sinner. It's an unburdening.'

'I can give you whatever you want.'

Without looking down, the woman snatched a duffel bag from the floor and tossed it across to Gross.

'Fill that with the contents of your eye-catching little container.'

'I can't do that.'

'Then you can't be saved.' She extended her right arm as if making to shoot.

'OK! I'll do it! I'll do it.'

Gross shoved the files, recordings and other paraphernalia into the bag and tugged it tightly shut.

'You've missed one.'

Gross glanced at the single file he'd left in the container. 'I can't. That one's—'

'Now, Damian. A job half-done is as good as none.'

He gripped the red file and shoved it into the duffel bag.

'Now your phone.'

He complied, whimpering.

'That's a good boy.'

'You've got what you came for!' He threw the bag onto the sofa; Now leave me alone. Please!'

'You want to be left alone?' She gave a ghost of a smile. 'Oh, Damian. I didn't come for these things.' She took a step towards him. 'I came for you.'

'I don't understand. What's in there can make you a bloody fortune!'

'I don't care.'

'That's not . . . natural.'

'Nature. Yes. Let me tell you something about nature. Nature abhors a vacuum.' She gestured to the raised container using her Colt. 'Get in.'

'No!'

'I'll give you three seconds to comply. If you fail to do so, I'll shoot you in the head. I don't want to. I *really* don't want to, largely because I know I'd enjoy it, which feels wrong.'

'We can discuss this!'

'But only a little bit wrong.' She raised her pistol.

'All right! All right!'

Gross hauled himself into the container.

'Now lie down! Just like you're going to beddy-byes. That's right, Damian . . .'

He complied, and as his body lay supine in the unit, its resemblance to a coffin became uncanny.

'When Red Fort updated your security pano last week, I had a poke around. Gave myself a few user privileges. I thought you'd approve.'

'Why?'

'Because I know you're a big fan of privilege.' She paused, then, as though addressing the room itself, added, 'User D3225. Security rights of Damian Gross are revoked. This order cannot be countermanded.'

'I am begging you . . . *Please!*'

'Retraction authorised.'

Gross screamed, 'No!'

She pointed the Colt directly at Gross's head.

He was weeping now. 'I will do anything you want. Anything! I can give you money!' The container's supporting metallic struts began to retract, lowering the unit until it rested fractionally below floor level. 'How much money do you want? Tell me and I'll make it happen! You'll be rich!'

The woman stood to one side of Damian Gross, gazing down on him. The thick Perspex slab began to slide across the container.

'I'll give it you all! Do you understand? Money! Money! Mon—'

The slab sealed shut, cutting off Gross's final word and every sound from his confinement.

The woman put away her gun and stood over Gross. He was trying to batter the Perspex beneath her shoes with his fists, but it was clear the soundproof covering was far too thick and sturdy for his blows to have any effect. As she studied him, he paused and pressed his palms together, as if literally praying for salvation. Sympathy. Anything.

'You asked me who I am.'

Gross's eyes widened. With exaggerated slowness, he desperately mouthed, 'I can't hear you!'

'Well, Damian Gross, I'll tell you.'

She took a step back. The previously displaced section of parquet floor was slowly sliding over the container. Gross, realising he was about to be trapped and completely hidden, redoubled his useless efforts, pounding on the Perspex.

'*I am Nemesis.*'

The wooden flooring completely slipped across the unit. The woman's final sight of Damian Gross was a chilling vision of his understanding.

He was trapped. And after spending so much energy and time to ensure he was entombed in his home, alone and unreachable, his aim had been achieved.

The quiet and neat electromagnetic poltergeists finished their job, sliding the sofa and chair back into their customary positions above the hidden container.

When Dugdale and his men would search for Gross and check this room, they would find nothing. And later, when the police would reluctantly be called in to investigate, they would go through the study, riffle through the bookshelves and desk and drawers but find nothing, although, in truth, their hunt for Damian Gross would not be conducted with their usual levels of care. Care was something that, even in his absence, would not be afforded to Mr Gross by anybody that knew him, no matter how slightly.

-43-

It's a big ship with only a small outside area set aside for the passengers. Even that's out of bounds because of the rough weather, but we surreptitiously dart through a couple of doors marked 'No Entry' and find ourselves on the outer port deck. Out here, the strong, biting winds are inescapable and the driving rain feels icy cold. Stacey miraculously manages to light a cigarette and I cling to the railings with one hand and find Jeremy Simmonds hip flask with the other. I'd topped it up with Glenlivet before leaving the hotel and I'm glad of it now.

Stacey joins me. 'So, go on. How do we find this ghosty?'

I take a mouthful of the whisky and relish the burn.

'We utilise the information we do have. We know Fenton "defected" and we know when. I imagine the defection boiled down to him telling Vauxhall Cross what he knew about the Russian networks he worked with. They'll have set him up with a new identity and off he goes.'

'And that helps us – how?'

'Well, there are a fair few intelligence watch lists out there. Some for criminals, drug dealers, sex offenders and the like. But there's also the protection list that Special Branch runs.'

'Never heard of it.'

'It's a list the Security Services provides them with. So, the most obvious example is, I don't know . . . Say a member of British Intelligence has their house burgled and a neighbour alerts the police. The address will trigger a notification with the coppers, who will automatically refer the incident to Special Branch, who will, in turn, alert Thames House or Vauxhall Cross to see what action they should take. There's all sorts of weird and wonderful people on the list.'

I take another measure of the whisky, simply to stave off the chill. Stacey says, 'Giz a draw.'

'A draw?'

'The hip flask!'

'Oh . . .' I hand it to her and she knocks back a mouthful of the Glenlivet.

'Nae bad stuff. You can't beat a Scottish single malt.' She takes another swig. 'So, I'm guessing one of these lists contains the names of people like Fenton?'

'Exactly! If anything happened to him, the Service would want to know about it PDQ. I also think that for the first few months after his resettlement the local bobbies would have been asked to do the occasional drive-by, just checking everything was in order and to make sure there were no cars in the area that had been reported missing, or strangers loitering that could be part of an obs team. That kind of thing.'

Stacey tries to take a drag on her cigarette, but the driving rain hasn't been kind to it. She tuts, then says, 'That kind of list must be top secret, though.'

'Not really. Don't forget the police wouldn't be informed why they're keeping tabs on certain addresses or why they've been asked to refer an individual to Special Branch. For all they know, it could be because he or she has just started work as a PA to a backbencher. Might be as innocent as that. Could be for anything.'

Stacey looks down at her beleaguered cigarette, accepts it's a lost cause and flicks it overboard. 'I meant more that the list itself would be top secret.'

'Well, that's the funny thing. You'd think so, but it would be available to anyone with access to the PNC network.'

'The Police National Computer network?'

'One and the same. And, believe me, that's abused by coppers on a daily basis, whether it's to check out potential new girlfriends or pull pranks on colleagues and register their cars as having been stolen. In other words, it's not some sacred cow that's difficult to peek into.'

'So you plan to access the list and see what new addresses or names were added to it, shortly after Fenton defected?'

'Exactly.'

'Smart.'

'Well, the idea just came to me in a flash of genius.'

She shakes her head, gives me back the hip flask and rams her hands deep into her pockets for warmth. 'One problem. I'm guessing it's a constantly expanding list, and we only have rough dates. There might be dozens and dozens of potential names.'

'We can narrow the list down, though. I mean, let's look at the area Fenton will have been relocated to. London's out of the question. Too much of a chance he'd randomly bump into someone he knows. And if I was a betting man—' I break off as the ship lurches wildly. Stacey's hands shoot from her pockets to grip the rail and I continue, '. . . I'd say it would be somewhere in England. His accent would make him stand out in Wales, Scotland or Ireland. I mean, not massively stand out, but just enough to make those places unsuitable.'

'And the house our lot gave him would be decent, but not exactly a mansion. We can use that.'

'Bravo, Miss Smith.'

'So we get a list of the addresses that fit our parameters, then go into housing records – tax records, the electoral register, and so on – and find out the names of the people at that address.'

I nod. 'Once we've got that shortlist, we discount any female names. Finally, we look at the names we're left with. Any of them with history, we can lose. I can't imagine we'll be left with many contenders.'

'That's brilliant, Novak.'

'Not really.'

I'm hoping she'll disagree with me, but instead she asks, 'So what's the risky part?'

'I've got lots of friends in the force who'd access the PNC network for me. But we'll be drilling down for this search. It's not just an in-and-out job. That makes it more serious. And the higher clearance we can get, the better. So, ideally, we'd need a Special Branch colleague. Those two issues combined make it a problem.'

'You've no contacts in Special Branch?'

I bristle slightly, but it's so cold out here that Stacey probably mistakes it for shivering. 'One or two, but they'd think twice about all the drilling down they'd have to do. What they do is monitored. If they start moonlighting, they're for the high jump.' I realise my left hand is virtually frozen to the railing and I'm pretty much soaked to the skin. 'Any chance we can go somewhere with a temperature above minus five? My whole body's turning cornflower blue and it's not a great look.'

Stacey scoffs, 'This isn't cold!'

'Oh, I'm toasty warm,' I reply, prising my fingers off the railing one by one. 'But I'm out of whisky and could do with a top-up.'

She laughs and we make our way back to the bar, where, a couple of Scotches later, I feel like I'm starting to thaw. Stacey buys a bottle of the Pinot precisely because I know it won't be chilled, and as she pours us both a large glass, she says, 'You never answered my question. What's the risky part?'

'The risky part is, I only know one person with a good enough contact within Special Branch. And my friend is not someone I want to involve in this.'

'Oh aye? Who is she?'

'How do you know it's a she?'

'Because you're always more protective of women. You're an old-fashioned sod.'

I mumble, 'It could be a bloke.'

'Is it a bloke?'

'No.'

Stacey laughs again. 'So, come on then! Who is this delicate wee lay-dee who couldn't possibly be involved in the world of Novak because she's far too fragile?'

It's time to tell Stacey about one of the most innocent, naïve and peaceful people I've ever met. 'Her name,' I begin, 'is Sophie Grace.'

-44-

I met Sophie Grace for the first time at a funeral and she seemed fascinated by my work. I guess that's because it's so utterly different to everything she's accustomed to in her own life. She's a mother to young twins and is all about local fundraisers, making jam, coffee mornings and being an invaluable member of the Crownly Ladies' Luncheon Club. She drives a classic Type 2 VW Camper ('Heavens! I'd be lost without the old girl!') and she's possibly the most good-hearted person I've ever met in my life in terms of not having an aggressive bone in her body.

Don't get me wrong about my reluctance to ask her for help. I like Sophie Grace a great deal, but she recently lost her husband, Christian, and I'll be damned if I'm going to bring any more trouble to her otherwise calm world of charity gymkhanas, church bazaars and bread baking.

'She was incredibly helpful on the Damian Gross case,' I tell Stacey. 'Although, in retrospect, maybe she was just lucky.'

'I can live with lucky, Novak. Lucky suits me right down to the ground. What was the Damian Gross case?'

I think back to the matter.

You see, Damian Gross is a gruesome Surrey businessman who's known to deal in stolen *objet d'art* and rare ephemera. He's also swindled dozens of vulnerable old people out of their life savings. Problem is, he's perceived as threatening and untouchable. Even after losing thousands to his get-poor-quick schemes, his victims remained reluctant to speak out against him. Frank had – injudiciously in my opinion – mentioned the case to Sophie whilst we'd been having brunch together at the Ivy Castle View. I'd been hired by the daughter of one of Gross's targets who wanted me to get him put away, but I'd faced problems accumulating any evidence worth a damn.

Sophie had tucked a stray strand of her long blonde hair behind her ear. 'Give me the names of a half-dozen of his victims and leave it to me,' she'd vowed over her eggs Benedict.

No, it was more than that. Looking back, I recall she actually said, '. . . and leave him to me,' before correcting herself. And I remember that for a fraction of a second, after hearing of Gross's crimes, she'd looked livid. I'd never seen her even mildly annoyed before that moment. Anyway, whilst running a bottle tombola at the village fete, she met some of the people he'd conned and before dusk had settled she'd presented me with three – three! – lots of signed statements which detailed Damian Gross's duplicity.

Armed with the evidence she'd gleaned, the CPS soon agreed to press charges. I guess there's no denying that Sophie Grace had been brilliant in getting people to talk.

I give Stacey the potted version and end on a downbeat note. 'Word on the street is that he's going to try something to wriggle out of the charges.'

'Pity,' Stacey replies. 'He should be locked away for good.'

'One can always hope.'

'Why don't you reach out to Sophie about persuading her Special Branch mate to do her a solid?'

I pull a face that suggests I'm loath to do so.

'You never know, Novak. She might be tougher than you think.'

-45-

Nemesis's Story

She dodged the patrols, climbed the perimeter wall and dropped down to the roadside. No cars. Perfect. She threw the duffel bag over her shoulder and started jogging. Less than ten minutes later, she reached her vehicle, parked off-road, a few yards into a sprawling wood.

As she neared the driver's door, her phone vibrated. She checked caller ID and pressed *reply*.

'Hello,' she said. 'Is everything all right? Are they OK?'

The man on the other end of the line replied, 'They're both fine! But they say they're missing you and can't sleep. They wanted to speak to you.'

'Did they ask politely?'

'Of course!'

'Did they say *please*?'

'Yes. Very persuasively.'

'Good. Put them on, then, please.'

A pause. 'You're on loudspeaker.'

The woman heard a two-tone cascade of, '*Mummy, Mummy, Mummy!*'

She removed her wig and slipped out of her navy blue jumpsuit to reveal Harris tweed slacks and a mint-green fluffy jumper.

'Hush now, darlings!' She ran her fingers through her blonde hair, opened the side door of her VW Camper and tossed the duffel bag, jumpsuit and wig into the back passenger well.

A young boy's voice asked, 'Have you finished work?'

She closed the side door. 'Yes. All put to bed.'

A young girl's voice: 'Will you be home soon, Mummy?'

She opened the driver's door and climbed in.

'It's awfully late!' the girl added.

'I know, darlings, and yes. I'll be home very soon. And if you're extremely good' – Sophie Grace started the engine – 'I'll read you both a bedtime story.'

-46-

'I like to think I'm good judge of character,' I reply to Stacey, 'and I reckon Sophie is a great mum and lovely person, but she's very *safe*. I don't want to make her feel awkward by asking her to do something that would take her wildly outside her comfort zone.'

'Folk like being outside their comfort zones.'

'No. They literally don't. They say they do. But they don't. It makes them uncomfortable. That's why it's called a comfort zone and not an uncomfort zone.'

'Look, let's ask her. If she's not up for it, well, so be it.'

I'm too tired to protest. 'I'll give her a shot.'

'Good man!'

'First thing in the morning.' I refill our wine glasses. 'Talking of tomorrow . . . we might have to part company.'

'Why? Not happening, by the way. But what makes you think we should?'

'Because whilst we were zigzagging across Europe, it was unlikely that any of Sandy Paige's men would come after us. Even we didn't know where we were going half the time. It feels as though I'll be easier to assess and monitor back home. Putting it bluntly, if Paige is still dead set – no pun intended – on having me killed, now is the time he'll try to do it.'

*

Despite the appalling weather, we're only running about twenty minutes late when we finally dock in Dover. Stacey persuades a van driver to drop us near the town centre, and after checking Google Maps, I begin leading us through a succession of Kentish backstreets.

Stacey realises I'm taking a specific route and asks, 'Have you got a plan?'

'I've always got a plan.'

We reach Pencester Road and an off-white, three-storey building. In large black writing, the words 'Independent Order Of Odd Fellows Club And Institute' run across its façade, just above the windows of its first floor.

Stacey quips, 'This place should suit you right down to the ground,' and I respond with a withering look. It's starting to rain again, so we huddle in the doorway. 'What are we doing here, Novak?'

'Waiting.'

'Right.' Stacey idly looks at a noticeboard beside the doorway, and reads out a message intended to summarise the Odd Fellows' raison d'être. 'This independent order holds these stated aims: to improve and elevate the character of mankind by promoting the principles of friendship, love, truth, faith, hope, charity and universal justice.' She rubs her palms together for warmth. 'Good luck with that, guys.'

I'm about to reply when a vehicle pulls up across the road from us. It's a mustard-coloured Morris Marina. One of the four-door versions, as opposed to the snazzier two-door coupés that were popular in the 1970s.

Stacey spares it a single glance of disdain and mutters to me, 'I thought my van was a piece of old shit. What the fuck is that thing?'

She chuckles, leaning into me as though I'm expected to join in with the laughter. I don't.

Stacey's eyes widen and she falls silent for a millisecond. 'It's your car. Oh my God, it's totally your car.'

I start moving towards it, calling over my shoulder, 'You're walking home!'

Frank Harvey opens the driver's door, gets out and meets me in the middle of the empty street. 'Y'all right, Novak? How are you? Are you well?'

He looks like he always looks. Short hair. Side parting. Suit and tie – Dunn & Co. Basically, he looks like he's going for a job interview in 1978.

I brush aside the hand he's offering me. 'Come here!' I hug him and he awkwardly pats my shoulder. 'Good to see you, Frank. Thanks for picking us up.'

'No problem.'

I step back. 'Stacey, I'd like you to meet Frank Harvey. Frank Harvey, this is Stacey Smith.'

They shake hands. 'Novak's told me a lot about you, Frank.'

'Yeah, well, I wouldn't believe half of what comes out of his mouth.' He winks at me and we load our suitcases into the boot. 'Do you want to drive?'

'I've been drinking.'

'All right, I'll be your chauffeur, but I'm on double time after midnight.'

I say to Stacey, 'Can't get the staff, these days . . .'

'Come on . . .' Frank sounds suddenly serious and he's glancing at his watch. 'We haven't got much time.'

*

We join the A2 and head north towards Lydden Hill. I see a petrol station and suggest to Frank that we use it.

He checks the fuel gauge. 'We should be all right. I've got us a B&B in Canterbury. Thought it was out-of-the-way but not too out-of-the-way. Landlady said she'll wait up til—'

'Let's fill her up, Frank.'

He doesn't take his eyes off the road. 'Sure.'

We pull in and I stick about thirty quids' worth of petrol in the tank. Knock on the window of the driver's door. 'Give us a hand, would you?'

We walk into the station shop together. It's late and there's only about half a dozen other people in the place. It's typical for its type, selling everything from Merlot to motor oil. The goods are overpriced and the shop floor is over-lit. It smells of steak bakes and the guy behind the counter is wearing a parka over his uniform because it's so cold. I pay for the fuel. Frank waits for me in the far corner and I tackle him by the pick 'n' mix.

'Why did you lie to me?'

He narrows his eyes. 'What are you on about?'

'Don't do this. I want to know why you lied to me. About Ekaterina. About the fingerprints. About God knows what else. Why did you lie to me, Frank?'

He considers the question for what feels like half an hour, eventually saying, 'Yeah, you're right. You deserve the truth.'

'Look, I didn't lie to you as such. Least, not how you think. I'd never heard of Ekaterina Karpin. But you ring me out of the blue, asking about the Romanov treasure. Then you ask about a woman with a Russian name. You don't have to be a long-jumper to make the leap. Ekaterina was connected with the royal loot. And if that was the case, she could be FSB. Possibly freelancing. But she was definitely connected with the Tzar's lost riches.'

'So what?'

'The Romanov treasure is bad news. Always has been. That's why I didn't want to give you anything that would send you further down that road. It's why I pretended Potter hadn't got a match for your dabs, an' all. When he came back with a Russian name, I thought, aye aye, don't want him chasing this one.' His voice becomes pleading. 'Just walk away from it. Just—'

'What's so different about this case? What's so different about going after this haul?'

I can see Frank is torn. His indecision doesn't stem from him wavering about telling me the truth. It's more nuanced than that: he doesn't want to vocalise his belief because that would somehow make it more real.

When he speaks, it's as though he's coaxing the words out of himself. 'The legend of the Romanov treasure was born in bloodshed. For over a hundred years, men have been searching for it. That's not something to be taken lightly. No one knows its secrets. Not really. Because . . . it's like the gold was forged in death and the diamonds cut from greed. I don't care whether you believe in such things, but this lost treasure . . . Marc, it's cursed. I swear to God. It's like nothing you've gone after before.'

I slap Frank's upper arm. 'It's all good.'

His uncertainty switches to anger and he shouts, 'It's not all good, lad! Were you listening to me for one second?'

Everyone in the shop has stopped to have a good gawp at us and I reply, 'Well, I think everyone in the room is listening to you now.'

'Do you think I lied for no reason? You know? For a giggle? I was worried about you! You've just made it ten times worse. Thanks for that!'

'I've got to do this, my friend. For reasons I can't tell you about yet. Part of a bigger hunt.'

'Bloody hell . . .' He rakes his fingers through his hair. 'It's Diana, isn't it?'

'I made promises.'

'Promises are like necks. Easily broken.'

I flash him a grin. 'There we go! Now, are you with me?'

He doesn't answer immediately and the other shoppers, aware that the flashpoint has flashed by, lose interest in our exchange. 'Christ . . .' Frank's tone is steady again, but remains deadly serious. 'I've seen you do amazing things, son. I've seen you defy the odds. But listen to me, you can't defy this curse.' I offer no response, but don't move. He shakes his head. 'And yes. I'm with you.'

-48-

Frederica House, the B&B Frank arranged for us, lies at the end of a cul-de-sac in the heart of Canterbury. It's homely, smells of dried flowers and, very pleasingly, the landlady looks and sounds like Mrs Wilberforce from *The Ladykillers*.

I get a reasonable night's sleep before being woken early by my phone's quiet ringing. I pick up and try not to sound too groggy.

'Hello?'

'Are you alone?'

It's Jeremy Simmonds and I reply, 'Yes, but I've got my memories to keep me warm.'

'I meant—'

'I know what you meant! I'm by myself. But I don't remember ordering a wake-up call.'

'We need to meet.'

'I'm in Canterbury.'

'So am I. Now, you're in Frederica House.'

I sit up and lean back against the headboard. 'How did you know that?'

'The landlady is one of our sleeper agents. She's actually a Bulgarian assassin who used to work in East Berlin.'

'You're joking!'

'Of course I'm joking! We just ANPR'ed your old Marina. Took about three minutes to track you down. Meet me in half an hour . . .'

I haul myself out of bed as we make arrangements for the rendezvous. Simmonds hangs up. I shower, put on a suit and tie and head over to the cathedral.

Thomas Becket was murdered here in 1170, killed in a conspiracy by assassins who were essentially working for the British authorities. The corner of the north-west transept where the priest had his skull smashed open is known as the Martyrdom, and a few paces beyond it, I find a door leading to the Great Cloisters, a tranquil courtyard that's all stone pillars and arches around an immaculately kept square of grass. I can see Jeremy Simmonds waiting on the far edge, with two women I take to be bodyguards stood a few paces behind him.

As we shake hands, I ask if he's had any luck tracking down Alexander Paige.

'We've followed up on the ideas you gave us. It's ongoing, of course, but things are progressing terribly well!' He sounds confident and breezy, so I assume he's lying.

'OK. Do you know where he is?'

'At this precise moment?'

'At any moment.'

He looks pained. 'Hate to be a mandarin about the whole thing, Novak, but the words *need-to-know basis* are sadly applicable to this sitch.'

'I think I need to know, Simmonds. You know, bearing in mind the *sitch* is he's trying to have me killed.'

'Are you looking after my hip flask?'

'Really? We're discussing my potential murder and you're switching the conversation to your hip flask?'

'Fine bit of silverware that, you know. Given to me by my grandmother. Granny Simmonds. Of the Shropshire Simmondses. For my twenty-first birthday. I was always quite upset she didn't bother to have an inscription engraved on it, but hey-ho. How did that coffee go down?'

'It went down very well, thank you.' Which is technically true. It went down the plughole *very* well. We begin to walk around the perimeter of the grass. 'Any intel on Paige's plans to have me taken care of?'

'We've a plan in place and I don't want you to worry about a thing. I'm co-ordinating the whole operation.'

Christ! Simmonds couldn't co-ordinate a shirt and tie, and I quietly groan, 'I'm dead.'

'Pardon?'

We turn a corner.

'I was about to say I'm dead pleased you're running point on this one.'

'Anything for an old friend!'

I'm about to ask who he means, when I realise he's talking about me. 'Thanks, man. And it's lovely to see you, of course, but I'm guessing something is wrong. For something to pull you all the way from London . . . it must be very wrong.' We pause and both look over at the cathedral. 'Why don't you tell me all about it?'

-49-

I arrive back at the B&B and Mrs Wilberforce greets me as though I'm her long-lost son. When she's finished with the hugs, she tugs me into the dining room, where Stacey and Frank are tucking into breakfast. They both break off to congratulate Mrs W. on the meal and she pulls out her pinafore and curtsies.

'What would you like, Mr Novak?'

'The full English is winning rave reviews, so I'd be a fool not to try it.'

'Oh, an excellent choice!'

She totters away and I take a seat with my two friends. We're alone in the room and Gilbert and Sullivan's *Pineapple Poll* is playing quietly from some decrepit speakers in the bay window. Reassuringly, the sound system, perched on a sideboard, is a low, squat record player that looks older than me.

I pour myself a grapefruit juice and we go through the usual tedium of 'How did you sleep?' etc.

With that out of the way, we establish plans for the day. Stacey reveals she'll be staying with an old friend in London and Frank needs to return to his place in the Smoke, so they'll be catching the train to St Pancras together. I say I'll give them a lift to the station and they both put down their knives and forks to applaud sarcastically.

Stacey says, 'What a ledge!'

As Frank pretends to wipe tears from his eyes, he asks, 'Would you really do that for us, sir?'

'You're both utterly hilarious,' I say, whilst I reach across the table and whip a sausage from Frank's plate. He tries to protest, but I shut him down with, 'That's for being an idiot.'

'Did you get in touch with Sophie?'

I can tell by Stacey's tone of voice that she doesn't think I have.

'Yes! We spoke as I was walking back from the cathedral. She's up for it. Actually, she suggested we all meet later today to form an overall plan of attack. I told her it wasn't necessary.'

'What d'you do that for, you bampot?' Stacey looks up from buttering a slice of toast. 'Get back on the phone. Tell her it's a cracking idea.'

Frank is polishing off his last piece of bacon. 'Yeah, sounds helpful. Let's meet in Guildford. Nearer for Sophie. I'll text her. Oh, and I'll ask her to do a bit of history revision.' He takes out his phone, adding, 'About the Romanovs and all that malarkey.'

'All that malarkey?' I don't bother to conceal my disbelief at his choice of words. 'The brutal assassination of an entire family, the end of a long and bloody civil war and the birth of modern Russia.'

'Aye.' Frank pushes his empty plate away. 'All that malarkey. I don't have a clue about any of it. There was one story I did donkey's years ago, but honestly, it's not my wheelhouse, as you youngsters would say.'

'Same here.' Stacey picks up her piece of toast. 'I wouldn't know Lenin and Stalin from Lennon and McCartney.'

'Oh very pithy, Miss Smith. I see what you did there. Top work.'

She plucks Frank's sausage from my hand, places it on her toast and folds the bread around it to make a sarnie. 'That's for being an idiot,' she informs me.

I shake my head but smile, then look at Frank. 'You definitely think we're right to bring Sophie in?'

'These are two big jobs you've got on your hands. You're trying to find some guy that defected and disappeared years ago, and we all know you're going to go after the Romanov treasure.'

'On top of that,' Stacey chips in, 'you've got Sandy Paige trying to put you six feet under.'

'Yeah . . .' I try to sound casual. 'That's what Simmonds wanted to see me about. I met him this morning.'

Frank puts his phone on the table. 'You spoke to him here in Canterbury? What the hell brought him out all this way?'

'He wanted to take me into safekeeping. I said no. I had too much to do.'

Stacey says, 'Aye, well, their idea of safekeeping isn't all that safe if Julia's anything to go by.'

Frank and I exchange looks and he asks, 'So, why the sudden interest in your well-being?'

Before I can reply, Mrs Wilberforce appears in the doorway carrying my breakfast. She lurches over and places it in front of me. She proceeds to go through the contents of the plate, pointing at individual items and naming them, as if I might otherwise have been baffled by the sight of two fried eggs. At the end of the roll call, I thank her and she retreats to the kitchen.

Frank urges, 'Well?'

'Full English – just what the doctor ordered!' I pick up my cutlery. 'Jeremy Simmonds has received intel on the ground that suggests Paige has more men who'll make another attempt on my life in the next twenty-four hours. Last time, he sent two killers to polish me off. This time, he's hired a small army of assassins. Pass the butter, would you, Miss Smith?'

'Don't be so cavalier about your own death,' she snaps.

'Why shouldn't I be?'

Stacey sounds furious as she replies, 'Don't forget you have people who rely on you!'

And it occurs to me that maybe I was wrong when I told Simmonds I was alone.

Frank repeats the words, 'A small army of assassins.' He looks ashen and doesn't need to say any more because I know exactly what he's thinking. He believes the odds I'm facing are too great and that this time, well, even I can't get out of this one.

-50-

Leonid's Story (cont.)
Arley, North Warwickshire. November, 1923

They never verbally agreed to keep the Red Diamond a secret, but something about the manner in which Leonid had acquired the gem, and the way they felt distrustful of almost everyone around them, meant it seemed natural to keep it hidden. Unused.

The closest they'd come to discussing it was weeks after they'd arrived in England. 'When the time is right . . .' Leonid had said, 'then we can trade it, or display it, or have it cut to be the centrepiece of a fine tiara for you!'

'Don't be so cavalier about it,' Maria had snapped. 'Don't forget you have people who rely on you! And using the diamond at this moment . . . letting the world know we have it. It could be the death of us!'

In the intervening years, he had become Leonard, Maria went by Mary and Georgy was known as George. The family's surname was legally changed to Alexander. They wanted to fit in. Live normal lives. Which, in England, they soon found meant earning very little money and existing in a near perpetual state of misery.

*

Leonard arrived home late. The coal dust from the pits was still lined in the creases around his eyes and across the back of his hands, but he was smiling. Laughing.

Mary, who had fallen asleep in an armchair by the hearth, stood up and said, 'Where have you been?'

As he approached her, she smelt booze on his breath.

'Have you been drinking? We can't afford it! You know we can't—'

He placed his palms on her waist and lifted her two feet into the air. Whirled her around. 'We can afford anything, my *krasivyy*!'

'You're drunk!' He lowered her to the ground and she struck his shoulder. '*Dzhoker*!'

'Yes, yes, I am drunk,' he merrily confessed, burying his hands deep in his pockets. 'I am also' – he threw two bundles of banknotes into the air – 'rich!'

Mary grabbed one of the pieces of paper as it wafted downwards. Examined the back of it – a detailed sketch of the Palace of Westminster. She turned it over and read, 'United Kingdom of Great Britain and Ireland . . . One pound.' She looked at her husband. 'They're not real!'

'They are as real as you and I!'

'How?'

'I was playing *durak* with the Vologda boys.'

Despite herself, Mary tutted, 'The Vologda boys! Layabouts!'

'Yuri has been a good friend to us. My only true friend in this country. I love that man like a brother.'

'Go on with your story!'

'I won a shilling or two.' Leonard shrugged. 'Then the *officers* came over. Sneering at the coins on our table. How would we like to gamble for real money? But no, you can't, they said. You have no stakes.'

Mary sounded appalled. 'You risked the diamond? Leonard, you promised we would—'

'What good is it to us if we simply keep it locked away? Yes! Yes, I was tired of living in another man's house! Tired of charity!'

'They've been good to us!'

'And now we can be good to them because . . . we . . . are . . . rich!'

Mary looked from her husband's face to the confetti-spread of cash on the floor. She started to laugh and weep at the same time.

George appeared in the doorway. Bleary-eyed and confused, he asked, 'Mama! Papa! What's happening?'

Leonard knelt beside his son's side. Took the Red Diamond from his pocket and held it before George's eyes. 'Did I not tell you it would bring us luck? And so it has proven to—'

His words were interrupted by a loud, rapid hammering on the door.

'Mary, take George to his room.' Leonard pressed the gem into the boy's hand, swept up the banknotes and stuffed them into his leather satchel. 'Who is it?'

Mary took George into the next room and hastily closed the door.

'Lenny, it's me! Andrei!'

Recognising the voice of one of his acquaintances from Vologda, he opened the door. 'My God!'

Andrei's face was torn and bleeding.

'What happened?'

'The officers . . . After you left, they became drunk! Angry drunk! They said you were a cheat! That your diamond was mere glass!'

Leonard grasped Andrei's shoulders. 'Well, so what? Let them moan like old women!'

'Yuri defended you. There was a fight . . .'

*

189

George strained to catch the conversation from behind the door, his mother hovering over him, also intent on not missing a single word. He listened as the wild man told his father, 'They killed him! They killed Yuri!'

The young boy looked down at the diamond in his palm as he heard his father begin to weep.

-51-

I arrive home at noon and find a tall, thin, mournful-looking woman at my front door. She's dressed like an undertaker and carries a battered, brown ox-leather Gladstone bag with the initials T. T. M. in gold letters about three inches below the lock fastening. Simmonds told me he was sending a professional over, and as I near my house, I say, 'Doctor Maldis?'

She nods, but does it sadly, as if acknowledging the fact is mildly traumatic. 'You must be Mr Novak? Best get on with it, I suppose.'

Once inside, Doctor Maldis refuses coffee, pulls a small medical kit from her coat pocket and says, 'Let's see if you'll live.' I lie on my couch and she inspects my abdominal injury. 'Astonishing.' She straightens her back and declares, 'You have remarkable powers of healing, Mr Novak.'

'Not really. The bullet wound is on my left-hand side. You've been examining my belly button.'

Silence.

I smile to show I'm trying to be light-hearted, but she seems thrown and annoyed. 'I know the difference between an umbilicus and a GSW.'

'I know. I was joking.'

'I spent five years at medical college.'

'I know. I was joking.'

'I also had an intercalated year.'

191

'That must have been very painful. Anyway! My stomach wound! You're giving me the all-clear?'

'There's nothing wrong with you.' She stands and repockets her slender medical kit. 'Physically, at least.' The doctor moves towards the door, empty-handed.

'Excuse me! You've forgot your Gladstone bag.'

'Oh no, that's for you. Mr Simmonds ordered the Toymaker to supply you with some of his . . .' She trails off, gesturing vaguely to the bag. 'Apparently you once chose to use an old gambler's gun, for some curious reason.'

'Someone was trying to kill me.'

'One sympathises.'

I'm interested to know if she means with me or my would-be murderer, but I let it slide.

She continues, 'I think Mr Simmonds quite enjoyed the fact you're as ludicrously old-school as he is, so he thought you might like . . .' Once again, she airily points to the bag. 'And if there's nothing else? I do have other calls to make, you know. Good day, Mr Novak.'

'Drop by any time. It's been fun!'

After Doctor Maldis closes the front door behind her, I take a seat, open the bag and begin examining its contents. There's an innocuous mobile phone, which, on closer inspection, it turns out isn't a mobile phone and certainly isn't innocuous. The handset unfolds into a two-shot, .380 calibre derringer-style pistol with a polymer case and metal workings.

I put it to one side and pick out what appears to be a tube of lip balm. I open its lid and the deception's maintained, but when I slide back the tip off the balm itself, I find the tube has been hollowed out and contains a tension wrench, three lock picks, a miniature blade for cutting through zip ties and a five-foot long Kevlar survival cord. I replace the items and slip it into my pocket.

Finally, I pull out what looks to be a tiepin. It's plain and unobtrusive and I know precisely what it is because I used a much more basic version when I dealt with kidnappers who were holding the wife of a very secretive millionaire. I hold it to the light and smile.

-52-

Over an early-afternoon conference call, Frank and I suggest meeting in the Three Pigeons, a snug little boozer at the top of Guildford's cobbled high street.

Stacey is having none of it. 'Not professional enough. Can't we book meeting rooms? Or, at a pinch, we could convene at your place, Novak.'

You see? This is why I choose to work alone.

'Stacey, I'm not sure you've grasped the company ethos of Novak & Stewart.'

We settle on the cafe bar of the Yvonne Arnaud Theatre.

'All right,' Stacey concedes. 'See you both there at five.'

*

Frank and I arrive a few minutes after four. We head upstairs and grab a table in the corner, overlooking the ribbon of garden that clings to the theatre and, a few metres beyond it, the River Wey. I get the drinks in whilst Frank takes the seat with its back to the wall and broad windows to his right, affording him the best view of the room itself.

We discuss the case over a couple of pints and Sophie Grace arrives dead on five. She's wearing a simple black dress and a fifties-style, mint-green cropped jacket. Big buttons and a collar so broad you could eat your dinner off it. She also manages to carry off a matching knitted hat that looks like a cross between a beret and beanie.

'Marc! You look absolutely divine!' I get my second enthusiastic hug of the day as she greets me like I've been released from prison after some long-standing miscarriage of justice has been uncovered. 'It's wonderful to set eyes on you again! And Frank! Come here, you incorrigible man!'

He makes a token effort to evade her open arms but ends up locked in a lengthier embrace than she gave me.

She eventually steps back and straightens his tie. 'This darling man is a mystery, Marc! Every time I see him, he looks younger!' She gives him, a dazzling smile. 'It's quite unchivalrous of you, Frank!'

He tries to say, 'Don't talk daft, woman!' but stumbles over his words and I end up grinning at my friend's face, suddenly the hue of a Crimson King beetroot.

'For God's sake, get the lady a drink and stop blushing like a schoolboy caught scrumping!' I tell him.

'I'm not blushing! It's warm in here. That's all.'

Frank heads to the downstairs bar and Sophie sits opposite me.

'How are the twins, Ms Grace?'

'Will you never call me Sophie? Wretch! And . . . oh, they're monsters. But they're *my* monsters.'

'And how are you? You must still be reeling after Christian's death . . . How are you coping – if you don't mind me asking?'

'I don't mind you asking. It's good manners, which I always approve of. But do *you* mind if I'm forthright with you?'

'Of course.'

'I've never understood . . .'

I wait, expecting her to finish the sentence. But she leans back, indicating that signalled the end of her thought process.

'Me neither,' I admit, although I'm not entirely certain what I'm admitting to.

We chat for a couple of minutes and she's full of news about the Crownly Ladies' Luncheon Club ('Daphne's plum jam is causing us no end of headaches! But she's such a dear, none of us wants to broach the matter with her . . .') and the feckless vicar's new fiancée ('Lovely woman! Well, girl. Well, zygote. Honestly. So young, none of us knew where to look! The whole thing is a powder keg waiting to go off, but none of it's her fault. Probably. He uses the pulpit like it's a crow's nest, of course, if you get my drift, Marc. Such a shame for her, though! She's simply adorable. She wears foundation like it's going out of fashion, true, but I say that's terribly *brave* of her . . .').

When Frank re-joins us, he's carrying a tray that holds what looks tantalisingly like four large Bloody Marys. Stacey – just a couple of steps behind him – is wearing ice-white trainers, three-stripe Adidas tracky bs and a black, round-neck bishop-sleeve top. I'm no Edith Head, but I do silently marvel at her ability to look so effortlessly cool.

Frank places the tray on the table. Stacey reaches his side and glances down at the drinks. 'Four Bloody Marys. Grand. What are you lot having?' She breaks her deadpan delivery with a smile. 'Hi! I'm Stacey! I'm guessing you're the amazing Sophie! This one' – she nods in my direction – 'is always banging on about you. Fuck! I bloody love your hat!' She takes the last seat at the table.

Sophie Grace beams. 'Stacey! Darling girl! We'll be great friends – I can feel it in my creaking bones! And this old thing?' She gestures to her headwear. 'My Auntie Violet knitted it for me! Blind as a bat, but an absolute mad thing with knitting needles and a yarn!'

Frank laughs.

'Right . . .' I look across the drinks at my three friends. Individuals, but hopefully not for long. 'Let's get started, shall we?'

-53-

I begin by recounting everything I know about Ekaterina Romanova. Sophie asks, 'Is she really one of the Romanovs?'

'She's distantly related to the Tzar and Tzarina, which sounds impressive, but if you extend the family tree wide enough, so are literally hundreds, maybe thousands, of other people. She seems to think it confers some kind of honour on her. And also some kind of obligation. Hence her involvement in the Romanov Foundation.'

Stacey gets straight to the point. 'Do you trust her? I mean, do you believe everything she's told you about Mr Pitkin, Fenton and the rest?'

'Do I trust her? That's easy. No. Do I think she's told me the truth? Substantially, yes.'

Frank adds, 'But the best lies are always heavily couched in truth.'

I nod. 'Exactly. I think the vast majority of what she's said is accurate. But I also sense there's stuff she's not telling me. And that her narrative has been . . . *edited*, shall we say.'

Sophie says, 'But we're going after Fenton?'

'Oh, yes.'

'Fabulous!' she continues. 'That's where I come in. I'll have my friend in Special Branch run the checks you spoke about. Should be a doddle.'

197

'It won't be a doddle!' I tell her, trying not to bite her head off. 'It'll take time and a lot of cross-checking.' Her casualness worries me, but I add gently, 'Thanks for doing this.'

'My absolute pleasure.'

Franks asks, 'Could Tania not give us a hand?'

Tania Wilde was a useful contact within Special Branch who's assisted me in the past. 'She's moved on, I'm afraid. Promoted to Thames House.'

'That's bloody inconvenient.'

'Selfish, I'd call it.'

We organise for Sophie to pass on her findings to Stacey, who'll investigate and confirm the identity of the individual she targets. When we've found out what Fenton is calling himself these days, and where he is, I'll take over.

Frank finishes his Bloody Mary. 'What do you want me to do, lad?'

I bring Sophie up to date on the situation regarding Alexander Paige, but before she can express her horror at my predicament, I say to Frank, 'If you wouldn't mind, I'd like you to ask a few questions. See if you can find out who Paige has hired to do the job on me. What's being planned. There's a pub in Custom House that might be a good place to start.'

'Aye. I know the one. I'll get on it as soon as we're done here.'

'Thanks. And, Sophie, I know it looked a bit like Frank was setting you homework, but he asked you to look into the Romanovs. You once mentioned something about research being vital for a lot of the work you do, so we thought—'

She interrupts me with a bright, 'It was fun to do! I've studied Russian history, so it wasn't terribly onerous.'

'Thank you.'

'I'll begin at the beginning,' she tells us.

She's clearly knowledgeable about the subject and gives us a potted summary of the events that culminated in the revolutions of 1917.

'To be honest, the names are different, but the events triggering any revolution are invariably similar. You've got a weak leader at the top. Disgruntled workers at the bottom. A power-mad, charismatic killer somewhere between the two.'

Frank interjects, '*Plus ça* bloody *change*.'

Sophie continues, 'In this case, our ineffective leader was the Tzar. Nikolai Alexandrovich Romanov. His family had been ruling Imperial Russia for over three centuries by the early 1900s. The workers weren't happy with the pay and conditions they were being forced to endure. Russia gets a drubbing in the Crimean War and loses another 25,000 soldiers in the Russo-Japanese conflict, then along comes the Great War. Russia's casualties were the highest ever sustained by any country in any war. All those failures could be laid at the Romanovs' door. Oh, and there'd been problems with food shortages for a generation. In the famine of 1891/92, as many as half a million Russian men, women and children starved to death. Things had got better on that score, but not much. No surprise that people wanted change.'

That change, she explains, came in the form of Bolshevik Party leader Vladimir Lenin. He demanded a Soviet government comprising councils of soldiers, normal citizens and workers. 'In other words,' Sophie points out, 'he offered change. But after the revolution, he established a rule of law that was even more autocratic than the Romanovs' imperialism. And although life got harder for the average Russian, he ensured obedience through massacres, gulags and the assassination of political foes.'

I ask, 'So where do the Romanov jewels come into this?'

'Their crown jewels were essentially a collection of riches that had been expanding for over three hundred years. Its value is beyond reckoning, and we'll never have a complete inventory of every item it included. In the years leading up to the revolution, we know that a lot of gems and precious metals were smuggled out of Russia for safekeeping. But Nicholas and his immediate family hung on to a lot of it.'

Frank says, 'What exactly did happen to the Tzar and his wife and kids?'

'Well, after the February Revolution of 1917, Nicholas II abdicated and power passed to the Provisional Government. Lenin was not yet in charge. The former emperor and empress and their son and daughters were placed under house arrest in the Alexander Palace, about thirty miles south of Saint Petersburg. The property had been commissioned by another Romanova. Catherine the Great. It must have reminded Nicholas of better days. They were moved after the October Revolution, allegedly for their own safety, to a still pretty grand house in Siberia. Which sounds lovely, but, at that stage, the citizens of Siberia were vehemently anti-royal and simply being in that region would have made the Romanovs feel even more vulnerable.'

Stacey says, 'I'm guessing their stay there didn't last long?'

'I'll get to that in a sec, but it's worth pointing out that while that was going on, some members of the imperial family managed to stay on amicable terms with the first new government and were actually allowed to leave Russia. That could indicate how some of the Romanov treasure was kept out of Bolshevik hands.'

'It's entirely possible,' I agree.

'And don't forget other Romanovs were abroad at the time of the revolution. They swiftly decided it was wiser not to return. Grand Duchess Maria Georgievna is probably the best known example. She was in England when the revolution began. Her husband wasn't so lucky and was shot by a firing squad alongside his brother and two cousins. You'll be amazed to learn Maria never set foot in Russia again.'

She pauses to take a sip of her Bloody Mary. 'Anyway, in April 1918, Nicholas and his family were shifted to the Russian town of Yekaterinburg, in the Urals. Their new home – Ipatiev House – was more or less a normal residence. It was a prison for them, of course, and they were treated badly. Regular searches, having to ring a bell when they wanted to use the toilet, windows in their rooms painted over, a ban on visitors and strict rationing. Having said that, the family was initially watched over by Russian soldiers. Problem was, these men began to quite like the bunch of fallen aristos they were holding captive. They thought the former Tzarina was aloof, but aside from her, their jailers became quite fond of Nicholas and his children.'

Frank pipes up, 'I can't imagine Lenin and his cronies were crazy about that.'

'True. And because of it, the security detail was changed so the guards were overwhelmingly men that spoke no Russian. I think we all know how the story ends. In the early hours of 17 July, 1918 . . .'

Sophie solemnly describes the facts of the Romanovs' slaughter. The abuse of their corpses. The chaos and brutality that engulfed Russia as Lenin's grip on power tightened. At length, she circles back to the treasure. 'The riches that were collected from the dead bodies, along with other pieces from the collection, taken from the Winter Palace for example, were sent to Moscow. There was an inventory and the majority was sold off in the 1920s, although between the inventory being made and the auction, certain significant items disappeared. But perhaps more interesting is what happened to all the items that never even made it to the inventory.'

Stacey asks, 'What sort of stuff are we talking about there?'

'Fabergé eggs, crowns, tiaras, gold, diamonds . . . Extraordinary artefacts. I mean, this is a collection that began to be made and assembled during the days and nights of the Byzantine Empire. So opulent, so magnificent and so vast, that it's impossible to say how much it would fetch if sold today. Hundreds of millions. Maybe billions.' Sophie leans back in her chair. 'Disappearing masterpieces are nothing new, of course. I still don't believe the real Mona Lisa was returned to the Louvre after it was stolen in 1911. How could Vincenzo Peruggia have wrapped it around his body, as he claimed. It's not on canvas. It's on wood! But the point with the Romanov treasure is there are literally tonnes of it missing . . . But no one knows what happened to it.'

'Somebody must,' I correct her. All eyes turn to me. I put my elbows on the table. Intertwine my fingers and rest my chin on my knuckles. 'And that lost treasure, ladies and gentleman, is the prize we're going to find.'

Sophie takes another well-deserved mouthful of Bloody Mary. 'Was that helpful?'

'It was horrific,' Stacey murmurs.

'Don't be blinded by the brutality,' Frank advises her. 'We're here to look at the evidence as investigators, not historians.'

'Historians are investigators!' Sophie counters.

Frank raises his palms. 'No disrespect. I just meant a detective would look at the narrative very differently. Or at least have different questions.'

Stacey asks, 'Such as?'

I reply, 'Like why does so much about that story not make sense?'

Sophie bristles. 'It's accepted historical fact!'

'Yeah, well, it's not accepted by me.'

'What doesn't make sense?'

'The diamonds and other gems!' I exclaim. 'The enormous amount of crown jewels the Romanovs are in possession of whilst they're at Ipatiev House. First of all, how did they get there? The Romanovs won't have been given the jewels whilst they were being held captive there. That makes no sense. So they must have brought them from their residence in Siberia. And they'll only have been there because they brought them from the Alexander Palace. Does that really make sense? That under armed guard and whilst they're under constant

GAVIN COLLINSON

supervision, they manage to smuggle so many crown jewels across Russia?'

Frank adds, 'And when they get to Ipatiev House they're subject to spot checks. Their personal effects would be examined at random. We know that from the journals of people who were there. They had no freedom at all within the house. OK, they may have been able to stash one or two diamonds. Could have swallowed them or crotched them. But a bloody big hoard like they had? Really? No one noticed them? I don't buy it.'

Sophie asks, 'So what do you think the truth is? How were they able to keep such a large amount of bulky valuables?'

Frank looks at me and I say, 'Well, one obvious explanation presents itself.'

Sophie admits, 'It's not obvious to me.'

Stacey says, 'Me neither, to be honest.'

'Well, wouldn't it be reasonable to assume . . .' I break off as my phone rings. 'Would you mind if I take this? It's Ekaterina.' I pick up. 'Hello?'

'Mr Novak! It's your favourite client! How is the case going?'

'So far we've eliminated Lenin and Trotsky, but Joe Stalin still can't account for his whereabouts.'

'I think we got off on the wrong foot.' Whenever she uses an English idiom, she puts on a version of my accent. It was cute at first.

I reply, 'I think we got off on the right foot. It was only after a few paces that we stepped into a bear trap.'

'*Da!* Well put! Mr Novak, I would like to extricate us from it.'

'Oh, right. What do you suggest? Couples' therapy or reinstating date night?'

I'm being sarcastic, but she says, 'More along the lines of the latter.'

I laugh. 'Single Russian. GSOH and KGB would like to meet English detective for fun times and possibly more. Must have moral fibre, open mind and a Glock 19.' I shake my head. 'I can't see it flying.'

'I understand that's what they said to the Wright Brothers, but the rest is history.'

'Touché.'

'A party! I am inviting you, and whoever else is working on this case with you, to a party. Thrown by the Romanov Foundation. It will allow us all to recalibrate. We can all get to know each other a little better and move forward in harmony.'

'Is that an invitation or a party political broadcast?'

She laughs. 'A little of both! But what do you say?'

'Where and when?'

I listen to her reply and let her know I'll RSVP ASAP.

As I repocket my phone, Frank asks, 'Who were that?'

'Ekaterina. We've all been invited to a party. Dress code – glad rags and concealed automatics. No jeans.'

Stacey is the first to respond. 'I'm in.'

Sophie adds, 'Same. When?'

'Tomorrow night.'

Frank isn't quite so enthused. 'Where's it being held?'

'That's the bit you won't believe.'

'Try me.' Frank gives a wry smile. 'Where's the party, Novak?'

I pause, anticipating their responses. 'Ipatiev House.'

-55-

My phone rings at 3.30 a.m. and I awake, bleary but immediately filled with dread. I pick up. 'Sophie! Are you all right?'

'I'm peachy! I just wanted you to know, we've found David Fenton.'

'You've been working on it through the night?'

'With my contact – yes.'

I'd never doubted Sophie's willingness to help, but I had underestimated her eagerness to get the job done so swiftly. She explains that a dozen people had been added to the relevant watch list during the date range I'd specified. There'd been an even male/female split, leaving us with six possibilities. Two had been in Central London and one in a small village in North Wales. Those were discarded. Sophie had investigated the remaining three. One, it turned out, was far too old to be Fenton and another didn't match the physical description given to us by Ekaterina.

'So who are we left with?' I ask.

'His name is now Thomas Maughan.'

'How certain are you?'

'I found recent photos of Maughan. They match with the ones we have of Fenton in his relative youth. He's our man. No doubt.'

'And where is he now? What's he doing?'

I hear Sophie laugh. 'You're going to love this . . .'

*

I manage to get some more sleep, but my alarm goes off in the early hours and I groggily rise from my bed like Frankenstein's monster stumbling from the slab in his creator's laboratory. Thirty minutes later, I'm showered, shaved and changed into a suit and tie. And within the hour, I've downed two cups of rather good Jamaica Blue Mountain and ordered a taxi.

My phone rings. I pick up and hear Frank's voice. 'Something very strange is going on. No one wants to kill you.'

'Yeah,' I reply. 'Trying hard not to take offence at that. What's so strange about no one wanting me dead?'

'I've just spent a lot of money for intel from the kind of men whose pints you really don't want to spill. They confirmed that Sandy Paige hired someone to do you in.'

'We already knew that!'

'But here's the thing. The contract was cancelled.'

'Maybe it used the wrong pronoun on Twitter.'

'What?'

'It was my hilarious cancel-culture joke. Sorry. OK, why was the contract revoked?'

'Nobody knows. But word is, the rescindment came from Paige himself.'

I should be delighted by this turn of events, but it simply strikes me as odd. 'Thanks for letting me know, Frank. By the way, Sophie came up with the goods. David Fenton is now Thomas Maughan.'

'Have you told Ekaterina?'

'I left her a message explaining I wanted to meet Fenton before I give her any information about his new life.'

Frank pauses. 'Why's that?'

'Because there's something not quite right about all of this, and for once I want to be one step ahead.'

'You be careful.'

'Hey, what could possibly go wrong?'

'I get stomach cramps every time you say that.'

My taxi arrives and I tell Frank I have to dash.

I'm en route to Guildford train station when the cabbie says, 'You're up early for a Sunday. You off anywhere special?'

'Yes . . .' I tell him the truth. 'I'm going to church.'

-56-

Jeremy Simmonds' Story

Sunday morning. Jeremy Simmonds sat at his desk in his office and re-read an unsigned letter. He finished it. Sighed. Looked up. It was his letter of resignation from his role within British Intelligence, but he felt far from resigned to signing it. He had his own office that overlooked the Thames, an assistant who was over thirty who didn't take it as a personal slight when he requested her assistance. His job title was long and vague, which always, in his mind, conferred a degree of status.

But, in truth, Jeremy Simmonds felt that life was passing him by. When his previous manager's position had come up for grabs, he'd assumed it would be handed to him without fuss.

All, 'There was really no other chap for the role . . .' and 'It'll mean a considerable boost to your salary, Simmonds, yet, after all your years of service, we feel it's richly deserved . . .'

But no.

The woman they had ushered in was new to the department and carried, in Simmonds' admittedly jaundiced eyes, all the poise and professionalism of a drunken go-go dancer.

His pen hovered over the bottom of the letter.

He heard a light tap on his door.

'Yes?' He paused. 'Come in!'

'Sorry to bother you, sir . . .' His assistant, Beryl, bobbed her head around his door. 'You've got a call coming through on the old Apex line.'

'Apex line? Who is it?'

'He won't give his name. But he says it's urgent.'

'Tell him I'm busy. Take a message.'

'Yes, sir.' Beryl went on her way but reappeared in the doorway a few seconds later. 'He asked me to stress it's very urgent. And pressing.'

'But he still won't give his name?'

'No, sir.'

'Dammit! Tell him I've asked you to find out what's so urgent and pressing.'

'Yes, sir.'

Beryl returned to her phone. Simmonds returned to his letter. He laid it on his desk, picked up his pen and—

'He's told me what it's about, sir.' Beryl was back in his doorway.

'And?'

'He says he's just murdered a priest.'

'Just murdered . . .'

'A priest.'

'Did he sound serious?'

'Deadly serious. Oh!' Her hand shot to her mouth. 'I wasn't meaning to make a joke.'

'That's all right, Beryl. Better put him through.'

'Yes, sir. Shall I ask him for his name, again?'

'Don't bother!' Simmonds gave the kind of sigh usually reserved for reacting to a bill that's unexpectedly hefty. 'I know exactly who it'll be . . . Will no one rid me of this turbulent detective?' He gave his assistant a half-smile. 'Thank you, Beryl.'

'Very good, sir.'

She retreated and, a moment later, Simmonds' phone rang. He put down his pen and lifted the receiver. 'My God, Novak! What the hell have you done this time?'

-57-

Twenty-eight minutes earlier

The priest appears to be winding up his sermon and I silently congratulate myself for not heckling at any point during his performance. He spoke about the pain, loss and hardships we must all face, but in a bad-news-good-news kind of twist, he assured the congregation that God is actually doing a great job and He's got the whole thing under control. So, really, don't worry about it.

He's frustratingly light on detail, however. There's no mention of how God will help a single mother pay her heating bills, feed her family and keep them clothed, or how a parent is supposed to remain equanimous when told that their child has developed cancer of the spine. Instead, he talks about God's love and chooses to dodge the nitty-gritty of real-world examples. I find this lazy and infuriating and guess it's why sermons never end with a follow-up Q&A session.

But, hey, at least we're into the home stretch and he's urging us all to be as Samson in the Temple of Dagon. That strikes me as a bit of a mixed message, but it's just one more generality that doesn't add anything to the sum of my knowledge.

Don't get me wrong. I enjoy the architecture and serenity of churches, but I'm left cold when they swing into action and start staging ceremonies and the like. It's as baffling as it is boring. But I'm told it brings comfort to many people and

I genuinely envy their faith. Their belief that there's a benign and all-powerful force looking down on us must be reassuring. More than this, I suppose, the notion that our existences are infinite and that every tatty little life is simply a preliminary to the good bit must be heartening.

Having said that, as I look about me, I notice very few happy faces. It's a well-to-do parish. Business leaders pack the pews. Rich as Croesus but as miserable as sin. If these people believe all the stuff pouring from the pulpit, they should be grinning from ear to ear, but instead they sit with expressions locked in Old Testament solemnity.

And yet . . . The priest *must* be right to a certain extent, surely? There must be more to life than is obvious and transparent. There has to be a meaning – no matter how vague – to it all. An intention for everything. So, inevitably, I wonder what mine might be, and whether I'm fulfilling that purpose.

'Think on *why* we were placed on God's good Earth . . . There will be times when the devil has you by the throat!' the priest informs his audience. 'But we must remain strong in our resolve! We must reach out to our Lord . . .'

I'm in a charming little church at the heart of a village just south of the Clandon Downs in Surrey. After the service concludes, we all file from the nave and the priest hovers outside the main entrance, like an actor meeting fans by the stage door.

'Welcome, welcome!' We shake hands and he continues, 'A new face in the flock, I see!'

He's about my age, that's to say late thirties, so I'm not sure why he's speaking like the vicar off *Dad's Army*.

'Are you passing through, or are you a new parishioner?'

'I'm here to see you, actually, reverend. Is there somewhere we can talk?'

His eyes dart to his right and the line of ladies queuing up to congratulate him on his turn at the lectern. 'I'm a little busy at the moment and I am rather bound to presently mix and mingle with these good people in the church hall. There's coffee and cake. You're welcome to join us, Mr . . . ?'

'We have a mutual acquaintance.'

The woman behind me clears her throat, an indication that I'm hogging the priest and should move along.

'And who might that me?' he asks.

'Ekaterina.'

It's doubtful he'd have looked as uncomfortable if I'd loudly announced I'd received his results from the STD clinic and it wasn't good news. 'Ekaterina? Goodness . . .' He pulls his shoulders back. 'Now there's a name I haven't heard in many years.'

'If you could spare me ten minutes before your coffee morning?'

'Of course!' He smiles as if his change of heart is something to do with Christian largesse. 'Let me see . . .' He calls to the curate who's waiting a pace or two inside the vestibule. 'Martin!' He's a much younger man wearing a navy blue duffel coat. 'Have you got a moment?'

Martin nods enthusiastically. Joins us.

'Could you possibly greet the remaining ladies and gentlemen? I need to speak to the new member of our congregation.'

The curate eagerly agrees and the woman behind me tuts, aggrieved at being palmed off with the leading man's understudy.

The priest puts his hand on my shoulder, gently guiding me away from the queue. 'We can talk in the vicarage.'

'If you're sure you can spare me the time.'

A spark of irritation flashes across his face, then he's all smiles again. 'Of course, of course!'

I wonder if Ekaterina has some kind of hold over this man of God, or whether they're linked by something more intricate.

We walk across the churchyard, passing two men digging a fresh grave. As we pass the gaping hole, the priest crosses himself. 'In the midst of life . . .' he murmurs.

-58-

Reverend Thomas Maughan stands a touch under six feet. He's fair-haired, trim and muscular and blessed with a youthful, unlined face that I imagine makes him good-looking to many members of his congregation. He wears circular tortoiseshell glasses that he nudges up his nose when he wants to buy himself time.

'This way, Mr . . . ?'

'Is this the vicarage?'

'Yes.'

'Impressive.' I mean it. The property lies about fifty yards from the church. A large Victorian house with broad sash windows and English ivy that covers most of the brickwork. It has a thatched roof and two huge chimneys. 'How long have you lived here?'

'A few years now.'

'I guess it's easier to believe in God's benevolence if working for Him lands you a pad like this.'

Maughan doesn't seem offended. He pushes open the wooden gate that bars his home's enormous gravel driveway. 'I take it you're not a believer.'

'Parts of your sermon resonated,' I admit. 'The notion that we all have a purpose. That implies the chaos isn't absolute, which would be . . . something of a relief.'

We begin to crunch across the gravel and the gate swings shut.

Maughan inquires, 'How do you know Ekaterina?'

'Professionally.'

He stiffens slightly at this. 'And what profession are you in?'

'I'm a detective.'

'How exciting!'

'It's pretty much like your line of work, padre. People come to me with problems. I try to solve them. Half the time, my flock have lost their faith. It's up to me to restore it. Or shatter it completely. Ekaterina is fine, by the way.'

'What's she up to, these days? And I must admit I'm mystified. Why has she sent you to me?'

'She seems to think that you can help with a matter that concerns you both.'

'Really?' We've reached the front door. 'How bizarre! I haven't seen her in years!' He shakes his head to convey profound disappointment. And, pointedly, he makes no move to open the door. 'I'm sorry I can't help you.'

'She thinks you might be able to assist in a quest she's embarked on.'

'A quest? What's she looking for?'

'The lost treasure of the Romanovs.'

I'm curious to see his reaction, but his response isn't what I'd expected. He begins to laugh, and as he looks at me, his focus changes, as though I'm no longer to be taken seriously. 'Lost treasure! That is so Katty! Lost treasure . . .'

I'm not falling for his dismissive mirth and he turns to unlock the door, which indicates I'm right. He might be trying to laugh off Ekaterina's search, but he's once again willing to talk to me. We enter the vicarage and he leads the way up a wide, central staircase.

'How do you know Ekaterina?'

Maughan says, 'We met a million years ago. At university.'

'Were you lovers?'

He stops and turns to me. 'What? Are you trying to shock me?'

'No. I'm trying to understand you. Let's face it, you had no intention of talking to me until I mentioned Ekaterina. Now you're trying to pretend you barely know her. Come on, padre. Lying lips are an abomination to the Lord.'

'Point taken. Look, you never told me your name.'

'Marc Novak.' I decide to take a punt. 'What scares you about Ekaterina?'

'My life now is ordered. It runs along fixed lines. Some would say boring, but that's the way I like it. Ekaterina represents the very opposite of all that. She's . . . She's dangerous.'

I believe he's telling me the truth, or, at least, part of it.

'Why does she think you can help in the search for the Romanovs' jewels? Actually, let me rephrase that. Can you help?'

Maughan hesitates. 'Follow me.'

-59-

Thomas Maughan leads me into his upstairs study, a vast room lined with books and shelves laden with religious figurines. The centrepiece of the latter is a two-foot tall statuette of the Virgin Mary. It's a classic depiction. Here, she's a pale-skinned woman garbed in fine clothes. She's wearing a spotless white dress under a blue robe, but, unusually, she's weeping.

'Sit down, Mr Novak.'

There's a round, oakwood table in the middle of the room and I take a seat at it.

'Thank you.'

The table is dominated by the black figurine of a stallion on his hind legs. As far as I can see, it's the only secular ornament in the room and although it works fine as a piece of artwork – conveying a sense of dynamism and muscularity – it jars with the religious adornments.

Maughan perches on the edge of the table. 'Back at university, I was interested in the Romanovs, but initially as religious figures.'

'How so?'

'Well, they may have had their critics whilst they lived, but eighty-two years after they were slaughtered, the Romanovs were elevated to sainthood. Quite literally. The Russian Orthodox Church canonised Tzar Nicholas II, Tzarina Alexandra and their five children in 2000. It was a controversial move. Many in the Church condemned it.'

'Why's that?'

'Nicholas was perceived to have been a weak leader whose folly led to the revolution. And, of course, his family's massacre was in no way instigated by any religious motivations.'

'That's arguable.'

'Maybe.' Maughan nods. 'In fact, some claimed the sainthood was a way of interpreting the Romanovs' killing as a ritual, or ritualistic murder. Some even claimed that the Russian Orthodox Church was actually blaming Jewish revolutionaries for the deaths.'

'Jews being blamed for the execution of a major religious figure. Who'd have thought it?'

He ignores my dig and says, 'The Church's relationship with the Romanovs is fascinating. The house where the murders occurred was demolished and a place of worship known as "the Church on the Blood" was built on the site. It's said its altar stands over the exact area that saw the horror unfold.'

Maughan has become more animated and less guarded, so I probe a little deeper. 'You said you were drawn to the Romanovs as religious figures *initially*. Where did your interest spread to?'

'Their incarceration! Their riches! Their treasure! And what on earth happened to it? I read everything I could find. You know how passionate one can be in one's youth. I interviewed experts and all kinds of academics but . . .'

'What is it?'

'Certain points just didn't add up!' He's talking faster now, warming to his subject. 'There were lies so obvious that it seemed strange no one had questioned them before.'

'Give me an example.'

'The incredible amount of jewels the Romanovs kept at Ipatiev House. Pounds and pounds of diamonds were sewn into the girls' undergarments alone! But the entire family was constantly being checked. Their clothes searched. Their every move scrutinised. How on earth could the guards miss all that wealth?'

'There's an obvious answer.' It's the solution both Frank and I arrived at separately, and hinted at, when we spoke to Sophie and Stacey in the theatre cafe.

'Well, maybe I'm being dense, Mr Novak. But how did the Romanovs somehow make their treasure invisible?'

'They didn't. Yakov Yurovsky, the man in charge of Ipatiev House, must have known about the abundance of riches. Anything else is unthinkable. So the question is, why didn't he seize the jewels? I can only think of one reason.'

Maughan impatiently gestures for me to continue.

'Why do we give anything up, or turn anything down? Ever? Isn't it obvious? He wanted something more valuable.'

'What could possibly be more valuable than crown jewels?'

'Power.'

Maughan gawps at me. 'What do you mean?'

'The Romanov Code.'

The priest smiles nervously. 'I don't follow . . .' He needlessly uses the tip of his right index finger to push his glasses further up his nose.

'What do you know about the Romanov Code?' I ask.

'I've no idea about any . . .' He begins. Checks himself. 'Actually, I suppose you could call it the Romanov Code, or the Code of the Romanovs. It's the code they lived by. A set of principles. All morally sound. I suspect they liked to think they were defined by it.'

'So it wasn't a physical thing?'

'The code? Oh, no. Unless you mean . . . There's a legend. That the Romanovs created a book. A single book. In it were notes stretching back centuries. The thoughts of everyone from Ivan the Terrible, their formidable ancestor, through to Peter the Great, Catherine the Great, Alexander I and even Nicholas II. It's said this book encapsulated the true Romanov Code. But more than that, it not only defined it, in the eyes of believers, it physically encapsulated it.'

'Would it be valuable?'

'Oh, utterly priceless. If it existed. Which it doesn't.'

I stand and walk to his side. 'Can you be absolutely sure about that?'

As if talking to himself, he mutters, 'If it did, it would be held by the Court.' And then louder, with more certainty, 'It's just another enigma!'

'Go on.'

But he remains still, captivated by the statuette's face. 'It's bewitching, isn't it?'

'The Madonna or the mystery?'

'Both!' He turns to me. Smiles. 'Let me get you a drink, Mr Novak. Coffee? Tea?'

'Tea. Well, a large G&T if there's one going spare.'

Another smile. 'I'm sure I can rustle one up.' He disappears for about five minutes and returns carrying a highball glass. 'Bombay Sapphire. That OK for you?'

'I'll force it down. Cheers.' I take the drink. Raise it in his direction. 'Your very good health.'

'Mr Novak, it's been many years since I spoke about all this. Maybe too many years.'

'We can remedy that right now.'

'Yes . . . Yes, I know.'

'Reverend, I don't pretend to know Ekaterina terribly well. But this case . . . I can sense there's more to it than an excitable individual who thinks she's in reach of some kind of priceless haul.'

'You're absolutely right.'

I sip my drink. Take a gamble with the kind of question that could have him ushering me out of the front door in seconds. 'Ekaterina said you worked with a man called Taras.'

'Really?'

'The kind of work that isn't entirely above board. On the Continent, I believe.'

I can see he's wavering, torn between truth and the more familiar sanctuary of fabrication.

I prod him a little with, 'You might have known Taras as Mr Pitkin.'

Maughan smiles at this, and this tiny show of affection serves as an admission – and he knows it. He purses his lips. I wait. He takes a deep breath and says, 'Do you know why they called him that?'

'The Norman Wisdom character. Clumsy. Gauche. But likeable. A hero in Eastern Bloc countries.'

Maughan is remembering now. 'Clumsy, gauche, likeable. Yes, that sums him up. He was a nice chap. But they also called him Mr Pitkin because Wisdom was a character from a world that wasn't theirs, whom they nevertheless accepted.'

I'm baffled by this last observation and say, 'Go on.'

'Are you here to blackmail me, Mr Novak?'

'If I wanted to blackmail a priest, you'd have to get to the back of the queue. Taras was involved with the transportation of some very high-end artefacts. Missing Romanov treasure. Did you know that?'

Maughan sits down. 'He occasionally used to imply it. Strongly. I didn't know if he was being frank or boastful. Until the end. I believed him then.'

I take another sip of my drink, but he's dried up. 'The end? Just before he was killed, you mean?'

The mention alone distresses him slightly, but he says, 'He knew it was coming, of course. Shortly before he died, I met him at his house in Rome . . .'

I want to interrupt. *He could afford a house in Rome?* But I choose to let the priest continue.

'He welcomed me in. We drank schnapps. As I left, he said, *It was fun, wasn't it?* I just laughed. At the time, I thought he'd meant the shots. Anyway, he gave me a gift and told me I'd been a good friend. Which I had. Not to be immodest, but I'd saved his life when the Carabinieri got a little over-zealous in Turin. Anyway, the very next day . . .'

The very next day, clumsy, gauche and likeable Mr Pitkin was found hanging by his throat above the Tiber.

'What was the gift?'

Maughan nods to the circular table and the equine figurine. 'It was a joke. You see, he always said I was a dark horse. And before the cogs start turning and wild theories start forming – it's worthless. I must confess I wondered if it was part of a lost trove worth millions. But it's painted alabaster, about thirty years old. Austrian. I've had it valued several times, just in case . . . No, if it had been worth anything, we'd be having this conversation in a villa on the South of France.'

'Or, more likely, you'd have been found dangling under a bridge, just like Taras. Look, you and I need the truth about what happened all those years ago because it's casting a shadow across both our lives. Let's try to work together.'

Maughan is gazing at the black stallion and seems to make up his mind. He turns to me. 'Agreed. I've already phoned Martin. Whilst I was mixing your drink. He's looking after the coffee morning. And I've got a rather fine bottle of Château Bélair-Monange in the cellar. It's not a 2017, but it should be very drinkable. What say I open her up and you and I can talk, man-to-man?'

'I say fabulous.'

'Good! Good!' He starts heading to the door. 'You quickly finish your G&T so it's expunged from your taste buds. We really should do the Bélair-Monange justice. Take a seat. I'll be right back. And Mr Novak . . .'

'Yes?'

'Bless you.'

I sit down at the oakwood table. Glance at the alabaster horse. Sip my drink. He's added way too much tonic, but I can still taste the sweet, peppery notes of the Bombay Sapphire. I wonder why Ekaterina wanted me to find this man and why she hadn't mentioned that she'd known him before they'd worked together for the Russian network. I wonder why Maughan was – and is – suddenly willing to open up. And I also wonder why people insist on drowning perfectly good gin with too much tonic.

I rub my eyes. It's been a long day. I feel weary. In need of a reviver. And fast. I drain my G&T.

A peal of bells rings out. So close, I assume it's from Maughan's church. A celebratory chiming. The sound of Sunday afternoons in sleepy English villages.

Sleepy.

I'm too sleepy. Far too sleepy. Heavy and fatigued. I rub my eyes again. Actually, it's *not* been a long day. It's still early. I shouldn't feel anywhere near as—

I glance into my empty glass. Sniff it. There's a slight metallic tang that I didn't notice as I gulped the bloody thing down. As I place the glass on the table, my hand blurs. Whatever he put into my drink, it's acting fast. I can barely keep my eyes open and my limbs are like lead. I put my palms on the tabletop, preparing to stand. But before I can, I spot a reflection in the glass.

An individual moving quickly towards me, right arm aloft.

I try to move around and spin out of my chair, but I'm too slow. I turn a little. Enough to see Thomas Maughan closing in on me. He's brandishing the statuette of the weeping Virgin Mary and even as I try to yell, 'No!' he brings it crashing down onto my skull.

-60-

Having seen Maughan's reflection, I'd normally have been able to dodge his onslaught with ease, but with some kind of poison coursing through my veins, my body is refusing to co-operate. I manage to move a little to one side, so although the Madonna clunks into my skull, it's only a glancing blow.

But still, the statuette shatters and I'm knocked from my chair. My shoulder hits the oakwood table and sends it crashing over. The figurine of the horse, that symbol of friendship given in another time, smashes as it hits the floor.

I land on the carpet and roll over, trying to push myself up and onto my feet. But the priest is nimble and vicious. Circles me. Delivers a right-footed kick to the side of my head that sends me sprawling.

My arms feel so heavy, but I have to find a way to—

Maughan brings the heel of his shoe down onto the side of my head, grunting with exertion as he repeats the attack twice more. Now he stands back. I look up at him.

The Reverend Thomas Maughan is wearing the traditional garb of a Church of England vicar. A white smock over a black cassock. There's a dark tippet – the long linen scarf-like item of clothing – around his neck and, of course, an ivory-white dog collar circles his throat. He also wears a silver crucifix on a heavy chain. It's large and ostentatious, with the body of Christ on the cross, gazing forlornly down, as if he's looking at me with a degree of sympathy.

Maughan is breathing heavily and there's a sheen of perspiration across his boyish face, now rendered a deep, angry red. His assault has taken it out of him, but adrenaline floods through his system and he's fired up. All in.

I manage to gasp, 'Don't do this! Don't cross this line, reverend.'

'I crossed the line a long time ago, Novak.'

He straddles me, effectively sitting on my chest, his knees either side of my torso. I feel his weight pressing down and although I struggle, I'm far too feeble to shift him a single inch. He removes his tippet. Coils one end around his left palm. Repeats the process on his right hand and then loops it around my throat.

I try to stop him, clawing at the linen, but he's strong, confident and resolved to finish this thing. He pulls the material sharply so it digs tight into my windpipe. I can't breathe. I manage to plead, 'Please . . .'

But looking at this crimson priest, I know there is no chance of mercy. Either I overcome him or I die, and whatever he drugged me with has left my body hopelessly weak. I try to strike Maughan's face and see my clenched fist barely makes any impact worth a damn.

My head throbs from the kicking and lack of oxygen. My vision blurs.

I turn my face to the left. On the carpet, inches from my eyes, I see the weeping Virgin Mary. Half her face is missing. I reach for the statuette . . .

Maughan shouts, 'Bastard!' and, relaxing his grip on the tippet, seizes the Madonna and tosses her to one side, far out of my reach. My fingers try to pull the material from around my throat, but the priest is too swift. Too committed. He tightens the ligature. Now I can't fight him. I'm just fighting for breath. My skull pounds and my vision gives me nothing but blurred, sliding colours.

I feel myself slipping away, and as if he senses my powerlessness and defeat, Maughan urges me to, 'Get this over with . . . Just *die* . . .'

-61-

Will Hay's Story
London, England. July, 1938

The great British film star, Mr Will Hay, walked into the cinema foyer and paused to acknowledge the cheers and applause of the circle of people, dressed in fancy frocks and dinner suits, who were clustered by the box offices to greet him.

He raised his hand in thanks and as the welcome died down, he cleared his throat, and despite the fact it was a little after seven in the evening, he said, 'Morning, boys!'

The expression was something of a catchphrase for Hay and his audience rewarded it with a further smattering of applause. He stepped forward and was introduced to the venue's owner.

Hay's manager said, 'This is Mr Leonard Alexander,' and the two men shook hands.

'Thank you so much for agreeing to officially open my picture palace, Mr Hay. I'm one of your biggest fans. I saw *Oh, Mr Porter!* five times. I saw *Windbag the Sailor* three times.'

The actor smiled and Leonard anticipated a vaguely amusing comeback – *Oh, really? And what was wrong with* Windbag? But Hay merely thanked him politely.

'And, Mr Hay, this is my son, George.'

A tall, expectant man in his early twenties stepped forward and began to wring the film star's hand. 'It's an honour to meet you.'

'You're very kind,' Hay replied, gently pulling his arm away. 'And how many times have you seen *Oh, Mr Porter!*?'

'Just the once, sir. But I've read *Through My Telescope* many times. It opened my eyes to the stars.'

'Oh, I see!' He sounded impressed. 'You saw *Porter* once and read my book quite often?' Hay looked to Leonard. 'There's hope for this young man!'

'There is indeed!'

Hay leant into George. 'Thank you, my boy.' As he was shepherded away to meet other people, he patted him on the arm and said, 'If we were all astronomers, there'd be no more war.'

-62-

M_y vision melts into an inky darkness, so when my eyes slip shut, it makes little difference. My lungs feel like they're on fire, but I have no moves left to escape my plight. I'm too feeble. He's too strong.

I can still hear Maughan's voice, and even that's becoming muffled. His words . . .

'*Think on why we were placed on God's good Earth . . .*'

But . . . Those aren't being spoken at this moment. They're from the sermon, when he'd looked down on me from his pulpit and lectured his 'flock' about kindness and love.

'*There will be times when the devil has you by the throat!*'

His pious proclamation. I feel the rage surge through me.

'*But you must remain strong in your resolve!*'

Yeah. Dead right. I really must, padre.

He won't win. I open my eyes. Not today.

'*We must reach out to our Lord . . .*'

I grab his crucifix with my right hand and snatch it to one side. The chain breaks and I'm left holding the cross, gripping it by the vertical section above the head of Christ.

Maughan knows immediately what I'm trying to do. Or, at least, he thinks he does. I hesitate.

He squeals, 'No!' and gives into instinct, glancing to his left to see what I'm about to do with his crucifix. That's the movement I paused for.

I swing the cross in a fast, tight arc, stabbing it deep into his right eye. He screams and falls back, but I don't relinquish my hold on the crucifix. Finally, the noose of fabric around my throat loosens and as I gulp in fast, deep breaths, I manage to raise my torso slightly. Maughan half sees this and shuffles forward, lunging for his cross.

But this time I'm too swift. Too committed.

With a yell of primal effort, I stab him hard in the left eye, driving the crucifix deep into his orbit, until the horizontal beam of the cross rams into his frontal bone, preventing me from forcing it any further into his head.

I start to push him with my left hand, expecting resistance, but he topples backwards and lands on the carpet with a heavy thud. I know immediately that he's dead.

For several seconds, I simply lie on the floor, choking at first. Gulping in air. Gradually, my breathing returns to normal and I unwind the tippet from my throat, drag my body over to the oakwood table and use it to haul myself to my feet.

I stand over the eyeless corpse of the Reverend Thomas Maughan. An inordinate amount of blood, pumped through his severed retinal veins and arteries, pours from his orbits and gathers in the carpet. The shattered Madonna lies beside his face.

And it's only now that I notice it again. The peal of church bells, still ringing joyfully through the cold, blithe afternoon.

-63-

I find Maughan's upstairs bathroom. First, working on the assumption that whatever he slipped me won't have fully broken down or been absorbed through my digestive tract, I force myself to throw up. It's a grim process, and I'm not convinced it'll do any good, but I spend a wretched few minutes with my fingers lodged halfway down my throat. That delightful interlude over, I drink far more cold water than I've consumed over the past six months combined. Finally, I splash some onto my face and, out of everything, this last action seems to help the most.

I stride through to the study and make a call, finally getting through to Jeremy Simmonds. He doesn't sound ecstatic to hear from me. 'My God, Novak! What the hell have you done this time?'

'I just killed a priest.'

'Catholic or Church of England?'

'I think you're missing the bigger picture.'

'Simply trying to establish what the picture is.'

'C of E.'

'Oh.' Simmonds makes a tutting noise, but I can't discern whether this strikes him as good or bad news. 'Are you in public? Did anyone see you?'

'I'm at his vicarage and no one witnessed the' – I glance down at the bloody corpse – 'altercation.'

'Altercation? Right. Is anyone with you now?'

'Only the dearly departed. The Reverend Thomas Maughan. Currently lying eyeless in Gaza.'

'You're in Palestine? Christ! What the—'

'No!' I interrupt. '*Eyeless in Gaza*. It's a quotation.'

'Yes, I know my Milton, thank you. *Eyeless in Gaza, at the mill with slaves / Himself in bonds under Philistian yoke.* I didn't think that would be your cup of Earl Grey.' He sighs like he's the one who's been half-strangled by a homicidal vicar. 'Right then! Let's get on with it. What happened?'

I give him a recap of my day so far and, to be fair, he listens attentively, only interrupting with moues of disappointment and disdain. A moment of silence follows my précis.

'And are you certain he's dead?'

'Simmonds, I drove a crucifix into his brain. Trust me, he won't be taking evensong.'

'First things first. Remove any trace of your presence at the vicarage. You won't have time to wipe your prints, but don't leave anything there that could identify you.'

I roll my eyes. 'That's brilliant advice. I'll take my business card off the mantelpiece. Look, can you actually help me?'

'Of course!' He sounds stung. 'You're one of our own. I'll do everything I can to extricate you.'

I'm certainly *not* one of his own and feel a little queasy that he considers I might be, but this isn't the time to quarrel about it. I manage a half-hearted, 'Thank you.'

'Not at all, not at all. Listen to me carefully, Novak. And, for once, follow my instructions to the letter. Get out of there, now! I can send a team round to take care of the situation, but I can't intervene if the police arrest you. The Fifth Floor is very clear that we're not to get involved with the boys in blue unless absolutely necessary.'

'I'd have thought me not ending up in Wormwood Scrubs qualifies as absolutely necessary.'

Simmonds' voice hardens. 'If the police take you in, you're on your own.'

'Understood.'

'Good. So leave now and contact me again on the Apex line when you're back in London.'

'Will do.'

'I'll ensure you were never there.'

'Thanks, again, Simmonds.'

'One last thing, Novak. I mean it when I say get out of there *now*. Straight away. This instant. It's far too dangerous to hang around.'

'Understood.'

'Do *not* linger in order to explore, investigate or find out more about Thomas Maughan.'

'Of course not. I'm leaving as we speak.'

I hang up, walk towards the master bedroom, check my watch and allow myself a quarter of an hour to explore, investigate and find out more about Thomas Maughan.

-64-

Thomas Maughan had evidently spent his last few years living a quiet life as a country vicar. Yet something in this man's past was so potent that my innocent mentioning of Ekaterina's name and a reference to the Romanov treasure were enough to reawaken something in him. Something so powerful that it meant he had no compunction about murdering me. So, whatever it was, I need to know about it so I can get some idea of who I've killed and what I'm mixed up in.

Annoyingly, I'm aware Simmonds was correct: I have very little time. If anyone arrives and finds the corpse, I don't imagine the police will have a great deal of patience for my claims that their much-loved priest tried to smash my skull with a statuette of the Virgin Mary, before attempting to strangle me with his tippet. I'd definitely be detained and it's more than likely they'd arrest me. It's also highly probable that, without evidence to clear me, I'd be sent down for the brutal murder of the Reverend Maughan.

I hurry through to his bedroom. It's a decent size, with religious prints scattered across the walls. Several minutes looking for hinged panels, concealed safes and compartments in the floating shelves yields nothing. I force myself to think about Maughan. Recall my slight irritation that he spoke like the vicar off *Dad's Army*. He was an old-fashioned man, so presumably he'd employ an old-fashioned approach to secreting his valuables. I check his mattress. Nothing. Open his double wardrobe. I spot a shoebox, half hidden by winter jumpers. Kneel down. Reach for it. Whenever you find a shoebox in a bloke's wardrobe, it's a knocking bet it'll contain anything other than shoes.

I place it on the bed and remove the lid. It holds a load of old fliers for church events. I toss those aside and find the items that their owner wanted unseen. If I needed more proof that he was a man with secrets and a dangerous past, it's right here in front of me. It's an interesting haul and includes four passports. Although all are for the individual I knew as Thomas Maughan, each one offers a different name and spread of personal information. I scan them quickly, noting the various countries of origin. 'The UK . . . America . . . the Turkish Republic of Northern Cyprus . . .'

Maybe I'm becoming cynical, but I doubt it's pure coincidence that he owned a passport for a nation that has no extradition treaty with the UK. I've known several people of interest to the British authorities who've fled to Kyrenia, slipped into Greek Cyprus and, from there, ghosted through Europe.

The final passport is burgundy and resembles those issued in the UK prior to the summer of 2020. But this one's dominated by a central insignia featuring a double-headed eagle. It has a line of Cyrillic text along its top border, immediately above the words, 'Russian Federation'.

I slip all four passports into my inside pocket. The only remaining item is a small blue book. It's old, battered and ornate. I read the title, *Poetical Works and Letters of John Keats*. It's an attractive tome with golden motifs on the front cover and spine, and I'd estimate it was published in the late nineteenth century. That's not to say this copy is worth a fortune. It's been bashed about a bit and lacks a dust cover, so I'm guessing it would only fetch a few pounds. I riffle its pages.

Nothing drops from them, but I doubt Maughan kept the book in his clandestine stash because he secretly enjoyed dipping into *Endymion* before calling it a night.

I thrust it into one of my suit's side pockets and check out the last item in the shoebox. Using my handkerchief as a makeshift glove, I remove it and hold the object to the light.

It's a PMM. A particularly ugly and nasty little semi-automatic pistol that was designed to replace the Makarov PM, although the fact it's heavier than a Glock 17, less accurate than a Berretta and packs all the penetrative punch of a water pistol made many shooters reluctant to swap their old Maks for this lump of steel. On the plus side, in terms of durability, the PMM is incredibly reliable and super easy to maintain.

I've not held one for several years, but back in the day, it was standard issue for agents working within Russia's Committee for State Security. Or, as it was more commonly known, the KGB.

I'm pondering this fact as I hear someone shouting.

'Thomas!'

I freeze.

'Thomas, are you there?'

I recognise the voice of Martin, the young curate I'd briefly met at the church.

I remain silent. But with more urgency this time, he calls up from the ground floor, 'Is everything all right, Father?' He hesitates, then adds, 'The police are here to see you.'

Another voice calls up from downstairs. This one's gruffer and belongs to an older man. 'Come on, Thomas! We need to see you, now! We know you can hear us!'

Given that what's left of Thomas is a ragged corpse currently sprawled across the middle of his study, the claim seems unlikely. But if there's anything worse than being caught by the police in the same house as the body of a priest you've just stabbed to death, it's being discovered in the identical scenario whilst carrying a Russian pistol once used by one of the most ruthless organisations in recent world history. So I decide to keep my mouth shut.

There's a moment of silence, but now the second voice bellows, 'This is a police matter, Thomas! And we're coming upstairs!'

I pull the magazine from the PMM's grip and check it's loaded with its complete complement of 12 Makarov-made bullets. The full dozen is there. I slam the mag back and make sure that the safety, on the top left of the piece, is switched to *on*, then wedge the pistol in the back of my suit trousers.

Martin shouts, 'We're in the sitting room, but we're coming up, Father!'

I hurry to the door and open it a couple of inches. 'Hello!' I shout to the visitors below. 'Don't bother coming up! I'll be right down.'

No one could confuse my voice for Maughan's and I immediately hear low chatter.

'That you, Father?'

There's clearly a third person downstairs because the question comes from a different voice.

I dash to the wardrobe. Close it. Rushing back to the door, I reply, 'You'll have to make do with me, I'm afraid!'

I jog down the stairs. The sitting room is beneath the study, so at the bottom of the steps I turn sharp right, meaning I can see the trio immediately.

There's the curate, Martin. Slight. Smiley. Barely out of his teens. I can see his duffel coat on a chair next to the patio doors. I can't help but like the guy.

The other couple of men are bigger and therefore bigger potential problems. Two uniformed policemen. On the left, a PC. Mid-twenties and below medium height, but he's got a heavyweight's physique that I wouldn't want to go three rounds with. He's not wearing his helmet, so I can see he sports a buzz cut, giving his features a drawn, military look.

The other copper is a sergeant. Mid-thirties. Tall. Not as muscular as his colleague, but he looks like he can handle himself.

I swiftly assess all three individuals. Martin I could batter whilst making a pot of tea and still fancy myself to serve up a pretty decent brew. The sergeant? Yeah. I could take him, and probably his hulk of a sidekick. But facing them both at once, especially with the Mickey Finn that Maughan slipped me still swishing around in my system? Possible. But problematic. It's not an avenue I'm keen to explore and I'm hoping I can defuse the situation using persuasion not pugilism.

'Good to see you again, Martin!'

I wasn't even introduced to him earlier, but I'm hoping my implied camaraderie with the curate is noted by the policemen.

Martin offers me a nervous grin. 'Hello,' he says.

I breeze into the sitting room. It's large and, unlike the study and master bedroom, it's furnished in a resolutely modern style. Immediately behind the three men, there's a long, snow-white sofa and, to my right, a light beige travertine dining table, easily large enough to accommodate thirteen diners popping round for a late supper. The three men clearly entered by a pair of patio doors, which I can see remain ajar across the room and slightly to my left.

The younger copper gets us underway. 'Could I ask what you're doing here, sir?'

'I wasn't aware we were living in a police state, constable. This is my friend's home. He invited me over. Can I ask what you're doing here?'

242

'Mrs Shawcroft, that's Reverend Maughan's housekeeper—'

'I know who she is!' I interject waspishly.

'She entered the premises via those doors' – he gestures towards the patio – 'to collect her handbag. She thought she heard a scuffle coming from the room above.'

'A scuffle?'

The sergeant asks, 'How did you get those marks on your face?'

'I had a bit of work done. It's residual swelling. I can get you a doctor's note if it would help.'

'And the curate here . . .' The sergeant nods to Martin. 'He thought the vicar was perturbed when he spoke to you outside the church.'

'Perturbed? Good word.'

'Care to explain that, sir?'

'Sure! It means agitated. Disturbed. Disconcerted.'

'Not the word!' The sergeant is riled but tries to remain calm. 'I mean, why was Reverend Maughan so perturbed to see you?'

I decide to gamble. I'm holding a weak hand, so may as well go all in. 'Thomas doesn't like his flock seeing us together. It's a very conservative parish.'

That hangs. The PC mouths, 'Oh . . .' and takes a step back.

But the sergeant doesn't appear convinced. 'Martin says he's never met you before today.'

'Well, maybe he swiped left. Sergeant, are you going to stop harassing me, or am I going to have to lodge a complaint with your chief constable, citing your blatant homophobia?' Annoyingly, I can't remember the CC's first name. Shame, I'd liked to have used it to suggest a friendship. I recall it's a cool name, but can't bring it to mind. 'It's the twenty-first century and your particular brand of prejudice has no place in—'

Something catches my eye. Something bright and near and so rapid that I can't process what it is. *Was*. But it breaks my train of thought, forcing me to pretend I'm too upset and appalled to even finish the sentence.

The PC says, 'It's nothing like that, sir.'

The sergeant smiles. He's a wily old devil. 'You're welcome to make a complaint as you see fit. I hope you don't feel I've disparaged you.'

'Well . . .'

'Or the Reverend Maughan.'

'To be frank, you did come across as being—'

The distraction again. This time, half prepared for it, I can make out what it is. A red droplet, falling from the ceiling. I try to remain focused on Martin and the policemen, but two feet behind them, the blood of Thomas Maughan is leaking through the study floor and dropping from the ceiling of this room.

The sergeant notices I'm distracted. This throws him and he furrows his brow. 'As being rather what? Are you all right, sir?'

'I don't wish to appear rude, but your presence here, and you interrogating me . . .'

I spot a third red droplet fall from the ceiling. And I see the snow-white sofa now has three crimson spatter marks nucleated across its middle section. If any of the three men turn around, they can't fail to notice the fresh blood.

-66-

'. . . It's all very distressing,' I conclude. 'That's all.'

'I'm sorry for that! You're just spending a pleasant Sunday afternoon with Thomas?'

'Yes.'

'Well,' says the sergeant, 'I'll call him down so we can assure Mrs Shawcroft he's OK, and we'll be on our way.'

If I lead the men upstairs, they'll find the corpse of their vicar on the study floor. But if they leave, they'll see the fresh blood marks.

The curate appears genuinely concerned. 'Are you sure you're all right?'

A fourth bead of blood drips onto the sofa, immediately behind the trio.

'What could possibly be wrong?' I ask Martin with a smile that even I find unconvincing.

The sergeant angles his head towards the ceiling and bellows, 'Thomas! It's Smithy! Police business, I'm afraid! Could you pop down for a minute? I just need a quick word with you!'

The room suddenly feels unbearably hot. I remove my suit jacket, hook it on my right index finger and, in an attempt to appear nonchalant, sling it over my shoulder.

The sergeant shouts, 'Thomas! Need to see you – now!'

I smile. 'You'll need to shout louder than that, Smithy. He's not in.'

'I thought he invited you over.'

'He did. Martin can confirm that.'

The curate nods.

The sergeant says, 'You said you were spending the afternoon together.'

'And so we are.'

Now he makes a meal out of looking perplexed. 'But he's not actually here?'

'He's nipped into town for a bottle of wine.'

Bugger! The moment the words leave my mouth, I recall Maughan mentioning his wine cellar.

Martin looks suspicious and blurts out, 'He's got dozens of bottles downstairs.'

The older copper nods in a this-is-making-me-uber-sceptical kind of way. 'Thomas always stocks a very fine cellar, so why on earth should he—'

'All right!' I yell. Another deep breath and I rake my fingers through my hair, deciding on which fabrication – several have already occurred to me – I'm going to regale them with. 'You're really going to make me say this? OK. I met Thomas at a pub in Soho. I was at the bar and asked if they had a bottle of Château Bélair-Monange. The barman told me he didn't, but he offered me a very good Merlot. So I said . . .' I shrug to indicate I'd accepted. 'Then Tommy asked for the same wine I'd just bought. The guy behind the bar said the one he'd just handed me was the last bottle. I was waiting for a friend and I'm *not* ashamed to tell you, I said to Tommy, why not join me so we could both enjoy the Merlot?'

Martin is nodding. 'He does love a good red, doesn't he?'

'Don't interrupt!' I hear myself retort, largely because I'm enjoying the little romance I'm spinning on the fly. 'That's how we started . . . Anyway, whenever we get together now, it's kind of our thing that we share a bottle of the Merlot that brought us together.'

'I think that's utterly beautiful,' Martin whispers.

'Me too, sir!' the PC chips in.

The sergeant appears less moved by the meet-cute. 'So he'll be back shortly?'

About two feet behind him, I see another globule of blood and—

And three more bombard the white sofa in quick succession.

'He'll be dropping in before you know it,' I assure the trio.

'In that case,' the sergeant assures me, 'we'll leave you be. We'll wait outside until the reverend gets back.'

He half turns.

'No!' I shout the word and all three men pause and fix their eyes on me with *WTF is going on* expressions that they don't bother to conceal. But if any one of them turns around, they'll see the sofa is now sodden with blood. They'll peer at the ceiling and see the crimson bubbling where—

'No what, sir?'

'I feel a fool for being so off with you. Why don't the three of you come through to the front room? We can have a drink while we wait for Tommy.'

The PC looks horrified. 'Can't do that, sir.'

'Why not?'

He gestures to the hallway.

'The carpet!' Martin says. 'The reverend is so particular about the carpet in the rest of the house. Never lets anyone walk on it without removing their shoes.'

'That's why we didn't nip upstairs earlier.' At last, the sergeant gives me a genuine smile. 'I couldn't be arsed to take my boots off. And I can't be bothered to get them off now, so we'll pop out the back way.'

'We'll wait on the patio,' his colleague intones. 'It's no bother.'

'Right then,' the sergeant continues, 'we'll just be on our way. I'm sorry if I offended you. Really wasn't my intention.'

Another trickle of blood cascades onto the middle section of the sofa, directly behind the policemen.

I laugh. 'These things are sent to try us.'

They half turn to leave.

No! If they see the sofa—

'One last thing!' I declare.

As they swivel back to face me, I discern their patience is wearing thin. They want to leave.

I feel my mouth go dry. 'I wanted to say, I'm sorry if I sounded belligerent earlier. And if I took offence a little too quickly. Apologies.'

'Don't worry about it,' the sergeant replies.

'I was just perturbed.'

'No problem, sir.'

'You see, I know it shouldn't be this way . . .' I start to tell the men.

Again, they begin to turn. I see all three of them about to head to the patio and wonder how they'll react to the damp, bloody sofa – white when they entered, and now looking like a butcher's block – and the trickle of blood that sporadically rains from the ceiling. One more droplet falls from above and—

'It's just that, even in this day and age, sometimes I feel like . . .' As they fully turn away from me, I toss my suit jacket onto the sofa and it lands centrally, resting across the crimson patches. 'There's so much I need to cover up.'

The policemen glance down at the sofa as they make their way to the patio doors.

Martin says, 'I appreciate your honesty.' He shakes my hand. 'What you said took courage.'

He turns, begins to walk away and—

No!

I see a crimson comma falling, as if in slow motion, towards the curate.

No!

A splash of fresh blood hits him on the shoulder.

If the God that Maughan blathered on about exists, his former colleague won't have noticed it.

But he stops.

I think my heart stops.

'What on earth was that?' he asks.

Martin pauses and moves his fingers to the red slick where the blood hit the top of his arm.

-67-

Leonid's Story (cont.)
London, England. July, 1938

Leonard jogged up the narrow staircase that led to his office. 'Maria! Maria! Mr Hay is here! The opening ceremony is about to begin!'

As she entered her forties, his wife had begun using her given name once more, and although he'd never requested it, she called him Leonid when they were alone.

Out of breath, he paused midway up the flight. 'He looks a lot younger than he does in his pictures. And he's not as funny! Maybe you were right . . .' He began walking up the final few steps. 'We should have got Formby.'

He pushed open the door to his office, a large, warm area that felt like a meld of workspace and drawing room. Its decor was a busy blend of Russian and English chintz.

'Maria?' He heard someone cough. 'Hello?' He stepped forward.

'Come in, come in . . .' a male voice said to him. The unexpected guest sat behind Leonard's desk, his face hidden by darkness. 'It's good to see you again, comrade.'

'My God . . .' Leonard began walking towards him. 'Is it you?'

An art deco table lamp on the desk provided a pool of feeble, golden light. The visitor angled his body so his face moved into it. 'You're a lucky man,' said Pasha.

'What are you doing here?'

'Waiting for you.'

'I mean . . . how have you been? It's good to see you again!'

The contrast between the two was striking. Leonard was comfortably overweight. He wore an expensive suit and his greying hair was immaculately gelled into side-parting respectability. Pasha, slightly younger, looked older. His face was lean and lined. His dark hair unkempt. He wore rough clothes.

'Is it?' He sounded surprised. 'Last time you saw me, I tried to kill you.'

'That whole period was madness! I never held it against you, Pasha. We were good friends once.'

'Before you fled with the diamond.'

'Is that what this is about?' Leonard sat at his desk in the chair normally taken by his assistant.

'Your famous jewel stone? I read an interview you conducted with *The Times*. *The Times*! My God, Leonid. You now suggest it's called the Red Diamond because it hails from Russia. I suppose that makes it easier for you.'

'Do you want money, Pasha? Do you want—'

'Easier than the truth. Insofar as it was red when you stole it because it was besmirched with the blood of Olga Romanova.'

'I can give you money.'

'I read you won some cash when you'd not long been over here. Used it to invest. Did very well for yourself and Maria. You're a lucky man. Then you used the diamond as collateral for a new venture. This will be what? Your third cinema in London?'

'Fourth.'

'Fourth. The Red Diamond has been good to you . . . It's given you all this!' Pasha's hand moved into the light and

Leonard saw he was brandishing a Nagant M1895 revolver. Standard issue to soldiers serving in the Imperial Russian Army during the Great War. Pasha put on an exaggerated American accent, 'Jeepers creepers, Mr Alexander. Ain't you the cat's meow?'

He aimed the revolver at Leonard's head.

-68-

'Pardon, Martin?'

'I said, what on earth was—'

'Thanks, my friend!' I slap my palm across his newly acquired red epaulette. 'Your comment about honesty and bravery . . . You've no idea how much that means to me.'

He smiles. 'That's nice to hear. Thomas is a lucky man. But I bet he'll never tell you that!'

'I'd be amazed if he did.'

The curate chuckles. I walk beside him, moving him onwards as if my hand, resting across his shoulder, is a sign of friendship and gratitude for his remark. He picks up his enormous navy blue coat from the chair by the door.

'You should put that on,' I tell him. 'It's cold out.'

To my relief, he nods. As he dons his duffel, he leans closer to me. 'And really,' he lowers his voice, 'that conversation with the policemen . . . it must have been a trial for you.'

'You know what, Martin?' He starts fastening the toggles and turns away. Takes a couple of paces. We reach the patio doors. The two coppers are already outside. 'You really have *no* idea . . .'

*

As Maughan's blood is drizzling into the room below his study, it seems likely he'll be discovered sooner rather than later. I need to get away fast, but just in case I'm picked up before I can escape the area, it feels wiser not to be carrying a fully loaded 9mm PMM. I race upstairs, wipe the pistol for prints and return it to the shoebox.

I'm about to head downstairs when something makes me pause. Strange, but I'm not sure what forces me to linger. I drift into the study. The corpse doesn't interest me. No, I feel drawn to the far end of the room, where I'd initially sat down after Maughan had expressed a willingness to talk. I walk across to the circular oakwood table that was knocked over when he attacked me. The figurine of the rearing horse lies on the floor, shattered. And amongst the fragments of alabaster, I see the item that had remained hidden in the belly of the beast for decades.

I kneel down, so I guess that for a moment it looks like my posture is one of supplication.

Perhaps it is, because there is no doubt in my mind that I'm in the presence of something preternaturally remarkable.

I'm looking at a Fabergé egg. More than that, it's one of the six Imperial Fabergé eggs that have been missing for generations. I'm also aware that it's one of only four for which photographic evidence exists. Having seen a picture of the artefact in front of me, I know it's the Alexander III Commemorative egg, created under the supervision of the legendary Peter Carl Fabergé over a century ago, for Nicholas II, who presented it to his mother, the Dowager Empress Maria Feodorovna.

I know all these things, but I could not have guessed how moving the sight of this relic would be. Put simply, it's beautiful. The photograph of the egg is hugely misleading. It's much smaller than I anticipated – about three and a half inches tall and a great deal more delicate. Historical records reveal the shell is decorated with over 3,500 rose-cut diamonds, yet in reality they appear unified. A brilliant array of largely geometrical patterns that somehow contrive to form an aesthetic singularity. And although I say it's beautiful, I don't mean as an outstanding piece of *objet d'art*.

I mean, it's inches away from me, but remains ethereal. It was kept for many years at the Great Gatchina Palace and went missing around the time of the Russian Revolution. Designed by an icon and once owned by the last Romanov emperor. I'm not a fanciful man, but it feels as though its history – and that of its creators – has elevated the artefact beyond its components of white enamel, gold and diamonds. It seems to glow.

This luminous, ominous Fabergé egg radiates a sense of its own opulent and bloody past.

I lean closer to it. My fingertips reach towards its bejewelled surface.

*

If I hurry, I can reach the railway station in seven minutes and – I glance at my watch – catch the next train out of the village in about ten. I tear through the hallway, swing open the front door and—

'Is Reverend Maughan in?' It's the parishioner who stood behind me as we all filed out of the church following Morning Prayer. 'I'd wanted a quick word about the flower and vegetable show.'

'You know what he's like after a long service!' I close the door behind me. 'I don't think he's in a fit state to see anyone right now.'

'Is the poor dear exhausted?'

I start walking across the gravel driveway. 'He's dead to the world.'

*

Nine minutes after leaving the vicarage, I'm on a train pulling out of the village. I remain standing, thinking about the Fabergé egg. My fingertips had been an inch away from a fortune, but I'd withdrawn my hand. I'm still not entirely sure why.

I recall Frank's warning about a curse but can't bring myself to admit that I might believe it to be true. Yet there'd been something about the artefact that bordered on the supernatural. I have no belief in curses, but I believe in connections. Whatever the Alexander III Commemorative egg ever was, it has become something more than originally intended. Luminous, gold and dazzling. Shadowy, base and blinding. Whatever forced that evolution is something I have no wish to be connected with. Whatever power the Romanovs still exert must be—

In the window in front of me, I see a reflection.

Thomas Maughan.

I spin around. No, it was the reflection of a much older priest, shuffling past me towards First Class. I shake my head. Force the Fabergé egg from my thoughts and focus on the case. The priest says, 'Good morning,' and I guess it must be, for someone, somewhere.

-70-

Pasha's Story
London, England. July, 1938

It had been decades since Leonard had seen a sidearm levelled at him. And here in his well-to-do office, so many years later, the same man who had held the weapon then rested his finger on the trigger now.

'Why don't you put the gun down, Pasha?'

'This is just a cheap single-action Nagant. Not one of the double-action versions that they gave to officers. But you know, in Russia these days, they make a few with the Red Star embossed on the handle. Right there. The award of such a gun is supposed to be one of the greatest honours that can be bestowed on a Party member. Isn't that . . . hilarious? Or sick? I don't know.'

Leonard watched his old friend in silence.

Pasha gestured to their surroundings with his revolver. 'You've tried to bring a little of Russia to England. Jesus! All the tchotchke. The lace. That watercolour of the Urals. Why are you trying to remake what you once loathed?'

'Because, even after all these years, I suppose it's still home.'

'Home sweet home, yes. A place of madness. Your words!' Pasha extended his arm so the revolver was closer to Leonard's face. He shouted, 'You despised Russia and made a new life here! But now you're trying to recreate the past!' He breathed

258

deeply. Lowered his voice. Lowered the sidearm. 'Well, I can help you with that, comrade.'

'What do you mean?'

'You're a lucky man.' Pasha smiled.

To Leonard, it looked like regret. Very gently, he asked, 'What happened after I left?'

'It was a shit-show. The truck broke down. Some of the soldiers broke down. We got rid of the bodies in the end. But . . .' He shook his head. 'Yurovsky went to work in a museum. A bloody museum! Can you imagine?'

'Did he find the book he was always after? That he spoke of when he was in his cups?'

Pasha nodded. 'That's why he didn't follow with the bodies immediately that night. He returned to the prisoners' rooms, eventually found it. But . . . they say he went mad with remorse. Gave the thing away. It's lost. Probably forever. It's a good thing! Everything from that bloody time should have been lost. You know it's all cursed, right?'

'Are you saying that in the end . . . Yurovsky felt contrition?'

Pasha paused. Coughed. Thudded his chest with his left fist. 'They say he felt horror and regret for his part in the slaughter. Good for him. Remember Ermakov?'

'A monster. Of course.'

'Did you know he murdered a man and chopped his head off for kicks, even before the revolution? That was the upstanding citizen they placed in a position of power. He's still around, of course. People like that are always still around. Boozing and boasting about his role in the massacre.'

'What about the others who had a hand in that night? Stepan Vaganov . . . Pavel Medvedev . . . Sergei Broido?'

'Vaganov got a bullet through his brain in 1918. The next year, I think it was, Medvedev died in prison. The authorities said it was typhus. His widow said he'd been shot.' Pasha shrugged. 'Broido got his last year. Convicted of being a Trotskyist and . . .' He aimed the Nagant at Leonard and made a motion of shooting it. 'All dead.'

'The younger men?'

'Netrebin was only seventeen at the time. He . . . *disappeared*.' Pasha started to pull a face, but a short fit of coughing interrupted him. 'And the kid,' he said as he caught his breath, 'Nicholas Sadchikov . . .'

'A rare guard, trusted by Yurovsky *and* the Romanovs.'

'Yes. When he heard about their murders, he was inconsolable. Took his own life. At least, that's the story. No, Leonid, out of all of us, you were the phoenix that flew from the flames. You're a lucky man.'

'Why do you keep saying that? Because of the past?'

'No. Because of the future. Your near future. I married, by the way.'

'Inessa?'

'I forgot. Yes, you met her once, didn't you? We married in '19.'

'Children?'

'No.'

'Is that why you say I'm a lucky man?'

'No. She was the love of my life.'

Leonard picked up on the past tense. 'And how is she? Is she—'

'You're to blame, Leonid. In that clearing, you looked at the savagery and said the world had gone mad. But you were part of that savagery! Leaving without sharing. Leaving me to the madness. You were to blame. You were part of it!'

'I did what I had to do to protect Maria and George! They're everything to me! I never—'

'I was working on the railways. When I got back, she was gone. It was as simple as that. Everyone claimed they didn't know what had happened to her, but we all knew. She'd been critical, you see. And so we all knew that she'd been taken to a gulag. I learnt years afterwards she'd died there. A nameless number on a list that was later misplaced. Her death, or I should say her removal from our life together, was so . . . perfunctory. I think that's the word. She was there. She was gone. There was nothing to mark *my* wife's passing. That is crushing.'

Leonid's breathing became strained. 'Oh, my God . . .'

'Every day. Crushing. That's why I say, you're a lucky man, comrade.'

-71-

The elderly priest continues on his way and as my train gathers speed, I find an empty carriage and make a call. There's no reply and although there isn't a friendly *I can't get to the phone right now* message, I hear an answer service click on. I say, 'This is Marc Novak. I need to speak to the Baron,' and hang up. Take a seat. Notice the palm of my right hand bears a light but distinct red blotch from coming into contact with the blood on Martin's shoulder.

I stare at the stain.

Guilt is starting to seep into me, but I know I can't allow myself the luxury of regret or self-recrimination. Not yet. I take a breath. Weigh up the redness. It looks like a birth mark, which is ironic, because it's the exact opposite. There are no toilets in the train, so employing the handkerchief and spit method, I try to expunge it.

'Out, damned spot . . . Out, I say.'

My phone rings before I've had time to fully wipe away the blood. I pick up, saying, 'Novak.'

I hear a familiar voice. 'Novak . . . This is the Baron.'

*

I've known the Baron as long as I've known London. For me, at least, he's always been a part of the capital. A detail in its tapestry. I've no idea what his real name is, or ever was. I

262

don't know where he comes from. I'm not even sure he does. Going by his accent, and various whispered rumours, he originally hailed from Belarus, Russia or Georgia, or maybe one of the smaller nations lying east of the Iron Curtain. I asked him once, very directly, 'Where were you born? Where did you grow up?'

He shrugged. 'I have forgotten both!'

Maybe he has, but, on reflection, I doubt it. He's the kind of professional that forgets nothing. The Baron is old-school and the only hard drive he uses is his brain. And I suspect nothing is ever wiped from it.

Crucially, he can acquire anything for you. An unused Penny Black from the stamp's first pressing in 1840?

'Impossible! Quite impossible . . . Come back Tuesday and bring the money.'

A Falcon 8X private jet, capable of Mach .9 and ready to fly for the weekend?

'Impossible! Quite impossible . . . Come back Friday and bring the money.'

But the Baron's real skill and passion lie elsewhere. He is gripped by the artistry of forgery, as drawn and transfixed by this field as an oenophile is fascinated by fine wines.

Now, without preamble, he tells me, 'Whatever you want, Novak, it can't be done.'

'Oh, I know it's quite impossible. That's why I called you.'

He clucks and sighs, but I know he's flattered. 'As I've gone to the trouble of making a telephone call,' he replies, 'you may as well tell me what madness you were after this time.'

'Information. Pure and simple. Well, probably not simple. Definitely not pure.'

'Concerning what?'

Out of instinct, I touch my inside pocket. 'Four passports. All fakes. But good. Very, very good . . .'

'I'm busy for the next fortnight.'

'Me too. I'll see you in an hour. Where shall we meet?'

*

Exactly sixty minutes after we spoke on the phone, I reach the building in Soho which the Baron instructed me to visit. I enter and it's immediately apparent I'm expected. There's a man standing behind the front desk wearing a dinner suit and a pair of matte black Moscot Lemtosh glasses. He glances down at a monitor on the desk, looks up and wordlessly nods me towards a passage to his left.

I make my way down the dimly lit corridor and emerge in a small, expensively furnished room. A door in the opposite far corner opens and a raven-haired woman slinks in.

Eyes me.

OK. I don't mind the fact she's looking at me like lions study gazelles on the Serengeti plains. And I've not got a problem with the expanding pink globe of bubble gum that inflates from her lips.

But I do object to the pair of .36 calibre Navy Colts – she holds one in each hand – that are pointed in my direction.

'Not quite the welcome I was hoping for,' I admit.

Maria's Story
London, England. July, 1938.

Leonard stood and tried to read Pasha's face, but as if he was ashamed, his old friend moved his body back so his features became hidden by the darkness.

'What have you done?'

'How often have you thanked your lucky stars that my gun jammed as you ran from the clearing?'

'Pasha, what have you done?'

'Now you will wish the bullet and a half-dozen more had found your skull. For what it's worth . . .' His voice cracked, and even in the shadows, Leonard could see tears gleaming on the other man's face. 'I'm sorry.'

'No . . .'

Leonard turned, ran to the door and began hurtling down the staircase. 'Maria!'

*

On the small stage, in the larger of the cinema's two auditoria a local councillor stood in front of the rich red velvet curtains and neared the end of his speech.

'Places like this,' he opined, 'aren't just for the community. They are the community! A place of warmth! A place to escape the news and the naysayers. Incidentally, ladies and gentlemen, I'm often asked if another war in Europe looms. I can assure you most, err, assuredly, it does not!'

Despite the fluffed line, the sentiment apparently merited a brief round of applause and, warming to the theme, the councillor added, 'Because the boys who fought on the battlefields of Flanders, the Somme and Gallipoli are now the men who work in the corridors of Whitehall, the Reichstag and Washington. They know war isn't an adventure. They will not look to remake that terrible past!'

More applause.

'And I say . . .'

The councillor spotted Will Hay frowning on the front row and remembered he wasn't on stage to win votes, but nevertheless he made a mental note of the phrases that had generated such approval and looked forward to employing them next time he was up for re-election.

'And I say, we are all honoured to have Mr Will Hay with us tonight, who has kindly agreed to join me on stage to officially open this wonderful new picture house! Ladies and gentlemen – my friend and yours, Mr Will Hay!'

The councillor stood back, and as the guest of honour made his way to the front of the auditorium, he did the old trick of milking the applause, as if it was intended for him, and not the third biggest box office pull in Britain.

Hay moved swiftly up the stairs, thanked the audience and the councillor and said, 'I'm sure we can all agree that this is proving to be a very memorable evening.' He spotted George in the front row, a few seats along from where he'd been sitting, and gave the young man a smile and a nod of acknowledgement.

*

Leonard tore down the stairs and along the corridor leading to the foyer. A cigarette girl, resplendent in a black and gold uniform with her pillbox hat worn at a jaunty angle, stood holding the auditorium's middle door slightly ajar, peering through it to the stage.

'Maureen!'

The woman whirled around.

'Sorry, Mr Alexander! Will Hay's on stage and I just wanted to—'

'My wife!' he shouted. 'Have you seen Mrs Alexander?'

'Not seen her since lunchtime. When she was here with you.'

'Are you sure?'

'I'd kiss the book on it.'

'What about George?'

She used her thumb to point over her shoulder. 'Front-row seat.'

Leonard muttered, 'He might know where she is.' He hurried to the door, opened it and rushed into the auditorium.

A few members of the audience craned their necks to squint in his direction, annoyed by the distraction and wanting to see who'd caused it.

Leonard bumped into an usherette, who said in a loud whisper, 'Nark it! Can't you see . . . Sorry, Mr Alexander! I didn't—'

But he'd moved on, inching down the central aisle, looking to see if his wife was sat somewhere in the audience.

'And, in short,' Hay was saying, 'it gives me great pleasure to declare this picture house officially open!'

The red curtains started to part and the applause began. Leonard, who had been scanning the central rows for his wife, barely noticed it.

He thought he'd spotted Maria, halfway along row F. Same hairstyle. Same size. But he couldn't make out the woman's face because she was leaning forward slightly, and the person in the seat next to her was holding a box of popcorn that obscured her. But now she recoiled, forcing her body back as far as it would go into the seat. First of all, Leonard saw it wasn't Maria. And then he registered that whoever the woman was, her mouth had dropped fully open and she was screaming. Pointing. Crying.

A moment later, more shrieks. More screaming. People shouted out in shock. The room became a cacophony of horror.

Leonard followed the direction the woman had been pointing, looked towards the stage and saw his wife. The parting of the curtains had revealed her.

Maria Alexander was hanging several feet above the stage, directly below the centre of the proscenium arch.

The thick rope that suspended her ended in a noose that held her neck at a grotesquely skewed angle. Her corpse swayed and rotated very fractionally, creating the image that she was a gruesome weight at the end of a compound pendulum.

Audience members were on their feet and rushing towards the exits. Leonard, staring at his wife's dead, discoloured face, allowed himself to be caught up in the fast-flowing tide of fleeing people. It swept him back up the central aisle. He spotted George tearing onto the stage, but he had seen death too many times not to recognise it here.

It was far too late.

For a moment, the world was a smudge of noise and colour. Leonard blinked and found himself in the foyer. Without realising it, he began striding along the corridor that led to the staircase up to his office. His gait quickened as a molten rage coursed through him. As he bounded up the steps, he yelled, 'Pasha! Pasha, you'll pay for—'

A single gunshot. So loud it sounded like an explosion.

As quickly as he had been galvanised into action, Leonard froze. He stood motionless in the silence for a moment. A picture of monolithic despair. A heartbeat. He physically crumpled. Tumbled down the stairs. Leonard lay at the foot of the steps, unable to shift from his mind the vision of Maria hanging above the stage.

For a moment, he'd been driven by a desire for vengeance, but even that had been denied him.

He knew the man that had killed his wife was dead. He knew that, this time, Pasha's gun had not jammed.

-73-

The shiny pink bubble pops and she sucks the gum back into her mouth. Chews it and smiles at the same time. 'Heya, Mr Novak!' She flashes a grin that I don't find remotely reassuring. 'You and me,' she reveals in a broad Bronx accent, 'we're gonna have some fun!'

'I only have one question for you . . .' I approach her without breaking eye contact and, using the tips of my index fingers, press the barrels of her pistols downwards, until both are aimed at the floor. 'What the devil are you wearing, Reggie?'

'Don't ya think it's cute?'

Reggie DeLuca is a friend of mine. In the few years I've known her, she's worked as a waitress at Cahoots, an analyst at GCHQ and briefly (and weirdly) a yoga instructor for Scotland Yard. Those are the legal jobs she openly admits to, but I'm sure her true CV would contain several lines detailing dodgier gigs.

Her black hair is lashed into a ponytail and I'm guessing her lipstick is called something like Electric Maroon. She's also wearing a cowgirl's outfit. Suede leather boots over blue jeans. A low-slung belt with holsters just below her hips, a black blouse with red and white embroidered detail and, inevitably, a Stetson.

'I think it's . . . an interesting choice.'

'It's so I blend in.'

'Right. Are you thinking of visiting Colorado circa 1875?'

270

She laughs. 'You don't know what this place is?'

'I'm guessing it's not that new Tesco Metro I read about in the *Standard*.'

'You're a sweet kid, Novak.'

'Ain't I just?'

'Come . . .' She slides her Colts into her holsters. 'Let's walk and talk.'

She places her hand against the wall by the side of the door. I don't even see the palm reader, but I know it's there because I hear the sound of metallic bolts sliding to one side. When Reggie opens the door, I see it's a slab of steel three inches thick, with a locking mechanism similar to one I once had cause to examine in the New York Federal Reserve vault.

'Follow me.'

'Always.'

And given that the New York Federal Reserve vault houses over five thousand tonnes of gold, I can't help wondering where Reggie is leading me.

I follow her into a labyrinth of narrow, dimly lit corridors. Each one is dotted with two-way mirrors, meaning we can see into rooms but the occupants don't even know they're visible. I suppose I'd been expecting something more exciting, not this.

Reggie tells me, 'You look disappointed. Were you expecting something kinkier?'

'Something more remarkable, to be honest. These are just normal rooms. A bedroom. A lounge. A library.'

'They're a lot more than that, sugar.'

'How so?'

'Every client comes to us with a very simple set of memories. Recollections of when they were happiest. When they were in love. Or were loved.'

'And you try to recreate that?'

271

''Zactly! So let's say they want to recreate the years when they were first married. We had a client recently whose wife died. He wouldn't accept it. Couldn't! So the Baron recreated the living room of the first house they shared. We hired an actor to play the wife. Trained her for months. Used AI to figure out how she'd react to certain circumstances and then – boom! We put the client in the replica of his old room and added his replica wife. First session – he cried flat out for an hour. After that, he just slips into the fiction. I've seen it. They chat for hours. They laugh.'

'It's obscene.'

'It makes him happy.'

'Reggie, I'm coming across this more and more. People's need to recreate the past. Why do you think that is?'

'We need certainties, Novak. The present is a mess. The future's unknown, sure, but it's as sure as shit scarier than it's ever been. The past is the only place we feel safe.'

I pause. Look through one of the two-way mirrors. A man is awkwardly positioned on one knee in what looks to be a dishevelled bedsit. He's in his fifties, gazing up at a twenty-year-old woman wearing nineties-style attire. He's holding a ring box in her direction. His face is fraught with eager anticipation.

'Don't you think that's real sweet?'

'That's what makes the past so dangerous, Reggie.' I turn away. 'We think it's safe.'

-74-

The Baron sits in a white, circular room. There's a table in front of him and he's studying a solitary piece of art on the far wall. It looks to me like a Russian mountain range, but I could be wrong. His eyes flicker towards me and he offers an enthusiastic welcome.

'Oh, it's you.' A mournful shake of the head. 'What madness have you become entangled in this time?'

Well, enthusiastic for him, that is.

'Oh, the usual.' I walk towards him. 'What madness have you created here?'

'I got the idea years ago. I was at Pinewood Studios. Wandered onto the 007 stage. I wasn't thinking or paying attention to where I was. This may sound foolish, but when I looked up, for a moment I really thought I was in the Louvre! The recreation of the gallery – for some film or other – was extraordinary. And now, using AI, detailed research and the best construction team in the world, we can replicate any room you care to mention. Barring churches and chambers of a certain size, you understand. All for a price, of course.'

'Of course.'

'You've seen the rooms, but we'll soon be upscaling. Bigger spaces. Bigger memories.'

I resist the temptation to say, 'Bigger profits!' because I've an important question on my mind. 'Why are people so obsessed with the past?' I ask.' 'With reforging it?'

'Perhaps we want to get it right this time.'

'You never cease to startle me.'

I'm rewarded with a brief but genuine smile. 'Sit down, Novak, sit down! And I didn't create all of this venture. I was merely a partner with deep pockets.'

I take a chair beside the Baron. Reggie stands by the far wall looking too much like a sentry for my liking.

'You know,' the Baron continues, 'if anyone ever approaches you to invest in a scheme to make rich people happy, and you can see that it will indeed bring them joy . . .' He taps the side of his nose. 'Sink as much money into the project as possible!'

'There's a definite logic to that.'

'Experts always tell us to follow the money,' the Baron opines. 'I'm not sure why. We all know where it leads. Where it's always led. To rich people.'

'And this venture goes straight to source?'

'Exactly.' He gestures to an ice bucket on the table. 'Help yourself to a drink. Pour me one while you're at it. It's only champagne. Crude and obvious, I know.'

I remove a bottle of rosé from the cooler. It's one of those champagnes with a label that looks like it's been hand-drawn by someone doing their art homework in a hurry. The maker's intention is to suggest, 'Hey, we don't take ourselves too seriously! We have a sense of humour!' but I've seen how much this wine costs and the price tag is no joke, believe me.

'I wouldn't worry. I'm a man with very obvious tastes when it comes to the finer things in life.' Reggie shakes her head when I offer her a glass, so I fill two flutes, hand one to the Baron and sink into my chair, asking him, 'How are you, my friend?'

'Business is good. My health is bad. Doctors? Crooks and charlatans!'

'What's wrong with you?'

'I don't like to talk about it.'

He talks about it for ten minutes and eventually loops back to why I'm here.

'So, how can I help you? You mentioned something about passports.' I reach into my pocket and he adds, 'One at a time, please.'

'Sure, but there are four of them, though, so you . . .' I trail off as I notice he's closed his eyes. 'Are you all right?'

'Perfectly.' He proffers his open palm. I place one of the passports in it. The Baron raises it to his nostrils and inhales. 'Ah, yes . . .' he murmurs.

I look across to Reggie, who shrugs in a way that suggests she's seen this a thousand times.

I return my attention to the Baron. He's running his fingertips over the cover, as if examining the texture.

'You're allowed to look,' I tell him.

'Don't be insolent.'

'Sorry.'

A minute later, with his eyes still shut, the Baron says, 'It's an American passport, of course. Or, at least, it purports to be. It's a fake, but a very good one. It's delightful, in fact. Absolutely delightful.'

'Can you tell me who made it?'

His eyelids open to reveal a look of chagrin. 'Impossible. Quite impossible.'

'How long will it take you?'

'That depends on how much I have to go off.' He closes his eyes again. 'Second passport, please.'

I place it in his outstretched hand. 'No peeking.'

'I told you not to be insolent.'

Reggie calls across, 'It's in his nature.'

'She's right,' I admit, 'for a change.'

Reggie pokes her tongue out at me and I smile.

We repeat the routine for all the passports and the Baron informs me, 'They're quite fascinating! And works of art, my friend. They should be displayed in the National Gallery for connoisseurs to admire, but, really, the public has no taste.' He pulls a jeweller's loupe from his pocket and uses it to examine the edges of the British passport. 'The details are exquisite.'

'Are there any telltale signs that indicate their provenance?'

'Of course, of course. I had thought I'd need them to be analysed to draw a conclusion, but I'm quite certain I know who created these beauties.'

'That's incredible! You've surpassed yourself.'

Reggie chips in, 'He ain't half bad!'

The Baron wafts away our compliments. 'Thank you, Regina . . . And Mr Novak. Where do you think these passports hail from?'

'Honestly?'

'Of course.'

I tell him truthfully, 'MI5 or MI6. Not sure which. But I believe they were issued by British Intelligence.'

'Not a bad assertion.' He takes a sip of champagne. 'But you're quite wrong.'

'Are you sure?'

'One hundred per cent.'

'Then who made them? Who issued this man with these forgeries?'

'There's no doubt whatsoever.' The Baron hands me back the passports. 'They were made and issued by the Russian Secret Service. That in itself may or may not surprise you. But there's something else. Something much stranger.'

I glance at the passports. 'And what's that?'

'Documents like those – I mean documents that are that good . . . they don't come cheap. And the exceptional ones like those, well, they are not so easy to procure. Whoever those are for –' he nods to the passports – 'the individual they were crafted for is not simply some sleeper agent or a low-level operative, or even a mid-range officer. To have gone to that much trouble and expense . . .' The Baron carelessly scratches his neck. 'He's someone the Russians care about. Maybe even love. Or fear.'

-75-

As I walk through the grounds of Ipatiev House, I straighten my tie clip. The place is defended like a fortress, with guards packing the place and – I glance upwards – a helicopter circling the estate.

It's another cold day, but the moment I saw the property in front of me, it suddenly felt even chillier. I pause. Take it in. The ornate arched windows on the lower floor. The plain, rectangular casements above them. It's a strange building, about thirty metres wide, built on the slope of a hill, so from some angles the ground floor remains hidden from sight. The intricate detail towards the top of its façade emphasises the swathes of plain stonework below.

The security guard who met me at the gates says, 'Keep moving!' so I stay still for a couple more moments, studying the site.

Ahead of me, I can see into the first-floor room that would have been set aside for Olga, Tatiana, Maria and Anastasia Romanova and, to its right, the chamber where their parents and brother, the Tsarevich Alexei, would have been confined. Below those two rooms, the basement where the last royal family of Russia and their friends were butchered.

I'm aware the building is simply a replica, but the *realness* of what I can see, its solidity and sheer presence, is unsettling.

Ekaterina Romanova appears at the front door. 'Welcome to Ipatiev House, Mr Novak! What do you think?'

'It's quite an achievement,' I reply truthfully, adding to the guard, 'You can get back to your crossword, now.'

Ekaterina nods at him and he marches towards the gates. 'Come inside, Mr Novak.'

I don't reply. Neither do I move.

She smiles, not unkindly. 'The ghosts of the past can't harm you.'

'It's not the ghosts I'm afraid of.'

'Then what?'

'Honestly, Miss Romanova, I don't know. But . . . This place looks like an exact replica of the original. Is the interior as accurate?'

She nods. 'Of course. The amount of detail we were able to research meant duplicating the first House of Special Purpose was a task we could achieve with remarkable precision.'

'But why would you want to? I don't understand. This is a symbol of horror.'

And here's that Ekaterina Romanova temper again, flaring like a firework. As sudden and striking as any rocket. 'It is a symbol of what my family endured!' she tells me. 'It is a symbol of captivity! Not just of the Romanovs' imprisonment, but the confinement of millions of my countrymen and women in the decades that followed the false revolution! You ask why it stands here.' She's so agitated she doesn't notice an old woman appear at her shoulder. 'It is a reminder because the people need reminding that—'

The woman gently interjects, 'Calm yourself, Katta.'

Ekaterina pauses, but she still stares at me as though I've said something rude about her parents.

'I didn't mean to offend you with my question.'

She takes a breath. Turns to the person who's joined us and softly replies, 'I don't want to be calm. We've all been too calm for too long.'

'I know, I know . . .' The woman looks at me. 'You must be Marc Novak! I've heard a lot about you.'

'Good or bad?'

'A little of both. I preferred the bad.' She beams at me. The kind of smile it's hard not to return. I'd say she's in her mid-seventies. Robust. Active. She has long, loose white hair which somehow contrasts with her smart check suit trousers and boyfriend blazer. 'I'm Helen Merrydale.' She offers me her palm and we shake hands.

'Helen is the head of the Romanov Foundation,' Ekaterina informs me.

'You look surprised by that, Marc.'

Remind me never to play poker with Ms Merrydale. 'I expected the organisation to be run by a Romanov. Or at least a Russian.'

'You disappoint me! Here at the Foundation, we continue the spirit of the Romanovs' work. They were pro-freedom right across the world.'

'There are many examples,' Ekaterina tells me. 'Like it is conveniently forgotten that Catherine the Great played a major role in tipping the outcome of the American Revolution, freeing what is now the USA from Britain. Through non-military and diplomatic pressure, of course. Catherine refused the British request for troops on the ground and she acted favourably towards the so-called colonists by offering to provide them all that she could without compromising Russia's neutrality.'

'Well, it's fairly obvious that a weakened Britain was better for Russia economically, but I take your point. Although I'd say it would have been more apposite to point out that Catherine the Great wasn't even Russian. And wasn't that great, to be honest. Didn't "her" Russia invade what's now known as Ukraine? That's not something you'd approve of, is it, Ms Romanova?'

Ekaterina regards me with a slight air of annoyance.

Helen says, 'You seem remarkably well informed, Marc.'

'I watch a lot of *Horrible Histories*.'

'Horrible . . .?'

Before I can reply, Ekaterina cuts in, 'It's a children's television show. Ignore such comments. It's his way of deflecting.' And to me, 'Let's all go inside.'

*

I'm taken to the one room in the building that isn't a match for the corresponding chamber in the original Ipatiev House.

'We had no wish to recreate the offices of Yakov Yurovsky,' Ekaterina explains. 'A monster and a murderer.'

The room is large and modern, clashing with the rest of the building with its array of screens, PCs and laptops. Helen switches on an enormous television and shows me a ten-minute film that's essentially a promo for the Romanov Foundation. The video is slick and convincing, highlighting the many worthwhile causes they've helped over the years, positioning the organisation as a global force for good, upholding the values of the Romanovs in the twenty-first century. I'm surprised at the level of buy-in that the film reveals. Sure, a lot of it shows people like Helen and Ekaterina meeting individuals on a grass-roots level, but several cutaways show the Foundation's heads chatting with presidents and prime ministers.

As it fades to black, Helen asks, 'What did you think?'

'Genuinely impressive. I had no idea your reach was so extensive. And I had the impression – falsely it turns out – that your organisation would be persona non grata in Russia. But I noticed a few shots of you guys holding meetings in the Kremlin.'

Helen says, 'Before the geopolitical climate became so heated, we had good relations with Moscow. We believe they'll be rekindled when the current situation evens itself out.'

'Why would any Russian leader have a problem with the Romanovs?' Ekaterina asks the question as though she's furious for having to do so.

'They weren't always so popular with the men in charge. This place is a testament to that.'

'The history of Russia is the history of the Romanovs.'

I could argue with Ekaterina about her claim, but I turn my attention to Helen. 'It was fascinating. Thank you.'

'Our pleasure,' she replies. 'And I believe you had something you wished to discuss with us?'

'Forgive me. My business is with Miss Romanova alone.'

Ekaterina says, 'Anything you tell me, you can tell Helen. We have no secrets from each other. I am searching for the Romanov Code on behalf of the Foundation. I have been for years. It's only right that Helen is kept fully up to date. All right . . . Did you find David Fenton?'

'Yes. Yes, I did.'

'Oh my God!' Ekaterina looks delighted and begins to gabble. 'How was he? How is he? What's he up to?'

'Well, to answer your questions in order. Annoyed. Dead. And not a great deal from hereon in.'

Her face falls. 'Dead? Are you saying he's dead?'

'I'm afraid so.'

'But . . . When did he die?'

'About half an hour after we met.'

Helen can't quite grasp it. 'Was there some kind of tragedy?'

'Almost.'

'What?'

'He tried to kill me.'

Ekaterina asks, 'What exactly happened?'

'I killed him.'

'But why would he want to murder you?'

'I didn't think to ask. I was a little preoccupied at the time.'

The two women appear to be in shock.

After a couple of seconds, Ekaterina says, 'David was a man of purpose and conviction. He wasn't a murderer. He was . . . lovely. He was—'

'Well, lovely David was back working for the Russian Secret Service.'

'Don't be ridiculous! He was like me! He ran away because he saw what they were capable of.'

I shrug. 'Maybe they reminded him what they're capable of, which is why he ran back.'

Helen inquires nervously, 'Is that what you think happened?'

I could hazard a guess but don't see the point. 'The authorities have accepted I acted in self-defence. But there will be an investigation.'

'Of course,' says Helen. 'A man has died, so . . .' She tails off as the significance of my words hits home.

Ekaterina, to her credit, has put her grief on the backburner and is already more concerned with what the police might be cooking up. 'Will the Foundation be dragged into this affair?'

'Would that be a problem?' I know damn well it would, but I want them to realise the full extent of the implications.

'Would it be a problem?' Ekaterina almost stammers with incredulity. 'If the Romanov Foundation is seen to be mixed up in the murder of a Russian spy? We'd be pariahs in the West, with observers assuming we were connected to the agent, and outcasts in Russia because they'd suspect we were involved in the killing! Fuck! Fuck, fuck, fuck!'

'Either way,' I agree, 'it's not a good look.'

Helen murmurs, 'This is a nightmare.'

I allow the silence to simmer for a moment or two, then reveal, 'I may be able to help you.'

Ekaterina looks suspicious. 'Why would you?'

'Because it's what I do.'

The head of the Foundation reacts with more grace. 'That would be marvellous. If there is any way you can keep our connection hidden . . . You've seen the work we do. We would be beyond grateful.'

'I'll do what I can.'

'What's your price?' Ekaterina asks.

'I don't have a price. That always seems to fox you. But it's really dead simple. I do what I believe to be right. It means I can sleep at night. It also means I do my clothes shopping in Cancer Research UK because I'm never going to be rich, but, hey, swings and roundabouts.'

'Mr Novak.'

'Yes, Miss Romanova?'

'I don't know why I like you so much.'

'It's my natural modesty. No one's immune to it. But before we start playing footsie under the table, I'm going to need a few answers. Top of the list – what's the Court?'

Helen and Ekaterina exchange glances and the latter replies, 'I've no idea.'

'If you're going to lie to my face, please do me the courtesy of trying to sound at least moderately convincing.'

She blushes. 'I'm sorry.'

'OK, let's take it from the top one more time. And this time I want an essay answer or I tell the police everything.'

Ekaterina pauses. 'Yes. I'm sorry.' She looks at Helen, who gives a tiny nod. 'We'll tell you everything we know.'

'How glorious. So, what's the Court?'

76

Helen pauses at the main entrance and says her goodbyes. Ekaterina walks me to my cab. I open one of its rear passenger doors and as I'm about to get in, she says, 'Catherine the Great may not have been great in the modern sense of the word, but she ruled Russia and its empires for over three decades. She founded cities, theatres and universities. She conquered countless lands. Was responsible for untold deaths. She also established Europe's very first state-financed higher education institute for women.'

'What's your point?'

'In her early days, Catherine's opponents often underestimated her because she was a woman. Mr Novak, because of her femininity, men couldn't see her for what she truly was.'

'And what was that?'

'Enlightened. Efficient. Cultured. But a killer.'

'I still don't get your point, Miss Romanova.'

'History repeats itself.' And as she turns to re-join Helen, Ekaterina adds, 'Catherine wasn't her real name, you know. Goodbye, Mr Novak.'

As my cab pulls away from the outer gates of Ipatiev House, I remove my tie and tell the driver where we're off to. I look back and see Helen and Ekaterina watching me depart. It's hard to tell what's worrying them the most. It's even money on the fact that now Thomas Maughan, the con artist formerly known as David Fenton, is lying cold in a mortuary somewhere, the chances of finding the Romanov Code have dwindled to pretty much zero. And it's even money again that the prospect of the Foundation being linked to the priest's death tops their angst list.

And now I know the truth about the Court, there's an outside bet that they're most concerned with me and what I'll do next.

To tell you the truth, I'm worried about all three, but for different reasons.

I face forward. Take a black tie from my suit pocket and loop it around my collar. I'm already half-regretting not asking Ekaterina to fulfil her side of our bargain, but I want to question her about the man I'm seeking in connection to Diana's death when we're alone. I've a feeling Helen Merrydale's presence would have made her less than forthright.

The cabbie glances in his rear-view mirror and spots my tie. 'You going to a funeral, mate?'

'Yeah,' I reply as I fashion a half-Windsor, 'I'm just hoping it's not my own.'

I pull my phone from my pocket and google 'Catherine the Great'. Turns out her real name was Sophie.

*

Nobody looks forward to a funeral, but I've been dreading this one more than most. Today, the friends, family and colleagues of Claudette Vale gather to bury her body and pay their last respects.

I arrive at the church in good time. A crowd has gathered around the main entrance and I spot Claudette's sister, Émilie, a few feet away from the cluster of mourners. She's tall, naturally elegant and has raven-black hair sculpted into a collarbone bob. She resembles her sibling, so much so that seeing her now, I'm taken back to the moment in the hospital where I looked down on Claudette's pale, dead face. I try to shake that thought as I approach Émilie.

'Hello! You probably don't remember me but—'

'Mr Novak!' She embraces me. 'Of course I do. We met at the ACTION fundraiser at the Waldorf. My sister always spoke of you very fondly.'

'That was kind of her.' I think back to our final meeting. Her overwhelming disappointment in me. Émilie won't know the circumstances surrounding Claudette's death and I'm glad I don't need to explain what happened, but my feeling of guilt remains immense. 'How are you doing?' I ask.

'Oh . . . You know.'

'And how are things with ACTION? I heard you've taken over the organisation.'

'Yes, yes I have.' She purses her lips. 'Things could be better, to be honest. Financially we're in deep water. Very deep water. I don't see how we can last another year. It's a wonder we've been able to keep going as it is.'

I'm about to change the subject when a familiar figure joins us. 'Ms Vale, I just wanted to offer you my deepest condolences. I knew your sister well. She was a great woman. I miss her very much.'

'I appreciate that.' Émilie touches the man's forearm. 'I don't think we've met.'

'No,' says Jeremy Simmonds. 'My name's Thom Peters. I worked with Claudette. Now you've taken over the reins at ACTION, I hope we can continue that relationship.'

'I'm afraid that's unlikely. I was telling Mr Novak, it's miraculous we're afloat as it is.'

I start to ask Émilie about her brother, but Simmonds interrupts. 'How so?'

GAVIN COLLINSON

'The strangest thing . . . Shortly after my sister died, I got a package through the post. Huge. Unwrapped it. It was an attaché case!'

'That's amazing,' I exclaim. 'How's your brother doing? Has he been able to get over from Christchurch?'

'Yes, he should be—'

Simmonds won't let it go. 'An attaché case, Ms Vale?'

'Yes! And here's the extraordinary thing! Miracle one – it was jam-packed with money! Miracle two – it arrived without any conditions, so we were able to use the cash immediately. There was enough to keep ACTION going, in the short term at least.'

Simmonds slowly nods. 'As you say, miraculous.'

'Would you gentlemen excuse me? You mentioned my brother and, funnily enough, here he is . . .'

Émilie drifts away and Simmonds fixes me with one of his headmaster stares. 'Care to share?'

I ignore his question. 'What are you doing here? If you've come for your hip flask you're out of luck. I left it at home.'

'Émilie Vale's piece of news . . .'

'What about it?'

'Know anything about the miracles?'

'They were never as good after Smokey Robinson left.'

'You know damn well what I mean, Novak! We picked up one of the men responsible for the death of Miss Winters. He told us they'd been ordered to give you an attaché case. He thought it was full of money.'

'Simmonds, if I'd been given a case full of money, don't you think I'd have used it?'

'Given the circumstances, you may have thought – incorrectly – that it was blood money and decided not to spend it on yourself due to some . . . misplaced morality.'

'Morality is always misplaced in my business.'

'You do talk absolute tommyrot sometimes.'

'Any news about Sandy Paige?'

Simmonds checks his watch. 'Good lord, is that the time?'

'Your changing-the-subject skills really need a bit of work.'

'I thought it was marginally better than *how's your brother doing?*'

'Simmonds! Come on!'

'We've been pressing forward. Finding out more regarding his child trafficking operations.'

'And?'

'And it's bizarre. Paige had every client interviewed at least three times. He provided them with kids illegally, but he made damn sure the children were going to homes where they'd be taken good care of. Loved. Brought up well. Trust me, that's not how trafficking rings normally function. It's unbelievable.'

I think back to Paige's wife, Louisa, revealing that her husband began the networks after they'd discovered they couldn't have kids themselves. 'Oh, I believe it.' I rub the bridge of my nose. Close my eyes.

In truth, my investigations had suggested Paige was running his operations along those lines. It seems there is greyness in all things. Perhaps his approach influenced me on a subconscious level and was partially responsible for my offer to him, allowing him to escape a custodial sentence. But examining my decision now, I know I chose poorly. I feel for the kids he supplied to wealthy families. I know the pain of padding downstairs one morning to find the woman at the centre of your world is absent. Forever.

I was a kid when I lost my mum and the period where we struggled to come to terms with her death . . . well, it never really ended. The children Paige trafficked were stolen souls. I should never have shown him a flicker of mercy. It could be argued that, ethically speaking, I'd been right to act the way I did. To give him an out. But, like I said, morality is always misplaced in my business.

I say to Simmonds, 'How are you getting on with tracking him down?'

'Dammit, man! I've already overshared!' He lowers his voice a fraction. 'I've told you before! The case runs on a need-to-know basis.'

'And I've told *you* before, *I* need to know.' He shakes his head and begins to head to the church, but I grasp his arm. 'You see, I think you've found him.'

He faces me. 'Not exactly.'

'Then how exactly? Please! I risked my life on this one!'

'We reached out via some of the contacts you suggested. We offered him a deal.'

'How cosy.'

'It's not a best-case scenario,' he snaps, 'but that's not the world we live in.'

'What's the deal?'

'He's given us details of all the trafficking networks he was involved in and several more that he had knowledge of. The intel he's delivered means many rings will be broken forever and we're hopeful that literally hundreds of children will be reunited with their families.'

'But Paige walks free?'

'He's retiring from public life. When the time's right, we'll put out a story that he suffered a stroke and would like his privacy respected at this difficult time. We're relocating him and Louisa to somewhere far, far away.'

'But he keeps his cash? And his liberty? Christ! Who brokered the deal? Your new boss?' I tighten my grip on his arm. 'You've got to overturn it!'

He angrily swipes my hand away. 'I made the deal! And an integral part of it was his agreement to call off the dogs he'd unleashed on you!'

'But we could have found him and—'

'Novak! I've been to too many funerals recently!' I've never seen Jeremy Simmonds this angry. 'Miss Winters'. Gerry Whittaker's. Claudette's. I didn't want the next one to be yours. And if you think that makes me weak . . . if it makes you hate me . . . well, join the queue.'

To my right, I see the hearse pull up to the church.

'Time to bury the dead,' Simmonds mutters, and hurries away from me.

77

I'm momentarily alone with Sophie at the wake and ask her, 'Have you been honest with me?'

She replies, 'I've never lied to you.'

'That's not quite the same thing. What haven't you told me?' She holds my stare but bites her lower lip. I add, 'Is it a lot?'

'It's a lot.'

'Sophie, you can tell me anything. And if you're ever in any kind of trouble, I'm here for you. Every time.'

'Really?'

'You know I am! Why didn't you tell me about whatever it is? Are you in some kind of danger?'

'Me, here now? No. My immortal soul, unbound from my corporeal body and co-eternal with Almighty God?' She nods. 'Yeah. That's in trouble.'

'OK. Let's talk after the meeting, yeah?'

'Marc.'

'Yeah?'

She pauses and, in this moment, Stacey and Frank arrive back at our table, laden with drinks.

'It's a *lot*.'

Stacey asks, 'What's a lot?'

'It doesn't matter,' I tell her.

We're in the White Swan, a cosy little pub in south-west London with pretty views across the Thames. It's one of those boozers that dates back to the 1600s and its rooms and layout are charming but higgledy-piggledy, as if its architect kept forgetting what he was doing and couldn't be bothered to check his notes. It's warm, but not too warm, and my second pint of Neck Oil, polished off a few moments ago, is starting to hit the spot. This could be an all-afternooner. But first we've got some business to get out of the way.

I'd sat next to Frank at Claudette's funeral and Sophie and Stacey met us here, at the wake, just a few minutes after we'd arrived. I tell them, 'I know what the Court is. And I know why it's so powerful and so secret.'

Frank says, 'Well, crack on with it, lad!'

Stacey adds, 'Aye, don't keep us in suspense.'

'Julia Grant told me the Romanov Code and all the Imperial treasures were only a small part of something bigger. The Dresden White Diamond, the Ivory Coast Crown Jewels, the Patiala Necklace, the Nazi Gold Train . . . In fact, priceless historical riches have been going missing throughout history. The Lost Inca gold, the Great Bell of Dhammazedi, the Treasure of Amaro Pargo, the Sceptre of Dagobert, the Three Brothers, the Crimson Angel, the Kruger Millions . . . it's staggering. And I asked Julia why so many of mankind's great treasures are missing. And she told me I was asking the wrong question.'

Stacey interrupts, 'What did he mean?'

'She said the question was wrong. So, the implication is obvious. It's wrong because all those things I've just listed, and hundreds more artefacts besides . . . they're not missing.'

78

Sophie frowns. 'But we know they are!' she insists. 'We know they existed and that they were either stolen or simply vanished!'

'Sure,' I agree. 'And some of it, like Kruger's gold, might have simply been melted down or broken up. But why take something as valuable as, say, the Irish Crown Jewels, stolen in the early days of the twentieth century, and then break them up into something worth infinitely less? It just wouldn't make sense. If you want to steal a bunch of diamonds, you could easily knock over a high-street jewellers. There has to have been a reason why the significant items were taken.'

I look at Frank. He remains silent.

I continue, 'That reason is the Court. A group of people with immeasurable wealth and influence. They exist around the world, and have done for centuries. To these people, members of the aristocracy are commoners. It's hard to stress how rarefied the Court is. They're supremely powerful, and their aversion to publicity is absolute.'

Sophie asks, 'But what do they do?'

I reply, 'The Court isn't an organisation as such. It's more a strata of global society. They'd see themselves as the top billionth of the world's population. An echelon as opposed to an establishment. Its numbers are very, very limited. Its might is very, very robust.'

Frank says, 'What else did you learn about them?'

'Not a huge amount. I only scraped the surface. Helen Merrydale is the head of the Romanov Foundation and their search for the Imperial treasure over the years is the only reason she knows anything about the Court. She told me what she knows, but there's obviously more to uncover. The point is, members of the Court will inevitably have some of the Tzar's jewels and, more than likely, the Romanov Code itself. But I'm not sure how far that gets us. We can't organise a meeting with the Court. That's not the way it works. And even if we could, how could we leverage anything out of them? What do we have that they would want?' I take a sip of my Neck Oil. Look across the four faces in front of me. 'Thoughts?'

Frank replies immediately. 'We need to drop this.'

'I thought you said you were with me.'

'I am, lad. That's why I'm begging you to just walk away.'

Stacey says, 'Come on, Frank! You obviously know something we don't. Share it with the group, man.'

'Many, many years ago,' he tells us quietly, 'I started out on my journey, like we all do, I suppose. Full of hope and swagger and ideals. And I'm not blowing my own trumpet, but I did well. I was working on a big national in my early twenties. By my mid-twenties . . .' He smiles. 'I thought I was the King of Fleet Street.'

Sophie gently asks, 'What happened?'

'I was writing a piece about why prime ministers sometimes institute a complete change of approach on a given policy. Not just a tweak or even an overall change. More a complete reversal of ideology. The weird thing was, although we can discern the change, it's never reported as such. Or, occasionally, it comes to light that a PM or a minister has done something utterly outrageous. Wasted billions. Transferred millions to a friend's business for goods that weren't needed. You know the kind of thing.'

'Aye,' Stacey replies. 'Only too well.'

'And the more I looked into it . . . Well, I stumbled across the Court. You know what I found out about them? Nothing! Just that they exist. But that one piece of knowledge . . . Within twenty-four hours, my career was in tatters. I was persona non grata in London and it was made clear that I was lucky to be alive and I should drop any idea of following up the piece, or my luck wouldn't hold.'

As Frank takes a mouthful of beer, I ask, 'So what happened?'

'I was banished to the regions. No bugger would touch me. Then someone took a gamble. Ended up working on the *Blackpool Chronicle*. It was the start of my comeback. In the intervening decades, I've covered some of the biggest stories of the day. And maybe a handful of times I've detected the Court's influence. Unreported. Unverifiable. But undeniable.'

Sophie says, 'And what did you do on those occasions?'

'I'm not proud of it. But I looked the other way. Look, we don't need to find the Tzar's lost treasure. We sure as hell don't owe the Romanov Foundation anything. If we want to live, we drop this.'

Nobody replies.

'The thing is—' I begin.

'Excuse me. Could we possibly have a quick word with you?'

The man cutting in looks to be in his thirties. Tall, lean, angular. He's wearing a black suit and tie just like me and Frank, but something tells me he wasn't at the funeral.

I shrug. 'Sure.'

I'm English, so if someone politely asks me for a 'quick word', that's my default response, even if I am engaged in a private conversation in the middle of a wake. I'd probably give the same reply if I was about to be wheeled into theatre for open-heart surgery.

'Thanks. This way, please.'

That's unexpected, but I assure everyone at the table that I'll be right back and follow the interloper downstairs, where he has a similarly dressed colleague waiting. 'If we could just step outside for a moment?'

The White Swan is so close to the Thames that at high tide its rear pub garden becomes partially submerged by the river. It's not unusual to see waiters wading through the waters to collect dead glasses. And although it's not quite that bad at this time of the afternoon, as we nudge through tipsy mourners, I see the Thames is relatively high and a boat bobs on the gentle waves just a few feet away from the last row of tables.

One of the men says, 'I'm afraid you're going to get your shoes wet.' He unbuttons his jacket so I can see its designer label and his Glock G43. I'm not massively impressed by either.

'Fine. But you could have told me. I'd have brought my pint.'

So now I'm in the back of what is technically a yacht. I recognise the vessel as an Iguana Commuter, but only because a former client of mine used to swear by them. About thirty feet long with a small cabin at the for'ard and wrap-around seating at the stern, its top speed is fifty knots, and even pre-owned, you wouldn't get a lot of change back from half a mill. More importantly, it's rocketing me up the Thames, leaving the pub and my plans for a boozy few hours with Frank and friends in its wake.

But, hey, I'm wedged between two men wearing Hugo Boss suits in the back of a sleek, strangely beautiful piece of machinery. Sometimes it's hard to know if you're being kidnapped, but if that is what's happening, at least it's an upmarket kidnaping.

We bank sharp starboard to avoid a tug, weave in between a couple of tourist boats and, with a clear run ahead, surge forward at full speed. I'd have to have been dead for a fortnight not to be galvanised by this turn of events. I feel fresh, cold air buffeting against my face and wonder what's waiting for me at the end of the ride. It has to be about a case. People warning me off the Court? Someone wanting me to delve deeper into the Romanovs' riches? Something to do with the Sandy Paige job?

Don't know. Don't care. Because, let's be honest, sometimes a little mystery can be good for the soul.

The man stands in solitude on the bank, smoking a cigarette and glancing at the boat just enough to suggest he's waiting for me. He's diminutive. A little over five feet tall, he's bald from the eyebrows upwards but sports a black pencil moustache. I can see from here that his grey suit is from the kind of shop where assistants use phrases like *forward fitting* and *skeleton baste*.

The captain presses a button on the touchscreen control panel and I hear the soft whir of lithium-powered hydraulics. Underneath the vessel, two side panels are opening and a pair of tank tracks slide gently into the water. Of course, as we hit land, they're fully extended, meaning we can literally drive from the Thames up onto the riverbank. There's a slight jolt as we leave the water, but nothing that would have caused me to have spilt a drop of my Neck Oil if I'd brought it along. The boat's deep V bow rises high, as if saluting terra firma, then falls as we move from the incline of the bank to flatter ground.

Across the way, Windsor, its castle and riverside buildings are easily visible, but I can only see three people on this stretch of countryside. The smoker with the thin moustache and, several paces behind him, two men dressed like the guys who picked me up at the pub.

The captain presses another button and the boat's wide metal ladder emerges and smoothly drops to the ground. The individual who initially approached me points to the stern. I stand to attention and salute both my kidnappers. They regard me with bafflement tinged with hostility. One of them nods to the figure on the bank.

The other says, 'He's dangerous, so you'd better behave.'

'If ever I do Tinder, I'm *so* having that line in my profile.'

No reaction.

'Tough crowd,' I mutter as I haul myself over the side of the Iguana. I step gingerly down the ladder and saunter towards the guy in the expensive suit. I take out my phone. 'Do you mind if I let my friends know where I am?'

He moves his open palm across his face as if swatting away the question. 'Don't be such a child!' His accent sounds English with maybe a tiny touch of Russian mixed in. He circles me, studying my appearance in the same way I imagine a potential buyer would scrutinise a heifer at a livestock market. 'Mr Marc Novak . . . Better looking than the photographs in your file suggest.'

'If ever I do Tinder, I'm so having that line in my profile.'

Still doesn't get a laugh.

'And you're taller. Your shoulders broader. But I expected a posher accent.'

'Well, I got kicked out of Roedean after my second term.'

'Roedean? Isn't that a girls' school?'

'Why do you think they kicked me out?'

'Ha!' He looks delighted. Flicks the last inch of his cigarette into the Thames. 'Your file mentions your humour! Analysis suggests it's often a diversionary tactic, sometimes a technique employed to buy yourself time and occasionally it's intended to throw your opponents off-guard.'

'What else is in the file?'

He shrugs. 'The usual. That nasty business with Precious Weeks. The Venice Case. Operation Sutekh. There's the mystery of what happened to your partner, Stewart. And your investigation into the death of Diana, of course.'

'All my greatest hits. So, if you've got the album, why did you want to see me live? Why did you have me brought here?'

'Come! Walk with me!'

He starts strolling along the riverside and I join him. His two bodyguards follow at an indiscreet distance.

'My name,' he tells me, 'is Aleksandr Antonov.'

'No, it isn't,' I tell him. 'Your name is Maksim Bulatov. Russian Intelligence. You flit between the FSB, the SVR and even the FSO. So, either you're very good at your job or workmates find you so annoying you keep getting moved on. The fact you've been awarded the Medal of Ushakov and the Hero of Russia Gold Star suggests it's the former. You've been in the UK on and off for decades. A dacha in Rublevka and a townhouse in Mayfair, I imagine. Known to be ruthless, pragmatic but unusually fair. You let Möller walk away from that bloody affair in Copenhagen, simply because you had a gentlemen's agreement.'

'I'm impressed.'

'You're not the only one who can read files, Colonel.'

'I'll have to update yours, Mr Novak. Your knowledge of Intelligence personnel is greater than we recognised.'

'Good idea. And don't forget to mention my good looks and broad shoulders.'

He stops and pulls out a packet of cigarettes. Extracts one. Lights it. Takes a drag and exhales. The smell of the smoke is noxious. 'I have an offer for you.'

'I'm listening.'

'I want you to find the Romanov Code.'

'Join the queue.'

'When you have it, give it to me. You'll be well paid and any expenses you incur will be settled. I'll make you a rich man, Mr Novak.'

'One teeny problem, Colonel. I haven't a clue where it is.'

'We know you met with Ekaterina, of course. And Thomas Maughan. Also the woman known as Julia Grant. We know you've been digging. Searching. Consider this to be a little encouragement.'

'Ekaterina told me the Romanov Code was Excalibur. Julia refused to talk about it. I mentioned it to Maughan and he tried to kill me. Is it really as powerful as people think?'

'It's a legend. And they're always powerful until the truth behind them is exposed. But in this case . . . You see, *sometimes* the strength of the legend is so strong it can lend force to the heart of the object that started the legend. It becomes self-perpetuating.'

'You presumably believe in its potency?'

'I believe in the potency of the order that commanded me to retrieve it. But . . .' He gazes across the Thames. 'Perhaps we shouldn't be too dismissive about these things.' He nods towards the castle. 'One of that place's former residents, your Queen Elizabeth I, maintained close trade relations with Tzar Ivan IV.'

'Ivan the Terrible?'

'Quite so. They regularly corresponded and it is known from their communications that he believed the paraphernalia of royalty wasn't simply symbolic. He felt it gave him actual, physical powers.'

'Well, maybe he should have been known as Ivan the Gullible.'

'The empire he founded was vast and feared by its neighbours. And the last time I looked, it lasted longer than the British's palsied attempt at global dominion. That's because we Russians are more resolute than you hand-wringing islanders. I want the Romanov Code, Mr Novak. You must acquire it for me.'

'I can't help you. Even if I wanted to, I—'

'That would be a pity. You come from a large family.'

'Is that a threat?'

'Yes. Yes, it most definitely is. And you have many friends. The intrepid journalist, Frank Harvey. The fascinating Mrs Grace. Even the remarkable Reggie DeLuca. Oh, and the worthless Stacey Smith.'

'Colonel.'

'Yes, Mr Novak?'

'If you ever say anything disparaging about that lady again, I'll ram your cigarette down your throat and I'll tear out your fucking heart while I'm there.'

He studies my eyes. Takes another drag on his biological weapon of a cigarette. 'Yes, I rather think you would.' He smiles. 'Forgive me.' He half turns to face the river and, as if musing to himself, says, 'Old Father Thames. So pretty. So calm.' He gives me a sideways look. 'About fifty people die in its dark waters every year. Did you know that?' His voice becomes harder. 'You have one week to find and deliver the Romanov Code. Should you fail to do so, you will be unharmed. But everyone you love, or even faintly care about, will be slaughtered. That isn't a threat, or even an area for negotiation, Mr Novak. It is a fact. It is a promise that my people have the resources to carry out.'

It's clear he's not bluffing, but he wants to make sure I completely understand his terms.

'Every person who means anything to you will be butchered if you do not find and deliver to me, the Romanov Code, within exactly seven days. And the countdown begins . . .' He glances at his wristwatch. 'Now.'

-80-

Lazarus's Story

At first, there was horror. But horror is a known thing. It's a kind of pain, initially overwhelming. Almost unbearable. Yet it must be borne by the sufferer and a sense of horror in itself cannot kill. It subsides with reason. So as he lay still and evaluated and grasped, the overwhelm shrank. He understood. The unknown had intensified his dread, but by gauging his situation, he was able to loosen the grip of appalment.

The terror and dread lingered, of course. He was trapped and alone and would possibly die in this coffin-like space. But he knew this. The knowledge acted as a kind of absolute. It was more than a reminder of his continued existence and assurance that he was not yet dead. It was an insistence of it. At length, he gleaned the irony of the assertion. The fact he would probably die very soon was a vivid confirmation that he remained alive. And this truth dictated that hope also remained. Such reasoning was neither optimistic nor capricious. It struck him as a simple piece of irrefutable logic.

He screamed and shouted until his throat burnt, but he knew this confinement was soundproof. He worried about oxygen. Thought back to the thing's construction and recalled that micro-vents below it allowed a tiny flow of air. If he was going to perish here, it would not be through asphyxiation. Terminal dehydration, he deduced, would end his life. Recognising this made him thirsty, but as the days passed, so did the feeling. Its absence surprised him. He enjoyed mild euphoria and heard himself laughing. Somewhere, he knew this was caused by a lack of fluids.

Thedelusions were harder to classify. Yes, he understood dehydration caused hallucinations, but could they also be attributed to a kind of insanity? The product of his abject dismay and helplessness?

He thought back to all the people he'd ever wronged and felt justified and wild, intoxicating righteousness. He had been consigned to this lonely, lingering death, which proved that any god or gods that governed our plane were not merciful, benign forces. They were like him. Self-serving and aware that cruelty is only punishable when those demanding penitence and reprimands are more powerful than those they seek to rebuke.

His sole crime, he reasoned, was letting the woman confine him. The events and sins that led to this incarceration were irrelevant. The people he had damaged were as inconsequential as the insects they had crushed underfoot when walking across a lawn, or the bacteria they happily killed when taking antibiotics, simply to feel well again. He had wanted to feel well. Their suffering had been a side-effect he could not be held responsible for.

He seethed about his victims. He regretted not causing them more hurt. He laughed. They were here with him, now. Jostling him. Tugging his elbow. Asking him questions. Apologising. Apologising again and again. He covered his ears with the palms of his hands and yelled at them to find their own coffins and he slept. Awoke. Became unable to tell which state was which. Until, eventually, the delirium faded. The hallucinations left him, as if they'd grown bored of his company.

And his clarity of thought returned. The old absolute remained. He was alive but would die. He neither embraced the fact, nor shunned it. He thought about nothing and experienced a kind of peace that reminded him of childhood and made him weep.

When the light came, it was immense and sudden. He believed it was death and met the sensation stoically. But aside from the light, there was cold air. He could feel it on his face. A form of passive interaction, like the way it made the tears on his face feel fresh again.

He blinked. Tried to speak, but the movement of his mouth pulled open cuts on his dried lips. He no longer understood what was happening and the old absolutes became instantly worthless. His instinct insisted he had passed over. He had survived death itself and—

Oh. Maybe not.

Someone was peering down on him. A woman in a mint-green jumper and cardigan and an akoya matinee necklace. Surely even the most unlikely god or goddess wouldn't greet the newly deceased wearing a twinset and pearls?

Or perhaps it was time to radically revise his view of the afterlife.

He managed to murmur, 'What is this?'

And the goddess smiled. And the goddess spoke.

'Mr Gross,' said Sophie Grace. 'This is your lucky day.'

-81-

Two hours earlier

I arrive back at the White Swan hours after I left, but most of the mourners are still here, drinking and reminiscing. The wake has evolved into a get-together. Slightly raucous. Very emotional. As I saunter through the downstairs bar, Émilie and her brother are laughing about something, although her smudged mascara implies she's also been weeping. She spots me and points downwards in the time-honoured way of saying she wants me to come over. I make a gesture suggesting I'll be five minutes and she mirrors it to convey both acceptance and a sense that she's giving me no longer than five minutes.

I jog up the staircase and find Frank, Stacey and Sophie clustered around the same table as earlier. At least I assume there's a table somewhere between them. If there is, it's hidden below over a dozen or so empty glasses and a crumpled sheet of empty crisp packets.

Frank spots me and roars, 'What the hell have you been up to?'

'I was kidnapped.'

Stacey says, 'Bloody hell, Novak! You'll do anything to get out of buying your round!'

I retake my seat. 'I'm serious.'

'Shit!' She plonks her pint glass on the table. 'I thought you were joking!'

There's a barrage of *'Are you all right?'* type questions, which I interrupt with, 'I'm fine, I'm fine.'

Sophie asks, 'What happened?'

'Well, I've good news and bad news.'

Frank says, 'Let's start with the bad.'

'Fair enough. The bad news is, if I don't find and hand over the Romanov Code within one week, the Russian Secret Service will murder everyone at this table and slaughter my entire family.'

There's a horrified silence. Sophie breaks it with, 'What's the good news?'

I get to my feet. Look at my three friends. 'It's my round,' I tell them. 'What's everyone on?'

*

When I get back to our table, I dish out the drinks and recount what happened with Colonel Bulatov. I leave no one in any doubt that the Russian will make good on his threat if we don't find the Romanov Code.

'Sorry to sound like the newbie,' Stacey begins, 'but how do we go about this? The book's been missing for over a century and we're supposed to locate it and seize it in less than seven days? It feels impossible.'

'It's not impossible,' I tell her. 'We now know a little about the Court. It's probable that one of its number holds the Romanov Code. Helen told me that, very occasionally, some of their ranks convene. The meeting could take the form of a party, but it's not unusual for business to be conducted at the same time.'

Stacey says, 'Some form of bartering, you mean?'

'Exactly. We've got two problems. *We* can't just trigger a meeting. We've got no idea who's part of the Court and what their etiquette is for these things.'

Sophie leans forward. 'Look, if bartering is done at these parties, if they're buying and selling lost masterpieces, isn't it logical to assume that such meetings could be called by, say, crooked billionaire businessmen with an interest in making money out of stolen treasure?'

Frank gives her a withering look. 'Aye. But do you happen to know any crooked billionaire businessmen with an interest in making money out of stolen treasure?'

As if oblivious to his sarcasm, Sophie beams her best smile. 'As a matter of fact, I do!'

I narrow my eyes. 'But could you convince him to convene a Court meeting?'

'Oh,' Sophie replies. 'I can be very persuasive.'

Stacey chips in, 'You said we've got two problems.'

'Yeah, no matter who we know that could help us get an audience with the Court, we'll need something to barter with. We can't just turn up with a box of chocolates and a bottle of Prosecco. We need something that makes us look serious. Something that we can credibly suggest we can trade for the Romanov Code.'

'You're right,' says Sophie. 'That is a problem.'

'One of the Romanov gems would be ideal,' Frank opines.

I shrug. 'Yeah, I'm sure I had one somewhere. I'll check down the back of my settee.'

He smiles. 'Cheeky bugger.' Takes a mouthful of beer. 'Sophie. If I got hold of the right bait, do you think your contact could set up the meeting?'

She nods. '*Absolutement, mon chéri.*'

'Then let's do this thing,' he urges. 'And do it fast.'

'Whoa, Frank,' I say. 'Are you telling me you can get your hands on some of the Romanovs' crown jewels?'

'I am.'

'At the risk of appearing over-curious,' I reply, 'how in God's name are you going to manage that?'

He takes a sip of his drink. 'You just leave that to me, lad.'

Frank's Story
Blackpool, England. July, 1981

The editor of the *Blackpool Chronicle* rested his cigarette on the edge of his desk, stood up and said, 'How are you, lad? Are you well?'

'Fair to middlin', Jock. How about yourself?'

The two men shook hands.

'Not so bad, Frank, not so bad. Welcome to the *Chronicle* and all that. Take a seat.'

Frank remained standing. 'Do we have to do this here? There must be somewhere we can get a drink. You can do the whole *best team in Blackpool* thing over a beer or two, can't you? It has to be time to . . .' He glanced at his watch and tutted. 'Bloody battery's gone again.'

The editor frowned. Gestured to Frank's watch. 'What the hell is that thing?'

'This, my friend, is a Casio C-80. LED lighting, built-in calendar, digital stopwatch and' – he lifted his wrist – 'fully functioning calculator.' A proud nod. 'You're looking at the future, Jock.'

'But it doesn't work?'

'Like I said, you're looking at the future.' He grinned. 'The light's an absolute bugger when it comes to draining the battery.'

'Aye, well, my old wind-up tells me it's half past four in the afternoon. Pubs won't even be open for another hour, Frank. And besides, that's not the way we work anymore! This is 1981! Times are changing!' Exasperated, he sank back into his seat, jammed his cigarette into the corner of his mouth and pulled out a bottle of Bell's from his top desk drawer. 'You drink in the office until your work's done and only *then* do you slope off to the pub.'

Frank shook his head. 'You're going soft, mate. You're—'

'Sit down!' The words were spoken with a force that took Frank aback.

'All right, all right.' He took a seat. 'Don't panic, Captain Main—'

'No, it's not all right, Harvey! I took a bloody big gamble hiring you, lad! You made a mess of it on Fleet Street by poking your nose into the wrong scandals and your oh-so-promising career went arse-about-tit. Don't forget that! And don't think you're doing us a favour working on a local rag! We've got a good readership and this is a grand little number! There won't be any holding hands under the table!'

'Jock.'

'What?'

'Piss off.'

Frank stood up, stepped from the office into the newsroom and didn't bother to shut the door. He pulled a packet of Camel Straights from his pocket and lit up. 'Blondie!'

A fair-haired woman, stood by the office's enormous, state-of-the-art fax machine, replied, 'Are you talking to me?'

Frank exhaled a nimbus of smoke. 'No, I was talking to Debbie Harry on the news desk, but you'll have to do. What's the best pub in this town these days?'

*

As he walked into reception and hurried towards the exit, Frank heard someone call his name. 'Mr Harvey?'

'Yeah?' He paused. Three people were hovering at the reception desk. An old guy. Mid to late eighties. A younger man, maybe early sixties.

'We spoke on the phone last night.'

Frank guessed this third man was about his own age, late twenties, early thirties maybe.

'Sorry to mess you about. I've just been kicked off the paper.'

'You only started today.'

'I work fast. Go on up, though. Tell your story to the editor. His name's Jock. He's a good reporter. Lousy editor, but good reporter. See you!' He opened the door to leave.

'No, wait! You don't understand. We want you to cover our story, yeah. But not for the *Chronicle*. We want you to write a book about it.'

Frank hesitated. 'Nah, not for me. Sorry. Good luck, though, chaps.'

The oldest of the three men approached Frank. He walked with a stick and wore a grey, full-length, cashmere coat and a black homburg. Something in his bearing made Frank pause. He spoke with a slight Russian accent. 'Mr Harvey, this is all very fortuitous. Yes?'

'What is?'

'Well, our story will take maybe fifty minutes to tell. The public houses will be open in around an hour. Perfect timing, wouldn't you say? It's as though fate has brought us together in this propitious moment!'

The old man smiled and Frank laughed. 'Fair enough. Do you know anywhere we can chat?'

'It's a beautiful day,' said Leonard Alexander. 'Why don't we take a stroll along the seafront?'

-83-

Frank's Story (cont.)
Blackpool, England. July, 1981

It was a sunny day but a cold one. A thin, biting wind blew through the Lancashire streets, so Frank and his three companions didn't make it to the seafront. They reached Binns – a large, beige department store close to the promenade – and Leonard suggested they visit the shop's cafe.

'Wouldn't have thought it would be your kind of place, Mr Alexander.'

'I like English tearooms. And they serve the best toasted currant teacakes in the north of England in this place. By the way, you must call me Leonard.'

They made their way up the escalators to the cafe, armed themselves with plastic 'wooden' trays, grabbed snacks from the counter and found a corner table. Frank settled for a coffee. Pulled out his Camel Straights and plucked one from the packet. 'So, what's the story, gentlemen?'

'First, let me introduce my son, Georgy.'

Frank shook hands with the man in his sixties. 'Please call me George. My dad's sentimental.' He spoke with fondness and no recrimination in his voice.

'And this is my grandson, Marius.'

The younger of the Alexanders gave Frank a friendly, informal salute. 'My friends call me Mya. My middle name is Yuri and so M-Y-A.'

'I get it. So how can I help?'

'Before we begin,' George said, 'I think it's only fair to tell you we're already talking to two other authors about potentially writing this extraordinary true account.'

Marius said, 'My grandad has an amazing story. He was there when the Russian royal family were shot. He was in the very room when it happened.'

Frank lit a cigarette. 'I'm guessing the Romanovs didn't think it was that amazing.'

'My grandson has a romantic view of history,' Leonard replied.

'And you have a realistic one?'

'I believe it's only history when it's been forgotten by those who were there.'

'Anyway,' Marius continued, 'he found a gemstone in the house where the massacre took place. He called it the Red Diamond. Have you heard of it?'

'Vaguely.'

'It allowed him to build our family's fortune. Long story short – I'm opening a nightclub in Blackpool. I think it could be more successful than Brian London's 007 ever was! And I'm going to call mine The Red Diamond. I want my grandad's story told so it will drum up some publicity for the place. Give it a bit of history. Lend it some weight. And it's a cool name, don't you think?'

George interjected, 'It's *much* more than that, Mr Harvey! My father's story *should* be told. Not just for him. But for those no longer here to tell it.'

The older man nodded. 'Maria, Yuri . . . even Pasha.'

Frank took a pull on his cigarette. 'All right, gents. Why don't you tell me your story from the beginning?'

*

The editor of the *Blackpool Chronicle* was beginning to wish he'd acted on Frank's suggestion, but instead found himself lying on the phone to his boss. 'Yes, I know you said I was taking a risk, sir, but Harvey is settling in already . . . it's like he's never been away.'

A minute later, he pulled out his bottle of Bell's, took a mouthful and walked to his office door.

'Do any of you lot know where Frank Harvey might be heading?'

The woman with fair hair raised her hand.

*

Leonard finished his story. George patted the back of his father's hand. Marius leant across and squeezed his shoulder. Frank lit yet another cigarette.

'Well, first of all, Leonard, I'm so sorry for what you've had to endure. Losing your wife like that. Losing so much. Do you regret taking the diamond? Do you mind if I ask?'

'I do not mind. Do I regret taking it? I don't know. Pasha stayed in Russia and lost his wife. We escaped. Yet I lost Maria. So . . . It's like that puzzle which is all the rage at the moment. The Rubik's Cube, I think it's called. One twist changes not just one aspect, it throws everything into disarray. There were many twists that led to Yuri's death, to Maria's death, to Pasha's suicide. Changing that one thing – my acquisition of the diamond – putting back that one twist alone wouldn't restore the cube to perfection.'

George murmured, 'Well said, Dad.'

Marius asked, 'So, what do you think, Frank? How would you handle telling my grandad's story? One writer said a first-person narrative was the way to go. Another thought telling it as though it was a collection of short stories that ultimately weaves into one narrative ... What would you do? How would you tell the story?'

Frank looked at Leonard. 'I wouldn't. I wouldn't touch that story, to be honest with you. And my advice, for what it's worth, is that if I were you, I'd walk away from it.'

Leonard said, 'Go on, Mr Harvey.'

'The Red Diamond has brought you a lot of wealth. But it's cost you, Leonard. Every time you've looked to it, it's cost you.' He paused. 'Marius, if you call your nightclub The Red Diamond and launch a book to lend its name some kind of lustre ... I wouldn't be surprised if it burns down on its opening night.'

The youngest Alexander shook his head. 'I can't believe I'm hearing this! You believe in curses? In the supernatural?'

'I don't believe in God and I don't believe in the Devil. But I believe in good and I believe in evil. And I certainly believe in luck.'

Marius retorted, 'You make your own luck.'

'I believe,' Leonard stated, 'that that is exactly what Mr Harvey is saying.'

Frank bowed his head to the older man as a sign of respect, thanks and affirmation. He broke the ensuing silence with, 'I'm sorry to have wasted your time, gentlemen.'

'Yeah, well, thanks a lot, Uri Geller,' Marius grumbled. 'You could have told us straight off that you thought some kind of black magic governs our lives!'

George snapped, 'Marius! Mr Harvey is the first writer who hasn't asked about fees and royalties and just given us his true thoughts. Apologise!'

Frank cut in, 'That's really not necessary. I can understand why you're pissed off, Mya. If it's still OK to call you Mya?'

Marius gave an unexpected smile. Shrugged. 'Sure.'

Leonard said, 'I apologise on behalf of my grandson.'

'Please don't,' Frank replied. 'Hard to believe, but I can fly off the handle, too. Look, Mya. Open your nightclub. Make loads of cash. Just don't call it The Red Diamond. Please, gentlemen, next time you use that diamond, make sure it's for the right reason. And when that time comes, maybe it'll be the right time to recount your story to the world.'

*

A lifetime later, Marius Alexander, now in his seventies and wearing his late grandfather's old full-length, cashmere coat and homburg, walked through the windy streets of Elephant and Castle. He strode along Newington Causeway until he reached the Mercato Metropolitano – a vast collection of bars, cafes and street-food vendors. Much of the place was outside, giving the MM a sense of being part-market. Communal. Artisanal. Marius smiled.

'Mya!'

He turned around and saw Frank Harvey approaching him. The two old friends embraced. Marius slapped the other man's upper arm. 'You were right! My grandfather would have loved this place!'

'Let me get us a drink in!'

'No, no, no. You bought the meal when we met up last month. Let me take care of this.'

They took a table in the French Corner and Marius poured them both a glass of Cabernet Sauvignon. They clinked glasses.

Frank said, '*Za drooz-boo!*'

'*Za vas*!' Marius sipped his wine. 'So, my friend, how can I help you? You sounded so serious on the phone!'

'When we first met . . . God, so many years ago . . . Do you remember, I told you, urged you really, that the next time you use the Red Diamond, it should be for the right reason.'

'I remember, Frank.'

'Well, Mya . . . I believe that time has come.'

-84-

Two days after meeting at the White Swan, Sophie phones me early and breathlessly states, 'Can't talk long! Got the school run! But Damian Gross has confirmed that the Court has agreed to a one-to-one with you. There's apparently a meeting later this week in Austria. You'll be invited. How are you holding up?'

'Sophie, you can't just tell me you've somehow convinced Gross to help us out with the Court and leave it at that! How did you persuade him? We need to have that talk.'

'Lordy, Marc. Whenever anyone says *we need to talk,* it's a sure-fire way of making the other person reluctant to utter a word.'

'I just want to know the truth about you.'

'Does it matter?'

'To me. Yes.'

'But why should ... Hold on a moment ...' I hear her addressing someone else. 'I don't know where your sports bag is, darling. Every night, I ask you if you have everything ready for school, and every night, you say *yes*, so whose fault is it if you're late because you can't find your kit? And what's that on the sofa? Exactly.' A pause. 'Are you there, Marc?'

'Still here. Everything OK?'

'Just Betsy being a bother.'

'It must be hard without Christian.'

'I understand why you want to know everything, I really do. When this is all over, we'll sit down and I'll reveal all. So to speak. Pinky promise.'

'I appreciate everything you've done for me, Sophie.' I pause. 'Whatever secrets you're harbouring, you'll still be a very special friend to me. Nothing will change that. Ever.'

She sounds horrified to hear this. 'Oh, no!'

'I mean in a platonic way!'

'Are you all right?'

'Yes! I just meant—'

'Not you, Marc. Thomas! What were you thinking? Marc, I'm going to have to go. Thomas has just thrown up on the Aga. Literally on the Aga! What would I say if I wasn't a lady?'

'I have no idea. Speak soon. Thanks again.'

Frank's already promised me I can use the Red Diamond as my 'in'. My item which, ostensibly, I'll be there to barter. But if the meeting is later this week, it means I'll be cutting it fine if I'm to convince the Court to part with the Romanov Code and deliver it to Colonel Bulatov within the seven-day window he gave me.

It's a deeply unsettling thought and when I hear a knock at my front door, I'm grateful for the distraction.

'Coming!'

I walk through to my hall and swing open the door. Stacey is stood on the step. 'Grab your toothbrush and a change of clothes!'

'Morning, Miss Smith. Any particular reason why?'

'Because we're going to the Amalfi Coast and our flight leaves in less than two hours.'

'Not sure I can spare the time for a break in Italy, right now.'

'This is strictly business, Novak.'

'What's in the Sorrento Peninsula that's so important?'

As she barges past me, hurrying into my house, she replies, 'The truth.'

We're hurtling down the A3 in my Morris Marina, and for the fifth time since leaving Guildford, Stacey demands, 'Can't you make this thing go any faster?'

'As I keep explaining, yes, I can. This car has been completely reconditioned and can match most modern vehicles. But I choose not to. We'll be there with plenty of time to spare. Anyway, you've got a nerve! You drive an Austin Morris J4! Want that valued, you don't go to a garage, you take it to the *Antiques Roadshow*.' We hang a left and filter onto the M25. 'So, are you going to tell me why we're off to the Amalfi Coast?'

'Thought you were looking a bit peaky and could do with a splash of sun.'

'Wouldn't that be lovely?'

'Remember when we all met up in the theatre cafe and you told us everything Ekaterina had told you about her time as an agent?'

I nod. 'Sure. One of the other low-level operatives shot his mouth off about transferring Romanov treasure. He ended up dead under a bridge.'

'The Ponte Milvio.'

'Well remembered. It spooked the hell out of Ekaterina and she got out as soon as she could.'

'Well, I did a bit of research using the dates she gave us. Some guy did hang himself, just like she said. Newspaper reports name him as Taras Zvyagintsev.'

I glance across at Stacey. 'That fits. She said he'd given the name Taras, but she'd assumed he'd been lying.'

'Aye, liars always assume everyone else is telling porkies.'

'Well, it's good to know Mr Pitkin's real name, or at least his legend, but I don't see how—'

'Let me finish! Ekaterina said he died, right?'

'Right.'

'And yeah, he did. But there's more to it. This kid, Zvyagint-sev, he was found under the bridge by an officer in the *Polizia di Stato* who hoisted him up. He was in a bad way, but this Italian copper got him in an ambulance and travelled with him to the hospital, where, sadly, he died from a heart attack.'

'This is good stuff! How did you find out about it all?'

'Our Ryan's going out with an Italian lass and I just went online and . . .' She shrugs. 'Pretty much all newspapers are archived on the net these days. She helped out because she'd shrunk his best jeans and wanted to get back into his good books.'

'And so the world turns.'

'Do you want to hear the best bit?'

'He never really liked the jeans and it gave him a great opportunity to pop down the market and get a new pair?'

'About Zvyagintsev, stupid!'

'Oh . . . Yes. Go on!'

'The copper that found him is called Silvio Salucci. He retired years ago and now lives on the Amalfi Coast.'

'I think I see where this is heading.'

'I got in touch and he agreed to speak to us. We're meeting him later today. We're going to talk to the last person who talked to Taras Zvyagintsev, also known as Mr Pitkin. If he did reveal anything about the treasure before he died, we're going to find out what it is.'

-86-

We land in Capodichino Airport a little before 2 p.m., hire a drop-top Mini Cooper from a dealership just outside Naples and by 3 p.m. we're zipping through the Italian sunshine. We hit the Amalfi Coast Road and find it's as picturesque as its reputation suggests. The Tyrrhenian Sea stretches endlessly to our left, whilst the views of the coastal countryside are uniformly stunning.

That said, the reality of tearing along these iconic roads isn't quite like it is in the movies. Progress is slow. On the straighter lanes, trucks and buses rumble along and don't bother to give way, and we're obliged to stop for a donkey in the middle of a street in one village and a flock of sheep wandering through the market square of another. Ironically, we make better time travelling through some of the tightest switchback roads I've ever encountered, where the traffic is sparser.

Stacey bubbles away in a good mood, chatting and laughing as though she hadn't read the memo about her life being in danger. She's great company. Cheeky. Funny. Insightful. She's enthusiastic about everything, from her childhood holidays to her current listening habits. She asks me what I think about true crime. I tell her I'm against it, but it keeps me off the streets. Stacey laughs and insists she meant the genre, not the thing itself. She recommends a podcast called *Piercing the Unknown*, then stops herself. No, that's more about unexplained mysteries. I counter that all mysteries are unexplained, otherwise they wouldn't be mysteries.

She takes me seriously and asks about previous cases. I clam up when she mentions Stewart, but she's sensitive to this and zings off on another topic of conversation. Something about the time she completed the Tromsø Marathon and fell in love with Norway. She's joyful as she recalls running through the early hours ('It never gets dark in summer! Even at night!') and when I ask what time she posted, she shrugs and says she never checked.

Stacey Smith is only a few years older than me, but it feels like she's lived so much more. She seizes life on her own terms and is contemptuous of anyone who tries to curtail that approach. I admire her for it. And yes, it's so different to the way I've done things. I can't help thinking that I'm like one of those competitors in Tromsø. I'm constantly running through the midnight sun, alone in a pack of people, yet completely unwilling to pause.

We hit a rare stretch of straight, empty road. I glance at my friend. She's laughing at another shared memory and I make a mental note to myself: Be More Stacey.

*

We reach Salucci's house towards the end of the afternoon. It's a remarkable building, nestling on a rocky spur that juts far into the ocean. We park up and make our way to the entrance.

Salucci's wife, an Englishwoman called Chloe, meets us at the front door with profuse apologies. 'Silvio has had to collect his mother from town,' she explains. 'I'm so sorry, but he won't be long. Come in! Come in!'

Stacey makes the mistake of complimenting her on her home, and now Chloe insists on showing us both around. To be fair, it's distinctive and interesting. We're told it was originally a maritime tower, but Silvio transformed the property into a stunning villa on three floors – two with terraces that offer incredible views across the ocean. The main space is a broad open area punctuated by pieces of modern art.

Stacey asks, 'Where's the TV?'

'We don't have one.'

'My God,' my friend splutters, 'how do you live?'

Chloe laughs. Next stop on the tour is the library. 'Silvio likes to read. To really immerse himself, you know?'

'I envy him,' I admit.

We're shown into a nursery next. 'The grandkids are toddlers and we don't like them going onto the terraces. So we had the study turned into a nursery.'

'This is more like it,' Stacey enthuses. 'Clutter!'

The room is vast. One corner holds a collection of toys. A scattering of Action Men and some smaller soldiers in the uniform of Roman centurions. A massive teddy bear wearing a tutu and a gaudy crown. A box of footballs, frisbees and racquets. Another corner is home to a mini-trampoline surrounded by crash mats and there's even space for a paint-stained table that's festooned with bright, bold artwork.

Stacey regards it all wistfully. 'It's lovely when they're this age, isn't it?'

Chloe nods. 'Doesn't last long though, does it?'

They exchange glances and I suddenly feel like the odd one out.

Simply to edge back into the conversation, I ask, 'Couldn't you just let them onto the terrace but tell them not to go too near the edge?'

'Really, Novak?' Stacey hoots with laughter. 'You can tell you're not a dad!'

Chloe is a little more temperate. 'I'm afraid that no matter how nice they are, you can't trust children.' She walks into the hallway, adding, 'Come through – I'll show you the dining room!'

I linger in the nursery. Something one of the two women has just said almost triggered a realisation in me. I can't tell what it was – not quite – but someone has just spoken a truth that holds the key to this whole case. Trouble is, I'm damned if I know what it was.

*

We're relaxing on the lower terrace. The weather is bright, the company charming and all would be right with the world, if it wasn't for the fact my friends' lives are all in danger and I'm stuck with a cup of indifferent mocha whilst everyone else is enjoying a proper drink.

Silvio Salucci is in his sixties. He's tall, tanned and rich, but I like him anyway. The four of us sit at a long metal table that's warm to the touch. He drinks Peroni, Stacey and Chloe sip Cervaro della Sala and I'm stuck with coffee. At least it's not as bad as the stuff Simmonds foisted on me. Our host tells us about Taras Zvyagintsev. Turns out Salucci recalls the young man as they met shortly before he swapped policing for international investment trading.

'The poor boy was in so much pain . . . it was terrible to see. It helped me make up my mind – to take up a new profession, you know?'

'What sort of kid did he strike you as, Silvio? Was he rich?'

The Italian considers my question. 'Not rich as in flashy. But I guess he was well-spoken. What my wife would call posh. Why do you ask?'

I'm thinking about something Maughan told me. He'd mentioned Taras having a house in Rome. 'No reason.' My lie is automatic, but the old policeman in Silvio Salucci isn't fooled. He eyes me with interest, but I quickly press on, 'Was there any unexpected upshot from your interaction with the boy?'

He laughs. 'These are strange questions, Marc!'

'I know, but it's important.'

Chloe says, 'Tell him about the woman, Sil.'

Her husband takes a mouthful of beer. 'Yes, that was unexpected! I retired from the service less than six months after accompanying Taras to the hospital. At my farewell party, a woman I didn't know appeared. She was very sweet. German, I think. Anyway, she thanked me for staying with Taras. For being with him in the ambulance.'

Stacey asks, 'What was her name?'

'I have no idea. We spoke for a minute, maybe less. Then she left. The party was already starting to . . .' His fingers circle the air to imply his leaving do was getting crazy. 'But I remember her because she gave me three little gifts.'

As he pauses for another drink, Chloe takes over. 'She gave him a black silk tie. Ever so nice. And a book of poetry she said Taras really enjoyed. How about that! Wasn't that thoughtful? But the third present. That was the strange one. You'll never guess what that was, Marc.'

'I think I can.' I place my cup of coffee on the table. Lean back into my chair. 'It was a tiara.'

Silvio looks flabbergasted. 'How on earth could you know that?'

'Because,' I tell him, 'no how matter how nice they are, you can't trust children.'

Silvio announces, 'I think you are a man with many secrets, Marc.'

'Maybe. But most secrets are just problems glammed up to look mysterious.'

He begins saying something in response, but Chloe spots that I'm distracted. She stands and gently takes her husband by the elbow. 'Come on, Silvio. Let's get a little something for our guests to eat. They must be starving after their trip . . .'

When we're alone, Stacey asks in a loud whisper, 'How the hell did you know that?'

'I should have seen it earlier! Taras was just a kid. Why would anyone trust him with the treasures of the Romanovs? I mean, it wasn't just that he was inexperienced. Ekaterina and Maughan both told me he was gauche and clumsy – that's part of the reason they called him Mr Pitkin.'

'Right. Agreed. He doesn't sound the ideal candidate for such a big job.'

'So what gets him the job? What always gets you the job? Nepotism.'

Stacey ponders this for a moment. 'You think Taras was part of the Court?'

'Come with me!' I begin to lead her through the Saluccis' home. 'Know how to tell a fake diamond from a real one?'

'Test for hardness?'

'Even easier. Hot breath on a diamond or a fake gem will mist over the surface. With a fake, it'll clear after a few seconds. With a diamond, it'll clear immediately.'

We enter the nursery and I stride towards the teddy in a tutu.

'Taras showed Ekaterina photos of the Alexander III Commemorative Fabergé egg. I know what happened to that. He also showed her a photo of the tiara known as the Russian Beauty. A priceless piece of headwear that belonged to the Romanovs long before the massacre at Ipatiev House. Its history was quite blood-free until it ended up the property of Imelda Marcos.'

'The woman with the shoes?'

'The woman with the shoes.' I remove the teddy bear's crown, move it close to my mouth, breathe on one of its sparkling stones and study what happens to its surface. 'The tiara was made for the Empress Alexandra Feodorovna. Much beloved of the Empress Maria. And, funnily enough . . .' The mist from my breath has instantly cleared. 'It's right here.' I pluck the streamers and brightly coloured pieces of cardboard from the headwear, reducing it in both size and gaudiness. As I toss it to Stacey, I say, 'Why don't you try it on?'

She catches it. Places it on her head. 'Is it real?' She looks at herself in a wall mirror.

I join her. 'You're looking at twenty-five natural pearls, God knows how many diamonds, all wrapped up in a piece of history that stretches back almost two centuries. It's real. And it's priceless.'

Stacey stands back as if judging it from a different angle. 'You don't think it's too much, do you?'

*

331

Back in the main living area, I call through to the kitchen. 'Chloe! Silvio! I'm afraid we're going to have to leave!'

They immediately appear and try to dissuade us, but we apologise and thank them for their hospitality and help.

As he walks us to the door, I ask Silvio, 'Do you recall anything Taras told you in the ambulance?'

He shakes his head. 'It was a long time ago, so not a great deal. I just remember he mentioned something. I didn't know what it was. To keep his mind active, to keep him with me and engaged, I asked him what it was. He told me it was a book.'

I ask, 'What was the name of the book?'

'I have not forgotten that. It was so distinctive. The book he kept talking about was called The Romanov Code.'

*

As we hurry back to the car, I explain to Stacey, 'So when Taras is killed, the Court thanks Silvio with the gift of the tiara.'

'Why give him something so extravagant?'

'They can afford it, believe me. Besides, it's one of the items that got him killed. Too many bad memories for them. Best be shot of it. Of course, the Saluccis naturally thought it was a weird present, along the lines of costume jewellery. The Court's gift to Fenton – AKA Thomas Maughan – was less palpable. They knew he'd saved Taras's life in Turin. So, they exerted their influence and one of the results was, well, even the FSB treat him with undue respect. The top-of-the-range passports and so on. He probably wasn't even aware of it.'

'But where does any of that get us?'

'Well, isn't the natural conclusion quite scary?'

'Look, Novak, I've no idea what the natural conclusion is!' We reach the Mini. 'Wait here!'

I tell Stacey I won't be a moment and jog back up the stone staircase that leads to the villa's lower floor.

'You came back, Mr Novak! Have you and the charming young lady changed your mind? Shall I open champagne?'

'Another time, Silvio. Another time. Right now, I just wanted to ask you one more question.'

'Feel free!'

'Thank you . . .'

I ask my question and Salucci rubs his chin as he considers it. 'Yes! Yes, poor Taras did mention something along those lines! It was decades ago, so it had slipped my mind, but I'm certain of it.'

And with that reply, I know why I've been dragged into this whole search for the Romanov treasure. I know the real reason why Taras Zvyagintsev was murdered. And I know the secret of the Romanov Code.

-88-

Lady Eleanor's Story
Salzburg, Austria.

The masked ball at Lady Eleanor's *schloss*, perched high in the mountains above Werfen, was proving to be a success. Wine flowed. The orchestra played. The laughter was loud but not uncouth. Yet everybody present knew the real reason for the party. The real reason for most of their meetings. Neither merriment nor friendship. They were gathered for their joint passions. Trade. Money. Power.

Lady Eleanor descended the broad staircase that led to the ballroom and the revels paused. She was applauded and demurely nodded her acknowledgement. The atmosphere felt charged. She scanned the rows of people below her. Every single face covered by strange, striking masks.

Her gaze paused. One individual in the sea of masks wore none.

She fixed on him, and as she reached the ballroom floor, he cut through the swathes of guests and approached her.

'You are breaking protocol!' She asked, 'Why aren't you wearing a mask?'

'I am,' he replied. 'You just can't see it. Isn't that the very best mask, Lady Eleanor?'

'You must be Mr Novak.'

'I suppose I must. Lucky me.'

*

Novak was escorted to a large, spectacular chamber. The walls weren't simply lined with amber panels; they were constructed from them. Gold and silver detail curved around gemstones that formed a decorative design and figurines depicting children and angels were dotted around the room. Novak didn't particularly like his surroundings. The chamber didn't even feel opulent. It came across as a parody of it.

Lady Eleanor, still wearing her mask, joined him. He asked, 'You've seen the Red Diamond?'

'Yes, of course. A fascinating stone. It's why you were given an audience. I'm curious about the jewel. And about you.'

'Well, thank you again for meeting me.'

'After you went to such lengths to request our meeting, to have refused you would have felt . . . discourteous. I'm afraid I must disappoint you, however. You told our intermediary you were interested in the Romanov Code. That remains the one lost artefact I cannot help you with. I've searched for that item for decades, but . . . It's lost, Mr Novak. Even to the Court.'

'I think you've misunderstood why I'm here, Lady Eleanor. Why I wanted to meet you. You see, I don't want your help.'

'Really?'

Novak paused. Looked about the chamber. 'This room. It feels familiar, but I've never been here before.'

'Fancy that.'

He gestured to a wall. 'Is that amber? Looks like amber. A *lot* of amber.' He flashed a smile at his hostess. 'It's a little garish for my taste. But, then again, flock wallpaper feels like a step too far for me, so what do I know?'

'You said you weren't here for my help.'

'Why don't you take off your mask, Lady Eleanor?'

She nodded. 'It's amber. Once known as northern gold and held in the same esteem as the precious metals we prize so highly today. As you say, a lot of amber. In fact, combined with the gold and silver incorporated into its architecture' – Lady Eleanor removed her mask – 'its weight has been estimated to be six tonnes.'

'Six tonnes of amber, gold and silver?' As the significance of the figure hit him, Novak laughed. 'Any chance of a selfie? The two of us by the pilaster in the corner?'

'One photograph and I'll have you incinerated.'

'Yeah, I'm pretty touchy about having my piccy taken at parties, too. I really am here to help you.'

'That certainly gives you novelty factor.'

'Don't patronise me.'

He held her stare, and after several seconds, she murmured, 'You're here to help me. Go on. Please.'

'Of course, Lady Eleanor.' Novak gave her another smile. Genuine, if a little resigned. 'You see, I've not engineered this whole situation and come to this castle to barter for the Romanov Code. I've come to tell you where it is.'

-89-

I insist on meeting Ekaterina in Opium, a glorious little cocktail bar and dim sum parlour in the hustling heart of Chinatown. That's partly because I anticipate she'll be angry on a volcanic scale, so I need our face-to-face to be in public. And it's partly because they mix an amazing Vesperanta and offer a seafood platter that's one of my favourites in London. I arrive half an hour early, find a discreet corner table and fortify my resolve with a couple of drinks.

It's going to be a long few hours.

Ekaterina arrives and sits opposite me. She's calmer than I expected. Meeker.

'Why did you tell the Court I have the Romanov Code? They've been searching for it for years. Now it looks like I've been concealing it from them, and every other antiquity hunter who's been questing for it. Novak, it places me in a great deal of jeopardy. Now . . . I need your help more than ever.'

'You can drop the act, Miss Romanova. I met with Silvio Salucci. The last man alive who spoke to Taras. He told me the poor lad had said the book belonged to the Romanova woman.' I take a sip of my Vesperanta. 'I don't know how it happened, but you slipped up and Taras saw the Romanov Code. I'm guessing you learnt he had the Russian Beauty and the Alexander III Fabergé egg . . . Did he show you the photos when he was drunk? Trying to impress you? So you told him about the Romanov Code. Offered a swap. A swap you never

337

intended to go through with, but then you realised what a stupid, *stupid* mistake you'd made with the offer. You should never have mentioned the book. And you should have simply *demanded* the artefacts you wanted. They were yours by blood, after all. He had what was rightfully yours! Made you look weak. That's why you had to kill him. And that's why it was done so publicly. So theatrically. You were sending a message to your opponents and potential enemies. Mess with Ekaterina Romanova and this is the fate that awaits you.'

She shakes her head. 'You're out of your mind!'

'Possibly. But I'm also right. Your story was the best kind of lie. So much of it was true. Your network did disband and scatter. But not because you were on the run from them. They were on the run from you. You were in it to win it from day one. You exploited the network to build up a collection of valuables. But the Romanov Code was the jackpot. That was the real prize. The game changer!'

She laughs at my claims. 'You seem to forget I hired you to find the Romanov Code!'

'And the way you did that was shrewd. Serving up bait I couldn't resist. Admitting to being a former spy. Claiming to have a treasure map in an envelope. Then later – only being interested in the Romanov Code, as opposed to the gold, jewellery and other riches. Good shout. But the absolute genius bit? You knew the Court and the Russian state and God knows how many other people were hunting for the Romanov Code. So you let it be known you were searching for it, too. Both through the Foundation and through private agencies like mine. It was the ultimate piece of misdirection. Everyone thinks you're looking for the Romanov Code, so it stands to reason you don't possess it. It's a ploy you've used brilliantly, right back since the days when you were working with Yulia Protopopov.'

For a moment, I fancy I see her mask slip. I catch a hint of pride in her own guile.

'Here's what I think happened,' I tell her. 'Years ago, you heard the rhetoric coming out of Moscow. You knew history would repeat itself. Russia would adopt an expansionist policy and that would make life difficult for émigrés in the UK. So you become an integral part of the Romanov Foundation. It's the perfect cover, and the cherry on the Medovik is that they even fund your apparent pursuit of the book. You use it to build up your contacts and influence. I'm guessing – and this is only a guess – that you used it to launder money generated by your other activities.'

She nods. It could be an indication that she's hearing me. But I interpret it as some kind of confirmation. 'There was a greater reason for my requisition of the Foundation. But please, continue. I'm starting to enjoy this.'

'You hired me because of Frank. You knew he had connections to the world of the Romanov treasure. Couldn't do any harm to let him know you were looking for the book. He might make others in the know aware of your pursuit. It all served to emphasise the narrative you were spinning.'

I pause. Finish off my cocktail. Over Ekaterina's shoulder, I gesture to a waiter, requesting two more.

'Do you have any other extraordinary theories, Mr Novak?'

'I think you were surprised when I found Maughan. Russian intelligence had never really let him go. He was embedded in a little village and I saw for myself his congregation included a great many prominent people in positions of power. Both politically and on a business level. I imagine he got titbits of intel from them and passed them on to the Kremlin. He was very, very low level. But they knew he was connected with the Court, or rather, that he was in their good books. Hence his top-of-the-range passports and sidearm. When I came asking questions,

I don't think he saw the level of trouble that signified. Until he contacted his case officer, who immediately twigged, panicked and ordered him to kill me. They couldn't afford anything to happen to him. The thought terrified them – supposing they got the blame. The Court would be displeased. Unfortunately, the act of trying to look after him got him killed.'

'David Fenton was always a fool.'

'Were you his case officer?'

'No.'

I believe her this time but keep scratching. 'Did you have some sort of hold over his case officer?'

And there's that half-smile again. That pride in her own guile. It has to be a weakness and so I use this moment to ask the one question that still perplexes me.

'Ekaterina, you're a genius. No doubt about it. I'm in awe of you. Truly. But one thing baffles me.'

'I'm delighted to hear it.' She beams. 'Ask your question, Mr Detective.'

'Why? What in God's name is so important about the Romanov Code that it's made you do all this?'

-90-

The waiter arrives and places two more cocktails on our table. As he departs, Ekaterina says, 'As a species, we look to recreate the past. Constantly. Unthinkingly. And, as you know, history inevitably repeats itself. These two truths are a powerful universal driver.'

It's my turn to prod her along. 'Go on.'

'My ancestor, Mikhail Romanov, was proclaimed the first Romanov Tzar in March, 1613, by the Zemsky Sobor. Essentially the Russian Assembly. Do you know where that epoch-defining event took place?'

'No. Enlighten me.'

'The Ipatiev Monastery. It was the start of a royal reign that continued for over three centuries. A golden age for Mother Russia! In 1917, the monastery was disbanded. Less than a year later, the Romanov dynasty was interrupted by the massacre in Ipatiev House.' She sips her cocktail. 'Ipatiev to Ipatiev. The names are only a quirk of what I mentioned earlier, of course. History repeating itself.'

Finally, I understand her mad plan. Her lunatic ambition.

'Ekaterina . . . You really think you can rule Russia?'

'My country's current leader is a man. All men are mortal. When he goes, there will be a power vacuum. There are no figures who are obvious successors. I've seen to that. I believe my people will look to their past. They will seek to replicate that past. Once again, history will repeat itself. I will be proclaimed the rightful successor in my Ipatiev House. The Romanov line will be restored to its predestined position of power.'

I let that sink in for a moment. 'I think I need this drink.'

'Is my ambition really so unbelievable?'

'Nepotism. Nostalgia. Brute force and bloodshed. It's got it all. I'm already looking forward to the movie. But . . .' I hesitate.

'You see it now!' She actually claps her hands in delight. 'You understand the significance of the Romanov Code!'

'The book! Of course! The encapsulation of all your family's ideals. A credo you hope to exploit. And so the book becomes more than a symbol of the Romanovs' code. It becomes a right to them! A proof of accession!'

'Brilliant!'

She's talking about herself, of course. There remains something charming about Ekaterina Romanova. I could genuinely like her, if it wasn't for her psychotic compulsions and complete disregard for any human other than herself.

'Brilliant, yes. But you forgot one thing.'

'What's that?'

'Me.' I raise my glass to her. 'I'm going to stop you.'

'Don't bother!' She leans forward. 'You can help me! I can make you rich. Powerful. Significant.'

'Yeah. I'm taking a diamond-tipped hard pass on that one, thanks.'

'Why?'

'Not because you want to rule Russia, Miss Romanova. And you think some little book and all your preening politicking is going to help you achieve that. No. That's just mad. And I quite like mad. Empathy, I imagine. And it's not because you've lied and manipulated me. I can even admire some of your artwork.'

'Then why?'

342

'Because of the boy you hung in Italy, just because he'd glimpsed a book. Because of all the people you've destroyed in your quest. And mostly because of what you tried to do to Julia Grant. She has a daughter, you know. Willow.'

Ekaterina nods deeply, as if acknowledging applause. 'You guessed!'

'Not at first. Although when Julia told me she thought Bulatov was trying to kill her simply for meeting me, I thought something was off. Like I said to her, the Colonel is cold and ruthless, but he's not psychotic.'

'When did you realise that was my work?'

'Much later. I finally grasped you had two men try to kill her because you knew it would look like Bulatov's call. That's why you had to murder the two assassins I injured at Julia's place. You couldn't afford to have them reveal the truth. As it stood, the whole incident would have had the bigwigs in Moscow doubting his reasoning and calling his stability into question. It was just a petty attempt to discredit him. Even fractionally. All because you see him as a possible contender for the top chair in Russia when it finally becomes available.'

Ekaterina holds up a finger. 'There was another reason.'

'Go on.'

'I didn't like her. She thought she could escape. She thought she could do something I could never do.'

I smile. 'But she did, Miss Romanova. Julia escaped. Along with Willow and her partner.'

'I'm afraid not. I would have killed her, of course. But Bulatov really did get there first. Took her from a service station. Never seen again.'

'I made that lady a promise. That I'd make sure she got through the ordeal. You still don't get it! Bulatov didn't take her. I did!'

She looks shocked. 'What?'

'I had my man Sebby Hughes attached to the detail guarding her. He faked her abduction at the service station. It was all hastily pre-planned by me, but the pieces fell into place all right. Sebby actually handed Julia over to a friend, who drove her to a private airfield where she was reunited with her daughter and partner. I couldn't even risk British Intelligence knowing about it at that point, so it was all very hush-hush and I feigned alarm when I was told about Julia's so-called disappearance. Sebby's contacts ensured that she and her family were secretly flown out of the country to safety. You see, I like to keep my promises.'

'What you did was dangerous and duplicitous.'

'I know! Worthy of your own machinations, Miss Romanova.'

'Now you're flattering me.'

'So, back to where we currently stand. The Court knows you have the Romanov Code. They'll ensure everyone knows the truth.'

She shrugs. 'Maybe it's time the truth was in the open.'

'That's great in principle, but in reality, one of the agencies searching for the Romanov Code is going to find you.' I pause. 'Actually, find *us*. They will send scary-looking men holding syringes. They will inject us. Render us unconscious and then . . . Well, that's all I can tell you.'

I finish my Vesperanta with a single gulp.

'And how could you know that, Mr Novak?'

I reach across the table. Take Ekaterina's cocktail and drain it in one shot.

'Ekaterina.'

'Yes?'

'Look behind you.'

-91-

I wake up in what looks to be Ekaterina's office in Ipatiev House. The one room that doesn't seek to replicate the original building. But it looks slightly different. Maybe because I'm viewing it at a right angle. I blink. My head rests on the floor. I roll over. Groan. Look up.

I see Ekaterina has been placed in a chair and she's coming to, regaining her consciousness as my eyes blink open.

'Novak . . . is that you?'

I try to stand but realise my wrists have been shackled by a pair of handcuffs, and glancing across at Ekaterina, I see she's been similarly inconvenienced. I shake my head. Sniff the air.

'Who did this?' she demands, glaring at her cuffs.

'Colonel Bulatov.'

'How do you know?'

'Only he'd have the chutzpah and manpower to break into your little fortress. And I recognise his brand of cigarette. He's been here recently.'

Ekaterina peers to her left. One of her guards appears to be asleep in the seat behind the room's main desk. 'Soldier!' she shouts. 'Soldier!'

I recognise the man as the guard who'd escorted me to the main entrance during my first visit.

Ekaterina bawls at him again, but he gives no sign of having heard her. No sign of anything.

I stagger to my feet and make my way over to him. 'What's his name?'

'I don't know. Pavel, I think.'

'Pavel! Wake up, mate! We need to know what happened here!' I spin his chair around and very gently shake his shoulder. 'Come on! You can hit snooze after you've—'

The guard's body topples forward and slumps heavily to the floor. Pavel is lying on his front, meaning his back is exposed. There's a circle of blood between his shoulders and a dagger handle protrudes from it. I drop to my haunches and check for a pulse.

'For God's sake, you can see he's dead! Why's he been stabbed, not shot?'

'Your compassion is boundless, Ekaterina.' I look up. 'Yeah, he's dead. Poor bugger. And I imagine he was one of the first to be taken out and Bulatov was relying on stealth as part of his attack.'

'Oh my God!' Ekaterina gets to her feet. 'Are you saying the Colonel's taken over Ipatiev House?'

'No idea. But it seems likely.'

I hurry to the door. Check it. 'Locked.'

'This is a nightmare!'

I nod to the blinds covering the windows. 'Can we get out that way?'

'They're perma-locked.'

'Bulletproof?'

'Damn near missile-proof.'

I lean my back against the door. 'Then it looks like Colonel Bulatov is holding all the cards. The question is, what does he want from us?' I glance at my watch. 'And let's hope he's in a merciful mood.'

'Why?'

'Because my deadline is almost up. If I don't hand him the Romanov Code in ten minutes, he's promised to slaughter my

346

friends and family. And knowing Bulatov as I do, whatever the circumstances, well, I've absolutely no doubt he'll make good on his vow.'

For once, Ekaterina is completely candid. 'I'm afraid your assessment is correct,' she tells me. 'You have less than a quarter of an hour to avert unimaginable bloodshed.'

-92-

'Tell me there's a way out of here, Ekaterina.'

'No . . .' She massages her temples. 'But there is a Beretta in my desk!' She rushes across to it and pulls open the bottom drawer. Then the one above it. 'Damn! They've completely emptied it!'

I frown. 'That's weird. Why would they do that? I mean, I get why they've taken the sidearm, but why remove everything else?'

'Does it matter?'

'It suggests they're looking for something but they don't know what it is themselves.'

'You're missing the big picture, Novak! You've seen what they did to Pavel, and probably the rest of my guards. Bulatov isn't bothered about the fact we're on British soil! This is a small war and we've got to get out of it now, or we'll—'

She's interrupted by a knock at the door. Neither of us responds, but we hear a lock being turned. The door opens and Maksim Bulatov enters the room, flanked by two men, both wearing paramilitary uniforms and both carrying Heckler & Koch UMP submachine guns.

I try to look pleased at his arrival. 'Good to see you again, Colonel! I was saying to Ekaterina, we really should get Maksim over for a drink or two and . . .' I trail off. Through the open doorway, I can see more soldiers dressed in uniforms identical to those worn by the two men with Bulatov. They're dragging the

348

bodies of Ipatiev House guards along the corridor. Every one of the lifeless bodies is drenched in red. 'How many did you kill, Colonel?'

'Me personally? None. I detest violence. Noisy. Unwieldy. Unpredictable. For example, my strategist told me we could take this place without sustaining any casualties of our own. But I've just been informed that two of my men lost their lives once we thought we'd secured the building.' He shakes his head. 'Two of my employees dead. That's expenditure I really don't need.'

'And Ekaterina's guards?'

'They put up a good fight! All dead, though. Why didn't they just run? They were outnumbered and outgunned, but instead of laying down their arms, they tried to defend this place. Mr Novak! I've worked with soldiers for well over a quarter of a century. But I'll never understand them.'

'Yeah, well. They have little things like a sense of duty and courage, which will always be alien to men like you.'

'Dear, dear, dear . . . You threatened me once. Remember? Threatened to tear out my fucking heart. And now you insult me.' He nods to one of his guards.

I step back, but the man moves quickly, slamming the butt stock of his UMP into my face. I feel my lip split and blood pours from my mouth.

I dab my handkerchief over the cut. 'What do you want, Colonel?'

'What do any of us want? Respect. Security. Good food and wine we can't afford.'

'I meant—'

'Oh, I know what you meant. I was using humour. You remember we discussed how you deploy jokes in certain situations. But your humour seems to have deserted you. Why is that, I wonder?'

'Massacres tend to have that effect on me.'

'Nobody else needs to die if you simply give me what I want.'

Ekaterina says, 'And what is that?'

Bulatov looks astonished. 'Isn't it obvious? The Romanov Code. Hand me that and I can return to Moscow in triumph.'

'Is that it?' It's hard to tell whether Ekaterina is more surprised or aghast. 'You just want the book? Why? Don't you want our intel? Our funds? Our assets?'

The Colonel laughs. 'Intel? Don't be so naïve! Some of your top people work for me. I'm sure some of my top people work for you. Our intel is already shared! Ha! That's Communism in action, Miss Romanova! As for your funds and assets . . . Russia is the biggest country on earth. We don't need your subscription fees.'

I ask, 'But *why* is the book so important?'

'Because it is history! Because of what it represents! A past that we can respect, but must not replicate.'

'Is the Kremlin really so worried about the power of an old book?'

'Mr Novak, men have been fighting wars over old books since the time of Christ.'

'Then perhaps it's time to stop.'

'History repeats itself. And as surely as the tide will continue to ebb and flow. Any person that tries to fight or deny it is nothing but a chronological King Canute. And now . . .' He steps over Pavel's body and sits in the seat behind the desk. 'I'd like the Romanov Code, Mr Novak.' He checks his watch. 'You've less than five minutes to give it to me, or I'll order the death of everyone dear to you.'

-93-

I approach the desk. 'I don't have the book. You know that! Ekaterina's had it in her possession all along!'

'I'm aware of this. Yes. But we had a deal. And I'm offering you a chance to keep your side of it.'

Ekaterina walks towards the Colonel. 'What you're doing is an outrage and—'

As she nears the desk, one of the soldiers swings his UMP in her direction, but he lowers the barrel as Bulatov gives a tiny shake of his head. Ekaterina spots the gesture. Pauses. And as realisation hits her, she beams.

'That's why I'm still alive! You've butchered everyone else in the building because they can't help you. But you need me alive, because without me you can't hope to get your hands on the book!'

Bulatov drums his fingers on the desktop.

Ekaterina gives a short, high-pitched yelp of triumph. 'I believe this is what they call a reversal of fortune, Colonel.'

I say, 'Would someone care to explain what's going on?'

Ekaterina takes a seat. 'In the basement of this building, there is possibly the most sophisticated vault in Europe. It has what is known as a shield door. That's to say a door that can withstand a laser cutter, acid or even explosive force. The only force capable of destroying it would be a military-grade strike. So it's protected by a paradox. The only way to get past the shield door would destroy the entire vault itself, rendering such an attack pointless. And the Colonel knows it.'

Bulatov nods. 'We hacked the records of the men who fitted it. Beyond the shield door, which can only be opened by a ten-digit sequence known only to yourself, there is a chamber. The shield door must be closed for the second door, the door within this chamber, to be unlocked. As with the first, it can only be opened with a ten-digit code. That second door leads to the storage area of the vault, where I presume the Romanov Code is housed. Now, I understand this second door could be penetrated by a military-grade laser. Something like a Lockheed Martin, that can produce a single beam of 58kW. But even then, piercing it would take some time. A lot of time . . .'

'Time you don't have,' Ekaterina reminds him. 'You've just carried out a massacre on British soil. It isn't going to be long before someone notices those men are missing. At best, you've got hours. But you certainly don't have days, which is how long it would take you to open that second door . . . And that's only if you can open the shield door. Which, without me, is impossible. Literally impossible.'

'True enough!' Bulatov stands. 'But this is not a reversal of fortune, Miss Romanova. I was aware of the situation long before today. We find ourselves in something more akin to a Mexican stand-off. I need the book. So I need you. But if you flat-out refuse to give it to me, I may as well kill you. What would I have to lose?'

'Then we're at an impasse.'

'Not quite. You will come with me!' The Colonel barks something in Russian to one of his guards and Ekaterina shouts in protest.

'No! You cannot do that!'

We're roughly pinned to the far wall. Sack cloth bags are pulled over our heads and I feel myself being pushed towards the door.

'Try anything en route,' Bulatov warns us, 'and it will not end well for either of you.'

I'm half pushed, half guided to the corridor and sense the same is happening to Ekaterina. She seethes, 'This is an outrage! I am a Romanova!'

'You are a Romanova in Ipatiev House,' Bulatov replies. 'You may wish to consider that fact before issuing any more shrieking protests.'

The short journey proves a painful one. The guards apparently delight in knocking us to the floor as we're propelled through the building. It's disorientating and humiliating in equal measures.

Eventually, I hear the Colonel tell us, 'You must be careful, my friends. We shall now descend into the most infamous basement in the history of the world. Where I have a little surprise for you.'

Ekaterina and I are guided down a flight of stairs. I count twenty-four steps and feel floor beneath my feet. I hear a door being shut and someone snatches the bag from my head. Ekaterina has hers removed, and as soldiers take off our handcuffs, we exchange glances. We're in the room that's a recreation of the chamber where Nikolai II Alexandrovich Romanov, his wife, children and friends were gunned down.

Something in the basement makes me shout, 'My God! This is madness! You can't be serious, Colonel!'

Because, to my right, I see a line of uniformed guards. Some grip UMPs, a few hold rifles and a couple are brandishing Makarovs. But every one of them is armed, and every single weapon is pointing at a line of people to my left.

'The tide of history seeps in, creeps out and seeps in again,' the Colonel insists. 'It's inevitable, my friend.'

'Stop this now!' I demand.

But our captor simply smiles.

There are five people in the line.

Stacey Smith, Sophie Grace, Reggie DeLuca, Molly Stone and Frank Harvey.

Maksim Bulatov tells me, 'I cannot be a chronological King Canute, Mr Novak.'

-94-

The Colonel checks his watch. 'You have precisely one minute to persuade Miss Romanova to give me the book. Otherwise, your friends will suffer the same fate as the Tzar and his family in 1918.'

'Bulatov! Listen to me! That's not the way her mind works! She doesn't care about any of those people or me! The only person you can threaten that would have any sway is her! You must see that!'

He shrugs. 'You are, in a sense, her colleagues. That must mean something to her.'

I look at my friends, forced to pose in a line-up that's ghoulishly similar to the assembly of Romanovs who faced their killers over a century earlier. I turn to Ekaterina. Plead with her. 'Please! Just give him the book! Is it worth the lives of five innocent people? Ekaterina! He *will* execute them!'

Sophie says, 'What's going on, Marc? We don't understand! We were all taken at gunpoint and—'

Bulatov shouts, 'Silence!' He adds to his soldiers, 'If any of that lot says another word, shoot them in the face.'

I see Sophie go even paler as she steps back into line.

'Ekaterina, please!'

She remains silent.

I grip the lapels of Bulatov's suit in desperation. 'It's possible Helen Merrydale knows the combination of the vault. They trust each other! We just need to find her!'

GAVIN COLLINSON

Ekaterina's voice is thick with scorn. 'Helen hasn't a clue! I've used the Romanov Foundation to launder money and cultivate alliances for years! She's never suspected a thing and has never even asked me for the opening sequences. Kill me and the book is lost forever. Helen can't help you.'

The Colonel says, 'You have thirty seconds, Mr Novak.'

'Ekaterina! I have the Red Diamond! You know that! It's priceless! I can give that to you! Give him the book and you can keep the diamond.'

'Do you have it here?'

'No!'

'Then no deal.'

Bulatov peels away and stands by the side of the armed men. Looks to my friends. 'Stacey Smith, Sophie Grace, Reggie DeLuca, Molly Stone and Frank Harvey . . . In view of the fact that your colleagues are continuing their attack on Russia by repeatedly refusing a simple request, the Special Executive Committee has decided to execute you.'

Frank looks at me and stammers, 'What? What?'

Bulatov turns away. 'As I said, history repeats itself. Raise arms!'

Every weapon picks out a pre-arranged target.

I make one last plea, in the form of a simple promise. 'If you do this, Colonel, somehow, some way – I will kill you.'

'Really? Well, that's a chance I'm prepared to take. We cannot fight history, Mr Novak.' He looks to his soldiers. 'Fire!'

-95-

There's a simplicity in death.

Grey-white smoke from the hot barrels of the sidearms fills the room and when I inhale, I can taste the sharp chemical tang of cordite and feel its caustic burn at the back of my throat. Visibility is further worsened by a heavy snowfall of dust from the plaster ceiling, loosened by the reverberation of the shooting. And yet I can clearly see the effects of the gunfire.

I look across to my friends. There'd been no time for any show of courage. No brave last words or declarations of love. The deafening cacophony of gunfire still echoes in my ears. The reverberation still finds my bones and seems to rattle them. The plaster dust coats us all. The living and the dead.

I push Bulatov out of the way, but for a moment I can't approach my friends. The sight of them shrieks at me. Their truth too appalling. Because the Colonel had been wrong in a way. History did not repeat itself. The victims here had no jewels and gemstones to protect them from the bullets. They lie contorted on the floor, their bodies drenched in blood.

I force myself to approach Stacey. My hand reaches for her throat, but I find no pulse.

Sophie's mint-green top is sodden w ith blood, so much so that I imagine – or maybe I can – taste the salt of it. I reach for her throat, but I find no pulse.

Reggie lies prone, half underneath Stacey's body. I pull her free. Turn her over. The blood leaking through her clothes is still warm. I reach for her throat, but I find no pulse.

I shuffle along. Molly Stone's still, pale and blood-speckled hand is resting on Frank's sleeve. I reach for her throat, but I find no pulse.

I drop to the ground. 'Frank, Frank . . .' I haul his body around and drag him towards me so his head rests on my lap. I reach for his throat, but I find . . . A pulse! 'Frank! Stay with me! Frank!'

I must be crying because my vision of him has become blurred.

I see his eyes flicker open. 'The girls?'

'They're all right,' I tell him. 'We all just need you to hang on! Do you hear me? Just hang on!'

He somehow musters a smile. Shakes his head. 'Too late. But wanted you to know . . .' He takes two quick shallow breaths. I lean closer to him and he whispers, 'Jock was right. I love you, lad.'

I hug him so tightly, it feels like I might crush his bones. And I wait for another breath but hear nothing more. There is nothing more. Because there is, after all, a simplicity in death.

96

Frank's Story (cont.)
Blackpool, England. July, 1981

Frank Harvey sat in a snug at the Oliver Arms, an apocalyptic little pub close to the ABC cinema.

Jock walked in, bought a couple of pints and took the seat opposite him. 'How do, Frank?'

'Y'all right?'

'What the hell are you doing in this place? It's probably the worst boozer in Lancashire.'

'One of the lasses in the office recommended it.'

'Tall, fair-haired woman?'

'Aye.'

'Yeah, she said she'd mentioned this hellhole.' Jock took a sip of bitter. 'Were you rude to her?'

Frank grimaced. 'Probably.'

'That's why she sent you here. Payback. Right! Have you calmed down yet?'

'I suppose so.'

'Good! Let's sort out your first story, then! Covering the wedding of Charles and Diana from a Blackpool point of view. I had wanted you to go to the Pleasure Beach on the day of the wedding. They're giving out free tickets to anyone called Charles or Di. But you said—'

'I said that the wedding day is going to be a bank holiday. Except some registry offices will be opening. I think we should cover a local wedding. Follow it. See how the married lives of our Blackpool happy couple differ from those of the Prince and Princess of Wales.'

Jock nodded. 'Not a bad idea. Run with it!'

Frank nodded. 'Can I ask you something?'

'Long as it's legal.'

'Why are you helping me out? You took a chance on me after I was kicked out of London. I was an idiot today in the office and here you are again. Actually, maybe I don't need to know why. But I just wanted to say . . . Thank you. It means a lot.'

Jock smiled. 'One day you'll be an old man. And you'll meet some younger bloke who's a hothead and impulsive and kind of smart but off the rails. He'll do things his way and to hell with the consequences. But you'll also see he's got a good heart. When you meet him, remember me, yeah? Remember this, lad.'

Frank nodded. 'Aye, will do.'

The two men clinked glasses.

'Time for some shots, yeah, Jock?'

'Not yet. Still got a bit of business.'

'What might that be?'

'You're covering the Charles and Diana story like you wanted to. No problem. But someone else already suggested that angle. So I'm teaming you up with her. She's young. A complete novice. But I think she's special.' Jock turned around. 'Come on over, luv!'

The fair-haired woman from the office picked up her drink and joined Jock at his table.

Frank groaned, 'Bloody hell!'

'Yeah! My thoughts exactly,' she shot back.

Jock laughed. 'Frank Harvey, I'd like you to meet your new partner. Molly Stone.'

97

Ekaterina's Story

Ekaterina Romanova glanced at the bodies of Novak's friends. He had howled a moment ago. A grim and terrifying wail that felt louder than the gunfire. Now he was silent, hunched over an old man's frame.

She turned to Colonel Maksim Bulatov. 'All right. I'll get the book for you.'

Novak raised his head and shouted, 'No! She's seen what you're capable of, Bulatov! If she steps foot in that vault, she'll just hole up and you'll never get the Romanov Code!'

'She can only hide for so long. She understands that. Don't you, Miss Romanova?'

'It's a simple business transaction. You get what you want, Colonel, and you leave me to mop up the mess here.'

He nodded. 'Quite so.'

Ekaterina stepped over the body of Stacey Smith, careful not to get any blood on her Miu Miu slingbacks. She unlocked, then opened the doors behind the five fallen friends to reveal a huge, metal arched door.

She said, 'This is the shield door. Immediately beyond it is a chamber. And beyond that is the vault containing the Romanov Code. If I could ask you all to stand back . . .'

Novak didn't move, but Bulatov and his men retreated a couple of paces.

Ekaterina placed her hands under a ledge in the door and felt the keypad. The covering meant that even if her body hadn't been blocking their line of vision, the sequence of numbers she entered would be impossible to see from any angle in the basement.

She pressed the tenth and final number and spoke three words aloud. 'Verification: Ekaterina Romanova.'

Click-click-click!

As the door swung towards her, she stood to one side. Looked back at Novak and the impatient Colonel Bulatov, a foolish man, she reflected, so eager for his prize to take back to the Kremlin that he was blind to the obvious truth, even after it had been spelt out to him. She would step inside the outer vault, close the door and, at that point, and in that place, she would be safe. She would wait.

She nodded. 'I'll be right back. You have my word.'

Novak yelled, 'You'll never see her again! But it doesn't matter. You're a dead man, Bulatov! I promise you that.'

Ekaterina gave the Colonel a pantomime grimace. 'Awkward!' Novak called her name and she paused. 'Yes?'

'Was any of it true? About the real you?'

She looked at him. Gave a sad smile. 'The postboxes.' She pushed her shoulders back. Businesslike again. Ekaterina Romanova walked into the vault's outer chamber and entered another sequence of numbers into a panel to the left of the doorway.

Bulatov called across, 'Don't let me down!'

'You can trust me!'

The door shut. Ekaterina was alone. She pulled out and switched on a PC built into the vault wall and confirmed all systems were running correctly. No problems.

'This place is invulnerable!'

She switched on a monitor that was intended to relay a visual feed of what was happening on the other side of the shield door, in the basement.

On the screen, Ekaterina saw the Colonel ushering out all the men who had shot the five people moments earlier. And now, finally, she allowed herself a deep sigh of relief. She could watch and wait. Days if necessary. In the storage section of the vault, she'd placed water and tinned food in case of such an emergency.

She peered at the screen. Novak was getting to his feet. She saw him shout something to the last of the guards as the line of soldiers trudged from the room. Bizarre! He was approaching the young man. Embracing him. Ekaterina furrowed her brow. Why on earth—

She saw the move. Slick and quick. Novak slipped the soldier's Makarov from his side holster. Slid it into the back of his trousers. He turned away and the guard hurried off to join the other men. Ekaterina wished she'd thought to have an audio feed installed, because she wanted to know what Bulatov was saying to Novak. It was clear he hadn't seen him take the pistol, but she wanted to hear the words they were exchanging.

Novak seemed calm again. In control. The Colonel appeared flustered. He pointed at the other man and—

Ekaterina's eyes widened.

Novak pulled the Makarov from his belt and aimed it at Bulatov's face.

Ekaterina moved closer to the screen.

Novak said a few words to Bulatov. Pulled the trigger. It would have been near-impossible to have missed from that distance. Ekaterina saw the Colonel's skull explode, spraying Novak with blood. The near-headless body wobbled for a ludicrous moment before toppling to the ground. Novak tossed the pistol aside, spoke a few words to the bodies of his friends, and walked from the basement.

-98-

Ekaterina's Story (cont.)

Ekaterina was an unusually resilient person, but now she put her face in her palms and wept. Not out of pity for the people she had seen murdered. Not out of its senselessness or her part in what had happened. She wept as a release. The tension and fear leaking out in her tears.

For almost twenty minutes, she cried. No thoughts other than self-pity and a sense of relief that she was secure.

Bulatov might be dead, but she intended to remain in the vault for days if necessary, until she knew it was absolutely safe to venture out. She wanted to be certain the Colonel's men had left and Novak wasn't lingering in Ipatiev House to exact his revenge. No problem. She could wait.

After about half an hour, she began to realise that events had apparently conspired to help her. Surely the British authorities would find the dead bodies and deduce they'd been murdered by the Russian state? History repeating itself. And she would be the brave Romanova who had somehow survived the massacre. She had a recording of Novak shooting the Colonel at point-blank range, so any claims he made about her could be dismissed as the inane, insane ramblings of an unfortunate psychopath driven mad by the slaughter of his friends.

And wasn't it obvious Bulatov had exceeded his authority by murdering her guards and the other five victims? Russian

Intelligence would disown him, both publicly and privately. That situation created a vacuum. A chance for her to step into his place? To position herself for power when the opportunity arose . . .

She had won. She felt it. The whole affair had been arduous and draining, but she had won.

Ekaterina stood. Entered a ten-digit sequence into the keypad on the secondary door. Nothing happened.

What?

She frowned, then remembered.

'Verification: Ekaterina Romanova.'

Click-click-click!

Yes, she felt thirsty. Needed water. She would enter the vault, help herself to some of the Evian she'd left there and, of course, look over the Romanov Code. Perhaps even now, in this bloody victory, she wanted to reassure herself it had been worth it.

The door to the vault swung open.

She looked inside. Blinked.

'What . . . ?'

She tilted her head in an attempt to process what she was seeing. Because as Ekaterina Romanova gazed through the vault's doorway, she was looking at the most mind-blowing thing she had ever seen in her life.

Ekaterina's Story (cont.)

Marc Novak flashed her a broad smile. 'Miss Romanova! What took you so long? Come on in! Join us for cocktails!'

Ekaterina blinked again, as if trying to dismiss what she was seeing and reboot visual reality with something – *anything* – that made sense. Because she should have been evaluating the inside of Europe's most impregnable vault. Instead, through the metal doorway, she was looking at the American Bar, the world famous cocktail lounge of London's Savoy Hotel.

She whispered, 'This can't be happening . . .'

'I know what you're thinking,' Novak told her. 'But don't worry! The American Bar operates a no-reservations policy. So, come on! Slide your slingbacks over the threshold and name your poison.'

Ekaterina stepped into the cocktail bar.

'What's up, hen? You look like you've seen a ghost!' Stacey Smith, dressed in a daring silk, Roberto Cavalli animalier-print dress, was taking a seat at one of the tables.

'Actually, sugar,' Reggie added, 'you look like you've seen six.' She wore a fifties-style polka dot swing dress.

'Yes, come on in, comrade!' Colonel Bulatov looked resplendent in his full military uniform.

Sophie Grace was wearing a green-tinged rabbit-print poplin midi dress. D&G. 'But do close the door, dear heart. There's a dreadful draught.'

Molly Stone, casually attired in jeans, black T-shirt and a Fred Perry jacket, called over her shoulder, 'What would you recommend for Miss Romanova, Frank?' She smiled. 'He introduced me to the joys of gin and he's my former husband, so I trust his taste in drinks and women implicitly!'

'I can recommend a Hanky Panky Highball. Or the Pocket Rocket.' Frank Harvey was crossing the art deco-themed room that seemed to perfectly show off his black Brioni three-piece suit. He paused. Rested his thumb in his waistcoat pocket. 'Actually, I can recommend anything on the menu. God knows, I intend to give all of them a whirl!'

Novak said, 'Actually, they do a rather wonderful vodka-champagne cocktail here. It's called the New Beginning. Yes, Ekaterina. I really think you could do with a New Beginning.'

-100-

Ekaterina's Story

Still dazed, Ekaterina took a seat at one of the small circular tables. She touched its edges to reassure herself that it existed. The other women and Bulatov were ensconced at one of the longer, oblong tables. Novak and Frank Harvey remained standing.

'What just happened?'

Novak said, 'We knew about your vault. Knew it would be impossible to break into. So we thought, why bother? You see, you've just witnessed a heist. And you didn't even realise it.'

'But how?'

'Well,' Novak continued, 'the Colonel and I decided to join forces. When we were both seized, he had us carefully transported to this place. It's a replica of Ipatiev House. Or, rather, parts of your Ipatiev House. Like you said, getting details of the original is fairly easy. The only snag was getting your office correct. When I visited you, I wore a tiepin that actually recorded the whole thing, so we got what we needed from the footage. The one problem, of course, was the desk drawers. We didn't have a clue what was in them. When you opened them, I thought the game was up.'

'That's why they were empty . . .'

'Exactly! There wasn't time to recreate all the corridors, hence the sack cloth bags placed over our heads. Sorry about that. And you were injected with a low-level dose of Valium that made you a little fuzzy. Just another way of diminishing your perceptual awareness. The basement was good, though, wasn't it? There was an extra step leading to it, though. Not going to lie – low-key annoyed by that, but, hey – nobody's perfect!'

Colonel Bulatov took up the story. 'I knew you would need, let's call it an *incentive* to open the vault. Which is why we staged the deaths of Mr Novak's friends. Pig-blood pellets detonated by remote control. Blank bullets. I'm sure you can guess the rest.'

'I didn't feel a pulse in any of their necks,' Novak mused, as if to himself, 'because I didn't bother trying to find one.'

'We bought out Pavel, which was easy, because you had him on minimum wage.' Frank took a sip of his Platinum Punch. 'That side of the sting was all organised and choreographed by an old friend of ours. Sebby Hughes. I'm just gutted he couldn't hang around for the after-work drinks.'

Ekaterina, still in a state of shock, panned across their faces. 'But I saw you shoot Bulatov in the head!'

'No. You saw me and Maksim acting out a little scene that was later enhanced with some special effects. Looked good, though, didn't it? When you switched on the monitor, we simply played the video. We shot the short film as part of the . . . Hold on . . . Cheers.' He took a mouthful of his drink. 'You know, this La Belle 1890 really is to die for.'

Sophie replied, 'I think there's already been more than enough dying for one day! Incidentally, Katty, you've probably worked it out by now, but when you entered the ten-digit sequence code into the replica vault, well, we rather had the number relayed to us.'

'And in case you were worried,' Frank chipped in, 'we also recorded your voice verification, so we can go straight to your Ipatiev House, open the vault and take the Romanov Code.'

Ekaterina shook her head. 'Helen won't let you within a mile of it.'

'Give over, luv!' Stacey gave a brief laugh. 'After we've shown her your video confession of how you've abused and misused the Foundation, I think she'll do anything we ask.'

'Your problem,' Molly informed her, 'is that you believed history always repeats itself. And it normally does. But once in every hundred times, we learn. We move on.'

'What's going to happen to me?'

Novak looked at his watch. 'Jeremy Simmonds' people should be arriving shortly. There won't be any fuss. You'll be taken directly to Moscow and handed over to an old friend of yours.'

Ekaterina looked at Colonel Bulatov and he nodded. 'Don't worry, my dear. We'll find you a real vault in Russia.'

-101-

I mix myself a Gibson and re-join Stacey and Reggie at one of the central tables. Bulatov and Ekaterina have left with the operatives sent by Simmonds, and Frank and Molly are chatting in the corner of the room. I feel a mild sense of elation, although I know that further dangers await. But for now, at least, I'm content to chink glasses with my friends and enjoy a cocktail.

As I take a seat in the replica of the American Bar, I say to Reggie, 'Please send the Baron my congratulations. And my thanks. Getting this whole thing ready so swiftly . . . We'd never have been able to pull it off without him.'

She replies, 'Yeah, well, he had a bunch of teams working round the clock. The rooms themselves were straightforward. His people are the best in the business. Getting the vault from the manufacturers, then adding the modifications – not gonna lie to you, that was touch-and-go. The only other problem was the first room had to be elevated. I'm not sure the geography was 100 per cent . . .'

I shrug. 'It was close enough.'

Stacey asks, 'What about this place? The bar.'

'Oh, this is for another client. We just placed your job next to it. We'll be extending this room tomorrow.' She sips her pale blue Midnight Kiss. 'And that woman. Ekaterina. She thought she could rule Russia some day, just because of an old book? Genuinely?'

She pronounces the third syllable as *wine*, which I always enjoy.

'The Romanov Code is a legend,' I reflect. 'Whoever holds the book holds the power of the Romanovs. Like Excalibur in the Arthurian histories. She was a Romanov and she really believed it was her destiny to restore her family's position of supremacy. All her politicking, planning and murders were to that end. She had networks of people in her employ, of course, but she became fixated on the book. I mean, simply as a relic its financial value must be extraordinary. But she, and many before her, felt its real value was something more . . . transcendent.'

'Baloney!' Reggie chops her hand through the air as though to convey the absolute certainty of her words. 'A thing is a thing is a thing!'

'I'm not saying the FSB and their masters in the Kremlin all believe in the book's power. But its reputation holds enough sway to ensure they aren't taking any chances.'

'No, it's more than that.' Stacey sounds uncharacteristically quiet. 'My ma was Catholic,' she says, and there's a firmness in her voice. 'She believed the wine in the chalice at mass became the blood of Christ. Not figuratively. Not symbolically. But the actual blood of Jesus. And that the wafer or bread handed to her by the priest was the real, honest-to-God flesh of Christ. That's what the Church believes. It's what millions believe. I guess it's the belief that's the important thing. In this case, for Ekaterina and the people she hoped to convince, it surely was. The book was some sort of totem. A sign and an assurance.'

Reggie looks sceptical. 'What do you think, Novak?'

'I think Ekaterina proved one thing. Like I always say, it's my clients that kill me. Or at least try to.'

'Sucks to be you, huh?'

'Quite the contrary.'

Reggie finds herself holding an empty glass and declares, 'Well, soldiers, I'm getting another drink!' As she gets to her feet, she asks, 'Anyone else want more ammunition?'

My Gibson is almost done. 'Get us both one of what you're having!'

'Sure thing, sugar.'

She makes her way to the bar. I'm alone at the table with Stacey and for something like a minute there's an easy silence between us. Perhaps it's too easy. Too much like the '. . . and relax' moment that follows anything that's painfully endured. As if reading my thoughts, Stacey says, 'Don't worry. I know it's not over yet.'

'If anything, what I have to do next is the riskiest part of the process. But if I stand any chance of . . .' I pause. Something strikes me. 'Where's Sophie?'

'Sorry!' Stacey replies. 'She said to pass on her goodbyes. She had to shoot.'

'Is she picking up the twins?'

'I think so. She said it was about the children.'

That's not quite the same thing. In fact . . .

I ponder the half-hints that Sophie Grace has given me about who, or what, she truly is, and for a moment, I wonder if she's seeking vengeance on—

'Ammunition, troops!' Reggie has returned with a tray that's pleasingly crowded with drinks. She dishes out some cocktails and I dive into one without waiting to hear what it is. Turns out it's strong and it's sharp and I like it. Before I can praise her mixology prowess, she points out, 'You didn't answer my question!' She retakes her seat. 'Do you think any of the Romanov treasure possesses otherworldly powers?'

Stacey scoffs, 'Novak doesn't believe in any of that blather!'

I hesitate. I'm recalling how my fingertips moved towards the Fabergé egg in the priest's study. The overwhelming sense

I had that touching it would be a terrible mistake. That the artefact held, if not a curse, then a kind of gathering of its own history, making it more than the sum of its physical parts.

'Who knows?' I feel myself shudder.

I've never completely believed in the supernatural, or in destiny for that matter. But if both are somehow at play, I feel that in the same way Maughan's Fabergé egg was *intrinsically* not for me, then, conversely, the Romanov Code is waiting for me. Is it fanciful to suggest I might escape the curse of its namesakes because it offers me redemption?

But if I'm wrong . . .

I reach for my cocktail, because, frankly, that's a possibility I don't even want to consider.

-102-

Bulatov's Story

Two days later, in the basement of the Ipatiev House used by the Romanov Foundation, Marc Novak opened the ingenious vault. Watched by Frank Harvey, Stacey Smith and Maksim Bulatov, he entered the storage section and emerged moments later carrying a small book. It was plain. Battered. Locked by a clasp. Novak handed it to the Colonel.

'Our business is complete, Maksim.'

Bulatov saluted him and took the book.

'Whoa, whoa, whoa!' Stacey sounded amazed. 'Aren't you going to open it? See what all the fuss has been about?'

Frank shook his head. 'The key's been lost for generations. Even Ekaterina didn't want to force it. You see, what's inside the book isn't the important thing. The really important thing is—'

'Oh, give it here!' Stacey snatched the book from the Colonel and wrenched open the clasp. All three men in the room gasped. 'Typical blokes! Never knowing when to just crack on and see what's there!' She handed the book back to Bulatov. 'I think you should do the honours, pal.'

He nodded. 'Lady and gentlemen . . . history!' The Colonel opened the book. Turned a page. Then two. Then clumps of pages, zipping through the entire tome. 'This cannot be!'

Frank and Stacey began laughing.

Bulatov let the book drop to his side. 'Empty pages. It was just a myth . . . Empty pages!'

'Look at it another way, my friend.' Novak placed his palm on the Russian's shoulder. 'It's history waiting to be written.'

-103-

The Romanov Code's Story

The four of them shook hands outside Ipatiev House. Maksim Bulatov's chauffeuse opened a rear passenger door of the gleaming eighth-gen Rolls-Royce Phantom. 'It's been fun,' the Colonel declared. He got into his car. The chauffeuse closed the door, slipped behind the wheel and gunned the purring engine. The vehicle inched forward. Stopped. The window closest to Novak slid down to reveal Bulatov's beaming face. 'Let's do this again some time, comrades!'

The Phantom glided away.

Silence for a moment.

Frank, Stacey and Novak began walking to the mustard-coloured Morris Marina.

They paused. The Colonel's car moved through the estate's iron gates and disappeared onto the roads beyond.

Stacey glanced at Novak. 'Did you make the switch?'

Frank replied, 'Course he made the switch.'

'Hey.' Novak pulled a small item from the poacher's pocket specially sewn into the inside of his suit's lining. Wrapped in brown paper, the package looked to be the size of a book. 'I made the switch. Now, can we get a drink, please?'

EPILOGUE 1

The Son's Story

Frank met Marius in the foyer of the National Gallery. They shook hands, then embraced.

'We couldn't have done it without you, Mya. I still don't know how you got your people to create the replica of Ipatiev House so quickly. And so brilliantly!'

'I only work with the best! Aside from you, of course!'

'And the Red Diamond gave Novak access to the Court. I think—'

Marius interrupted, 'Speak of the devil . . .'

'And he shall appear.'

Novak reached them. Shook Marius's hand. 'I don't have the words to sufficiently thank you . . .'

Later, across the road from the National, the three men sat in a booth at the Chandos. They drank beer and swapped improbable stories.

Marius rose. 'And now, I think, one for the road!' He walked to the bar without waiting for a response.

Novak nudged his friend. 'He still won't give me his real name. I don't think anyone knows it. I'm not even sure he does.'

Frank shrugged. 'Maybe he just comes from a cautious family.'

'Maybe.' Both men tipped back their glasses and drained their pints. 'You never did tell me, by the way.'

'Tell you what?'

Novak nodded to Marius. 'How do you know the Baron?'

*

Jeremy Simmonds' assistant, Beryl, held the envelope aloft. 'I found this in your out-tray, but you hadn't addressed it, so I didn't know whether you wanted me to forward it or . . .'

She paused. Simmonds seemed more interested in the jiffy bag she'd handed him moments earlier. He ripped it open, tipped it to one side and caught the hip flask that fell from it. 'So, he did return it. At last.' He looked up. Although she didn't know it, Beryl was holding his letter of resignation.

'What shall I do with it?'

'Let me ponder for a moment . . .' Deep in thought, he idly turned over the hip flask. Paused. Smiled. Laughed. 'Well, I'll be damned!' He grinned at his assistant. 'Get your coat on! We're going for that drink we're always saying we should have!' He stood, placed the flask on his desk and brushed past Beryl. 'I'll just get my coat!' He hesitated. 'The American Bar? Novak recommended it.'

'But what should I do with this letter?'

'Just bin it, Beryl!' He strode into the corridor. 'I was having a bad day when I wrote it!'

She nodded. Tiptoed over to the desk and took a peek at the flask. She frowned, uncertain what had changed his mood. It was just his usual hip flask, although she'd never noticed the inscription on its side before.

To Jeremy. With heartfelt thanks. N.

Beryl tossed the resignation letter into the bin and called after Simmonds, 'The American Bar will do very well!'

*

It fell to Frank to return the Red Diamond. He arrived at the old people's home at noon, and was greeted by a couple of members of staff who knew him by sight. He asked, 'How is he this morning?'

'Today is a good day! He complained about his eggs Benedict and ordered a second portion!'

Frank laughed. 'Good to hear!'

He walked to room 6. Knocked on the door.

'Come in, Frank!'

He entered. Smiled. 'You're looking well!'

It wasn't a lie. The home's most distinguished resident was one hundred and five years old and, although frail, remained mentally alert. He wore grey trousers, a crisp white shirt, offset by a burgundy cravat and the inevitable blue blazer. 'Do you mind if I don't get up?'

He sat in a wicker chair by a large and ancient gleaming brass telescope and French doors that overlooked a rose garden.

'You stay right where you are!' Frank approached him. Dropped to his haunches. 'It's always good to see you, old friend.'

'Who are you calling old?'

He chuckled. 'Fair play. I wanted to return something. And to let you know something important.' Frank felt overawed. He hesitated. 'Your father was right.'

'He was a good soul. I still miss him.'

'Aye. You're not the only one. On the same day the Romanovs were murdered, he put the Red Diamond in your hand . . .'

The older man nodded. 'I've told you the story many times. As many times as he told it to me. My father said, "I believe that one day it will do great good."'

'Well, thanks to your son and some other friends of mine . . .' Frank took the Red Diamond from his pocket.

Pressed it into his friend's palm. 'It really has done, Georgy. It really has done.'

'Thank God, and thank you . . .' The eyes of the son of Leonid Pavlovich Kiselyov filled with tears. 'Tell me how.'

EPILOGUE 2

History

Less than 24 hours before Frank had given George Alexander closure, Lady Eleanor walked with Marc Novak, side-by-side, down a broad corridor. Deep red carpet underfoot. Masterpieces flanking their every step. The couple reached a set of imposing doors, and although Lady Eleanor held back, anticipating Novak would open them for her, he'd been distracted. She smiled at the look of astonishment on his face.

He stood starring at the final painting in the passage. 'Is that what I think it is?'

Lady Eleanor didn't even look up at the work. 'Last seen in public in 1913. I always felt it was grotesquely overrated. She's terribly plain. The background – dull.' She finally spared the painting a glance. 'And why hasn't she got any eyebrows?'

'Maybe Leonardo ran out of paint.'

'Our people made the swap. We paid Vincenzo to spin his little tales, although why we couldn't have hired someone with more flair for verisimilitude is beyond me. It's fortunate we did take it, of course. That grubby little reproduction has been vandalised so many times, the French may just as well have hung it in a firing range. Dear God. Shall we continue?'

Novak hesitated. 'Since arriving here, I've seen dozens of works of art like this. You don't want me to sign an NDA?'

Lady Eleanor replied, 'If you say nothing, I shall honour my NDA to you.'

'How so?'

'My non-death agreement with you. An implicit promise to let you live, Mr Novak, despite all you have witnessed. The minute you utter a word, you can be assured that the agreement no longer stands.'

'Non-death agreement? You just made that up, yeah?'

But Lady Eleanor's only response was a faint, unreadable smile.

They entered the room beyond the doors and she gestured to a Louis XIV chair.

Novak shook his head. 'I'm not staying.'

'Very well. I wanted to let you know that the book has been analysed and confirmed to be the Romanov Code. I imagine you'll want to be appraised as to what will become of . . . such an extraordinary relic.'

'Nope! I don't give a damn what you lot do with it. Ironically, it's about the only first edition I'm not remotely interested in. It's a book written by royalty. I can't think of anything more tedious and trite and out of touch. Use it as a paperweight for all I care. I'm only bothered about the money.'

Lady Eleanor looked disappointed. 'How predictable. But very well. We agreed on the sum of eleven million.'

'We did.' Novak paused. 'But you can make it ten million. On one condition. I need a favour.'

'A one-million-pound favour. Is it legal?'

'I doubt it.'

'Thank God.'

'Oh, I'm not sure God would approve. You may have heard that once upon a time I was hired to find out the truth behind the death of Diana, Princess of Wales. I uncovered what really happened, but the majority of the men responsible escaped me.'

'How?'

'The ultimate escape. Death. But I believe one of the perpetrators remains.'

'Go on.'

'Ekaterina Romanova told me she knew where he is. I believed her. And I also believe you could get me that information. His whereabouts. The Court is the most powerful organisation I've ever encountered. You can help me do this thing. I know you may have moral qualms but—'

'I can help you.' She nods. 'Find the bastard and kill him. You can have your eleven million. But for reasons I can't divulge, I cannot be seen to be a part of your mission of vengeance.'

'Understood.'

'Really?'

'No. Just felt like the right thing to say.' Novak extended his hand towards her. 'But thank you.'

Lady Eleanor glanced at his palm and flared her nostrils. 'Oh, put it away, Mr Novak. Eleven million pounds. The full amount will be in your account within the hour.'

'I don't want it.'

'Excuse me?'

'What would I do with eleven mill? Here . . .' He handed her a piece of paper. 'These are the details of the account I want the money transferred to.'

She read the details aloud. Repeated the first word of the instructions. 'ACTION.' She stared at her guest. 'I think you're a fool.'

'Yeah. It's a recurring theme.'

'But . . .'

'You look flummoxed, Princess.' He winked at her. 'Don't you worry about it!' He turned to leave.

'I'm afraid I simply don't understand!'

'There are only two things you need to know.'
Lady Eleanor arched an eyebrow.
'My name is Marc Novak and I've got the best job in the world.'

'Remember that the evil which is now in the world will
become yet more powerful, and that it is not evil
which conquers evil, but only love.'
– *Olga Romanova, four months prior to her death.*

Marc Novak will return.

THE ROMANOV CODE
DECODED

I genuinely thought I'd invented the Romanov Code, the actual book written by Russian royalty that enshrined and evolved their credos and codes of conduct. But after writing this novel, I've spoken to a couple of historians who told me they've *vaguely* heard about it, but it should be considered a myth, or, at best, a legend that stretches back many decades. I've found no mention of it online or in any texts, but the book's possibility is seductive, isn't it? It's enticing to think that maybe, just maybe, the tome survived and is waiting to be found. The romantic in me hopes it'll come to light. The realist doubts it ever existed.

And speaking of the real and the unreal, Leonid Pavlovich Kiselyov and his friends and family are fictions, but the other characters we meet in the Russia of July 1918 are genuine historical figures. The terrible Peter Ermakov, the haunted Yakov Yurovsky and the young soldiers such as Kabanov were real-life participants in the tragedy at Ipatiev House.

Although the main thrust of what happened there is undisputed, various witnesses and historians have inevitably given slightly differing accounts of the massacre and the events that immediately followed. So although we'll never know the entirety of what unfolded and why (and on whose orders), I tried to embed my characters in an authentic version of that hellish moment in history. Details ranging from the state of the former Tzar's shoes, to the casual killing of Tatiana Romanova's French Bulldog and the language employed by Ermakov's men are largely uncontested. For the slaughter and its immediate aftermath, I predominantly stuck to facts that most eyewitness accounts agree upon.

Incidentally, the Red Diamond, as it appears in this story, is a fiction. But the extraordinary amount of jewels found in the clothes of the corpses and the fact these gems served as a kind of bullet-proofing for the victims is again taken from recorded historical reality.

The sections of *The Romanov Code* that deal with masterpieces and priceless treasures going missing are also based on fact. Fascinating to think that the Romanovs' elusive riches are out there somewhere. By the way, if you happen to stumble across one of the lost Fabergé eggs, do let me know. Lady Eleanor has become a good friend of mine and I think I'll be able to secure you an excellent price for it. My cut is a very reasonable 15 per cent and, believe me, my terms are much more agreeable than those generally offered by Colonel Maksim Bulatov. *Za lyubov!*

Gavin Collinson, May 2023

For more information on The Romanov Code *and Marc Novak, visit gavincollinson.com*

AND FINALLY . . .

If you enjoyed this book, please consider leaving an online review or sending me half a million in cash. The choice is yours. Should you go for the first option – thank you! Every single piece of feedback helps enormously and I'm grateful to everyone who takes the time to share their thoughts. Should you go for the second option, used notes are preferred, but I'm not fussy.

Back to the subject of gratitude . . . I'd like to thank my family and friends for their patience, support and feedback as I wrote *The Romanov Code*.

Big thanks also to the best agent in the business, Kerr MacRae, and the Welbeck Publishing team, especially Jennifer Edgecombe for such unwavering positivity and support, Loma Halden for being so fantastically forensic and Simon Michele who created this book's striking cover. I'm especially grateful to my editor, Cat Camacho, who deserves huge praise, not simply for spotting where my narrative was being derailed, but for her ideas in terms of getting it back on track. Thanks, Cat. You worked wonders and your input has been invaluable.

Barry Ryan – thanks for your constant faith. It means a hell of a lot.

Writing can be a lonely pursuit. And that's fine. Lonely is good. It's a kind of realisation, isn't it? But writing is also about how individuals respond to ideas. I'm lucky to have a bunch of people around me who offer sage advice, encouragement and the occasional, much-needed 'You're joking, right?' So thanks to Helen Burgess, Andy Fowler, Ann Challenor-Chadwick, Clair Challenor-Chadwick, Merle Nygate, Sam 'Elvis' Presley, Megan Skinner (Kia ora!) and, of course, the extraordinary Jonathan Zane. Rachel Brooke – you legend. I think your 'No f'ing way!' is my favourite piece of feedback ever. The next round is on me, and please thank Millicent for the Mercato!

This book is dedicated to Mr Rik Kershaw-Moore. An inspiration, unwavering support and the kind of man you want by your side when going into any battle. Thanks, old friend.

Gavin Collinson

ABOUT THE AUTHOR

GAVIN COLLINSON

Before becoming a full-time writer Collinson's career lurched from campsite management to journalism and marketing within the movie industry. He later enjoyed stints on *Coronation Street* and *Emmerdale* before working on *Doctor Who* for over eight years. Since leaving the TARDIS, he's written for the stage, radio and computer games as well as authoring the Marc Novak series of books. He scripted the 2021 interactive thriller *The Lonely Assassins* (starring Jodie Whittaker) which was hailed by *Engadget* as 'the best *Doctor Who* game ever made'.

A fan of classic film and TV he's delivered talks and events on topics ranging from James Bond, Sherlock Holmes and *Ghostwatch*, to Leni Riefenstahl, Charles Dickens and Alfred Hitchcock.

He was raised in Blackpool, Lancashire and now lives in Guildford, Surrey.